Ash and Blood
Relic Hunter Book 1

A Novel by Ann Bakshis

Published by AB Books, 2022

Twitter: @Abakshis
Facebook: @AnnBakshiAuthor
Instagram: abakshis_author
Tik Tok: @abakshis_author
Email: abakshisauthor@gmail.com

To my bonus daughter Emily.

Continue to strive toward your success and never look back at all of the pain that you're leaving behind.

Other Books by Ann Bakshis

Wasteland Series:

    Wasteland

    Sirain Rises

    Rebirth

Looper

Fallen Series:

    Zerah Prophecy

    Second Coming

    Reawakening

    Wanderers

The Arliss

Sinister

Nine Kingdoms Series:

    Unleashing the Shadows

    Beware the Seer

    The Loss of Another

    Promises Broken

    The Righteous Man

    A Selfish Purpose

    Moment of Reckoning

The Celestials:

    Born in Darkness

    Necessary Evil

Table of Contents

Chapter One

Rain drips through a crack in the rotting wood frame around the thick-plated window by my cot, the water falling into a brass basin, clinking loudly with each drop. The nip in the air is typical for these early fall mornings, driving me to remain under the thick, heavy, woolen blanket—the only warmth currently in my room—for a little bit longer. The owner of the hostel I live in refuses to turn on the furnace until at least mid-October, which is still weeks away, though it's been getting colder earlier with each passing season. It angers me that the man allows his tenants to suffer far longer than necessary. There's a lot of things the old man declines to do for us, but after living here for several years I've grown accustomed to it and know how to compensate ... like I have with other situations in my life that haunt my dreams and living nightmares.

A brutal life during a brutal time. One forged in pain and despair that never seems to subside. Misery an everyday occurrence, and sometimes a necessity for survival.

My stomach rumbles, desperately crying out for nourishment, prompting me to sit up and swing my legs over the side of the old, war-time cot with its spindly legs and forest green hammock. I rest my feet on the deeply scuffed oak wood floor. Cold rises through the seams in the boards from the levels below, as does the noises of my fellow tenants, each preparing for their trek of the day. Tossing the blanket aside, I wait a few seconds, tolerating the chill from the stale, bitter air seeping into my bones. I stand, then reach over to

6

the pile of dirty clothes sitting on the frayed, horrendous, floral-upholstered armchair across from me, snatching a pair of jeans from the top.

The fabric is rough against my dry skin, adding to the drab of the day. After slipping them on, I rummage through the tiny closet by the door to my room and remove a thick, dark blue hoodie, donning it over the heather gray tank top I slept in. Next, I put on tattered, white socks, followed by black leather boots with well-worn soles. I run a comb through my long, raven-colored hair, pulling it into a ponytail before securing the hood for the sweatshirt over my head, concealing myself from the fractured world I live in.

Snatching the canvas knapsack off of the floor, I make sure my kard—a dagger with a medium-length, gold blade and ivory-encrusted handle—is in the outside pocket, then strap the bag across my back, confirming the weapon is in easy reach should I need to use it. I have yet had a cause to wield it in the many years it's been in my possession. I open the door and step into the dimly lit hallway with its flickering bulbs which are embedded into holes in the ceiling, peeling, green velvet wallpaper that coats every inch of the slanted walls, and squeaky floorboards warped from both age and neglect.

My room is on the third floor of the six-story hostel, a few meters from the narrow staircase with its uneven rises and exposed nails. The railing to safely guide those adventurous enough to attempt an escape has been missing since before I arrived, forcing me to rest my palm against the wall to steady myself while descending. When I reach the first floor, both the ramshackle lobby and the common room are empty of residents, with the exception of Vin, the hostel's manager.

He's sitting behind the horribly paneled registration counter on a stool in his little, untidy alcove, flipping through the glossy pages of a torn magazine he's probably read dozens of times. His sunken features are currently hidden by a mane of scraggly, copper-saturated hair that's draped around his face and nearly brushes the collar of his long-sleeved, crimson-colored shirt. He's somewhere in his early forties, and always smells of cheap cologne and clove cigarettes, but I've never seen him smoke. He doesn't say a word when I pass, escaping the wretched confines merely to be met by bleaker ones outside.

Many of the structures lining the crumbling, primordial brick road the hostel sits along are in some stage of collapse, or are complete rubble, and have been ever since the great wars ended here decades earlier. Their charred remains loom like slumbering, shadowy giants waiting to pounce. Fragments of shattered glass still stick to the ruts between the sections of sidewalk and along the partitions, clinging out of desperation to avoid being swept away into nothingness like everything else in this world. A few of the buildings have been repaired, such as the hostel, while others were left to decay and rot over time. Burnt edifices and discarded possessions are all that remind us of a former prosperous and refined time, which will never be again. One I hardly remember.

No one really speaks about the societies that came before us. The great cities with their golden domes, granite statues, and rich heritages. People who were nearly able to outlive time itself, fables of grandeur that were solely told at bedtime. Those monoliths and assemblages are now buried under mounds of ash, rubble, and bone. Never to be resurrected, except for those few deemed fortunate to have found a sliver of peace.

Such as the town I live in.

History didn't learn from its awful past, nor its mistakes, and the people paid a heavy price for such arrogance. The fighting started out as simple squabbles, minor skirmishes between rising factions who were tired of being controlled and manipulated by the one percent that owned and ruled everything. Each vying for control over the many populaces, carving up the lands as if it were meat, sacrificing more than just their souls to obtain it.

It quickly escalated into all out genocide.

Governments were toppled and scorched, allowing zealots and heretics to rise from the corpses, chewing on the survivors like manna. New borders and territories were demarcated, erasing countries that had managed to outlive most civilizations from the face of the earth. Maps were, and still are, being constantly redrawn, eradicating the vestiges of our ancestors, and those who came before them. It took years for many to forget, even costing the lives of those who refused to acknowledge the true alterations, persecuted for clutching onto antiquated philosophies, rules of law, and forgotten deities.

History rewritten to accommodate a new reality, a crueler world.

The world leaders called it the Cleansing, and nothing was ever the same afterwards. There are those who still try to reignite the passions of our descendants, hoping to bring back what has already been lost, praying for the return of a habitual society, but it's all done in secret, behind closed doors or buried sanctuaries, and out of the eyes of the Watchers.

No one knows who these shadowy figures are since they appear like smoke and vanish just as quickly. The only thing you notice are their long, black robes with the tapered sleeves and elongated hoods. Nothing underneath is visible, not even a face or a fleck of skin, adding to their mystery and the fear they tend to generate.

While making my way through the center of town or its outskirts, I've spotted a few randomly materializing from the ruins of nearby buildings, terrifying their target into running. It's almost instinctive for the person to know a Watcher is after them, but not one has ever given chase ... at least that I'm aware of. Perhaps it's simply a group of individuals entertaining themselves by scaring the shit out of people using misguided qualms as a tool for their own amusement. However, it's best not to find out the hard way that I'm wrong.

Heading down the splintered sidewalk, the rain soaks me with each passing second, causing my already chilled body to freeze further. I remain close to the buildings so not to be splashed by the random car rolling by, which would add to the misery of the day. Keeping my head lowered, I go steadily toward the town square while those desperate to escape the pummeling raindrops scurry pass, rushing into the closest shelter no matter how feeble it may be. When I reach the roundabout at the center of everything—a derelict, three-tiered water fountain made from marble its focal point—I wait a couple of minutes for traffic to die down before crossing a few of the roads that branch outward like spokes on a wheel, leading to other sections of town.

My destination is a small café called Safran where most mornings I procure breakfast, as well as look over the notice board to see what odd jobs are available to earn some money. The moment I open the heavy, wooden door with its thick, stained-glass window, I'm engulfed in fragrances of cinnamon, freshly brewed coffee, and raw dough. Splintered and discolored ecru-colored tile encapsulates the floor in most places while missing in others, exposing rotting subflooring along the wall joists. Striped sienna and pale yellow wallpaper with permanently stained outlines of long-gone paintings adorn the walls, and a few porcelain knickknacks of various design take up residence on the shelves behind the counters that wrap around toward the rear of the shop. Light fixtures consisting of a single bulb encased in wire mesh cages hang precariously from beams for the ceiling, and there are pocket-sized speakers positioned in a couple of the corners producing pre-wartime melodies of some woman waiting for her love to come home.

Festus, the owner of Safran, is busy attending to a line of customers, so I lower my hood and make my way to the back where the notice board is kept. There isn't anything new pinned to the disintegrating cork, and most of the listings are months old, meaning they've either been forgotten by the requestor, or no one bothered removing them after taking the job.

"Magdalene," the older man says in his thick, eastern European accent. "Here." From his side of the counter he hands me a plump blueberry muffin and large coffee in a paper cup with a plastic lid. "Sit, so we can chat when I'm done."

I thank him, then after removing the knapsack I take a seat at one of the few tables away from the growing line that is now out the door. It's more than likely the weather that's propelling everyone in here today since I've never seen this place so busy. I nibble on the soft, warm muffin and sip at the piping hot liquid while carefully avoiding the occasional odd glance I know is falling upon me from those waiting to be served considering I'm the only one seated.

Over the course of twenty or so minutes, the crowds dissipate, and Festus instructs those working in the kitchen to clean and prepare for lunch. He speaks to his employees in the local tongue, which is Hungarian, or something similar. It's difficult to be precise with how altered the new world has become ever since the wars ended. Languages and cultures have either blended into new ones or died out altogether. I seem to be the lone person he addresses in English, even though I understand him perfectly when he's conversing with everyone else no matter the dialect.

Making his way over to me, he wrings his beefy hands with their hairy knuckles and discolored nails on a yellowed towel tucked into the waistband of his heavily stained apron. His filthy, beige pants sag with each step, and the buttons on his dark blue shirt are straining to remain closed because of his immense girth. He's somewhere in his sixties with a rotund body, splotchy skin, bulbous nose, lackluster gray eyes, pale lips, and has lost most of his thinning, brown hair. Some of it having migrated to his ears. The legs of the chair scrape harshly along the floor as he pulls out the seat across from me, then groan when his weight is applied to them.

Resting his arms on the shaky, green Formica table, he leans forward and smiles, exposing heavily stained, crooked teeth. "Is it all right?"

Nodding, I reply, "Of course. How much do I owe you?"

He waves away the question. "Nothing. You good customer." Then he points toward the notice board. "Nothing new came in, as you saw." He sizes me up and down, scrunching up his fat face. "Woman like you would do well working the dens."

"I'm not one for degrading myself in the red-light district." I finish the coffee, which has grown tepid. "Do you know of any jobs that aren't posted?"

Sweeping his arms out, he replies, "I can ask around. Of course, they might not be the type you're looking for, given who some of my customers are." He winks and chortles. "In the meantime, I do need someone to go to the rynek and pick up a package. I'll pay you for the delivery."

After I finish chewing the last bit of muffin, I ask, "Why can't you go?"

Festus' laugh fills the room, rattling a few of the semi-empty coffee pots resting on their burners. "And leave those idiots to mind the store?" He gestures to the workers wiping down the counters, restocking the cabinets, and those still in the kitchen. None of them look up, probably having heard this drab before. "They'd steal everything not nailed down before I'm a block away." He leans forward and lowers his voice as if the walls suddenly grew ears. "Go see the old woman in stall twenty-four. Her name is Dalma. Tell her I sent you. It shouldn't take more than a few minutes. I'll even let you borrow my umbrella."

After agreeing to run his errand, I clean up my mess—discarding the cup and crumbs into the trashcan by the front door—and strap the knapsack across my back. He rushes into the back, nearly knocking over a couple of unsuspecting busboys stepping out of the kitchen with trays of fresh tarts and cookies, returning with a pale blue umbrella, which I don't open until I'm outside and several meters away from the shop's entrance.

Heading in the opposite direction of the roundabout, I wander down the sidewalk until the road it flanks dead ends several blocks later. Across the way is the pebble-covered, muddy parking lot for the rynek, a market that's housed inside of a one-story, abandoned warehouse that used to hold armaments for the fighting factions, and those determined to end their reign. Scars from old battles have caused dents in the dull metal siding that wraps around the lengthy, narrow structure. Divots are still visible in the strips of grass dividing the street and lot, causing several power poles to lean precariously, their wires dangling too close to the ground. There are very few cars occupying the large expanse, causing me to wonder if the building is even open for business.

I check the road before crossing, hurrying over the gravel, failing to avoid the visible puddles, and splashing mud all over the bottom of my already filthy jeans, soaking me further. The handle for the door is a simple beveled bar bent and welded to the warped tin, secured by two additional bolts at the top and bottom. When I pull the door open, the interior is surprisingly warm, bright, and inviting. Fragrances of newly carved wood, foreign spices, warm wax, and hot baked goods fill the air, tantalizing my senses. There aren't any windows, so the rain pelting the roof reminds everyone inside how horrible of a day it truly is. The concrete floor is covered in pebble-coated footprints, which expand throughout the entire space.

I've only been in the rynek a few times. Usually during the summer when it's sweltering and the fresh fruit at the local market has gotten too expensive, so I buy from the farmers who come here to sell the remnants before it rots. There are roughly a handful of people milling about either looking at the various wares for sale or setting up their own booths for the day. I collapse the umbrella before stepping farther inside, being mindful of how I carry it to avoid whacking anyone who might get too close. Slowly meandering the wide aisles, I decide to take my time and peruse the booths while the crowds are still away. I'm always intrigued by the homemade items for sale, such as juicy preserves, hand-woven blankets, freshly baked breads and pies, various assortments of dry goods, fabrics, hand-stitched clothing, candles, soaps, and furniture.

Mostly I envy their talent.

Eventually, I locate booth twenty-four along the back wall and an old woman assisting someone interested in purchasing one of her clear glass antique oil lamps. It's void of the fuel required to burn the cotton wick, but I'm sure that's sold separately. Nothing like gouging people for their very last coin.

The woman I assume to be Dalma has to be somewhere in her late sixties or early seventies. Her spine is curved, hunching her over ever so slightly, but enough that I'm sure it interferes with her walking. She's short in stature with stubby legs hidden behind knee-high socks, the seams of which need to be sewn, while bits of patchy flab spill over the tight hem. I wouldn't be surprised if they're cutting off her circulation, or perhaps that's what they're meant to do. The rest of her is robust, masked by her dress made from a woven material in a mustard color with a chevron pattern. A heavily frayed, off-white sweater that's coming apart at the cuffs and collar is draped over her shoulders, exposing excessively dry, pale skin and Hadassah-like arms. Her long, gray hair cascades loosely down her back, while her sunken light blue eyes stare intently at the woman trying to bargain for the lamp.

On the tables lining the front of the booth and the shelves behind toward the back are chipped sets of China, hand-stitched blankets, porcelain and ceramic statues, outdated coins that are no longer worth the metal their stamped on, tattered books, and copious amounts of jewelry, some of which are tangled into haphazard piles. I wouldn't be surprised if most of these items were taken from abandoned homes, stolen memories of families long gone and forgotten.

While waiting for her to finish with the current customer, I rifle through one of the boxes of jewelry, curious about what I might find, though I'm not sure why since I have very little use for such trinkets. Surprisingly, an item down at the bottom of the mess catches my eye. It's a tarnished, blue compass rose pendant on an equally blemished silver chain. Resting the folded, wet umbrella against my leg, I gingerly pick up the necklace from its notch in the velvet-lined chest to have a closer look. The metal is slightly warped around its thick edges, the directional points are severely worn down, and the blue behind the compass rose itself seems to be some sort of stone, possibly sapphire or tanzanite, maybe even simple colored glass.

"You have excellent taste," the old woman says, startling me, her voice cracked like her complexion. Unlike Festus, she addresses me in what I assume is Hungarian, not realizing I'm from a different expanse of this broken world.

"It caught my attention," I reply in her dialect, setting the pendant down since I'm sure I can't afford it. Plus, I didn't come here to shop, tempting as it may be. "Festus sent me to pick up a package."

Nodding, she shuffles toward the back of the booth, her boots scrapping against the rough concrete, then involuntarily groans as she bends down and rummages through a pile of brown paper wrapped parcels, each tied with coarse brown string, emerging with one the size of a book. "Here," she says, handing it to me.

I take it from her, swing the knapsack over onto my chest, and tuck the item inside. Picking up the umbrella, I start to step away when the woman's knobby fingers with their swollen knuckles gently touches my arm, stopping me.

Glancing between me and the pendant, she asks, "You're not going to buy?" She seems disappointed, a childlike scowl on her thin, pallid lips.

"I don't have the money to purchase such lovely things," I reply, trying not to feel guilty for disappointing her.

She narrows her suddenly vivid eyes, a spark rising to the surface that hadn't been there before, and stares guardedly at me. "What's your name?"

Normally I don't have an issue providing people that wee bit of information, but something about Dalma feels different. It's almost as if she's probing, not truly inquiring. "Magdalene," I respond, unsure if it was a wise decision.

Studying me with great intent, she doesn't say anything for a few awkward seconds, annoying me. "Do you have job?"

"Only when they're available."

She hobbles closer, her light blue eyes boring into mine like daggers. "Tell you what. You help clean my house and I'll give you the pendant. There's junk everywhere, and I'm too old and frail to take care of it by myself."

"I'd prefer cash for work."

She shakes her head, triggering the tendrils of her brittle hair to swish against her shoulders, getting into her face a bit. "No money. Necklace is yours if you clean. The house is small. Shouldn't take more than a couple of days."

I hate being idle, and who knows when Festus will be able to find something for me that actually pays. As much as I don't want to be around Dalma more than I have to, I feel drawn to the necklace, a tremendous need to have it in my possession no matter the cost, and it should only be for a few uncomfortable hours, so what's the harm. "All right. You have a deal."

She smiles, exposing horribly stained teeth, several of them missing. "Festus has my address. You get it from him. I see you tomorrow morning." She pats my arm, turns, and busies herself in the stall as new customers approach.

Making my way to the entrance, I sense her stealthy gaze on me, and an icy chill runs down my spine. I involuntarily shiver as the warmth I had been feeling evaporates. At the door, I open the umbrella before stepping outside where I get covered in more mud while trying to avoid the ever-growing puddles. The café has just a couple of patrons when I return, so after closing the umbrella, I side-step past them and retake the seat I occupied earlier, making sure the knapsack is across my chest so I'm not resting against it. Festus has one of his younger employees bring me a cup of coffee, which I very much appreciate. Even though I had the umbrella to shield me from the torrential downpour, the dampness of the weather still managed to seep into my bones, so the hot liquid is very satisfying. I make a mental note to do laundry when I return to

16

the hostel since these are my favorite pair of jeans ... actually, they're my only pair, and I'll want to wear them tomorrow.

Festus is carrying a freshly toasted sesame seed bagel with a side of plain cream cheese, and when he sits, he places the food down in front of me. My mouth watering at the tantalizing meal, I open the bag and hand him the package.

He clutches it tightly, tucking it between his arm and chest, protecting it from being seen or noticed by those in the shop. "Did Dalma give you any trouble?"

I start spreading the cream cheese over the warm surface of the bagel, salivating as it melts into a gooey delicacy. "No. In fact, I'll be cleaning her house for the next several days. She said you have the address." The first bite qualms the gnawing in my stomach from the encounter I had with the older woman.

He nods, a pained smile creasing his lips. "I'll give it to you before you leave, along with the money I owe you. Just so you know, she lives two towns over in Latium." He jabs a finger behind himself, indicating the direction. "Do you have a way to get there?"

Before answering, I have to swallow the bite still in my mouth. "Vin has a motorbike he hardly uses. Hopefully he'll let me borrow it. If not, I'll find an alternative mode of transportation."

Festus nods to the half-drunk coffee. "Let me know if you want more." Taking the umbrella, he retreats behind the counter, disappearing into the kitchen.

When I'm done, Festus hands me several ralods—the currency of the new world—and Dalma's address on a torn piece of parchment. I shove both into my bag, don my hood, and return to the hostel, leaving puddles on the floor by the door while I drip dry for a moment.

Vin is still hunched over the counter reading his magazine, but there's now a fire roaring in the fireplace in the corner of the common room, easing a bit of the gloom and adding some much-needed warmth in the dank room.

Resting against the roughly textured, poorly stained clapboard panels that make up the section of half wall he's sitting behind, I wait for him to notice me, but when he doesn't I try to grab his attention. "Vin ... Vin!"

He slowly lifts his head to meet my gaze, his long, graceful fingers pausing in turning one of the glossy, crinkled pages. The whites of his green eyes are blotched with red, his lips chapped and dry, and his nails chewed and smoke stained. A heavy aroma of clove and something bitter lingers in the air around him, causing my nose to prickle and my eyes to practically water.

"Can I borrow your motorbike for the next couple of days?"

He stares at me for a few seconds before answering. "It needs gas. Where are you going?" he replies in his Irish lilt.

"Latium. There's a gas station between there and here, so I can fill it up for you."

"Sure, you can use it." He gets down from the stool and goes through the door at the back, leading into his darkened apartment. Returning, he tosses me the keys which are attached to a small ring and an old grenade pin. "It's in the alley. Just return them when you're done."

Heading upstairs, I place the keys into the knapsack so I don't inadvertently lose them. Once I'm in my room, I change out of my soaked clothes and into dry ones consisting of black sweatpants and a long-sleeved, yellow shirt, then gather all of my dirty garments and shove them into a large duffle bag. Checking the water in the basin under the window, I discover it's quite full, so I take it down the hall to the communal bathroom and dump the contents into the sink. When I return to the room, there's only a few drops of water on the floor. I clean it before replacing the basin, then pick up and carry the duffle bag down to the basement and into the poorly lit laundry room with its chipped popcorn ceiling and torn linoleum floor. After unloading everything into one of the antiquated washers, I add powdered soap from a box on the shelf by the door, and return to the common room once the machine is started.

Before taking a seat on one of the couches, I glance over the ragged spines of several paperback books resting on the tall shelf beside the fireplace, select an old mystery, and get comfortable in front of the fire.

The yellowed pages practically crumble in my hands, but not from use, purely from age. The spine is bent and broken, having been perused by many of those living in this place. Reading is one of the few respites available to us. I'm surprised any books still exist considering the trials those who orchestrated the Cleansing went through to ensure no written word of any kind remained. Perhaps they felt fiction was harmless, allowing us one true escape from the horrors real life awaited us. Also, there isn't a television anywhere in the hostel, and I'm not sure I'd want to watch hours of propaganda videos or news reels showing the ongoing bloodshed still occurring in segments of the world. It's horrible enough being reminded of the carnage by simply stepping outside onto the street.

Sometimes I wonder what everything was like before the factions rose to power, creation turned to dust to appease the tyrants and zealots. How society functioned as a whole instead of the splinters it is now. Wars aren't new, and sometimes they seem never ending, but between the conflicts there must have been brief moments of serenity, a life worth living, joy and happiness in place of rage and torment.

When enough time has passed, I set the book aside and head down to the basement, tossing my wet clothes into the dryer, then return to the common room. As the day draws on, several of the residents return from wherever they happen to scamper off to in the morning, and go into the kitchen to cook an early dinner or join me by the fireplace to warm up and dry off. Most of us living here keep to ourselves, but there are a few who socialize with each other.

I'm just not one of them, and prefer it that way.

With the kitchen now nearly empty, I place the book back onto the shelf, head up to my room, and rummage through the corrugated box under the cot where I keep food provisions stored, removing a can of soup. After picking up a pot, bowl, and spoon from the top shelf in my poor-excuse for a closet, I return to the kitchen and make dinner. Thankfully, there's a can opener in one of the shambled drawers under the cracked, aquamarine tiled countertop. Once it's heated, I take my concoction to one of the two-person round tables between the kitchen and the stairs leading to the basement, sit, and eat, the hot liquid warming my insides since the fire was barely able to thaw out my bones.

The front door bangs open, brought about by a sudden gust of wind. In walks a tall man with broad shoulders and frame, in addition to medium-length, wavy, brown hair, that clings to his face, obscuring it from view. His black leather jacket is slick from the rain, his black jeans heavy with water, and the soles of his thick boots are caked in mud, leaving dense prints all over the already grimy tile. Slung across his strong back is a heavy duffle bag which thuds when he drops it onto the floor. Returning to the door, he has to force it shut before going back to the counter to garner Vin's attention.

"Are there any rooms available?" he asks, pushing his soaked locks away from his square face, speaking in a deep British accent once Vin tears himself away from the magazine.

"At the moment, I don't have any for rent, but I will tomorrow. You're welcome to sleep on the couch." He nods toward the sofas and roaring fire.

"I appreciate the offer." Reclaiming the bag, the rugged-looking man makes his way over to the one closest to the fire, sits, then removes his jacket and boots, placing them not too near the flames to aid in their drying.

After I finish eating, I clean my dishes and bring them back up to my room before retrieving my laundry. I spend the next hour putting everything away, then go down the hall to the bathroom to brush my teeth and use the facilities. Once I return to my room, I turn off the lone light in the ceiling, lie down on the cot, and go to bed, encasing myself in the woolen blanket as the coldness of the night tries to bite me like a ferocious animal.

Chapter Two

The rain stopped sometime during the early morning hours, so after stripping down to nothing and donning my tattered, pink robe—the soft fabric pilling under my arms and around my waist—I pick up the partially filled basin, along with a bar of soap and clean towel off of the end table at the foot of the cot, and go into the bathroom to discard the water and take a quick shower. I dump the rainwater into the sink, claim one of the five filthy stalls in the cramped space, set everything down on the lone bench anchored into the wall, and close the mildew-stained, vinyl curtain in the small alcove in front of the shower itself, blocking everyone from seeing me naked. It takes several minutes for the water to heat up, but it never gets hot, just barely lukewarm.

When I'm done, I wrap my hair up in the towel, slip the robe back on, grab my things, and return to my room where I dress in jeans, a dark red T-shirt, black sweatshirt, and a heavy coat since I can already tell it's cold outside from the draft wafting in through the crack of the window frame. Also, the sky is heavily overcast, so I won't be surprised if it rains again. After putting on socks, I don hackneyed sneakers, run a comb through my hair before securing it into a ponytail, and make sure I have everything I need in the knapsack, then head out the door. Vin isn't behind the counter when I reach the lobby, and the only person around is the man who came in last night.

As I turn for the back door, he clears his throat to capture my attention. His movement was so quick that I didn't even hear him approach. The warmth he exudes could ignite the building.

He smiles, exposing perfect pearly white teeth. A woodsy aroma seizes my nostrils, causing me to inhale deeply. The cut of his pants is tighter today, highlighting his firm calves and sculpted thighs. His navy blue sweater clings to his generous biceps and what I can only assume is a chiseled chest given his physique. Now that the hair is away from his face, I notice his piercing hazel eyes that seem to absorb my essence, drawing me into pools I'd happily drown in.

"Excuse me. Can you tell me where I might be able to get something to eat?" His voice is rich and intense, though I don't think he means to be.

I can't help but feel my cheeks flush, causing me to become almost mute from embarrassment since it's obvious he noticed by the way his eyes light up and the corners of his mouth curls tighter. He appears amused by my lack of speech.

It takes a few seconds to find my voice. "There's a café down the street," I reply, using a fake Hungarian accent, which I do with most people—except for Festus and Vin—gesturing in the shop's general direction. "It's called Safran."

He continues to grin, a thick leash tugging at my core. "Thanks."

Biting my lip from unrelenting mortification and humiliation at my behavior, I leave and enter the narrow alley filled with dumpsters, garbage, broken glass, the occasional rat, and aged, rotting debris. Vin keeps his motorbike in a make-shift garage constructed from chicken wire and wooden pallets against the brick structure a few feet from the door.

After removing the ring from the knapsack, I use one of the keys to unlock the provisional gate, then duck inside because of the extremely low roof, grab the handlebars, and pull the clunky machine out. Every inch of it has been spray painted a matte black to mask the mismatched parts, silver duct tape holds most of the seat together, and the tires are badly worn. Once it's clear of the confines, I straddle it and put the key into the ignition.

The air around me falls eerily silent as if time has stopped. Though it's a bit blustery, none of the gusts seem to be touching the alleyway. Almost like it's been warned not to attempt disturbing the unsettling stillness. Staring down at the fuel gauge, my breath heavy in my chest, I sense someone watching me. A malevolent presence daring to latch onto my soul. Slowly lifting my gaze, it falls upon a dark cloaked figure at the end of the alley. His face is completely obscured under the hood of his long, black robe. He stands rigid, motionless, almost statue-like. A sense of dread envelopes me and pulses through my veins with ferocity, though I don't understand why. I force myself to blink and he's gone.

Once again, the sound around me returns, the wind tousling my hair. Shaken from the brief encounter, I turn over the engine as quickly as possible and head down the alleyway, traveling east once I reach the end. When the road I'm on ceases several blocks later, I go south for roughly a half mile, then east again, stopping at a quaint bakery on the edge of town beside a thrift store where I buy most of my clothing. Standing in line for the counter, I work on shaking the nervousness from my body, shoving the dreadful vision from my mind as best I can, hoping the aroma of cinnamon, glazed sugar, and freshly made bread dulls the anxiety clawing just under the surface. But it simply leaves me feeling frightened and deeply troubled. The older woman behind the glass counter stares at me, concerned when I can barely request my order, my voice hardly a whisper. Frustrated customers clear their throats angrily behind me while I hold up the line, adding to my already brittle nerves.

After purchasing several freshly made donuts and stuffing the bag into the knapsack, I continue until I'm in the next town where I stop at the lone gas station that's still functioning in a several mile radius. The pumps have obviously been patched since the metals are multi-toned in various hues of red. A single attendant station sits in the center of the concrete island, an older man bundled up inside.

Before unscrewing the cap for the tank resting between the seat and front tire, I hand over a few ralods to the man, then put in as much gas as I can, hoping it'll be enough to last the next several days.

Soon I'm back on the nearly empty road, feeling a bit better the farther I get from Kern, and practically gleeful when I reach the small town of Latium twenty minutes later. It takes me a bit to find the street Dalma lives on, which is lined with a mixture of delipidated bungalows, remnants of torn down homes, and a few livable dwellings. Hers is a single-story house covered in faded white shingles and roofed in slate tiles, some of them broken on the ground or dangling over the eaves. Under every window, along the front path, and brimming on the side of the crumbling asphalt driveway are nicely kept flower beds, though the buds are starting to wither back under the soil to hibernate until spring.

Parking the motorbike along the side of the house, I place the keys into my knapsack and proceed to the front door, knocking to announce my arrival. The shuffling of feet can be heard from the other side, and when Dalma answers I'm slightly shocked to see a cane in her hand, the top of which is in the shape of a wide ring with pieces missing from its center, almost like a puzzle box.

"Don't look so surprised," she grouses as I continue to stare, then she waves me inside, closing and locking the door behind me. The dress she has on today is red and white checkered, and made from woven material similar to the one she wore yesterday. Her hair is pulled back tight behind her head, and her light blue eyes have a coolness to them, which matches with the atmosphere of the dwelling.

The hallway I enter extends all the way to the rear of the dwelling, doors lining both sides. The walls are adorned in pink floral wallpaper that appears to encompass the entire house from what I can tell. Stained, cream-colored Berber carpet covers every square inch of the floor, extending into the living room on the left. There are a few oil paintings of lush landscapes with wind swept clouds adorning the walls, and what looks to be a hand-carved side table from a long forgotten time rests between two of the doors on the right, which are currently closed. Old black and white photos in thin wire frames are nestled on top of the table, and like the paintings, they're images of scenery, no personal or family pictures amongst them.

Turning to face her, I ask, "What is it made from?" I'm fascinated by the cane.

She purses her lips, annoyed by the question. "Blackthorn wood. It's been in my family for generations." Using the cane, she points to the end of the hall. "Let's go into the kitchen. My breakfast is getting soggy."

I follow her, then through the last door on our left. The kitchen is small with cheap pressboard cabinets barely holding onto their anchors in the walls. Peeling gray linoleum covers the floor, and the appliances date back to before the wars. The air is fragranced with stale tea and spoiled fruit. Tiny gnats hover above the drain in the stainless-steel sink, unable to figure out a way either into the smelly piping or out into freedom. A table capable of seating two rests in the far corner by one of the few windows in the cramped space, a bowl of cereal drowning in milk waiting to be eaten. Before sitting, I take off my heavy coat and knapsack, remove the bag of donuts, then set it on the table. Dalma eyes them ravenously, nearly salivating, so I offer her one.

She greedily snatches it from me and takes a giant bite, nearly moaning from the taste. "This is definitely better than cereal," she says, licking powdered sugar off of her lips. "I don't recall ever seeing you at the rynek before. How long have you lived in Kern?"

Waiting until the donut has been devoured, I answer, "Nearly five years. I've only been to the market a few times, but mostly during the summer." I have to clear my throat to loosen a few stuck crumbs. "Do you have anything to drink?"

She stands, pours me a glass of juice from a finely etched carafe, then retakes her seat, setting the drink in front of me and placing the pitcher within arm's reach on the counter since there isn't much room on the table with the two of us sitting and eating. "Where are you originally from?"

Sipping slowly, I allow the cool liquid to soften my dry throat, relishing the bits of orange pulp. Normally, I don't acknowledge the truth about my background since it reignites childhood traumas I'd prefer to forget. So I'm vague with my response. "West of here."

She frowns, powdered sugar falling from her lips and into her lap, her eyes hardening ever so slightly. "There are lots of places in that direction."

Searching my mind for an alternative response, other than the one that will satisfy her, Dalma continues to stare at me, and it quickly becomes obvious that she won't relent. Going against my better judgement, I decide to be truthful. "I grew up in the former United States and left when I turned eighteen."

Her eyes widen as she licks the sugar from her gnarled fingers. "Your Hungarian is flawless," she states, then drinks her juice.

I shrug my shoulders, feeling indifferent to the comment. "Languages come easily to me."

Setting down her glass and wiping her fingers on a dishtowel crumpled on the counter beside her, she studies me and I swear I can see the thoughts roiling around inside of her head. "The wars continue to rage overseas, so are your parents still alive?"

Honesty in situations like this isn't necessarily warranted. The truth being, I don't remember my parents. Not only their names, but what they looked like or what might have happened to them when I was a child. Instead, lies—or half-truths—are best and have been my greatest and only companions for quite some time. They've kept me alive.

I shake my head since my mouth is filled with another donut, then reply after swallowing its remnants. "They died when I was young, or so I was told. I really don't have any memory of them."

Clearly intrigued, Dalma leans forward in her seat, clasping her wrinkled hands on the table, resting them against the wooden surface at the wrist. "What *do* you remember?"

As if the nightmare of that day were happening right in front of me, my heart races, my pulse quickens, and I begin to sweat. The orange juice turns sour in my stomach, the light coming in through the windows dims, and my head starts to pound. Everything blurs, and the voice that comes out of my mouth is haunting and quiet. "The smell of the rain as it hit the blood torn ground; the gunpowder from the bombs that were ignited; the screams of people dying, even though I couldn't see them." Soaked wood beams, shattered sheetrock, broken glass, torn furniture, and remnants of splintered toys flash all around me, forcing me to relive the terror I felt at not knowing, or understanding, what was happening.

Closing my eyes, I find myself standing in what was once the basement of my home, not a scratch on me even with the devastation encompassing me. Shouts of confusion, orders being barked, and beams from flashlights searching the area consume me, threatening to overtake and drag me back into that horror. Opening my eyes, the sights, sounds, and scents still cling. "I mostly remember being pulled from the rubble of my home, wrapped in heavy blankets, and being passed from one pair of arms to another. No one spoke to me while I was carted off to one of the many orphanages that sprang up over the years."

Dalma pats my hand, pulling me out of whatever trance I had slipped into. "Sounds awful." She holds my weary gaze for a few seconds, then finishes the remainder of her juice.

A shiver crawls down my spine as I drop my hands into my lap. "I couldn't wait to leave it all behind." The images, smells, and sensations evaporate, leaving me feeling hollow and small.

It takes a bit to finish eating due to the weight of the room pressing upon me, and as she cleans up the glasses and her soggy cereal, I pass through the dining room with its solitary table made from cedar and six high-backed chairs, then into the narrow living room at the front of the house. Sitting on the couch with its dark, Jacobean floral pattern under the picture window, the twill charcoal-colored drapes closed to block anyone from spying inside, I start sorting the several haphazard stacks of old newspapers and magazines covering the floor, creating neat and tidy piles.

"I'll take care of those," the older woman says, batting the air as she sits beside me. "You clear away the trunks and boxes from around the couch, and place them in the dining room. Just make sure to leave me a path into the kitchen."

Before breaking my back, I check inside each prior to lifting them. Most are filled with blankets or pillows, while a few contain exquisite jewelry boxes either hand carved from wood, soldered from metal into intricate designs, or molded from delicate glass. Thankfully, those are also empty. Once those have been relocated, Dalma has me transfer the many vases—made from cut crystal, ceramic, earthenware, or porcelain—covering the coffee table, end tables, and floor to the dining table. Their styles range from bud to pedestal to amphora. Lastly, are the table and floor lamps, some with colorful shades, but most without. I make sure to move the ones that aren't plugged in, per her instructions. When I'm finished, I join Dalma on the couch where she's hardly made a dent in the stacks.

Even with most of the mismatched furnishings now in the dining room, the living room still feels cramped and now overheated. I'm sure the latter is due to the excursion in moving everything around, which is one of the reasons I had taken off the sweatshirt before starting.

Picking the garment off of the back of the couch, I ask, "Is there anything else that needs to be placed into the dining room?"

She shakes her head. "No. We're done for the day here, but I could use your help at the rynek. I'll meet you there in an hour."

Back in the kitchen, I place the remaining donuts in my knapsack and strap it across my back after donning both the sweatshirt and heavy coat. Heading out the door, I remove the keys for the motorbike and return home. In the alleyway behind the hostel, I secure the machine into its garage since I intend on walking to the rynek. Instead of stepping inside of the lodging to sit a bit by the fire and warm up now that I've cooled off from the ride, I retreat to the other end of the alley and make my way to the café. Stepping over the threshold, a bell above the door tinkling to announce my arrival, I'm surprised to find the man from the hostel sitting at one of the tables toward the back. I avoid his lingering gaze as I stand at the counter and order a large coffee from the barista, who isn't Festus.

He bursts through the kitchen door a few seconds later, his arms loaded with a tray of freshly baked baguettes. "Magdalene!" he exclaims as if there are hundreds of people in the shop and he needs to be heard over all of them, when there are just four. "Are you done with Dalma already?"

"I'm helping her at the rynek shortly, so I thought I'd stop in to get some coffee," I reply in the dialect he uses with the staff, throwing him off.

He gapes at me, puzzled, then his face lights up. "And you need hot food. Sit. I will bring it to you."

After claiming my steaming cup of coffee, I take a seat at the first table along the row of windows, placing my back toward the man from the hostel. Festus returns a few minutes later carrying a plate of crepes filled with strawberry jam and fresh whipping cream that's rapidly melting.

He joins me at the table while I start eating, then bends forward to keep our conversation private. "Why you not speak in your native tongue?" he whispers in his typical broken English.

Keeping my eyes averted from his quizzical stare, I respond, "I didn't really think about it." Which is an utter lie. "How long has that man been in here?" I subtly nod to the one behind me.

Festus scratches his stubbly jowls. "At least an hour. He's only had a single cup of coffee and a muffin that he finished a while ago." My companion narrows his gaze, boring it into me, which is something he's never done before. Just like this morning, a disquieting feeling tugs at my core. "It's almost as if he's waiting for someone."

Ignoring the comment, though unnerving as it is, I ask, "What do I owe you for the crepes?"

He chuckles, breaking the sudden awkwardness between us. "Nothing, of course." Then, he slaps the table with his beefy hand, stands, and returns to the kitchen.

I hurry to finish—anxious to be away from the stranger who won't stop looking at me—leave a few coins on the table, then swiftly make my way to the rynek. The parking lot is a little fuller today, the vehicles covering many of the puddles I couldn't avoid the day before. Dalma is sitting on a folding chair in her booth when I arrive, a large, woven basket in her lap. She gestures for me to take off the knapsack, which I do, storing it under the farthest table in the back to keep out of people's reach.

"Since I can't leave the stall unattended, I need for you to pick up items I've already purchased, then take them out to my car. After that you can head home."

Glancing around the lengthy structure, I ask, "Which booths?"

She hands me a piece of paper with the information written down detailing what I should be receiving from each vendor and the quantity. Taking the basket, I make my way to the first row of stalls by the entrance and start collecting. While waiting in line for the vendor who specializes in dry goods, I catch sight of the man from the hostel meandering about the rows, his hands tightly clasped behind his back. His gaze darts from table to table, carefully looking over the wares and trinkets, obviously searching for something in particular. He catches my stare, smiles sweetly, and works his way through the growing crowd over to me.

"Following me?" I chide when he's closer, still using my fake accent. The unease I sensed earlier at the café dissipates and is replaced by a tender warmth, a charged thread passing between the two of us, soothing my disquiet.

Brightness flickers at the corners of his eyes and his grin widens. "I heard several people mention this place, so I thought about checking it out." He holds out his hand, which is solid like the rest of him. "I'm Rowen."

"Magdalene," I respond, gripping the basket under my arm since it has barely any contents to reciprocate the gesture, shaking his firm, cool hand. A brief surge of intense heat passes between us, but is gone before I can fully enjoy it. "But you probably already knew that considering how loudly Festus shouted it when I entered Safran."

Shoving his hands into the pockets of his pants, he says, "Thank you for recommending the place. Do you have any more suggestions on where to eat in this small town?"

I can't help but leer at his enchanting smile, my composure melting in his presence. "Many of the restaurants didn't reopen when the wars ended. Everyone either buys their food from here or the grocer at the other end of town. There's a kitchen at the hostel, but be wary about leaving your things unattended. They have a tendency to disappear, which is why I keep mine in my room."

"I appreciate the advice."

When I'm next in line, I tell the man what I've come for, and he places Dalma's parcels into the basket. Moving onto the next booth, Rowen accompanies me without hesitation or prodding. He stays close to my side, acting as a buffer between me and the other patrons. I find the move both endearing and comforting. The sense of needing to protect is wafting out of his pores like the scents of the handmade soaps resting in their holders at the table we're standing in front of. His own woodsy aroma intensifies as if he's on guard, ready to pounce on anyone who might disturb our private meeting.

"How long will you be in Kern?" I ask after gathering more packages, the basket becoming a bit weighty. It feels as if Rowen wants to relieve me of the burden, but is uncertain, fearing I might view the gesture as too intrusive.

It's not unusual for me to detect other's emotions, the sort of disposition is afflicting them in the moment, what reactions may come about if they're challenged or angry. I've had the ability all my life and it's served me well.

He frowns as if something devastating has just happened, though I don't see how. "Just a few days, then I'll be off traveling again."

Surprisingly, my heart shatters a tiny bit, but I brush it off as nothing, a simple overreaction to desires that could never possibly be fulfilled. It's not often a handsome man notices and engages me in conversation. Normally, they're too caught up with themselves to bother with someone so plain. Or, they only want one thing, which is what the red-light district is for.

My mood wants to grow sullen, so I keep asking questions to block the negativity from enveloping me. "What brought you to our little part of the world?"

Sucking in a deep breath, his manner turns cold, hostile. His body stiffens, and the tantalizing aroma I smelled on him vanishes, replaced by something darker, more menacing. "I'm hoping to reclaim a very precious item that was stolen from me many years ago."

I try not to let the sudden shift in the air frighten me, so it takes a great deal of effort to speak with a fresh lump caught in my throat. "Sounds like a difficult prospect given the current climate of the world." Trembling ever so slightly, I keep focused on my task while unconsciously continuing the discussion, which I now hopes ends soon. "There are a lot of people who had things pilfered from either themselves or their families. I wouldn't be surprised if a few such items wound up in this place." I nod to the rows of stalls around us.

The chuckle escaping his lips is strained and forced. "True, but unlike them, my search has narrowed the location down to this very town. Now, all I have to do is find it."

"Then, maybe, it's in here somewhere."

Smiling, he replies, "Perhaps." Walking away, he disappears into the growing throngs of people, vanishing from sight in a matter of seconds, drawing the darkness I was sensing with him.

It takes me a little over twenty minutes to complete Dalma's list and return to her stall where she's currently busy. I set down the basket to help those waiting, taking my cues from the old woman when someone asks a question. As the crowds begin to thin, she reaches into the pocket of her unraveling sweater and hands me a set of keys on a small, tarnished hoop, an angel with broken wings dangling among the metal.

"Put the basket in the trunk. My car is an older model Lada in dark green. It's probably the only one in the lot that color." She snickers.

After putting the keys into my jeans pocket, I pick up the basket and head outside. There aren't as many vehicles in the lot as there was when I first arrived, which makes locating hers a whole lot easier.

The car is boxy in style with an elongated hood, tiny wipers, narrow tires, and rusty bumpers. The dark green is more of an olive and the doors have a few dings in them. Balancing the basket with my leg against the rear bumper, I fish out the keys. I slide it into the lock, the release gives, and the lid pops up, bouncing the entire automobile. With the keys back in my pocket, I set the basket inside of the mostly empty trunk, pushing a red and black checkered blanket off to the side to make room since it's such a cramped space.

An unexpected chill runs through me as the wind once again comes to a sudden and drastic halt. The rustling of leaves and the sounds of birds chirping cease like they've been muffled in thick clouds, which seem to loom dangerously close overhead. Gently lowering the hood, a reflection in the rear windshield snags my attention, causing my heart to stop and my breath to catch.

A figure in a dark cloak looms behind me, his face obscured by a lengthy hood. The darkness I felt from Rowen returns, penetrating deeper into my body, latching on as if to drain my life away. Dread creeps into my bones, penetrating my core with terror. Closing my eyes, I count to five in my head, then quickly turn around, fluttering my eyes open in a mad hurry ... merely to find no one there, and the parking lot devoid of people. After slamming the lid shut, I dart back into the warehouse, nearly colliding with those trying to leave, desperate to put as much distance between me and the car as possible. When I'm at Dalma's booth, she gasps at my appearance.

"Are you all right?" She places her hands around my trembling arms, a troubled expression gripping her face, practically contorting it. "You're so pale."

I shake my head, partially to answer her, but to also to rid the image from my mind. "It's nothing. I was merely startled by something in the parking lot. I'll be fine."

She tapers her gaze, holding me firmly, her gnarled fingers pinching me through the coat. "What did you see?"

Pulling myself free, I reply, "It wasn't anything. Really. What else do you need from me today?"

"Nothing." She fusses with a small bag hidden in the outer lining of her dress. "Here's a few ralods for the extra work." Taking my hand, she places the money into my palm. "I'll see you in the morning."

I grab my knapsack out from under the table where I left it, shove the currency into my pocket and leave, making sure to secure the bag across my chest instead of my back with my hand resting on the grip of the kard, though I don't remove it. Heading back to the hostel, I cautiously observe my surroundings, scrutinizing every shadow I come across and scurry faster at the littlest of noises. Blowing past the front desk where Vin is sitting and reading, I head straight to my room and lock the door. After discarding my bag onto the chair by the cot, I remove the money from my pocket and set it down on the end table before collapsing into bed, shaking uncontrollably, tears welling in my eyes.

It can't be a coincidence that I've seen two Watchers in one day, both here in town and when I'm the only person around. But I can't figure out what I could've possibly done to warrant their attention. I had hoped they were merely figments of people's imagination, or sick individuals intent on terrorizing everyone. However, I no longer believe that since the pair I saw appeared and vanished within the blink of an eye, which isn't humanly possible.

So who, or what, are they? And why the interest in me?

Chapter Three

The sun has set, and my nerves are frayed. I need to eat, but am reluctant to leave the safety of my room. After several minutes of procrastinating, I get up and search in the box under the cot for something to cook, selecting another can of soup, which I have plenty of because they're cheap to buy. Taking the pot, bowl, and spoon, I go down to the kitchen to heat it. When I reach the first floor, there's a fire burning in the fireplace with only a few of the residents milling about. One of them is Rowen, who's standing at the front desk speaking quietly to Vin. Reclaiming the book I was reading yesterday from the bookshelf once my food is ready, I sit at one of the tables to enjoy my dinner and block out the world around me by submerging myself into a fictional one.

There's a tap on my shoulder, pulling me back to reality. Rowen is there, grinning like usual. "Mind if I join you?"

Setting the book aside, I begrudgingly gesture to the chair across from me, and he sits. "Did you find what you were looking for at the rynek?" I inquire, making sure to use my fake accent, which becomes tiresome after a while.

"As a matter of fact, I did."

A twinge flutters in my stomach at the thought of what it might be, but it's not unpleasant. His hazel eyes sparkle even in the dull light. I can even see the flicker of the flames from the fire dancing in his irises, bending in rhythm with his breathing.

Filling my spoon, I ask, "Will you be leaving us now?"

He leans forward, and the woodsy aroma hits me square in the face. It's a scent I could pleasantly get used to if given the opportunity.

"I plan on sticking around for at least a couple of more days." He pauses while I continue to eat. "Do you have plans for tomorrow?"

Awestruck by the inquiry, it takes me a few seconds to recall what I'm doing. "I'm helping a friend clean her house and don't know when we'll be finished."

"Then how about I cook you dinner? Say around six?"

I'm enthralled by the invitation, as well as flattered, yet a voice in the back of my head begs me not to agree to the offer. I disregard it. "That would be nice."

"Great." He stands and heads upstairs while I return to reading and finishing my food.

After cleaning the dishes, I put away the book and go back to my room where I hide for the rest of the night, praying that tomorrow is better.

Sitting on the edge of the cot the following morning, I eat the remaining donuts and drink water from a tin cup while debating whether or not to go to Dalma's since I'm still alarmed from seeing the two Watchers. My fear is they'll be out again today and might snatch me this time ... if that is indeed their intention. I wish I knew more about them so I can determine if I should simply be anxious or completely terrified. Perhaps I'll ask Festus his take on the mysterious men the next chance I get.

Eventually, I put on clean underwear followed by jeans, a black tank top, and a bulky gray sweater. Next are my socks and sneakers, then I drag a comb through my hair before braiding it. I remove the keys for the motorbike, strap the knapsack across my back, and head out. The day isn't as cold as it has been, so I should be fine simply wearing the sweater. Before stepping into the alley, I check both directions, making sure I'm alone, then quickly unlock the make-shift garage and haul out the machine. When I enter the neighboring town, my anxiety starts to subside, but it doesn't completely dispel until I'm standing on Dalma's front porch.

"I was starting to worry," she says upon opening the door, letting me inside. Her dress of choice today is an olive green housecoat that sweeps the floor. Her long, gray hair is tied into a chignon with a few loose strands framing her round, wrinkled face.

"Sorry." I step into the living room, set the knapsack on the couch, and remove the sweater since I'm already sweltering due to the heat inside of the house, which is much stronger today than yesterday. "Where do you want me to start?"

After closing the door, she waves for me to follow her down the tight hallway, through the last doorway on our right, and into a bedroom. The first thing I notice is the number of crucifixes adorning the darkly painted red walls. There have to be at least fifty, if not more, varying in size—some as small as my palm, while others stretch more than a foot in length. Also, the materials are an assortment of wood to ceramic to glass, either clear or colored. A few of them are laced with intricate scrollwork, bejeweled with exquisite gems, or feature porcelain flowers that appear brittle to the touch. My gaze slowly moves away from the display to the rest of the room.

Surrounding the non-descript, queen-sized bed are piles of blankets and pillows, along with dozens of books in both paperback and hardcover. The mattress itself is bare and doesn't appear to have been slept in for quite some time, which is rather odd considering it's probably the only bedroom in the house, and I didn't see any covers on the couch in the living room. A light layer of dust covers the many trinkets resting on top of both the dresser and chifforobe, making the room appear neglected. The lone window above the wooden headboard is draped in a heavy, dull white curtain, blocking out the sun, casting an even gloomier feel into the small, dank space.

"I need the books moved into the living room," Dalma states while I continue to linger in the doorway while she fusses about, picking up a few items of clothing and tossing them into a closet along the far wall, closing the accordion-style door to mask whatever else might be lurking in there. "Place them either on the coffee table or stuff them wherever you can on the shelves."

Moving across the room to pick up the first pile by the nightstand, a thick, beveled crucifix made from blackthorn wood captures my attention. I try to ignore it, but it draws me in, almost as if it's beckoning, calling for me to touch it, to stroke the finely stained wood. A high-pitched ringing, almost like a shrill bird singing, flitters into my ears, but it doesn't hurt. Instead, I find it rather soothing. My gaze continues to linger on the crucifix as I sense there's something familiar about it, though I don't see how that's even possible. They normally petrify me due to my upbringing in the orphanage. Strangely, this particular one doesn't. In fact, it has the opposite effect, which I find rather unnerving.

Shaking my head to clear it, I take the books and carry them into the living room, delicately placing them on the coffee table due to the fragility of a few of them, then return to the bedroom. Dalma is sitting on the edge of the bed, flipping through one of the thicker volumes, the yellow pages practically crumbling in her shriveled fingers.

Rattled by the display, I ask, "Why do you have so many crosses?"

At first, she doesn't look at me when she answers. "Because I collect them." Lifting her head, she cocks it to the side and stares at me. "Do they make you uncomfortable?"

I bite my lip before responding. "Not exactly, but I'm not a fan of them. There was one in every room of the orphanage where I grew up, only ..." My voice trails off while I try not to relive the horrors of my upbringing, those dreadful screams and voices riling up to assault me. Instead, I turn and focus my attention onto the one specific cross, again feeling its pull ... its persuasion.

Dalma's soft hand rests gently on my arm. "Who were they?"

I pull away, ice filling my veins. "What?"

"Your imprisoners, my dear. The ones who took you from your home."

The rage that's taken me years to suppress boils to the surface as the memories of those monsters takes hold. "They weren't anyone," I snap. After picking up the stack I had been reaching for, I bring it out to the living room. When I return, Dalma is still sitting on the edge of the bed, a pained expression on her face. "It doesn't matter anyway," I say as if she asked a question, when all I had to do was simply look upon her to know one was lurking behind her sorrowful gaze. "They're dead, and I'm here."

She stands, closes the book, and sets it aside before making her way over to me as I loiter by the door. Stretching her arm up, she places a palm on my cheek. "Fires have a way of cleansing a lot more than just our souls, my dear."

Shock and horror stricken me. My throat grows dry, and I start trembling. "H-How did you know that?" I falter. "There's no way you could've known what happened."

"I'll tell you, but first you must do something for me." She cups my face in her warm, delicate hands, and this time I'm not able to pull away. "There's something in this room calling to you. A beacon begging to be found. Go to it."

I study Dalma's consolatory face for a few seconds, then without thinking move past her and step over to the blackthorn wood crucifix hanging beside her bed. It's no bigger than my palm and can easily be overlooked among the menageries. Lifting it off the wall, I'm surprised by its hefty weight, as well as how smooth and supple the wood feels. Carefully running my nimble fingers along the beveled edge, I find a notch which allows me to slide open a hidden door, exposing a small compartment containing a tiny, glass vial capped in wax. Inside are splinters of wood, and I swear there's bits of blood on them.

"What is this?" I ask, showing the item to Dalma, who's now grinning.

She comes over and takes the vial from me. "The wood within this vessel was procured centuries ago from a crucifix that has long since been forgotten and destroyed." She retakes her seat on the bed, patting the firm mattress beside her, indicating for me to sit, so I do. "The reason I know about your life is because I've watched it, though from a great distance. And I'm not the only one."

Furrowing my brow in confusion, I say, "I'm not following."

"This was a test." Dalma gestures to the crosses. "I purposefully hid the one in your hand among these fakes, hoping I was right about who you are." She stares at the contents of the vial as if transfixed by them. "It was rumored you had returned, but I needed to be sure."

I smirk, not believing a word of what she's saying. "Did you fall and hit your head this morning? Because you're not making any sense."

Looking at me, her eyes soften as she chuckles. "I do sound batty, don't I?" But then her expression turns serious and rigid. "What made you decide to take this?" she asks, tapping the crucifix still clutched in my hand.

Shrugging, I respond, "I don't know. It was instinctive." I leave out the part where the thing was summoning me to take possession of it.

She seems intrigued by the reply. "Was it the same when you spotted the compass rose?"

I nod.

Lifting her brow, she asks, "Anything else?"

I should mention her cane, but think better of it. So, instead I answer, "The kard I keep in my knapsack."

Her eyes brighten. "Show me."

Before standing, I set the cross down onto the bed. Dalma follows me into the living room, where I unclasp the pocket and carefully brandish the weapon, holding it flat against my palms. Even in the faint light of the room, the gold of the blade shimmers radiantly.

She practically oohs at the sight. "Where did you find it?"

"After escaping the orphanage, I went back to the house they found me in. The weapon was buried under the ruins. It took me quite a while to dig it up, but I knew it was there and couldn't leave until it was mine."

"You have only the one?" she inquires, her tone worrisome.

I put the blade away, then turn toward her before answering. "Yes, why?"

"Hunter blades come in pairs, so I wonder where its mate is." Noticing the puzzled expression on my face, she smiles, but the hardness I noticed in her eyes when we first met returns. "Why don't you step into the kitchen and make us some tea? I'll be right back." She disappears down the hallway before I can object.

Now that she's aware of the weapon, I feel compelled to carry the knapsack with me into the kitchen, draping it across the back of one of the chairs for the small table. It takes me a few minutes to find a teakettle, mugs, and a container filled with tea bags. The water begins to boil just as Dalma rejoins me, so after pouring, I set the drinks down on the table and take a seat.

She reaches into the pocket of her housecoat, removes the compass rose and its chain, then hands it to me. "Guard this like you do that weapon."

I place it inside of my bag. "Explain all of this."

Before responding, she dunks the tea bag several times, then sips at the drink, prolonging the excruciating silence. "There are certain things I'm aware of, such as you burning down the orphanage with those horrible people inside."

I wince at the shear mention of them. "Who told you since there's no way you could've possibly witnessed it?"

She looks at me thoughtfully, her gaze sharpening. "No one saw it, Magdalene. The atrocities they committed against you are visible to someone like me." Reaching out, her tender fingers graze my cheek. "They're etched onto your soul, blackening it."

Glowering, my arms instinctively cross over my chest as a way to protect the scars I bear on the surface. "They deserved what happened to them."

The older woman wraps her faintly shaky hands around the mug. "I'm not disputing that, and the rest of their victims probably thanked you for ending those malicious lives. Though they would've done it secretly so not to draw too much attention from the authorities, or whomever is acting as ruler over there." She takes a sip after blowing away a bit of steam. "Have you befriended anyone since arriving in Kern?"

"Just Festus and Vin, who manages the hostel where I live."

"That's good," she comments, as if approving my choices, then her tone turns bitter. "What about that young man I saw you speaking to at the rynek yesterday?"

"I just met him. He's staying at the hostel, but I don't know anything about him." I clutch the mug and rub its handle with my thumb, an unpleasant thought desperately grasping at my mind. "What does this have to do with the crucifix, or the compass rose, or even the weapon?"

Setting down her cup, she replies, "Everything, my dear. It's also why you understand languages and can speak them fluently, though you've never been formerly taught." She reaches out and clasps my hand inside of hers, holding my jaded gaze with her rigid one.

44

"You're what's known as a relic hunter. A being sent to locate and protect sacred objects from those who intend on doing the world harm with them."

Leaning back in the chair, a laugh unwittingly escapes my lips. "You can't be serious?"

Dalma scowls, releasing me with a hard squeeze. "Don't snicker at me like I'm an old fool," she spats. "This isn't the first time you've been here, nor will it be your last."

I can't help but to keep chuckling. "I think you've been peddling antiques for far too long. You're starting to believe the old wives' tales people create to sell their discarded wares to the gullible masses. Stories like those should never be taken seriously."

She points a crooked finger at me. "Then how do I know about you? Magdalene Leech, the girl who survived the apocalypse."

Ice fills my core and fire in my veins as alarm bells ring loudly in my head. The amusement I had been experiencing promptly vanishes, replaced by panic. "How do you know my last name?"

"Caught your attention, have I?" She briefly purses her thin lips while picking up her cup, then a smug expression crosses her face. "Perhaps Festus informed me."

"I've never told him, and before you bring Vin into this, that's not the name I used when I first registered at the hostel." My voice rises not only from fear, but deep-seated anger and pent-up torment. "That name died the moment the orphanage burned to the ground."

Her foul grin pushes my buttons, goading the animosity broiling within. "Oh, but it didn't. Nor has it all the other times you've ended his wars."

My throat closes, and it takes several long seconds to find my voice. "Wh-Whose wars?" I stammer, feeling ill at ease.

She reaches into the pocket of her housecoat, removes the small vial with the splinters of wood, and sets it on the table between us. "His father's."

Glancing down at the relic, I become spellbound by it. My heart pounds heavily against my chest, a loud thump reverberates in my ears while the world around me disappears. I imagine hearing the hammer against the bolt as it sinks into taut flesh and bone, drenching the ground with blood, the smell of which invades my nostrils. Hot iron mixed with sweat and grief. The wails echoing in the distance are gut wrenching and painful to hear. The shards themselves seem to pulsate with life, heaving and relaxing in rhythm with my breathing the longer I hold them with my gaze.

"It's why you're here," Dalma says through a fog that's encapsulated me. "And they're all watching."

When I'm finally able to break whatever spell has beseeched me, I shake my head to clear it. "This isn't real." Pushing back the chair, I stand and grab my bag. "I'm sorry, Dalma, but I don't believe you." I retreat to the living room, don my sweater, and strap the knapsack across my shoulders.

"Then why are you running?" she calls as I fly out of the front door, letting it slam shut behind me.

My trembling fingers fumble removing the keys to the motorbike from the bag, and it takes several long seconds to get the contraption running in order to leave. I have to concentrate heavily on the road and my driving so not to total the bike since my head is reeling, my entire body shaking violently from the conversation.

It's impossible for her to have known the things she did, but I'm struggling to come up with a viable explanation. No one is aware of what happened before I escaped from the fallen States. Nor have I ever disclosed my last name to anyone outside of the orphanage and those who found me in the rubble of my home. There must be a logical reason why these certain objects have drawn me like a moth to a flame.

But the kard was buried under three feet of mud and debris, the compass rose was upside down and mixed in with other jewelry, and the vial containing the wood shards ...

This can't be real.

When I'm back in Kern, I head straight for the café, parking the motorbike in the alley behind the building. There are only a few customers when I enter, but I move past them and take a seat at the farthest table toward the back. A young man behind the counter brings me a large coffee, which I never requested, while Festus finishes ringing up orders. I'm quaking too horribly to pick up the paper cup, so I simply place my hands around it, trying to warm them up since I still feel chilled from being with Dalma.

"Magdalene, is everything all right?" Festus asks in his typical broken English, sitting across from me, the chair groaning from his weight, a troubled expression on his plump face. "You don't look too good."

I can't bring myself to look into his sorrowful face, so I simply continue to stare at the scorching brown liquid simmering in the cup. "It's been a rough morning."

He wipes his hands on the towel sticking out of the top of his apron. "Have you eaten?"

I nod.

He cocks his head to the side, folding his beefy arms onto the table. "Do you want to tell me what happened?"

"I don't even know where to start," I reply, finally taking a sip of the scalding hot liquid. "Dalma is ... she's—"

"Crazy," Festus responds, chortling. "But she has a good heart."

I glare at him. "How long have you known her?"

He scrunches up his face and shrugs his shoulders. "Oh, all of my life. Did today not go well?"

Sitting back in my seat, I keep my hands wrapped around the paper cup while it rests on the table. "Do you know if she's ever traveled overseas?"

He startles at the question, then clasps his burly hands together, placing them into his lap. "Not that I'm aware of. Why?"

"Because she knew things about me that no one else does, or even should," I blurt out. "She claimed to have been observing me for years, though from a distance."

"Damn it," Festus mutters out loud, but I don't think he intended to since he's quick to cover the mistake by clearing his throat. "Come to the back. We'll talk in private." He stands and goes around the counter, then disappears into the kitchen.

I hesitate in following, but eventually do, leaving the barely drunk coffee on the table. Moving past the half-empty display cases, I enter a kitchen decorated in pale blue tile, scratched linoleum flooring, and rustic cabinets with matching countertops. Flour covers a good portion of an island nestled between the ovens and sinks. The few young men and women working ignore me as I stroll past, white caps on their heads and grease-stained aprons adorn their bodies from chest to waist, concealing their raggedly torn clothes underneath. Beside the rear door is a closet Festus uses for an office. He barely fits inside, let alone a ramshackle desk, a cracked, brown leather chair with wheels, and now me.

He motions for me to close the door after I enter, then has me sit in the chair while he leans against the creaking desk that bends due to his weight. "What did she say to you?"

Resting my arms on my thighs, I debate what specifically to disclose, but if I'm to get any sense of reality back I have to be honest with him. "She mentioned my past. The one I had before escaping to here. How the orphanage I was raised in burned to the ground with my tormentors inside, and that I'm the one responsible for it. She even knows my real last name, which I've never disclosed to anyone since arriving in Kern. Not even to you."

He crosses his arms over his barrel chest, not offended at being slighted by the comment. "Anything else?"

"That I'm something known as a relic hunter. A person who can sense sacred objects even when they're not visible to the naked eye, and how I'm supposed to protect them. Or some sort of nonsense like that. She alluded that I've been here before during other so-called wars, which I apparently helped end. Even making it sound like the reason I exist now is to stop the ones currently raging."

He scratches his prickly chin. "Something must have spooked her."

I expel an exaggerated breath. "If anyone should be scared, it's me. Yesterday, two Watchers appeared and vanished near me within the blink of an eye."

Festus grows ashen, his hands reaching for me, clasping my arms in a firm, powerful grip. "Where did you see them?" he asks, fright fixed on his face, shock tugging at the corners of his weary eyes.

I'm taken aback by his abrupt handling of me. So much so I nearly forgot that he asked a question. "In the alley behind the hostel, and in the parking lot at the rynek. I was planning on asking you about them."

He violently pulls me to my feet, throws open the office door, and hurries us into the kitchen. "Everyone leave!" he shouts, startling his employees, as well as the few customers I notice in the shop. "The café is closed until further notice. Get out!" He turns his attention toward me while everyone scrambles to obey his orders. "Go to the hostel and don't leave it until I get back. Do you understand?"

"What's this all about, Festus? Tell me."

He shakes his head, finally releasing me. "I can't. Not here. Just do as I say. Please, Magdalene."

He rushes to lock the front entrance, leaving me in awe. Eventually, I stumble out of the back door, take possession of the motorbike, and return to the hostel. Once the machine is secured in its makeshift garage, I head straight for my room, tossing the knapsack onto the floor, along with the keys and my sweater, then start to nervously pace. Taking down the braid to allow my hair to hang loose, I sit on the floor, lean against the cot, pull the bag over, and remove the compass rose, twirling the coin-sized pendant between my quivering fingers.

How could Dalma have known what I'd done?

None of the adults survived ... I made sure of that. If the flames didn't find them, then bullets did. I had witnessed enough executions by the age of fifteen that I easily handled their weapons, which I hadn't done until that very day. Still, those assholes got off easy for the atrocities committed against the children they vowed to raise and protect. The government had fallen long before the Caltraves ever rose to power, but they weren't the only clan seeking to claim control, which is why the wars over there continue to this day. Entire towns were leveled so those monsters could rule. Families massacred. Homes torn to splinters. The once pristine streets ran thick with bodies and blood in the early months of their incursion. Smoke darkened the sky, blocking out the sun, placing everything into perpetual night.

It ended by my hand alone.

To this day, I can still hear their screams, smell the burning flesh, and feel the heat from the blaze that consumed everything in its path. Little ones clung desperately to my sides, too afraid to move while we stood at the end of the property line, watching the only world we ever knew turn into ash. Not one of the children was left behind. I got them all out, even if they were already dead or dying from wounds inflicted upon them from our enslavers. I couldn't permit any of them to succumb to the fires, it would've pained me too much. Those around my age buried the ones who didn't make it, leaving their graves unmarked since the rubble was the only thing needed to indicate they had once lived. Their faces I'll never forget, though sometimes I wish I could.

They haunt my dreams every time I close my eyes.

On the opposite end, I have no recollection of my parents, my homelife, or my past before the age of eight. Just the bright beam from a flashlight cutting through the din while I wallowed in the basement of a shattered structure, burst pipes spilling cold water around me, slowly filling up the cavity I was desperate to escape from. Arms roughly prying back sheetrock, panes of broken glass, and destroyed furniture, searching for me as if desperate. Little did I know what awaited upon my rescue. For years, I attributed my memory loss to trauma endured when my neighborhood was bombed. Amnesia for the sake of self-preservation. But now, after what Dalma said, I'm starting to wonder if the real reason is because I wasn't alive until that very moment.

A life created from ash and blood by powers unbeknownst to mankind.

A person to rid the world of those destined to destroy it.

My existence wasn't an actuality until it became a necessity.

It still doesn't explain how she knew the truth about my past. I went to Festus hoping he could dispel her lies, but the way he reacted simply affirms the old woman's ramblings. And now he's gone off to God knows where because of the Watchers, who I still have no clue about what they are or why they've taken a sudden interest in me. I doubt the Caltraves sent them since they wouldn't dare cross the ocean and interfere with another faction or zealot's holdings, which there are plenty of here already. Though none are currently in Kern or its surrounding villages.

Lightning streaks across the sky, followed by a loud clap of thunder that rattles the entire building. As the winds pick up outside from the storm rolling in, the temperature begins to drop, blowing cold air in through the crack of the window frame. I slip on the sweater, then secure the chain for the compass rose around my neck, tucking the pendant under the bulky garment. Moving to the cot, I lie down and curl up into a ball, pulling my discarded blanket over my exhausted body, and enjoy the horrible weather, getting a bit of comfort from it.

The knocking on the door rouses me from a comforting nap I didn't intend on taking. Rowen appears sheepish on the other side, almost ashamed to have disturbed me. His wavy, brown hair perfectly frames his square face, and I find his smile enchanting and alluring. Then I realize why he's at my door.

"Shit, what time is it?" I ask, flustered and nearly forgetting to use my fake accent. Running my fingers through my hair, I attempt to get out the tangles.

He clasps his hands behind his back. "Almost seven." His cheeks blush, curls tugging at the corners of his mouth. "I was afraid you forgot."

"No, I accidentally fell asleep. I hope the food isn't ruined. I'm starving."

He smiles and bows slightly, nodding toward the stairs. "Follow me."

Laughing quietly at the gesture, I close the door and we head down to the common room where there's a table covered in an embroidered red cloth with candles burning in silver holders and a lone rose resting in a bud vase in the center. A bottle of wine sits on the table, two empty crystal cut glasses with long stems are beside a basket filled with rolls, and bowls brimming with stew, steam wafting into the cool air. The entire first floor is empty of people, including Vin, which is a first. I feel myself flushing with color, mainly from embarrassment at the fuss Rowen made when I thought it was going to be something simple.

"I didn't know dinner would be so formal," I say as he pulls out a chair, motioning for me to have a seat.

He sits across from me, ease and confidence seeping from his pores like cologne. "Seeing as the world isn't always full of nice things, I thought it wouldn't hurt to create an elegant night the both of us can enjoy."

"Where did you get all of this?"

After uncorking the wine, he pours the dark red liquid into our glasses. "I borrowed some of it from Vin, and purchased the rest at the rynek." He places the bottle back onto the table. "Did the storm lull you to sleep?"

Reaching for the glass, I smile. "Yes, since I find them quite soothing, which is weird."

Rowen's hazel eyes sparkle as they cast an affectionate linger my way. "I love them. Especially the sound rain makes when it's pounding against a tin roof."

A pleasant shudder snakes down my spine since I'd been thinking the exact same thing.

Noticing my reaction, he beams, a subtle bit of his natural aroma tantalizing my brain.

Caught in the moment, the quietness of the building becomes very apparent. I swear the entire world has disappeared. "How did you manage to scare everyone away?" I ask after swallowing a bit of the luscious liquid.

"I bribed them all with food." He laughs. "Be grateful they left some for us."

Furrowing my brow, I ask, "Are you serious?"

"Of course. I had to bat them all away like flies until it was ready. The wine, however, I wasn't going to share with those vultures."

We dig into the hearty stew, and I instantly salivate from the exquisite flavors rolling around inside of my mouth. I haven't eaten anything since the donuts this morning, so I try not to inhale the cuisine, nor consume too much of the wine.

The silence is a bit unsettling for my taste, so I intend on breaking it. "Rowen, where are you from?"

He gazes at me, a hunger in his countenance that I must have missed earlier. "It's kind of hard to say because the new world hasn't established boundaries yet since they're still being contested. The best way to put it is I'm from a country formerly known as Romania, though I grew up in England. I come from the town of Tomis at the base of the Carpathian Mountains." He drinks from his glass before continuing. "How long have you lived in Kern?"

"Since I was eighteen. I moved here from a village along the former Austrian border." It's a lie I tell some, but not all, like Dalma and Festus.

"What made you decide to stay?"

I have to finish chewing a piece of carrot in order to respond. "It's quaint, peaceful, and I feel at home here." The second the words leave my mouth I know them to be false. Crossing the treacherous ocean years ago was a means to get far from the Caltraves before they could seek me out. Especially, knowing my execution would be the only thing that could satisfy their need for justice after what I'd done to members of their clan. Where I landed mattered very little to me. It wasn't until I reached Kern that I stopped, mainly because I was compelled to by every fiber of my being. Still to this day I have yet to figure out why.

He nods, agreeing with my statement. "It does have a charming atmosphere and the people are nice. Do you work?"

The wine in my glass needs refilling, so I pour a bit more. "Whenever I can find it, which isn't often. How about you?"

"I pick up the odd job here and there. Basically, I'll do anything, even if the pay is awful, just to keep busy. My hands hate being idle." There's an underlying current in his words, and it tugs hard at me.

"Sounds like me." I chuckle to disguise the warmth spreading across my body, so my cheeks don't flush. "Hobbies?"

He finishes chewing. "Well, traveling for one. If I can find a worthwhile destination that isn't teeming with conflict."

"That has to be difficult."

"It is, but I seem to manage." Pause. "Have you been anywhere other than Kern and your home village?"

Something about the inquiry triggers alarms in my head, but they might simply be from the conversation I had with Dalma earlier. I try not to let it rattle me. "No, I haven't," I reply after a brief hesitation.

"What about boyfriends?" It's clear the question makes him uncomfortable, so I don't know why he asked it.

I snicker. "No. My life is too marred to allow anyone that close."

Rowen bites his lower lip as if preventing himself from asking a follow-up question and suddenly becomes tense. Clenching his jaw, he tightens the grip on his fork, his knuckles turning white.

Furrowing my brow, I tilt my head. "Are you all right?"

He smiles, but it's not welcoming like before, and his expression appears pained, almost hurt, but not due to a physical ailment. "I'm fine."

We allow silence to fill the void while continuing to eat. After our bowls are empty, I help clean up and pack away the leftovers, then we take our newly-filled glasses of wine and sit on the couch in front of the cozy fire. The alcohol has started to cause my mind to grow fuzzy since I'm not used to drinking, so I decide to nurse what I have left. Rowen is gripping the crystal as if it's a lifeline. I fear he'll shatter the glass. His mood grows sullener with each passing second, leaving me confused and uncomfortable.

"The food was really good," I say, trying to restart the conversation, though secretly I'm not sure I want to. "Thank you for making it."

"I love to cook," he replies, cheering up slightly. "My girlfriend always enjoyed the dishes I prepared." Again, his mood sours as he stares into his glass, sorrow tugging at the corners of his woeful eyes. "Red wine was her favorite."

I debate whether or not to reply given his new disposition. After a few moments, I decide to. "It's mine, also, though I don't drink it often. If you don't mind me asking, where is your girlfriend now?"

He raises his gaze to meet mine, and there's a tenderness in the way he looks at me. A desperate longing that I find bewildering considering we just met. "She's missing, and I'm desperate to find her."

"Oh," I utter, my heart sinking at a loss I can only imagine. "How long has she been gone?"

"For quite some time." He adjusts his position on the couch, turning slightly toward me. "You see, she was taken from me during the night while we slept, and I was powerless to stop it. I still bear the marks inflicted by those who wanted me dead because of who I am and what she is." He sets down the glass on the end table beside him, then starts to unbutton his long-sleeved, gray shirt.

I seize his hand, stopping him. "You don't have to show me." Mortification at his abrupt need to expose his wounds stuns me. Not that I wouldn't mind seeing what's underneath

"But I want to." The affection in his voice surprises me.

Observing the desperation in his eyes, I pull my hand away and he continues to undress, wrapping my stomach into knots in heightened anticipation. Even with the light cascading off of the fire casting odd shadows across his bare chest, I'm still able to distinguish his well-defined muscles from the numerous scars covering his tanned skin. I find myself drawn to them, much like I was to the crucifix, but for completely different reasons. The rough, jagged marks remind me of the ones I carry, though I doubt we received them in the same manner.

Setting my glass down onto the coffee table, I move closer to Rowen, bending slightly forward so my fingers can carefully trace the deep scar running diagonally across his chest, ending at several healed puncture wounds right where his heart is. His skin ignites at my touch, and I can feel his pulse racing faster the longer I'm near

56

him. He leans toward me, his hot breath tickling my face, grazing my ear, and sending tingles down my spine. I sense longing from him, a want that is ancient and forbidden. The woodsy scent from his flesh beckons me to clamor for more than a simple touch. So much more. Placing my palm over the healed wounds, the thread I felt connect us earlier strengthens, edging me ever closer, teasing me to take a bite.

Rowen pushes an errant strand of hair behind my ear, and I close my eyes, relishing his lingering touch. Wishing to feel his hands on more than just my face, his body pressed against mine, and a soft caress between my legs. His tender lips brush the tip of my ear, sending tingles down my spine that I never want to end.

"Oh, how I wish you would remember me," he whispers, then an ache of deep regret and mourning washes over me, floating out of his mind and slamming into mine. But I keep the agony at bay, not wanting to disrupt this intense moment.

Until the words sink in.

How I wish you would remember me.

"What did you say?" I ask, the fantasy in my head broken as I move out of his hold, an unease replacing my bliss.

"Magdalene—" he begins, but I abruptly stand, nearly knocking into the table and spilling the wine.

Trembling, I back away from the couch and wrap my arms around myself for protection, and to quelch the panic and fear attacking, wanting to claim my body and paralyze it. "Who are you?"

Getting to his feet, he outstretches his arms as if to pull me into an embrace. "Please, let me explain."

"No." I shake my head. "No, I don't want to hear anymore craziness today. I'm not who you all think I am." My emotions become so overwhelming that I start to cry, allowing my speech to return to its normal American accent since I've lost the focus, and desire, on maintaining the ruse.

His eyes widen. "Did something happen?" He reaches for me, the fondness and concern in his voice irresistible.

But I can't get dragged into the madness erupting around me, so I bolt to the other side of the room. "Go away, Rowen. I can't be a part of whatever you're trying to do. Not you ... not anybody."

I run up the stairs, slam the door to my room, and lock it. Sliding down the rough wood, I pull my knees up to my chest as I sit on the floor and bawl.

Chapter Four

I haven't left my room in several days, with the exception of using the bathroom and taking the occasional shower, which doesn't help my brooding demeanor like I want it to. Need it to. The self-isolation is mostly so I don't run into Rowen. His comment haunts me, drilling itself into my mind, burrowing deep into my conscious so I'll never be rid of it.

It torments me every time I close my eyes, and even when I'm wide awake.

During the middle of the night, I snuck down to the common room and snatched a couple of books from the shelf by the fireplace, wanting something to read to prevent boredom. There are enough dry goods in the box under my bed that I don't need to go into the kitchen to cook something. At least I was prepared for that.

If I'm not delving into a fictional world, then I spend the time twirling the compass rose between my fingers, thinking over the conversation I had with Dalma, as well as the brief one with Festus. I know he said not to leave the hostel until his return, but I need answers to the lingering questions plaguing me. And there's really only one person I can ask.

After dressing in jeans, a dark green top, and black hoodie, I slip on socks and my boots, then strap the knapsack across my back. Running a comb through my hair, I pull the dark strands into a ponytail and make sure the pendant is hidden under my clothes before stepping into the hallway. When I reach the lobby, Vin is the only one around, his nose deep in a different magazine. Opening the back door, I check the alley, then hurry over to the motorbike, freeing it from its cage. The sky is slightly overcast, but the temperature is surprisingly pleasant. I speed down the roads, keeping aware of those around me as they rush past, paying close attention to anyone who might be wearing a long, dark robe.

Dalma's car is in the driveway when I arrive, my body tensing up since I anticipate a hostile welcome. Standing nervously on her front porch, my fist lingers in the air for a few seconds, then slowly descends on the door. Several long minutes trickle by before she answers, but it's not her who greets me. A young man somewhere in his late twenties stands on the other side of the threshold. He has a round face, short, dark blond hair, and stunning emerald-green eyes. I guess his height to be around six feet, and he has an athletic build. The color of his fleece pullover enhances the intensity of his irises, and his jeans hug his waist as if sculpted to his frame. There's an intensity about him that I find off-putting and bothersome.

"Who is it?" Dalma calls out from somewhere in the house. She rambles into the hallway from the kitchen just as the young man steps aside, exposing me. She's donning the same housecoat from our last visit, and her long, gray hair has been set into a bun on the top of her head. "Oh, it's you." The cold greeting is what I was expecting given how I ended things. "Well, don't loiter. Come inside." She turns her attention to the other visitor. "We'll talk later."

He nods, then leaves without so much as truly acknowledging my presence.

I enter, closing the door behind me, and follow the older woman into the kitchen where she sits at the table and resumes eating a bowl of soggy cereal. After removing the knapsack, I set it on the floor and join her.

"Who was that?" I gesture toward the front door.

"Just a neighbor," she replies with great animosity, then glares at me, milk dribbling down her parched lips after she's taken a spoonful. "Why are you here?"

"To get answers. I tried asking Festus, but the second I mentioned seeing a couple of Watchers he immediately closed the café and disappeared. That was a few days ago. Do you know who they are?"

She sets the spoon into the bowl, wipes her chin on the paper napkin in her lap, then grasps her hands together, placing them on top of the table. "I've never actually seen one myself, simply heard stories like everyone else." She waves her hand dismissively. "I'm sure it's nothing. Simply a tactic to instill fear into the weak minded by those wanting to rule the world. I wouldn't concern yourself over it."

"Then why did he get so scared?"

Dalma snorts. "That man spooks easily. Always has." She picks up her mug of coffee, and drinks. "Is that all you wanted?" she inquires, her callous manner returning.

"No." I swallow the lump that's formed in my throat and request a glass of water, which she willingly provides. "I'm hoping you can tell me more about the past I supposedly had. The life before this one."

After reclaiming her seat, she watches me very carefully, her cool blue eyes narrow and focused. "There have been many. The last being nearly a century ago when a demon by the name of Rowen tried to steal the Perpetua Chalice. You stopped him before he could take possession of it, but at a great cost."

My pulse races and I break into a sweat, even though there's a nip in the air. "Ro-Rowen? Do you know what he looked like?"

The old woman startles by the change in my countenance, her body shuddering slightly. "I do, but I'm no longer in possession of the book his life was detailed in. It was pilfered from my booth at the rynek a few days ago. I was planning on giving it to you when you were ready."

"Did you read through it before it was stolen?" I ask, my anxiety soaring.

Her nostrils flare, then she jabs a crooked finger in my direction. "You want to know if the man I saw you talking to was him."

I don't answer, refusing to admit the truth.

The smirk creasing her lips is all the answer I need, but she speaks anyway. "Yes, it is, and I was shocked to see him out of his cage. I thought that bastard would rot in Hell for eternity like all of his kind should." She slams her palm against the table, rattling both the bowl and mug. "He's more than likely the one who took it. I should've known. Demons can't be trusted." She grabs my hand tightly, nearly pulling me out of the seat. "What did he say to you?"

"Nothing, really." I pull free. "Wait, did you say demon?"

She scowls, then clicks her tongue against the roof of her mouth. "He's a follower of Lucifer, an inhabitant of the underworld, and one of the many minions that slink their way across the Earth, looking to create nothing but death and destruction for their master. Who do you think is responsible for what's happened?" She tosses her hands into the air. "Normal humans would never do this to each other. Only those depraved enough could conjure such horrors as the Cleansing and relish in it." She purses her lips. "What did that bastard want?"

"He told me he was searching for something, but wasn't specific. Then later that day said he found it at the market." I bite the inside of my cheek, omitting the rest of the evening mainly to prevent further questions and possible accusations that I know she'll make. "I haven't spoken to him since."

Dalma relaxes, letting out a contented sigh. "Good. Maybe he'll leave now that he has what he's looking for."

As much as I want to believe that's the reason he came to Kern, his comment from that night tells me otherwise, but I don't dare breathe a word of it to anyone. Lifting the hand I held against his chest, I stare at it while recalling the intensity of the night we had dinner. I can still feel his hot skin pressed under my fingers, hear the rapid beating of his heart which quickened at my touch, and sense the desire drifting in the air between us. Like before, my stomach flutters at the thought of him ... of being with him in every way possible. My cheeks grow warm, and I know I'm blushing.

"Magdalene," Dalma calls to me from a distance. When I lift my gaze to meet hers, she carries a vexed expression on her face. "Did something happen between the two of you?"

"No," I answer rather quickly, then reach for the glass of water, consuming its contents. "What else can you tell me about my previous lives?"

She waits several seconds before answering. "There really isn't much. Whenever the ancient relics were, or rather are, in danger of being found or used, you're sent to combat the evil and reclaim them. After the enemy has been defeated, you hide the items and return home." She sips her coffee. "Oh, and you've never lost any of the battles you've forged. Not once. No matter what it cost you in the end."

Placing my hands in my lap, I say, "If any of that is true, I would think a dire situation such as that calls for an adult to handle, not a child."

She stares at me, puzzled. "A child? No, no, you were never that young, with the exception of when you stopped the near execution of the world, but that was before your service began." She shakes her head adamantly. "No. You've always returned as an adult, looking exactly how you do now." Setting down her mug, she scrunches up her already wrinkled face, severely creasing her forehead and the crow's feet at the corners of her eyes. "How old were you when you were sent to the orphanage?"

Leaning back in my chair, I cross my legs at the knee and my arms over my chest. "Eight, but I was fifteen when it burned."

Her troubled gaze wavers. "But you didn't cross the ocean right away."

Pressing my lips together, I inhale deeply through my nose before responding. "I spent a few years liberating other orphanages the Caltraves, one of the fanatical groups in the former States, were operating. I couldn't bear the thought of them doing harm to other innocent children like they did to me. It took time because of how well hidden the structures were."

"What made you decide to finally leave and come here?"

"At first it was to keep the Caltraves from hunting me down. But now I realize it was a feeling ... an instinct that drew me to escape. It took over a week to travel by sea, then many more crossing the heavily scarred terrain since most of the rail lines had been damaged or destroyed. When those became inaccessible, I rode buses or hitched for rides until I settled in Kern. That was five years ago."

"Do you know what lured you to the town?"

Reaching under my sweatshirt, I pull out the chain with the compass rose, allowing it to dangle between my fingers. "I didn't figure it out until yesterday. It's one of the reasons I decided to venture away from the hostel and see you, even though Festus told me not to leave until he returned." I tuck the pendant back under my clothes. "I haven't figured out why it called to me. Where did you find it?"

She doesn't answer right away while nursing the remnants of her coffee. "Honestly, I didn't even know I had it until the day you spotted it among the pile of jewelry. Only a relic hunter can sense the artifacts. That's when I realized its significance ... because of how you looked at it."

"Do you know what it's for?"

She shakes her head. "No, I don't."

I pause briefly because my mind is starting to become muddled since I neglected to eat breakfast this morning. The only thing in my stomach is the water Dalma provided, and that's not nearly enough to deal with the realizations rapidly falling upon me. "Are there any others like me?"

She smiles. "No, my dear. You're the only relic hunter in existence. There have never been more than one roaming the lands. If something unfortunate happens, then the hunter is replaced with a new volunteer. It helps to prevent competition and rivalry."

"And I was always brought back as an adult?" I inquire, my thoughts spinning out of control, causing my head to pound.

"Every time."

I rub my temples, hoping that'll ease the discomfort brewing. "What about my memory?"

Dalma tilts her head. "I don't know the answer to that, but I presume it was intact given the nature of what you do. It would be very difficult for a relic hunter to be successful if she doesn't know her entire history, or retain the knowledge of what she's already dealt with and defeated."

"Then why is it different this time?" I utter more to myself than to her.

Her sagging shoulders rise very little. "I wish I knew."

Staring at her, I ask, "What, exactly, are you?"

She chuckles, and I know immediately she's going to avoid giving a real response. "A friend, and I'm going to leave it at that." Standing, she places her dishes into the sink. "I hate to cut our conversation short, but I have to be at the rynek shortly."

I thank her, remove the keys stuffed into my pocket for the motorbike, place the knapsack across my back, and return to the hostel. Once the machine is secure, I enter through the back door of the building, finding Vin alone, right where I left him. Stepping up to the counter, I wait until he notices me before tossing him the keys.

"Is Rowen still here?" I ask, praying the answer is no.

Vin slides the ring into his pocket. "He left the day before yesterday. Before I forget ..." He turns, jumps down from the stool, and retrieves a brown paper wrapped package from the back counter, then hands it to me. "Festus dropped this off for you about an hour or so ago. He paid me to make sure I delivered it as promised."

I'm stunned to realize it's the same parcel I collected for him from Dalma. Pulling on the rough twine holding the bundle together, I discover a leather-bound journal being held together by matching thread tucked into the wrappings. The skin is soft and severely worn, a few cracks expanding down the weathered spine. The mystery behind the gift widens when I find the parchment inside is filled with odd lettering and tiny drawings, almost like it's some sort of code or forgotten language. The ink is partially faded in places and the pages are flaking around the edges.

"Wow, what kind of writing is that?" Vin asks, angling his head to get a better look.

My gaze doesn't leave the page. "I don't know."

Flipping back to the beginning, I stare at the bizarre images, slowly realizing the handwriting is, in fact, my own. As the seconds tick by at a glacial pace, a memory washes over me like a subtle wave and I'm able to comprehend the symbols making up the line at the top of the first page.

If you're reading this, then I failed to stop him.

Knots form in my stomach, and a dark cloud settles over me. "Is Festus at the café?" I ask, scrutinizing the ominous words while I work on digesting them. They sink into my head like a lead weight.

Having returned to his magazine, Vin doesn't look up when he replies, "He should be."

After closing the journal, I tie the leather strings around it, leave the wrappings on the counter, and head out the front door. The streets are a little more crowded with people out enjoying the nice day now that the clouds have finally cleared. We all know winter isn't too far away and beautiful moments like this will quickly be in short supply. When I reach the roundabout, I wait for the circle of cars to finish their dance around the fountain in order to safely cross. Through the windows lining the sidewalk, I spot Festus in his shop joyfully tending to customers.

Every bit of noise ceases, my hearing muffled by an unseen force that presses hard upon me, practically suffocating. A cold chill pierces my core, stronger than any previously experienced.

As the vehicles parade by—the sounds of their engines complete silence—between the flicks of metal roofs I notice a tall, dark figure standing across the way close to the entrance for the café, a long hood covering his face while his black robe dusts the ground, obscuring his feet. I become utterly petrified by the sight. The thing moves its head, so I follow his roaming gaze.

Glancing toward the other intersections for the circular junction, I spot a couple more wearing identical cloaks, their faces covered and every bit of flesh on their hands hidden in the folds of the thick, lengthy garment encasing their bodies. There are another two right beside the fountain. Turning, I notice a lone one standing several meters behind me. Terror grips me, freezing me into place.

The traffic clears and people traverse the roads, seemingly oblivious to the intruders as if purposefully masked from the danger being imposed upon me. Looking back at the Watcher by the café, the thing doesn't move while it's knocked into by multiple individuals, each of whom seem to pass right easily through him like vapor. He simply stands there, and yet I know he's smiling.

The blast is deafening and earth shattering.

I'm thrown sideways and backwards, hitting the brick exterior wall of the building next to me, then fall to the ground, hard. The ringing now permeating my ears prevents the sounds of agonizing screams to fully register. Pain sears through my entire body, and as I try to sit up, I notice my hands are badly cut, there are tears in my jeans with bits of shrapnel poking out of the skin, and I can taste blood—its bitter iron—in my mouth. Shards of glass, shattered bricks, splintered wood, torn metal, and splotches of crimson cover every inch of the sidewalk, as well as the streets. Plumes of smoke soar into the air, blocking out the sun, filling my lungs with toxins. Bodies lay strewn about, many appearing lifeless and in pieces. Entire limbs have been severed, allowing the victims to bleed out in a matter of seconds. Others moan and writhe, their death throws being the last things they will ever experience.

Grimacing, I work on pushing myself into a standing position, grunting loudly from the sharp pain, then focus my attention on what remains of the café where thick smoke billows from the fragmented edifice. Fire eats away at the interior, and whatever bodies remain inside. The structures closest to where the blast originated have structural damage, one already on the verge of collapse. Vehicles caught in the devastation smolder while their drivers are slumped over the steering wheels, unconscious and helpless. A car now sits where the fountain should be, its demolished stone beneath the twisted, scorched metal. Those not too badly injured start tending to the ones who are, but I focus my attention on the Watchers.

They haven't moved, are free from injury and debris, and each one is staring straight at me. Everyone appears unaware of their presence, adding to the horror clutching at me. It's thick talons threaten to rip apart what survived.

Stumbling backwards, nearly losing my footing due to the injuries my legs have sustained, I turn to run, but momentarily forgot about the Watcher behind me. With a wave of its arm, I'm thrown against the structure I collided with when the bomb went off, smacking my already injured head, causing blood to trickle into the collar of my sweatshirt. Everything blurs for a moment, stars replacing the smoke and clouds. Pain radiates down my spine as my back is adhered to the building's rough surface. The thing doesn't touch me while I'm being pressed harder into the brick, as if it means to make me a permanent part of the exterior. He keeps the arm raised above his head, an invisible power securing me into place.

"Where is it?" the thing hisses, coming closer, its face still obstructed from view.

"Where's what?" I moan, my entire body throbbing, blood still pooling around my collar and dripping onto the sidewalk from the wounds in my legs.

He flicks his gloved fingers, forcing my arms to extend outward as if I'm being crucified. "The cardinal stone. We want it."

Breathing becomes difficult since it feels like my chest is caving in. "I don't know ... what ... you're talking about."

He widens his hand, and my arms are slowly being pulled free from their sockets. I scream from the immense pain, but no one seems to care, or even notice. It's almost as if what's happening to me is separate from the rest of the world, on a completely different plane of reality. Tears stream down my face while my body rises higher, still plastered firmly against the building.

"We know you found it. Give us the cardinal stone."

My throat closes, and I'm on the verge of passing out when the force holding me releases and I drop to the ground. Through hazy eyes I catch sight of specks of ash floating skyward and the Watcher is gone.

"Magdalene," a familiar voice says, kneeling beside me, cradling me against their stable frame.

The person gingerly picks me up, wraps an arm around my waist, and assists me into the first alley we come to as rapidly approaching sirens wail in the distance. I garner enough strength to distinguish a set of black eyes staring back at me. They alter to a warm hazel, then everything goes dark.

Chapter Five

A supple embrace holds me firm, cradling me in its comfort while something weighty nestles me into place. The crackling of logs lures me out of a deep slumber. Opening my eyes, I find myself lying on a king-sized canopy bed with soft blue, satin curtains tied delicately around the thick, intricate, wooden posts that reach high toward the vaulted ceiling. The pillow under my head is bulky, and slightly propped up against the plush headboard. Heavy satin blankets swath every inch of the solid mattress, inviting me to stay nice and snug in their warmth. Along the far wall is a massive stone fireplace, a fire blazing behind its wrought iron screen, keeping the ashes and flames from filtering into the room.

A panel of windows line the wall to the left covered in dark blue drapes that are currently closed, obstructing the sun's rays ... if it's even still out. A Renaissance-style armoire and dresser with hand-carved lattice work sit along the wall by a partially opened door. Behind the dresser is a gold-framed mirror, its glass tarnished and chipped. An antique couch with matching high-backed chairs covered in powder blue jacquard create a small seating arrangement in front of the fireplace. Several elegant paintings adorn the room, many depicting a stunning mountainside characterized in lush colors and delicate brush strokes. Carefully sitting up, I spot woven rugs concealing stone floors.

I glance around the room a little longer, taking in its beauty and wonder since I've never seen such opulence before. Tossing back the covers, I gingerly swing my legs out over the side of the bed, noticing I'm still wearing my jeans and dark green tank top. The shrapnel from the blast has been removed and my wounds are bandaged, along with the deep cuts on my hands and the lacerations on my arms that I didn't know existed. It takes a great amount of effort for me to stand, but my legs give out instantly from the not only the pain, but fatigue. Using the bed, I pull myself back up and brace my aching body against it while moving around, grabbing the back of the couch for support when I'm close to it. Laying on its cushions is my blood-soaked hoodie with its torn sleeves and ripped hem. Underneath are my boots caked in dried blood and ash. My filthy knapsack rests on one of the chairs, so I carefully step over to it and remove the kard, which is still surprisingly in the outer pocket. The weapon feels heavier than normal, but that could be due to me being weak from the attack and subsequent injuries.

Limping over to the door, I prop myself against the wall before turning the thick brass handle. The hallway on the other side is painted a soft yellow with a dimpled, crystal light fixture protruding from the ceiling, which isn't vaulted. The stone flooring from the bedroom continues down the expanse, sending a shiver through my body from its coldness. A few feet away on the left is a narrow wooden staircase leading down, voices raised in anger wafting up from below. Unsure of which direction to go, I decide to follow the argument. With a firm hold on the ivory grip of the kard, I slowly descend, bracing myself against the wall for support.

"How could you bring her here?" a male voice booms in a heavy British accent, his anger and rage all consuming.

"I had to," a familiar voice counters furiously. "You know that."

Heavy feet pound on the floor as if someone is pacing. "It was reckless of you to have gone to Kern knowing what was there," the same person scolds.

There's an exacerbated sigh.

"That's exactly why I did it. If I hadn't, she'd be in their hands, and you know what they would've done to her." The man's voice cracks with emotion. "I couldn't risk it."

"Did any of them see you?" someone inquires in a calming, sultry tone with a Latvian inflection.

"I don't believe so, but it was so chaotic, and I was solely focused on the one Watcher attacking Magdalene. I'm not sure if the others took notice."

"How many innocents did they slaughter?" another person asks, this male sounding American.

"Around forty."

Someone lets out a deep, guttural groan. "Knowing that she's been let loose, the rest will come looking for her. What are we supposed to do now?"

"I'm not sure," the one with the heavier British accent replies, sounding tense.

When I reach the bottom of the stairs, I glance to the right, finding an arched doorway leading into a brightly lit, terra cotta-colored kitchen with stone flooring, red oak cabinets, and white marble countertops. In the center is an island where four men and two women stand, bickering. None of them notice my presence, so I debate whether or not to turn and run, even with my body in no condition to take such drastic measures. Instead, against better judgement, I step farther inside.

"Who are you?" I demand, clenching my teeth, the tip of the blade pointed in their direction, my hands shaking uncontrollably to the point I fear that I might drop the weapon.

They all turn and stare at me. I don't recognize any of them, except for one. Rowen's clothes are disheveled, torn, and bloody, but he doesn't appear to be injured. His wavy, brown hair contains bits of debris and ash. Dark smudges cover his chiseled face, his broad shoulders are slumped forward, and he looks utterly exhausted. When he moves toward me, I raise the blade higher, though I'm too weak to properly wield it.

"No one is going to hurt you, Magdalene," he says, lifting his hands as if to defend himself from a possible attack.

Glaring at each of them, I spot a kard identical to mine lying on the countertop for the island. "Where did you get that?"

Rowen looks to see what I'm pointing at, then moves his attention back to me. "You gave that dagger to me a long time ago. It's what I used to destroy the Watcher."

A wave of dizziness washes over me, followed by a pounding in my head and a tremor that racks my body, causing me to drop the blade, but Rowen catches me before I can hit the floor. His movement was so swift that I barely perceived it. He picks me up and cradles me in his muscular arms, his hold loving and consoling. The woodsy smell his body seems to normally give off has been replaced with the odor of smoke and blood. My nose wrinkles at the stench, then I wonder if I smell the same.

A woman with long, burgundy hair snatches a towel off of the counter and uses it to take possession of my kard. She grimaces at the weapon—almost as if she's scared to touch it—sets it on the countertop beside its twin, and tosses the towel aside, afraid it'll bring her unimaginable torment. At least, that's what I sense from her. Her dark eyes glare at me, and I know instinctively that she's incensed by my presence, enraged that Rowen has placed them all at tremendous risk for something so petty as a hunter's life.

It's as if I can see into her mind ... detect her thoughts, much like I did with the caretakers at the orphanage. This is something I haven't needed to do in a long time, and am glad to have the ability, though I'm not sure where it came from.

"I'm going to take her back upstairs. Can one of you bring something for her to eat and drink?" Rowen doesn't wait for a response before leaving the kitchen, carrying me gingerly to the bedroom I was just in. After setting me on the thick mattress, he adjusts the pillows so I'm in an upright position, tucks the blankets tenderly around me, then sits on the edge of the bed. His hand lingers by mine, desperate to hold it. "You need rest."

"Where am I?" I ask, my voice cracking due to tiredness.

"My home." He smiles, and there's a brightness behind it. "The one I told you about."

"Why did you bring me here?"

He pushes a strand of hair behind my ear, and I savor his touch, wanting to feel his hot skin against mine, our bodies pressed firmly together. Blushing, he replies, "To keep you safe." His fingers graze mine, and the tugging of a cord I felt before returns. "You need to sleep so your body can heal. I'll be back in a little while to check on you." He leans forward as if to kiss me, but changes his mind, which surprisingly saddens me.

The door isn't closed long before the woman with the lengthy, burgundy hair enters carrying a silver serving tray containing a bowl of soup, a roll, utensils, a cloth napkin, and a glass of water. She's around my height with an apple-shaped face, an athletic build, full red lips, and light gray eyes. Her black pants are tight, emphasizing the curves of her hips, as well as the firm muscles of her legs and ass. The red bustier with its silver accents pushes her breasts not only close together, but high upon her chest. Underneath is a long-sleeved matching blouse, the buttons of which are open, displaying the tops of her breasts and the deep cleavage caused by such form fitting garments. Her black boots go up to her thighs and have long, spiked heels.

After setting the tray onto my lap, she abruptly leaves without saying a word—though the heavy disdain is clearly visible on her face—closing the door behind her. I eat slowly, uncertainty and confusion weighing heavily on me, along with trepidation and exhaustion. When I'm done, I place the tray onto the empty side of the bed, slide deeper under the blankets, and try to get some more sleep.

The sun must have set because when I wake the room is much darker than it was before. The tray has been removed, and I notice Rowen lying on the couch with his eyes closed, the blaze in the fireplace now simply cooling embers, adding little warmth to the frigid room. Everything hurts, making it difficult to move without softly moaning, but I need to find something to help ease the pain. I'm in the process of pushing myself out of bed when Rowen is suddenly at my side, the scent of fresh lavender instead of the woodsy aroma wafting off of his clean skin. His hair is damp and he's wearing flannel lounge pants and a white T-shirt, which shows off his sculpted biceps. The tender ropes of the muscles drawing my unwarranted attention.

I find myself wanting to caress their edges with the tips of my fingers before kissing them, leaving a mark to show they belong to me.

"What do you need?" he asks, breaking my daydream and helping me back under the blankets, then turns on the amber-colored glass lamp on the nightstand beside the bed. The shadows being cast across his face from the pale light are both haunting and enticing.

"Do you have anything for the pain?" I manage to inquire once my sanity has returned.

"Yes, we do. Let me get it." He heads out the door, returning a few minutes later carrying a bottle of pills and a glass of water. "I had Ulrich go to town earlier and buy these for you since we didn't have any on hand, and I knew you'd be wanting them." He hands me the bottle and places the glass on the nightstand, then sits on the edge of the bed.

My fingers ache while I turn the cap on the plastic container, then dump three small capsules into my hand. After downing them, I set everything back onto the nightstand and prop myself up against the headboard as best I can so I'm in a sitting position, the blankets tucked gently around me.

"What time is it?" I ask when I'm finally situated.

"A little after midnight. Are you hungry? It's been hours since you ate."

I shake my head. "No, I'm just sore. Thank you for saving me from that Watcher."

He grins awkwardly. "I just wish I'd gotten there sooner." Then takes my hand since it's above the blanket, clasping it tightly. "I'm sorry about Festus."

As much as I want to keep holding onto Rowen, I pull out of his grasp, not quite sure what to make of the situation, which seems to upset him. "Vin said you left."

"I moved out of the hostel but remained in Kern."

"Why did you stay?"

His face softens. "You know why."

"But I don't." I let out a frustrated groan and decide to change the subject since the conversation is making me uncomfortable. Especially with the thoughts I know are rolling around in his head. Several of which cause my pulse to quicken and my heart to skip a beat. "What is this place?" I ask as calmly as possible.

"Burmstone Castle. We're at the top of one of the many ridges for the Carpathian Mountains. The closest town is Tomis, which is several miles west along the base. We're nice and isolated, so you'll be safe here."

"How many people reside in the castle?"

He scoots closer before answering, resting one of his legs on the mattress, leaving the other to remain over the edge, his foot firmly planted on the floor. "There are six of us."

"Are they all like ... you?" I ask, hoping the question doesn't irritate him.

"You mean are they demons? Yes, but they won't harm you. I promise. We aren't anything like the Watchers, or the other creatures roaming the Earth who are hiding in plain sight."

Looking down at my hands, which are clasped tightly in my lap, I recall Dalma's words. "Demons can't be trusted."

He glowers. "The old woman at the rynek told you that."

"That's not all she said to me."

He grimaces slightly. "I wondered if she knew who I was. I'm sure she explained about the book I stole."

Glancing at him, I ask, "Where is it?"

He points to the fireplace. "I didn't want her giving it to you because it documents my life *before* the two of us met. I feared it would turn you against me, knowing the things I've done. It's not who I am anymore, or who I want to be." He sidles up beside me, his face close to mine, desperation clinging to the surface of his eyes. "What do you remember?"

"You mean from before?"

He nods.

"Nothing. I didn't know about any of this until just a few days ago, but you already knew that." There's a sharpness in my tone, shocking not only him, but myself as well. "It's why you made the comment after dinner the other night."

He bites the inside of his cheek. "I was simply suspicious because of how you didn't react when I entered the hostel, or even when I asked about where I could get something to eat. It's one of the reasons I followed you from the café to the rynek. I needed to be sure I wasn't losing my mind and that you had, indeed, forgotten about me."

Surprisingly, his words sting. I pull my knees up to my chest and wrap my arms around my legs, cocooning myself from the anguish he's exhibiting at a loss I know I should be feeling as well.

"I wish I knew why I don't recall anything from before. According to the old woman, Dalma, I always did. But for some reason, this time is different."

Rowen furrows his brow and his eyes widen. "You mean it was done to you on purpose?"

"It would seem that way. Yet, I must have known something like this was a possibility. Festus gave me a journal filled with cryptic writing that apparently I created because I recognized the penmanship as my own. I was holding it when the attack occurred, but don't know what happened to it."

"I didn't see anything when I picked you up off the sidewalk." He stands, goes over to the armoire, opens its doors, removes a heavy knitted coat, and dons it, then slips on a pair of boots. "I'll go back and look for it. Stay right here." In the blink of an eye, he's gone in a puff of black smoke that quickly dissipates.

I wondered how we arrived at the castle so quickly since it should've taken hours, if not a full day or more, to travel this great distance by car.

I guess being a supernatural creature has its privileges.

Not knowing how long he'll be gone, and with my bladder full, I carefully get out of bed, make my way around it, pass through an ornate wooden door by the other nightstand, and turn on the light switch beside the doorway, illuminating a gorgeous bathroom constructed from pale stone. A porcelain toilet sits in an alcove with its own covered entrance by a bay of windows. A circular, sunken tub tiled in red marble lies in the center of the room with a flat showerhead dangling from the ceiling directly above it, and a tall, silk laden privacy screen shields the bath from the doorway. Along the far wall is a lengthy vanity with brass fixtures, two stone sinks, and neatly folded towels, as well as basic toiletries you'd find in any home. An immense mirror is adhered behind it, and the image reflected in its pristine glass shows a young woman with smudges covering her weary face, a cut above her brow, dark circles under her tired blue eyes, and raven-colored hair sticking up in every direction from a ponytail that's unraveling.

It's a face I truly don't recognize.

"Magdalene!" Rowen shouts frantically from the bedroom.

"I'm in here."

He rushes into the room, then lets out an exhalation of relief when he sees me. "I didn't find it." He pauses, noticing my reflection in the mirror. "You probably want to get cleaned up. I'll see if Doreleska or Hollis have clothes you can borrow, then get some more bandages and ointment since you're going to want to replace the ones you have on. Everything else you might need is under the sinks. I'll wait for you in the bedroom."

After the door is closed, I first use the toilet, then rummage for soap, finding an unused bar smelling of lavender wrapped in pale pink paper. Setting one of the towels along the edge of the tub, I turn on the water, allowing it to warm before pulling the chain that dangles with the showerhead, activating it. I discard my tattered clothes and toss the bandages into a receptacle by the vanity, but leave the compass rose around my neck. Cautiously stepping down into the deep tub, I stand under the pulsating water, enjoying the warmth as it pummels my sore and battered body.

Images from the bombing infiltrate my mind, vexing me further. The screams, the smell of burning flesh, the sight of blood rolling over the bricks for the roads, and the crushed, twisted metal of the vehicles, entombing their drivers. Why would someone attack the café? It had to have been the Watchers who instigated the violence, though I'm not sure why. Was it to get my attention? I had already noticed them several days prior. And what did the thing mean by the cardinal stone?

Lathering, I try not to open my healing wounds, which are many. The ones on my legs aren't as deep as I thought they would be. Bruises have formed nearly everywhere there's a corresponding injury, but are more prevalent along my arms where the Watcher tried to pull them from their sockets. When I go to wash my hair, I have to be extra careful due to the bumps on the back of my head and the scabbed-over lacerations. It feels good to rid myself of the grime, cleansing the horrible day from my skin, watching it spiral down the drain into oblivion.

I linger a bit longer under the gentle rain of the water, relishing the moment since the showers at the hostel were so horrible. After turning it off, I reach for the towel, dry, then wrap it around my body, securing it above my chest. When I enter the bedroom, Rowen is no longer wearing his heavy coat or boots and is sitting on the bed, a goofy grin on his face and lust in his eyes when he notices I'm simply wearing the towel.

I blush in response.

"Do you know how ridiculous you look?" I comment, snickering, once my composure has returned.

"You used to find me cute," he replies, pretending to be hurt by the remark. "Doreleska had some things you can wear." He pats the pile of clothes beside him. "If you're up for it, everyone is in the library. Demons don't need a lot of sleep, so we're awake most nights."

Standing, he hesitates to leave, but does with great trepidation. Once the door is closed, I look through the garments, noticing there isn't any underwear or even a bra, but that doesn't bother me since I've gone without plenty of times. Before dressing, I spot a tube of ointment and a pile of bandages on the dresser. I apply small amounts of anti-bacterial cream and tape the cloth compresses onto my more serious injuries, which, thankfully, there are few. The charcoal-colored leggings fit snuggly, swathing my curves and hugging my hips. The chunky, beige sweater is slightly oversized and shows a bit of my midriff, which really doesn't bother me. The only thing to cover my feet are white, low-rise ankle socks. Returning to the bathroom, I carefully run a comb through my hair, working out the rest of the knots, then decide to leave it down so it'll dry, and make sure the pendant is hidden under the sweater.

Exiting the bedroom, I traverse the stairs I used earlier, and at the bottom instead of turning right I go left, entering a lengthy corridor covered in white wainscotting, gold trim, and dozens of paintings, many depicting men in regal attire from an age long since passed. Tall, colorful vases rest in small niches, along with Edwardian-style tables topped with dark marble and granite statues. I next come upon an oblong entrance hall with a winding staircase leading up to the second story and down to a lower level. The floor is a tile mosaic depicting a circle with a horizontal 'z' that has a short line through its center.

Following the muffled voices, I proceed to the farthest archway, go through a small vestibule decorated in the same style as the corridor, and pass a bathroom on the right adorned in ivory granite. Then, I enter a library consisting of shelves made from dark cherry wood, with woven rugs covering much of the hardwood floor, low-hung chandeliers that cast minimal light, a robust table with intricately carved legs and crimson cushioned chairs, and a matching seating arrangement next to an active fireplace. The temperature of the room is sweltering, but doesn't appear to be bothering anyone. Perhaps they're used to it.

Rowen is immediately at my side, his arm around my waist to help steady me since I'm not quite sturdy on my feet yet. The lavender scent has now been replaced by a woodsy one, begging me to inhale deeply and nuzzle my face into his chest. He guides me to one of the chairs at the table where two of his housemates are currently playing a game of chess, while the other three are reading. I sit next to the woman who brought my food, her pointy nose deep in what looks to be an anthology, the felt spine cracked and shedding. Across from her is a dark-skinned man with short, black hair, wide-set eyes, an oval face, and a narrow chin with a bit of stubble. Next to him is a woman around my age with long, blonde hair tied at the base of her neck. She has an alabaster complexion, a petite nose, rosy cheeks, and is thin as a rail. Rowen introduces them to me as Doreleska, Ulrich, and Hollis.

The pair playing chess are Pierce—who's in his early thirties like Rowen, burly, with medium-length, dark brown hair, a square face, wide nose, and dimple chin—and Kagan, who's the oldest. He has a solid frame, brown eyes, short, honey brown, spiked hair, and a full beard that barely stretches below his chin. He's also the self-proclaimed leader for the group.

Hollis closes her book, using a slender finger to mark her page, and stares at me as if transfixed. "How are you feeling?" she asks, her Irish lilt thicker than Vin's.

"Tired and sore." I grimace slightly, readjusting myself in the plush seat.

She cocks her head and blinks her long lashes for several seconds. "You know, I've never met a relic hunter before."

"Considering Magdalene is the only one, it's not a surprise," Kagan comments without looking up from his game. His is the voice I heard booming from the kitchen, furious that Rowen brought me here. "There's just one in our group who's ever encountered her. The rest of us were never stupid enough to go after sacred objects."

"We did enough damage without them," Doreleska adds, chuckling, her Latvian voice sultry.

Pierce glances at Rowen, narrowing his gaze. "Why *did* you want the chalice? You've never told us."

"And I'm not going to," he replies bitterly, squaring his jaw in frustration.

"That's because he doesn't want to upset the girlfriend." Doreleska jabs him in the arm since he's sitting on the other side of her.

Grabbing the rear of her chair, Rowen shoves it backwards, nearly causing the woman to fall onto the floor. "Fuck off."

She manages to steady herself before toppling over, then stands and pulls back her fist, ready to strike.

"Stop it," Kagan orders, finally breaking away from the chessboard, glowering at the pair. "I'm sick of the two of you fighting."

Doreleska grumbles as she lowers her arm and retakes her seat. "I hate being trapped in this goddamn castle," she grouses, pouting her full red lips. "Loverboy gets to prance around the countryside while the rest of us are stuck inside of this monstrosity for who knows how long."

"Leave then. No one is forcing you to stay," Rowen practically shouts, tossing his hands into the air. "I'm sure Hollis would love to finally have a room all to herself."

"I like my roommate," the young woman says mournfully, as if Doreleska has already vacated the premises. "I don't want her to go."

"No one is going anywhere," Kagan affirms, growling slightly, his brown eyes becoming menacing. "Especially now that the Watchers are searching for Magdalene. It's not safe for any of us to wander farther than the castle grounds. Tomis is as far as I'm willing to permit you all to travel, but not unaccompanied or weaponless."

"Yeah, thanks for that, Rowen." Pierce glares hatefully down the table at Rowen and me. "I didn't escape Hell just to be trapped on a mountain for all eternity with you."

Smirking, Rowen rests his arms on the table and leans forward to get a better glimpse of his friend. "Who knew a demon as powerful as yourself would be so scared of a few Watchers."

Pierce's nostrils flare and his face reddens. "It's not them I'm afraid of, asshole. Besides, not all of us have access to hunter's blades like you do. We're stuck with swords that have been cast in iron, or some other ineffective armament. Thankfully, Kagan wrapped those guards and hilts in strips of leather so we can use them."

The older man grins at the compliment. "It took some doing, considering that particular metal can be fatal to our kind."

"Which is why I prefer more modern weapons," Doreleska adds, gesturing her long, slim fingers as if they were guns, aiming both at Rowen. "Quick and easy." She pretends to fire several shots, which only makes him angrier.

I look at Pierce. "Who *are* the Watchers?"

"Servants of the underworld," he replies, resetting the chess game since it appears Kagan won. "Normally, Lucifer tasks them with bringing us runaways back home."

"This time it feels different." Doreleska shivers. "I mean, why are they after the relic hunter? The God of Hell knows better than to steal his brother's possessions. Fuck, he hates it when one of us tries to. If anything, those monsters should've snatched Rowen's ass, not gone after Magdalene."

"Very troubling," Ulrich states without lifting his head to formally engage in the conversation, rubbing his chin.

"Why can't you use the blades?" I inquire, bewildered by the remark. "They're just simple instruments anyone can wield."

Pierce, Doreleska, and Kagan stare at Rowen. Hollis laughs at the exchange, while Ulrich keeps reading.

Rowen shrugs his shoulders. "I told you she doesn't remember."

Doreleska tilts her head back and lets out a frustrated grunt, then stands and goes over to one of the bookshelves beside a series of stained-glass windows depicting nature scenes through the seasons. Life on the mountainside when it isn't winter or raining. She removes a bulky, hardcover book that's closed, secured by a tarnished clasp. As she sets it on the table, I notice an embellished, white shield with a red cross adorning the cover. A hint of recognition rises to the surface, but I'm not able to grasp onto it long enough to recall the image's meaning. After opening the lock, she carefully turns the cream-colored parchment with her nimble fingers and highly polished nails. Words penned in multiple languages fill the pages, along with hand-painted pictures of ancient times long since burned from our memories. When she reaches a drawing of two gold-bladed kards with ivory handles crossing each other, she stops and slaps the Latin description below with an open palm.

"Your weapons are called the Blades of Solace, named after their creator, the archangel Solistine. Their purpose is to brutalize and raze demons from the Earth, sending us to infernal cages no one has ever been able to break out of." Raising her head, she glowers at Rowen. "Except for one." She turns her attention back to the book. "In order for one of us to touch the handle with our bare skin, the kard must be bequeathed to us by a hunter. Otherwise, we'll get burned."

"Which is why you used a towel," I state.

She nods. "Rowen can only handle the one you gave him, so he marked it in case your blades somehow get mixed up."

I pull the book over, turning back to the cover, and tap on the image. "Whose symbol is this?"

Ulrich finally looks up, his brown eyes dancing in the firelight. "That represents the Knights Templar. A few of them stayed here during the First Crusade. Years ago, Hollis, Kagan, and I spent months retrofitting this entire place for electricity and indoor plumbing, making it more livable for us younger demons." He chuckles.

"And us older ones thank you for that." Pierce smiles, saluting him.

Doreleska growls, obviously annoyed at being interrupted. "As I was going to say, all sorts of people have lived in this castle, which is why the books in the library are in various languages and subscripts. There's even a tome older than dirt filled with odd symbols and lettering. None of us have been able to decipher it."

"That's because it's written in hynafol glyphs," Kagan states, breaking momentarily from the new game with Pierce. "There isn't anyone alive who can read that ancient language. I doubt even the angels wandering around out there are able to understand it." He gestures toward the darkened windows.

The writing in the journal Festus gave me, could that have been what was used?

"Can I see this tome?" I inquire, my voice cracking ever so slightly.

They all stare at me strangely.

"Sure." Doreleska goes to another shelf and returns with a thin, leather-bound book, the spine of which is badly broken and the pages practically falling out. "As you can see, there have been others wanting to know what's written inside. But from what we can tell, no one has ever deciphered it."

On the cover are two glyphs: a crucifix with a star at the center of the crossbar, a triquetra inside its points; and a deer, whose horns extend beyond the body, then curl back around its legs, glancing off of the ground.

I know immediately what they mean.

"It's for a relic hunter," I utter, surprising everyone.

Ulrich puts down his book and practically stretches across the table, peering at the item in my hand. "You can read that?" he asks, astonished.

"That's not possible." Kagan's chair is virtually knocked to the floor as he thunders his way over, and forces Doreleska to relinquish her seat.

"Well, Magdalene can read, write, and speak every language imaginable. Why not this one?" Rowen interjects, beaming with pride.

The older man furrows his brow. "I can, too, but I've never met or known anyone who has been able to understand hynafol glyphs. Let alone a hunter."

"Maybe it's different for her because she searches for relics and not demons," Pierce comments, still in his seat. "Glyphs and sigils were one way the ancient gods and goddesses hid their powerful weapons and sacred treasures. Even from each other."

"Does it say who wrote it?" Hollis asks, giddy with excitement, rushing around the table to stand behind me.

Opening to the first page, it takes me only seconds to comprehend what's written. "Someone named Daimon, but there isn't much in here about who, exactly, he was. I would assume he was a relic hunter given the nature of the cover." I glance through the rest of the pages. "From what I can decipher, he simply documents his victories ... brags about them, actually. He doesn't mention the relics that were reclaimed or what he did with them after winning his battles." I'm not even halfway through the tome when I discover the rest of the pages are blank. "Looks like he wasn't able to finish."

Doreleska crosses her arms over her chest. "I wonder why."

Hollis retakes her seat, looking dejected. "Maybe he died."

I close the book and return it to Doreleska, who places it back on the shelf. Kagan and Pierce resume their chess game, and Hollis and Ulrich delve into their reading while I review the hefty book still on the table. Rowen moves into Doreleska's seat—who growls at being displaced and retreats to the seating area close to the fire—drapes an arm along the back of my chair, and leers over my shoulder while I review the contents.

The various religious wars that have been forged across the world from the beginning of time are heavily documented, in addition to who started the conflicts and who won them—if there really is such things like winning a war. As well as what changes came about, if any.

I skim over the stories, hoping to find something useful, and locate a brief narrative about a small village near the eastern shores of the Adriatic Sea that was once home to some sort of sacred temple enshrined to the sun goddess, Olwen. Apparently, during the rise of the Ottoman Empire, an unknown power leveled the town—including the temple—killing everyone. There were no witnesses to its demise, only the destruction that was discovered sometime later. Even though there isn't much to the story, it's the name of the village that rattles me: Cresidio.

I know that place, I think to myself. *But how?*

My heart catches, sweat breaks out over my brow, and knots form in my stomach, so I close the book, abruptly stand, and head for the door.

"Magdalene, are you all right?" Rowen asks, chasing after me, placing a hand on my shoulder, and drawing everyone's attention.

I stop and do my best to muffle the trembling desperate to come out in my voice. "I'm fine. Just tired."

Hollis joins us, wrapping her arm around mine as if we're old friends. She's slightly shorter than me and the bright purple sweatpants she's wearing are nearly falling from her tiny waist. The matching top hangs loosely around her small bust and she's barefoot, which surprises me given how cold the floors are even with their rugs.

"Let me get you something to sleep in since I doubt you want to keep on that bulky sweater."

Leaving Rowen behind, the two of us head toward the entrance hall, then up the winding staircase. Her room is across from ours and identical in design, but colored in shades of purple instead of blue.

"I have a few things you can borrow." She opens the dresser by the door to the bathroom, then proceeds to toss out clothes in all manner of style and color into a pile on the floor. "Take your pick."

Kneeling on the floor beside her, I select pink cotton sweatpants and a matching T-shirt.

She glances sideways at me, smiling wide, and giggling a bit under her breath while the two of us refold and tuck the clothes back into place. "You know, Rowen is madly in love with you." She waits for a response, but I don't give one. "I've never seen a demon so infatuated with a mortal before. I think it's kind of sweet. Not many of us get the chance at finding love. Mostly, people hear the word demon and run the other way. Or kill us." She leans against the dresser as I shut the drawer. "But, come to think of it, you really aren't a mortal. I mean, you've been around at least several centuries, if not longer." Tapping her finger against her chin, she scrunches up her exquisite face. "Where do you go after you win your wars?"

Standing, I reply, "I don't know. Like Rowen said, I have no memory of the past. My earliest recollection is from when I was eight and being pulled from rubble that was supposedly my home, but that was during this lifetime. I have no clue about the previous ones."

She narrows her gaze while crossing her arms over her chest. "You saw something in the larger book Doreleska showed you. I noticed it on your face when you got up. What was it?"

I had hoped no one had seen my expression, and have no intention of divulging what I felt upon seeing that name. "Nothing. The long day has finally caught up to me and the pain pills are wearing off."

She gives me a wry grin. "Uh-huh. Well, if you need anything, don't hesitate to ask."

When I'm back in Rowen's bedroom, I make a beeline for the bathroom to change, tossing the clothes I was wearing onto the cushioned bench at the foot of the bed. I fill the glass on the nightstand with water, take a few more pills, then turn off the lights and try to fall asleep. However, I can't stop thinking about Cresidio. The name eats away at me, gnawing on my memory for sustenance. I want to return to the library and scour the books to see if I can locate more information, but I'd prefer to do it alone, without so many prying eyes watching my every move.

If only I could see Dalma to ask, or peruse the scores of books she has in her home. She must know what happened in the town square since she was getting ready to head for the rynek shortly after I left. Is she wondering what's become of me, or has she assumed I was killed in the blast? Maybe tomorrow, Rowen and I can sneak out of the castle and pay her a visit, along with stopping by the hostel to gather my things. I don't want to keep borrowing everything from Hollis and Doreleska.

Chapter Six

In the morning, I find Rowen snoring softly on the couch. His hair is rumpled and his clothes askew, exposing a bit of his tight stomach. My hand lingers in the air above him, wanting to stroke those roped muscles, if only for a second. Instead, I take the clothes from earlier, step into the bathroom, use the facilities, then undress to check my wounds, applying more ointment and bandages where needed. After dressing and placing my hair into its usual ponytail, I toss the sweatpants and T-shirt onto the bed, grab the glass to refill it with water, and take a bit more pain medication. The aches aren't as bad today, but they're still plentiful.

Since I don't want to disturb Rowen, I quietly exit and go down to the kitchen to get something to eat. The room is empty and the kards are still on the island. Scanning their handles, I notice one has an 'R' scratched into the bottom of it. I'm glad he did that since I wouldn't want to be the one responsible for injuring him unnecessarily.

Searching through the cabinets, I find only a few boxes of dried goods, but the fridge is better stocked with fresh fruit, vegetables, eggs, and meat. Something tells me that demons don't really need to eat, that it's purely out of habit from when they were mortal. I pour myself a bowl of cereal, along with a glass of orange juice, and sit at one of the stools for the island. The morning sun blazes through the bare windows overlooking the grounds, adding warmth to the chill seeping from the old walls.

When I'm nearly done, Rowen enters still wearing the same clothes and makes himself breakfast similar to mine.

I wait until he's seated beside me before saying, "I was wondering if it would be possible to return to Kern today so I can get a few of my things."

"We'll have to be quick so Kagan doesn't notice we're gone."

Since he's open to the idea, I decide to push further. "That's not the only place I want to visit."

His demeanor quickly changes. "We can't be running around when there are Watchers looking for you. It's far too dangerous."

"Dalma needs to know that I'm all right. Maybe you can bring her to the castle?"

"No," he grumbles, avoiding all eye contact.

"It won't take that long. Just a few minutes."

He drops his spoon into the bowl, annoyed by my persistence. "No, Magdalene. She can't know anything. Not where you are, not who you're with. Nothing. No one can."

I shove my empty bowl away. "Why not?"

"Because it's not safe," Rowen responds furiously. "Not for you ... not for any of us."

"Is your plan to keep me prisoner?" My voice rises and cracks in astonishment. "Aren't you curious to know why the Watchers are after me? What they want?"

Face reddening, his anger intensifies. "No."

I grab the kards and stand. "Then I'll just find a way back to Kern without your help."

"I'll take you," Kagan says, stepping through the doorway dressed in jeans, a long-sleeved, brown shirt, and a pine green-colored vest. "We need to know what's happening beyond these walls."

"But last night you said you didn't want any of us leaving," Rowen rebukes, furrowing his brow.

"And having thought more about the situation, I've since changed my mind. Magdalene is correct. We need to know why they're suddenly interested in her since Watchers don't go after relic hunters ... ever."

Rowen stands, taking his dishes and mine, and places them into the sink. "Then I'm coming, too."

"I need you to stay here and help setup traps along the mountainside in case we get visitors. Use the blueprints down in the vault to make sure there aren't any secret passageways these old fossils are known to have. If there are, board them up. Magdalene, come with me and I'll get you a proper sheath for those blades."

Kagan turns and leaves, so I hurry to catch up, avoiding the rage filtering through Rowen at being left behind and tasked with doing something he feels the others are perfectly capable of handling without him. He flinches slightly when I murmur inside of my head that I wish he'd calm down and stop overreacting, leading me to wonder if he has an ability similar to mine, or whatever this thing is that's been my saving grace for years.

Reaching the entrance hall, we head to the lower level, then through a set of double doors and into a darkened great room. We turn left down a narrow corridor that leads to several other rooms, one of them being a weapons storage where Kagan turns on the lights. The stone walls are filled with swords, shields, maces, daggers, bow and arrow sets, and lastly guns in various calibers and makes. Below those are cabinets that probably house the ammunition. He rummages through an antique armoire constructed of cherry wood at the far end, removing a double scabbard made from worn brown leather that straps across the back.

"You can give Rowen back his blade when we return."

I place the kards inside and put the contraption on while the older man takes two long, thick knives with a smooth blade on one side and a jagged, almost serrated, on the other.

"What kind of weapon are those?" I ask as he holsters them around his waist.

"They're called sword breakers and date back to the Middle Ages." After tightening the belt, he closes the armoire door. "I prefer the older-style daggers, knives, and swords compared to the guns Doreleska and Pierce enjoy using." He points to the wall of armaments.

Heading for the great room, I say, "I need my knapsack since it has the key to my room."

He shuts the door to the weapons storage after extinguishing the light. "Then I'll wait for you in the entrance hall."

I go to the top floor, enter Rowen's bedroom, and snatch the bag off of the chair by the fireplace, situate it across my shoulders, then head downstairs to meet up with Kagan.

"You weren't awake when Rowen flew you here, so he didn't have to worry about you falling. Normally hunters can do this themselves, but without your memories I sincerely doubt you recall how, so I'm going to handle the traveling." Wrapping a powerful arm around my waist, he pulls me against his side. "Hold onto me tight and close your eyes. This can get a little disorienting if you're not used to it."

Gripping him tightly, I ask, "Do you know how to find the hostel?"

He doesn't answer, which tells me he does.

I close my eyes, and seconds later cold air spills around us while a sudden fierce wind kicks up and works on prying me loose. I freeze due to lack of proper attire, my lips chattering while my hold on Kagan intensifies out of panic. A few moments later my feet touch solid ground, and when I open my eyes, we're in the alley behind the hostel. Kagan releases me, and I spot Vin's motorbike secured behind the chicken wire with bits of debris from the attack resting on top. The smell of burnt wood and scorched plastic still permeates the air, causing my stomach to constrict and bile to rise, acid burning my throat.

"Let me go in first," I suggest, swallowing hard while Kagan steps toward the door. "Vin will more than likely have his nose buried in one of his magazines, so he shouldn't really notice us."

After opening the door, I cautiously enter the common room, noticing Vin at the registration counter with his copper-colored hair draped over his face, blocking us from view while slowly flipping through the glossy pages spread onto the countertop before him. As we head upstairs, I remove the key from my bag and unlock the door when we reach it. The interior is in shambles. Everything has been dumped out of the dresser, which is now tipped on its side. Clothes lay in piles on the floor in the closet. The mattress for the cot has been ripped open and the stuffing from my pillows is strewn everywhere.

"I doubt you normally live like this," Kagan says, closing the door.

Searching for my duffle bag, I find it buried under the remnants of the cushioned chair. "The Watchers had to have done this." I start shoveling clothes and toiletries into the bag, gathering everything I own that isn't ruined. "The one Rowen killed was trying to find something called a cardinal stone. He said they knew I had it, but I have no idea what he was talking about."

The knock on the door surprises me. Kagan holds a finger to his lips, indicating for me to remain quiet. He removes one of his knives, pushes me behind the door, then guardedly turns the handle.

"Is Magdalene here?" Vin asks, though I can't see him. "I thought I saw her."

Kagan keeps the weapon hidden behind his back; his body positioned to block out the room's mess. "No, she's still recovering from the bombing. I'm a friend of hers and she asked me to pick up a few things."

He lets out a long, deep breath. "I hope she's all right. It was horrible what happened. I'm in shock, as are many of us. We all thought the violence from the wars had finally left this part of the world, but I guess we were wrong. Well, let her know I say hi and that her room will be here when she's ready to return."

"I'll tell her." Kagan closes the door while I let out a sigh of relief, then finish collecting my things.

After securing his weapon, he takes the duffle bag and slings it across his shoulders. "Now where?"

I tell him how to find Dalma's house, then he wraps an arm around my waist, and I close my eyes as I cling to him tightly. Again, bitter cold seizes me, this time nearly taking the air from my lungs. The journey isn't long and we're standing on the front porch a few seconds later. Spotting her car in the driveway, I knock. The shuffling of feet can be heard on the other side, along with the locks on the door giving way. Dalma stands there in a bright, paisley housecoat with her hair pulled back into a braid. Her smile is brief.

"Why did you bring that thing to my home?" she spats in Hungarian, pointing a craggy finger at Kagan, hissing under her breath like a snake.

"I'm not thrilled to be near you either," he replies in the same dialect, his voice thick with animosity.

I grip the door, fearing she'll close it on us. "Can we come in?"

Her stare bores into the older man for a several long, excruciating seconds. "Are you going to kill me?"

A smirk tugs at the corners of his full mouth, the whiskers of his beard ruffling a bit. "Don't give me cause to."

Pursing her lips and scrunching up her face, she expels a loathsome huff, then backs away and proceeds down the hall, entering the kitchen. Once the door is closed, we follow, and since there are only two seats at the tiny table, Kagan is forced to stand. Dropping the knapsack onto the floor, I remove the scabbard, resting it against my leg as I sit. Dalma pouts while sipping her coffee.

"I thought you were dead," she says after a few seconds of tense silence. "Where have you been hiding?"

Kagan holds out his hand, stopping me from answering. "She's safe. That's all you need to know."

Her hard gaze shifts from me and over to him. "If she's with you, or that other one who's been wandering Kern for the last couple of days, then she's far from safe."

"Magdalene would be with the Watchers right now if it wasn't for us." His deep voice booms, rattling the entire dwelling.

Dalma grumbles, her stare falling back to the coffee in her mug. "A lot of good people are dead because of those bastards. Including a very close friend of mine."

I place my hand on hers while it rests on the table. "Do you know why they would've targeted Festus or his café?"

"No," she answers, her voice wavering and distant. "Unless they were after the journal he had me obtain for him, but it was full of nonsense. Symbols and letters no one could possibly understand. It was worthless."

"Where did you find it?"

She takes a sip before responding, lifting her head to look at me once again. "In an abandoned castle in the city of De Lamar, which is along the Durance River in a country formerly known as France. It wasn't hard to locate. Festus told me precisely where to find the book."

"What was the exact location in the castle?" I inquire, hoping the information will ignite some of my memory.

"There's a loose brick for the fireplace mantel in the drawing room. And before you ask, he didn't divulge how he came about this piece of knowledge."

Kagan stiffens. "Was there anything else with the journal?"

Raising her head, she glowers at him, the aggression returning. "No."

I tap her arm, drawing her attention back to me. "Why didn't Festus go get it himself?"

She chuckles, the lines around her mouth intensifying. "Because he was terrified to leave his shop, which is why I was astonished when you told me he did. I've been trying to figure out where he could've possibly gone during those few days before he died, and I haven't come up with an answer."

I look at her, puzzled. "Why was he so scared?"

Dalma scowls. "Festus was afraid of his own shadow if it looked at him the wrong way. It's a wonder he survived this long."

Scooting my chair, I try to give myself a better position at seeing both Dalma and Kagan equally. "Did he tell you if there was any significance behind the journal?"

"Don't be stupid, of course he didn't," she snaps. "It doesn't matter anyway. The damn thing more than likely burned up when he did."

I decide not to correct her on the assumption. "When the bombing happened, the Watcher who attacked me said they knew I'd found something called a cardinal stone. Do you know what that might be?"

"No, I don't. Unless it's the pendant I gave you, but I don't see how it can be mistaken for a stone when the thing is clearly made from metal." She takes another sip of coffee, her glare returning to Kagan, fury pulsing behind her ice-cold blue irises. "Is that all you wanted?"

He doesn't respond, but I do.

"I was wondering if you've heard of a small village called Cresidio."

Dalma slowly turns her attention to me, her hand frozen in midair with the handle of the mug between her quaking fingers. "No."

"Don't lie to her!" Kagan shouts, his voice booming.

The old woman slams down her mug, nearly shattering the ceramic. "What do you want with the relic hunter?" she demands. "If they find out that you have her—"

"They already know," he says, interrupting Dalma.

She frowns, then presses her thin lips together, making them nearly undetectable. "And you're still walking among the living?"

Kagan comes over to the table, rests his palms on its dingy surface, and leans close to her. "Magdalene isn't here for you. She's here for us."

The old woman's face grows ashen. "That's not possible. They'd never allow her to help your kind."

He sneers. "Well, I guess you don't know everything." Kagan pushes himself upright, then crosses his arms over his burly chest. "Tell her about the village."

Dalma's body goes rigid, obviously infuriated with being told what to do. "Why can't you? I'm sure you've all heard the story as much as we have."

"Just that Belial was responsible, nothing more."

A brutal image flashes in my mind, blocking out the rest of the world around me. One of a man covered in thick, gray scales that are razor sharp, a round face with bony protrusions jutting out of his chin and cheekbones, a wide nose with flaring nostrils, piercing black eyes that have bottomless depths, and two prominent horns on the top of his head that curl slightly forward before winding back toward his copious mane of silver hair.

I shake my head to get rid of what feels like a memory forcing its way to the surface. My anxiety skyrockets, my breathing becomes labored, and the room presses hard upon me, threatening to bury me alive.

"Magdalene," Dalma whispers, gently placing a hand on my cheek, wiping away a tear I didn't realize had fallen. Her face is filled with concern and despair.

Kagan kneels beside me, the same worried expression creasing his brow.

Sharp pain erupts at my temples, forcing me to close my eyes. Screams echo in my ears, so I cup my hands over them to shut out the blood-curdling noise. The smell of burning flesh becomes overwhelming, and I double over, falling out of the chair and into my past.

Chapter Seven

When I open my eyes, I find myself in a hut, a ruggedly woven grass mat under my small body. The dress I'm wearing, with its short sleeves and knee-length hem, is made from textured sackcloth that has been dyed dark blue. Brown leather sandals cover my small feet, a matching belt around my waist, and my medium-length, raven-colored hair dangles in front of my face. Clutched in my sweaty hand is my most prized possession, a palm-sized piece of obsidian rock. It's black surface stays warm in my grasp, and its smooth contours give me comfort whenever fear tries to take hold. At the moment, I can't recall how I came to own such a unique rock, just that I carry it with me always, usually tucked inside of one of the pockets of my dress.

"There you are," my mother says, entering through the thatch door, her voice angelic and light. "Did you fall asleep?" She's tall and elegant, her face gentle with a pleasant smile that elevates her stunning blue eyes. Her dress is identical to mine, and her long, black hair is beautifully braided down her back with yellow flowers woven into the delicate curves.

Stuffing the rock into my pocket while sitting up, I ask, "Did I miss it?" My voice is quiet and child-like, an odd sound to my own ears.

She reaches out her hand to take mine, her skin always smelling like lavender. "No. Come on. Your father is waiting."

After helping me stand, she guides me outside into a warm, summer day with clear blue skies and soft, gentle breezes. The grass under our feet is a lush green, and the forest lining the boundaries of our village with are in full bloom, along with many of the floral bushes that circle the huts scattered across the open expanse. Today is the annual celebration of the Shrine of Olwen, our benevolent sun goddess. My father is guardian for the temple and cleric, as well as counselor, to all who live here. He, with help from many of the villagers, have spent the last several days preparing for this yearly observance, and he's selected me to be the anointer for the traditional pyre. Something I've been looking forward to for a long time.

In keeping with tradition, a deer has been slaughtered and skinned, and has been skewered onto the pit for roasting. Around the roaring fire at the heart of the village, several men play music on hand-crafted instruments while others dance in rhythm to the enchanting melody. Children scamper about, playing and laughing, all wearing garments identical to mine. I wish to go join them, but know I'm expected to prepare for my part in the ceremony that will be starting soon, so the merriment will have to wait. When we reach the shrine constructed from stone, my father is busy decorating the pyre with flowers and offerings, such as fruit, vegetables, and tiny pieces of parchment where everyone has written their wishes and blessings for the upcoming year.

"Magdalene," he says, smiling as my mother and I approach. He's tall with a strong physique and chiseled features. His eyes are a brilliant blue, hair is dark and flows to just beneath his ears, and his face is soft and kind. The garments he's wearing are different from the rest of the villagers, given his position and responsibility. Instead of the normal blue pants and matching blouse, he has on white linen trousers and a corresponding button-down shirt that is tucked in at the waist and held together by a leather belt similar to mine only thicker. He appears overjoyed to see us, which isn't unusual. My father is very loving and adores his family with every breath he takes.

In his firm hand is the Scepter of Ignis, a sacred staff that harnesses the power of the sun by only those whom Olwen has deemed worthy. The rod is made from blackthorn wood, the handle twisted and knotted. On the bottom is a round, bronze pommel. The top has a radiant yellow gem with a bronze encasement in the shape of the sun, its rays wide. He holds it out toward me. "Are you excited to do the honors?"

Nodding, I take the short scepter from him and wait for the entire village to be called inside by the musicians now lingering at the door, having moved away from the spit. Once everyone is seated, my father picks me up and places me on a stool in front of him so I'm above the pyre.

He holds up his hands, drawing silence from the gatherers. "Today is our holiest of days. Olwen has once again blessed us with prosperity, kindness, and love. We are her humble servants, devoted to preserving her spirit from generation to generation so no one forgets the modest beginnings of our world. Without her caring rays, the harvests would falter, the rivers would run dry, and everything we hold precious would grow cold and dark. We owe her our lives and faithfulness from now until we depart this world."

I turn and stare at my father, noticing he's smiling at me in return.

"For that we give her thanks and adoration," he continues. "Almighty Olwen, we praise you and offer up our prayers for the coming year in hopes that you'll continue to guide and protect us."

Holding the staff securely in my hands, I tilt it, focusing the light being emitted—though I'm not sure how it's generating—from the gem onto the offerings. Smoke begins to smolder, a tiny flicker of flame seeping up from the ashes of previous celebrations. The fire gradually grows, consuming the fruits, vegetables, flowers, and parchments. Cheers erupt at the successful ceremony, my father kissing my cheek in affection and pride.

I jump off the stool, hand my father the scepter so he can return it to its crypt, then run outside with the rest of the children to play and dance. The adults prepare our large feast, and the remainder of the day passes with great joy and happiness.

A few days later, a strange young man wanders into Cresidio appearing lost and confused. We never have strangers stumble upon us, so it's odd that one should emerge as if out of nowhere. He's very weak—nearly collapsing under his own weight—and is sweating profusely, probably due to a fever. After lengthy discussions, several of the village elders bring him to the healer, who's my mother, to be tended to. She has them lie the young man on the mat I normally use to sleep, and asks me to go down to the sea and fill the pitcher with water while she rummages through her medicinal oils and herbs, which she keeps in an apothecary table my father built for her. I do as she requests, returning a short time later with a full bucket. While she prepares a special tea that should ease the young man's suffering, I sit off in the corner and study him.

He's younger than my father, perhaps close to my mother's age, of average build and height with short, brown hair, dark, narrow eyes, overly pale skin, and thin, pallid lips. He stares at me with a fierce, haunting gaze, which causes me to shudder. There's something odd about him, but it could simply be because he's a stranger. However, the more I gaze upon him, the colder the air around me becomes. Shoving my hand into the pocket of my dress, I remove the piece of obsidian which warms me while I rub its smooth, soothing surface. Gradually, my anxiety subsides, but not the menacing cloud I now sense lingering over the entire world.

When the tea is ready, my mother gives it to him, helping him to sit up and drink it. Within a few minutes he's fast asleep, and I pray he stays that way for a long time.

"What's wrong with him?" I ask, standing and making my way to his side.

My mother stops me from disturbing the young man. "I'm not sure, but he needs rest."

I show her the rock. "Could this help him?"

She smiles, enfolding her hand around mine. "No, sweetheart. You keep it safe for me. Remember, it's Olwen's special gift and will protect you always. Now, why don't you go help your father in the temple?"

I nod, put the rock back into my pocket, and leave. When I arrive, he tells me to sweep the floor while he prepares the altar for our traditional early evening prayers. The floors are hardly covered in anything, so I know it's purely busy work to keep me out of the way.

"Excuse me."

I stop and look up, finding an older man wearing brown, twill pants, an off-white blouse, and heavy boots caked in mud lurking in the narrow, open doorway. He's tall with olive skin, short, dark hair, and a scar jutting across his forehead, just above his eyebrows. Strapped around his waist are two daggers, the handles of which appear to be pure ivory, and flawless. He carries nothing else with him, which I find peculiar considering the distance he would've had to travel to reach our village since we're not near anything but the sea.

The uncomfortable feeling I had with the young man resurfaces and intensifies. He wasn't carrying any sort of satchel or provisions either when the men found him. During recent nights as I pretend to sleep, I've heard my parents discussing rumors of possible raiders infiltrating our lands, pilfering towns and villages for the sake of conquering fields that don't rightfully belong to them.

Could these two be part of that group?

"I was wondering if you wouldn't mind helping me." The man's accent is peculiar, even though he's speaking our language.

I grow nervous at his presence, so I shove my hand into the pocket of my dress and stroke the stone for comfort.

"What do you need?" my father asks, his voice surprisingly deep while he stares at the man with suspicion.

"I'm looking for the Scepter of Ignis and was told I'd find it here."

My father's jaw tightens. "Sorry, but I've never heard of such a thing."

The man furrows his brow. "This is a Shrine of Olwen, is it not?"

My father steps over to me, places a hand on my shoulder, and presses me firmly against his side. "There are dozens of such places around the region. Perhaps one of them has this thing you're looking for."

The stranger rests his hands on the hilts for the daggers, clearly trying to intimidate my father, who seems to be growing angrier by the second. "I know for a fact the staff is here because it was used quite recently."

My father scowls. "As I already said, we don't have the scepter. Now leave before I have you thrown out."

The man steps closer, his grip tightening on the weapons. "You're making a big mistake, Kaliel. One that could cost you everything."

I feel my father becoming nervous, almost jittery, then he forcefully pushes me behind him. "How do you know my name?"

The man smirks, his arrogance shining brightly. "I know a lot of things about you, and your family. Such as your daughter is Magdalene and your wife is Hera. You're the guardian for this temple, and the staff as well."

"Who the hell are you?" my father asks, his hands balling into fists.

"My name is Daimon, and I'm a friend." The grin he projects looks to be unnatural and menacing.

Friction fills the already heated air, and after several long seconds my father lets out a heavy sigh, his eyes downfallen. "The staff you seek was destroyed several years ago. I'm afraid you've come here for nothing."

Daimon seems to ponder the information, clicking his tongue against his teeth. "That's most unfortunate. Sorry to have bothered you." He turns and leaves.

"Father," I begin, but he shushes me and hurries toward the door, peering outside. When I join him, the man is nowhere in sight. "Why did you lie?" I ask as we return to the altar.

Kneeling on the floor in front of me, he takes my hand, squeezing it tenderly. "Because the scepter must be protected at all costs, dear one. From both friend and foe. The crypt is the only place where it will be safe. Now, go back to sweeping."

Standing, he releases me and returns to trimming the wooden platform with flowers and decorative rocks. Even though he's humming a happy melody, I notice the troubled expression weighing heavily on his face. His brow creases and his body quivers ever so slightly. After several seconds of watching him, I return to cleaning the floor, greatly unsettled by the encounter.

Later that night, my mother shares her mat with me since the young man is still asleep on mine. She wraps a woolen blanket around the two of us, holding me securely in a warm, loving embrace. My father has decided to remain in the temple out of fear Daimon might try and steal the scepter while we slumber. I don't envy the immense undertaking and long night he has in store.

"Magdalene," my mother whispers, rousing me from a fitful sleep. "Get up, we have to leave."

"What?" I mumble, not quite understanding her request, nor comprehending the terror in her voice and the panic in her eyes.

"Now, dear one," she orders, shoving a few of our things into a satchel clutched in her hands.

Glancing around the hut, I notice the young man is gone. Screams reverberate in the night, piercing the thick walls of our home. My mother grabs my hand, pulls me to my feet, and we dash outside, the bag now around her shoulders. Night has settled in, but the stars and moon are nowhere to be seen due to the heavy amount of smoke filling the sky. Villagers run in the direction of the sea, fleeing something I have yet to notice.

My mother shoves me toward an older woman, whose face and arms are covered in ash and scratches. "Take Magdalene. I'm going back for Kaliel."

She snatches my mother's arm before she can get too far. "Hera, don't. It's too late. We must go."

Tears stream down my mother's face. "I'm not leaving without my husband."

After dislodging herself, she disappears into the throngs of madness, and I finally catch a glimpse of what everyone is running from.

Men in dark armor made from stone fling maces and swords, slaughtering everyone they come across, while others lay torches against our homes, setting them aflame. Not a word is spoken amongst them, the only noise the clanking of their boots and the sounds of bones crunching by their hands and under their feet.

The old woman grabs my hand and begins pulling me along with the others. However, I shake loose, determined to find my parents, not wanting to be taken from them, even if it is by a friend.

"Magdalene, no!" she hollers as I desperately race toward the temple, her sharp nails narrowly clasping the back of my dress.

Dodging between huts, I try not to look at the faces of the fallen, their blood turning the pristine ground into rotting sludge. The men in the strange armor continue to attack those trying to defend our village, leveling all in their wake, even the children ... my friends. No one is being spared. When I reach the temple, the entrance is blocked by these creatures, so I hide behind a barrel just outside of our hut and peer around its fat edges. Through the legs of one of the monsters, I spot my father being held by another one of them while the young man who was staying in our hut paces in front of him, his hands clenched behind his back. However, I don't see my mother. Reaching into my pocket, I grip the stone tightly, willing the world to right itself, praying for Olwen's intervention and to save our people before it's too late.

"Where is it?" the stranger demands, his voice hissing almost like a snake, clearly recovered from whatever was ailing him.

"It's not here." My father appears pained as he struggles against his captor. "We don't have the scepter."

"Liar." The man slashes at my father's stomach with a serrated blade, adding to a wound already inflicted.

Blood soaks his garments and agony etches on his face. I go to scream when a hand covers my mouth.

"Don't alert them," Daimon whispers, crouching beside me. "Stay here and keep quiet, no matter what."

He stands, unsheathes his daggers—the blades made from pure gold— steps around the barrel, and flings them at the guards, hitting each squarely in the chest. Their bodies disintegrate, ash wisping the ground in place of corpses. The weapons instinctively return to Daimon, soaring through the air and directly into his awaiting hands. He throws them again at those approaching, cutting them down with ease. When he enters the temple, I hurry to follow after making sure no other guards are around, then hide behind one of the benches, spying the encounter through the gap between the wooden seat and the backrest.

"Let him go, Belial," Daimon orders, his legs shoulder-width apart in preparation to fight. "He doesn't have what you're looking for."

As the young man turns, his façade falters, revealing a creature with thick, razor sharp gray scales, a round face with bony protrusions jutting out of his chin and cheeks, a wide nose, piercing black eyes, and two prominent horns on the top of his head that curl slightly forward, then back toward a copious mane of silver hair. His simple garments turn into a flowing crimson cloak that encases his entire body, giving the appearance that he's dripping in fresh blood.

I gasp, then quickly cover my mouth and hope none of them heard me.

"Daimon, I was wondering if you were going to appear." The thing's voice drips with poison and conceit.

Moving closer, I make sure to stay hidden, squatting near the floor and under benches whenever possible.

"These people have done nothing to you. Let them live in peace. Leave before it's too late."

Belial chuckles, sending shards of ice down my spine. "Overconfident as ever. It'll be your downfall."

Daimon throws one of the daggers, but the creature swings with his own blade, knocking the weapon to the ground. The man hurls the other one. This time the demon steps sideways and the blade sinks into my father's chest. His body slumps against the guard and all life leaves his eyes.

I force myself not to shriek, biting my lip until I draw blood while tears flood my face and I quake from both terror and rage. Belial saunters up to Daimon, who's scrambling to retrieve his daggers since, for some reason, they didn't return to him this time. The creature wraps a large, scaly hand around the man's neck.

"Such a pathetic thing," he taunts, lifting Daimon off of the floor, who's writhing from the torment. "How you ever became a relic hunter I'll never know." With one swift motion, Belial snaps the man's neck, causing his head to loll to the side, then tosses the body across the altar, knocking everything onto the floor. "Search for the staff."

110

The guard holding my father's body drops it, then goes about tearing apart the temple while the demon proceeds down the narrow aisle and steps outside into the escalating chaos. Swallowing hard, I decide to fight instead of run. This is my home ... my people ... my family, and I will defend it no matter what might happen.

Crawling toward my father, I make sure to grab hold of the gold dagger that was knocked to the floor. My sight becomes blurred from the tears that refuse to cease falling, but I don't have time to wipe them. Shaking, I carefully remove the other blade from my father's body, choking back my grief as it becomes overwhelming. Both weapons in my hands, something commanding starts to course through me, clearing my eyes and focusing my mind. I find myself standing, gripping the ivory hilts tightly as possible. With one smooth motion, I throw the weapon into the guard's back. He becomes ash and the dagger returns to me just like it did Daimon.

A new purpose consumes me, seizing my core, and I surprisingly welcome it.

Staring down at my father, I want to sit beside him, to hold his head in my arms and mourn, but an urge to protect the scepter clutches me, forcing me to move past my own feelings toward something greater. Running down the aisle of the temple, I hesitantly glance out into the darkness, spotting Belial and several of his men slaughtering those who still remain. Exiting the structure, I dart for the tree line, my little legs pumping as hard as they can. When I'm close, I spot a pile of clothes on the ground, blood soaking the dark blue material. A lump forms in my throat as I get closer, discovering my mother's body face down.

This is why she wasn't at the temple. She went to get the scepter and use it on the invaders.

Kneeling to weep over the loss, I set down the blades and remove the obsidian stone from my pocket, place it in her open palm, then rest my head against her back.

"Mother," I whisper. "Come back to me." My tears soak her dress. "Olwen, please, save us."

Sounds of heavy footsteps approach, branches breaking in their wake. Using my mother's corpse as a shield, I lie on the ground behind her, hiding from the armored men as they step out of the trees. Grasped in their hand is the Scepter of Ignis. They must have found the crypt and broken into it. My father always thought it was foolish to keep such a treasure where everyone would expect it to be. So, he built the vault several meters outside of the village's boundary, knowing it was safer there than in the temple.

Rising, I pick up the daggers and hurl them at the two guards, cutting them down in seconds. With only a simple sash around my dress, and the weapons now back in my hands, I tie the piece of material to one of the blades and use it as a sling, draping it across my chest. I pick up the scepter with my free hand, firm up my grip on the remaining blade, and head back to the village.

Belial and his men are standing in front of the temple—which is now burning—when I approach, as if anticipating my arrival.

"What a good little girl," he says, tapping his fingers together, the light from the fires casting odd shadows across his horrid face. "Why don't you give that to me for safe keeping?"

Fury broils inside of me. I stare at the monster and know what must be done to stop him ... to stop all of them. "You murdered my family."

The gem starts to glow, its eternal spark igniting. An energy like none other flows up my arm, grasping my heart in its vice of hatred and revenge. I allow the sensation to wash over me, envelop me, give me the confidence I need to follow through with my fateful decision.

"Be careful with that." Belial takes a tentative step forward, anxiety clearly visible on his face, a flicker of fear in his eyes. "You don't know how the staff works."

The corner of my mouth curls up in a crooked smile. "Oh, but I do. More than you could possibly imagine."

I go down on my knees, lay the scepter flat against the ground, then pierce the stone with the dagger just as Belial and his men rush toward me. Fire leaps outward, consuming everything in its path ... including me.

Chapter Eight

$\mathcal{S}$weat soaks my clothes, my pulse races, and the sharp headache I had been experiencing evaporates. I inhale deeply as if coming up for air after nearly drowning. Both Kagan and Dalma are at my side, helping me back into the chair. The older woman fetches a glass of water, which she has to hold against my trembling lips, tears raining down my cheeks.

She wipes them away with a towel from the counter. "What did you see?"

"My parents ... the village ... Belial and Daimon."

"What else?" Dalma gently coaxes.

I stare at her worried expression while she kneels in front of me. "The Scepter of Ignis."

The older woman stands and refills the glass. She hands it to me since I'm now calm enough to hold it on my own, and retakes her seat. "A relic left behind by the sun goddess, Olwen. One, if in the wrong hands, can have irreversible effects on all life."

"Belial murdered my parents for it. Him and Daimon, with his carelessness." I glare at her, the ache in my head returning, now accompanied by one in my heart. "Did you know?"

Her face falls and she fidgets nervously with her fingers. "Not all of it. Just that Cresidio had been leveled when the scepter was destroyed, killing not only Belial and his followers, but the villagers as well."

"Who did it?" Kagan asks, standing beside me with a hand on my shoulder.

Gazing into the glass, wishing it would swallow me whole, I reply, "I did. Decimated hundreds of people with the simple shatter of a gem." I clutch the tumbler tightly against my chest, and gawk at the dingy floor. "All I kept thinking about were my parents, and my father telling me how the scepter had to be protected at all costs. I killed more that night than Belial and his soldiers did."

"You saved the world, Magdalene," the old woman says, though I'm struggling to believe her. "Including yourself."

I shake my head, lifting my eyes to meet hers, tears continuing to flow down my face. "But I didn't. The flames consumed me as well, so I don't know why I'm still alive."

Dalma rests her hand on my arm. "Because they didn't. That was the moment you became the relic hunter, thereby protecting your life."

Kagan nudges me. "How old were you?"

I finish the water before answering. "Eight."

The old woman leans back in her chair. "The same age you were when you returned this time. That can't be a coincidence."

"But why take away my memory?" I protest.

Dalma shrugs. "I don't have the answer to that, and I doubt others like me do either."

"Maybe now that you have some of it back, we can start piecing things together." Kagan picks up the duffle bag since he apparently dropped it to tend to me when I fell out of the chair. "We should get going."

I set down the glass onto the table, stand, reach for the scabbard, and strap it across my back.

"You found the other kard," the old woman comments. "Where was it?"

Kagan clears his throat, obviously not wanting me to give a truthful answer.

"I had loaned it to a friend."

Narrowing her gaze, she furrows her brow. "Be careful who you permit to use those, Magdalene. It might come back to bite you on the ass." She doesn't follow us to the door, but we take care to shut it after stepping outside.

Making sure the duffle bag is secured around his shoulders, Kagan says, "Dalma wouldn't have been able to enter the castle if Rowen had brought her."

"Why not?" I ask, adjusting the knapsack, wiping my face clean.

"Did you notice the sigil on the floor of the entrance hall? It protects us against angels like her."

"Meaning Festus was probably one as well."

Kagan nods.

"Why am I not surprised?" I groan.

He snorts. "Angels can be devious and deadly just like demons, so it's no wonder she's kept the truth from you. Like all creatures—mortal and immortal—they only divulge information when it suits their needs. Not for any other purpose."

"Do you think she's hiding anything else?"

He contemplates on how to respond for a few moments. "I wouldn't put it past her."

I take one last look at the door before wrapping my arms around his waist and closing my eyes. While we travel, my thoughts dwell on Daimon and why the daggers didn't return to him the last time he threw them. Also, his sudden appearance at my side behind the barrel troubles me since I never heard him approach. It starts me wondering if my memories aren't the only thing absent. During recent occasions when I've used the blade to defend myself, I never let go of it for fear of losing my most prized possession. Maybe there's a way to test if they'll come back to me like they did when I was eight.

Kagan shakes me, and when I open my eyes we're back in the weapons storage. He hands me the duffle bag. "Go unpack while I see how far everyone's gotten with the fortification, then we can work on recovering more of your memory."

Before I turn to leave, a thought pops into my head. "Can I ask you something?"

He removes his knives, placing them on one of the shelves. "Sure."

"Yesterday you were upset with Rowen for bringing me to the castle, but you told Dalma that I'm here to help your kind. Why were you mad if you were going to have to find me anyway?"

Scratching his beard, he replies, "Because he did it without my permission. I wasn't ready to inform the others about the truth of what's happening. Rowen has now forced my hand."

I look at Kagan, puzzled. "They don't know?"

He chortles. "Demons can't be trusted. Isn't that what you said to him? Well, it's true. Even if the cause is a worthy one."

"Does that include yourself?"

"You'll need to make that determination. I can't do it for you." He playfully winks.

Slinging the hefty bag over my shoulder, I ask, "What about Rowen?"

Kagan inhales deeply, then slowly exhales. "You gave him one of your blades, so you must have believed him to be honest and reliable. Unless he managed to trick you somehow, then Dalma is correct. That decision might bite you in the ass."

Unsettled by the remark, I trudge upstairs. After dropping the bag onto the bed, I pull open drawers in the dresser, happily surprised to find a few of them empty. Something tells me Rowen did this in anticipation of my return. I unpack, even finding a bit of room in the armoire. Storing the last of the items in the bathroom, I toss the empty bag onto one of the chairs in the seating area, adding the knapsack and scabbard on top of it. The clothes I wore yesterday during the attack are still where I left them, so I toss them into the trash bin since they're too damaged to be salvaged.

"I was starting to get worried," Rowen states upon entering, smiling cheerfully. His hands and clothes are caked in dirt, with a few streaks of mud on his cheeks. "None of us expected the two of you would be gone for so long."

I lean against one of the bed posts while he rummages for clean clothes to change into. "It was only an hour or so."

He appears confused by the comment. "No, it's been closer to three."

That can't be right. Three hours? How long was I unconscious? It only felt like a few minutes. Why didn't Dalma or Kagan say anything?

"Hey, are you okay?" he asks, coming up to me, noticing the distress on my face, and places a hand under my chin, lifting my troubled gaze to meet his soft one.

"I'm fine," I reply, but I doubt he believes me considering the worry in his eyes.

"Wait here while I get cleaned up. Kagan wants us all in the library shortly." Rowen lays his clothes onto the comforter, then steps into the bathroom, closing the door gently behind him.

Sitting on the edge of my side of the bed, I take off my boots, setting them by the nightstand, and curl up on the thick mattress while reliving the moment my world forever changed. The instant when my life was no longer my own. I'm awestruck that a child had the forethought to singlehandedly fight a band of demons. That shouldn't have been possible. Watching my father murdered, finding my mother dead ought to have broken me, crushed me into submission. Instead, it fueled my need to defeat the persons responsible, end the lives of those who took everything away from me. It's the same desire I had when I slaughtered the caretakers at the orphanage. I saw them as monsters, beings who needed to be extinguished before they could cause further harm, to prevent more innocent blood from being spilt.

Will I eventually feel that way about the ones I'm living with now? Do I pose a danger to them, and vice versa? What if this is all some sort of trap and I'm playing right into their hands, too stupid not to see right through it?

Kagan said I'm here for them, which shocked the hell out of Dalma. So, what sort of relics will I be hunting to keep out of the hands of the Watchers, and whomever else might threaten Lucifer's reign, if that's indeed who I'm assisting? Will I recognize these artifacts like I do the sacred ones?

The sound of the bathroom door opening pulls my attention back to the present, and when I spot Rowen simply wearing a towel around his waist, his powerful chest and abdominal muscles exposed, I can't help but blush, then reluctantly turn over to give him some privacy so he can dress without my lingering stare making things awkward.

He laughs. "You know, you've seen me in a lot less."

Though tempting as it is to turn and have a quick peek, I decide against it, biting my lip out of frustration. "Maybe when I get that part of my memory back, we'll get reacquainted."

The bed jostles, and Rowen pulls me onto my back. He's wearing jeans and nothing else, so the scarring on his chest is visible. It tugs at my heart. "Have they started to?" Anticipation permeates his face.

Knowing what he wants, the answer he prays that I'll give to him, I place my warm palm against his soft, smooth cheek and stare into his hopeful eyes. "At the moment, just the incident that caused me to become the relic hunter has risen to the surface."

Leaning back on his heels, he helps me sit up. "What do you mean?"

Using the headboard, I prop myself against it, crisscrossing my legs. "When we were at Dalma's, I had asked if she ever heard of a village called Cresidio."

He shivers, shaking the bed slightly. "That's a haunted place. It's rumored ghosts wander the woods surrounding the village ruins. Some have even been seen running into the sea simply to disappear under its treacherous waves. No one dares to enter what remains of the temple. Not even demons. It just shows how profoundly scarred the land is to horrify all matter of creature who dare visit. Including the immortal ones."

The image of the kard piercing the yellow gem nearly overwhelms me, so I pull my knees up to my chest, putting myself in sort of a protective shell. "It's also where my life changed forever." Tears work their way to the surface, wetting my lashes. "Kagan and Dalma started to argue over who was going to tell me about what happened in Cresidio when the name Belial was mentioned. It triggered a memory, knocking me unconscious. I thought I'd only been out for a few minutes, but then you said we were gone several hours, so it must have been longer and neither of them bothered to tell me."

Rowen delicately sets a hand on one of my arms that are now wrapped around my legs. "I've heard of Belial. He's also known as the Prince of Darkness, and a cruel servant of Lucifer's." His mouth falls open when realization dawns on him. "You were the one who defeated that bastard? How did you do it?"

I grow sullen, anguish and guilt at having survived consuming me, plunging me further into despair. "I don't want to talk about it. Not yet, anyway, since I'm still trying to come to grips with what happened ... with what I did." Staring at his chest, I bend slightly forward and put my hand over the healed puncture wounds surrounding his heart, a deep ache pulling at my core. "Who did this to you?"

He wraps his hand around mine, squeezing it while I continue to stare at the marks. "A vile person I hope to never come across again."

Using the tips of my fingers, I gently graze the jagged flesh, tracing the lines as if they were rivers that need to be carefully traversed. "Why did he do it?"

Rowen wipes away a few of the tears as they fall, then reaches out and places his hand under my chin, lifting my sorrowful gaze to meet his adoring one. "Because I fell in love with you."

The link I felt between us that night at the hostel returns, strengthening, entwining itself so intensely around my core with such veracity that I might snap if it were to break. My pulse quickens with heightened anticipation as he leans into me, his lips briefly brushing against mine, their warm, sensuous touch sending shivers winding down my spine in an endless loop. Our breathing hastens while his mouth lingers right before mine. When he realizes I'm not pulling away, he kisses me deeply, his tongue invading my mouth and mine his. Intense heat consumes us as we wrap our arms around each other, reclining on the mattress until the length of his body presses into mine. The memory of how we met grasps my mind, melding fractured parts of myself that I hadn't realized were there.

Chapter Nine

I hate the desert. Not just because of the heat and dry air, but for the scorpions and snakes as well. Anything that slithers, has sharp nails or talons, and is covered in scales reminds me of Belial and the night my life ended. I suppose I should be grateful for surviving the blight that destroyed my entire village, but it was at my hand alone that caused such devastation and death. Not the monster who feigned being ill only to attack us while we slept. Having been a child at the time should've exempted me from responsibility, but I knew what I was doing when I pierced the gem, unleashing Olwen's power onto the world. What lies before me now is my punishment: a slave to the holy immortals who consider themselves above everything. The ones who command and control every aspect of my life, including anyone that I might wish to share it with.

Wearing a light gray linen blouse, matching pants, and dark gray heels, I stand under the elegantly painted archway separating the Gallery of Honor from the Grand Central Gallery inside of the Cairo Museum where reclaimed artifacts stolen by Nebuchadnezzar II are currently being displayed. Later this evening, they're to be shipped to Athens by way of the Mediterranean Sea—a trip that should take an estimated four days—then after spending a week in Greece it's off to Paris. The final stop of the lengthy voyage will be the Smithsonian in Washington DC until they're permanently placed in the Silam Museum in Jerusalem. It's going to be an exhausting trip, but a necessary one. My main purpose is to ensure one of the sacred relics hidden among the treasures is properly restored when the exposition is over. So, I have to travel with it until the very end of the tour.

My raven-colored hair is braided and neatly tucked under a silk scarf wrapped around my head. I have barely any makeup on, just some rouge to brighten my cheeks. At the moment, I'm pretending to read a map of the facility while actually scrutinizing the visitors, monitoring who approaches the Perpetua Chalice—which sits on a marble pedestal draped in dark blue velvet under a locked glass case—and whoever else might be scoping out the place like I am.

The chalice is a modest object; no valuable gems, precious metals, or fancy filigree are embellished upon it. It's simply been carved out of a solid piece of wood that had once been a part of the sacrificial cross. There are even minuscule traces of blood coated on a few sections from when the bolts impaled flesh and bone. The cup is small, no bigger than the size of my palm, yet very powerful if filled with the right liquid. Thankfully, very few know that last part, which is why many have failed to harness the chalice's gifts when they were lucky enough to briefly procure the item.

I'll be grateful when it reaches its final destination since it will be housed in a safe buried under several levels of underground decking and a fake put on display in its place. But for now, the genuine chalice needs to be protected ... by me.

Folding the map, I step into the throngs of visitors, mingling with a group being escorted by an older male guide, then make my way over to a large display case filled with gold coins, hand-carved statues, ancient weapons, and jewelry that's been freshly polished to bring out the exquisiteness of the metals and gems. Briefly glancing at the chalice, I notice that only a few individuals have stopped to examine it. Many think it's not nearly as valuable as the rest of the items, but how wrong they are. I hear them mumble to each other under concealed breaths, and sense their hidden thoughts due to an added gift that I have.

Unfortunately, if anyone should attempt to steal the cup at this very moment, I'll be forced to rely on the museum's security to handle the culprit since my weapons are back at the hotel. I couldn't chance bringing the kards just to have them confiscated by some idiot, in addition to being accused of *pilfering weapons that resemble those kept behind bulletproof glass on the second floor ... not to mention they would've been difficult to conceal given the outfit I'm wearing. It bothers me that the museum should have a set of hunter's blades, let alone on display, so it begs the question as to which stupid bastard lost them, though they're probably dead, and it serves them right for being so careless. Of course, me being without mine doesn't aid the situation I could possibly find myself in.*

Relying on others for assistance has never been part of my rapport among our little community. Therefore, I'm stuck with poorly trained men in stiff uniforms and itchy trigger fingers to come to my assistance should a thief attempt to pilfer the chalice. But that's only if the person isn't a demon. Those creatures can easily overpower mortals with a simple thought, then the chase for me would be on.

And I loathe running ... especially in heels.

Standing between two of the smaller display cases, I review the brochure featuring the entire exhibit, my sight perched on the cup while pretending to peruse the information on the glossy pages in my hand.

Someone bumps into my shoulder, not hard, but jarring enough that I nearly fall over.

"I'm so sorry." The tall, young man with broad shoulders, slicked-back, wavy brown hair, square face, and piercing hazel eyes gently cups my elbow in his hand to steady me. His navy blue suit is tailored, accentuating his biceps and the power in them. The smile he gives is charming, along with his British accent, and there's an earthy aroma to him, bordering on woodsy, which pleases me. Something tells me it's his natural scent, one I could easily get used to.

"That's all right," I reply, using an American dialect I've become comfortable with over the years, though I can fake many different types. "No harm done."

Returning to the brochure, I keep a sharp lookout for those approaching the chalice, scrutinizing a few. Pretending to verify the information on the paper to what's written on the plaques inside of the display cases, I notice the young man reading over my shoulder.

"You know, they have more right over there." I point toward the entrance where a carton of them sit.

He reddens from embarrassment at being caught. "Thank you. I'll go and grab one." Then he heads in that direction, vanishing amongst the hordes of visitors.

I continue to wander the expansive room, marveling at all of the items, wondering if this is the entire collection, or could there be pieces still missing, or perhaps they're being kept down in storage due to the limited space available? The desire to know the full extent of available artifacts is one of the downfalls about being a relic hunter. I usually don't know until either happening upon them or am advised ahead of time. Even then the truth isn't always disclosed, making my job even more difficult. Also, the craving to use the sacred objects for myself continually loiters under the surface, tempting me to break the rules that govern my existence.

I have yet to disobey one but there's always a first time for everything.

Gradually, I make my way to the chalice, its power drawing me in with each methodical step, beckoning me to take full advantage of the opportunity afforded and snatch it under the eyes of all who are watching. My senses tingle at the majesty such a tiny relic beholds. If only those traipsing around the museum were privy to the ability that could be bestowed upon them, this plain looking cup would've been stolen from its hidden crypt long ago.

I mean, who wouldn't want immortality? Although, it does have its drawbacks, which I'm reminded of daily.

The remainder of the day I spend wandering the various halls, always returning to the Grand Central Gallery. Fifteen minutes before closing, an announcement is made and the lights flicker. I wait until the last possible moment until ushered out the door and into the waning sunlight. There is still some time to kill before the train from Cairo leaves for Alexandria where I've booked passage on the same boat the artifacts are to be shipped. The hotel I'm staying at is just down the street from the museum, so it's an easy walk. Prior to heading up to my room, I eat an early dinner at the café off the lobby since I have no intention of dining on the train.

Once upstairs, I change into khaki shorts, a short-sleeved, button-down shirt in olive green, and low-rising boots. After removing the scarf, I stuff it and the clothes I was wearing into my lone suitcase, make sure all the protective hexes and sigils I placed around the room are gone, then strap my rucksack containing my papers, tickets, and kards over my shoulders so it sits nestled across my chest. Back downstairs, I check out at the concierge and pay the bill before having the doorman flag me a cab. With the suitcase loaded into the trunk, I claim the seat in the rear and we're heading out into the night, merging with the heavy traffic. Thankfully, it's a short ride.

When I've reclaimed my luggage, I pay the driver, extract my travel papers and passport from the rucksack, then step into the ornate station with its alternating shades of slate in a chevron pattern on the floor. There's also a narrow, inverted pyramid that lights up while it hangs from the gold and blue embellished ceiling. The walls are made from sandstone, elongated sconces with drastic points adorn the walls, adding to the illumination. Since the trip was last minute, the ticket I purchased simply allows me to board the train, not to an actual seat, so I intend on spending the three hours sitting in the club car. It takes me several minutes to locate the appropriate track number, joining the line that has begun to develop along the platform.

When it's my turn, I hand over the documents to the steward, while another claims my suitcase, adding it to the stack to be stored in the baggage car. He stamps my ticket, hands everything back to me, then steps aside. After placing the papers into my bag, the initial step up into the train is quite high, but I manage by gripping the handrails along the sides. Turning left at the compartment door, I make my way pass the reserved seats—many of which are reclined with slumbering souls nestled under thin blankets—and follow the signage for the club car, which is several carriages back.

The interior is an emerald green with silver accents. Small lamps with Tiffany-style shades sit at the center of each table, in addition to identical sconces on the walls. The ceiling is brown leather, curved like a woman's hip. The booths are rustic with bench seating. There are only a few people taking refuge in the lengthy car, so I sit in a booth at the rear, facing the direction I just came from, and making sure the rucksack is between me and the cool steel for the exterior wall.

The steward assisting the bartender comes over, and I request a glass of red wine. Through the tinted window on my left, I spot other trains readying to pull out of the station, or newly arrived ones unloading weary travelers. When my drink is delivered, I twirl it for a few seconds, allowing the delicate liquid to cling briefly to the sides before cascading back into a pool. The taste is hearty and robust, gliding down my throat like silk. Moving my attention to the other passengers, I notice that a few more of the booths are now occupied, as well as several of the leather upholstered stools. One face in particular catches my attention.

Though he no longer has on the navy blue suit, it's the carved muscles of his biceps and the wavy brown hair now dusting his shirt collar I immediately recognize. The young man who bumped into me at the museum. At the moment, he's wearing a short-sleeved, black T-shirt, cream-colored cargo pants, and hiking boots that look to have been newly purchased given their cleanliness. His hair is no longer slicked back, but allowed to freely frame his face, hiding a bit of the charm I caught earlier. It can't be a coincidence that he's on this particular train, given its destination and the cargo it'll be pulling shortly.

While he chats up the bartender after having been offered a cold beer, a disquieting chill settles into the room, one I've felt before. Given how the conversations around me continue, I must be the only one who detects the change. I surreptitiously unclasp the latch on the rucksack and slide my hand inside, gripping the pearl handle for one of the kards. The lights briefly flicker, which isn't uncommon when the electricity for the train is being moved off of the main switch for the station to independent power. What everyone doesn't notice in those infinitesimal seconds is the addition of a passenger, one who materializes out of thin air and carries with him the stench of death.

Nestled in a booth at the opposite end is a bald man with thick muscles, a strong jaw, dark, narrow eyes, and heavily tattooed arms. The symbols of which are ancient and pagan. It's obvious he's proud of them since they aren't covered up, but on display like armor. He stares intently at me, a deep-seated rage searing under the surface, his mind focused on ending my life in a most gruesome way.

"Is this seat taken?"

I'm momentarily startled by the question, my gaze falling upon the young man from before as he stands in the aisle holding his cold beverage, waiting for a reply.

I smile, though it strains me given the current circumstances I now find myself in. "Please," I reply, gesturing to the bench across from me.

Glancing toward the other table, I discover the man is no longer there and the chill I was feeling seems to have dissipated.

"I wanted to apologize again for bumping into you," the young man says, drawing my attention back to him, though my senses are now heightened at the impending threat I know is out there.

"It's fine, really." Removing my hand from the rucksack, I leave the weapon inside and wrap my fingers around the stem of the glass. "Did you enjoy the exhibit?"

"It was quite breathtaking." Lifting the pilsner to his lips, he winks.

I lean back in my seat, my grip never wavering from my drink. "Do you always come onto women so strongly?"

He chuckles. "I'm a horrible flirt. What can I say, you caught my attention."

Lifting my eyebrow and my glass, I reply, "Somehow I don't think that's hard to do." I drink a bit of the wine, savoring its flavor.

His laugh is contagious and lights up his entire face. "Well, for someone like me, it's very difficult."

A stillness sinks over the carriage, the lights flicker once again, and the smile on the young man's face vanishes when his hazel eyes become completely black, but only for a moment, then everything returns to normal.

I go for the kard, but the demon across from me grabs my arm, stopping me. "I'm not going to hurt you, Magdalene," he whispers.

"Why wasn't I able to detect you?" I growl, furious at being so readily deceived.

He releases me. "I concealed my true identity from your mind, tricked it into believing I was a mortal so you couldn't distinguish me from any other human being."

"Tricks like that on a hunter take days to mastermind, and we just encountered each other a few hours ago."

"At least that you're aware of." He casually picks up his glass and consumes the contents. "This wasn't my first trip to the museum, just like it wasn't yours. This time, however, I allowed you to see me, which is why I purposefully bumped into you."

"What do you want?" My fingers grip the stem of the wine glass tightly, while the anger in my voice cuts through the air like a hot knife.

Relaxing against the back of the booth, he responds, "Just to talk. Spend some time getting to know each other before I steal the Perpetua Chalice from its crypt." He signals the steward to bring another beer, and orders me more wine, even though I'm not even halfway done with the one I currently have. "I'm Rowen." He holds out his hand for me to shake.

I cross my arms over my chest, rebuffing the gesture. "Well, don't you sound confident. Arrogance has a way of getting people killed."

He smirks, recalling his hand, resting both arms on the table. "And seeing as I'm immortal, such rules don't apply to me."

"There are ways to remedy that." I nod toward the rucksack on the seat next to me. "Was that your friend who made a quick stop in here a couple of minutes ago?"

Rowen's face hardens and he clenches his jaw. "What did the person look like?"

I describe the man, including the impressions I was getting.

His knuckles turn white as he balls his hands into fists, which he's forced to hide when the steward returns with our drinks. "He's not with me," Rowen replies firmly once we're alone.

"Like I'd take your word for it." Knowing there's not only a demon in front of me, but another stalking me, the wine loses its appeal, so I push away both glasses.

128

Rowen's demeanor sours, his eyes narrowing as he looks out of the window. Fury broils inside of him, wrath coating his insides like oil at being blindly led into the den of a very dangerous wolf. Him the lamb for slaughter.

"What do you have to be upset about?" I ask, puzzled by his thoughts.

He turns sharply toward me. "How did you …" His voice fades.

Feeling amused, I can't help but grin, then reclaim my partially consumed glass of wine, finishing it. "Hunter's instinct."

"Bullshit," he replies, then laughs. "You're an empath."

"A gift not bestowed upon me by my wardens, but extremely useful."

The train rocks as the cars carrying the precious artifacts are attached at the tail end. After several additional minutes, we pull out of the station into a cloudless night. The interior lights dim, giving a romantic feel to the atmosphere, adding to the allure of my table mate.

Setting down the empty glass, I pick up the other, cradling the stem between my slender fingers. "So, Rowen, why do you want the chalice? You already have what it promises to give."

His taut shoulders relax the farther we get from Cairo. "Are you sure that's all it does?"

Sitting forward, I rest my drink and my arms on the table's smooth, wooden surface. "I'm not sure. Why don't you tell me and I'll let you know if you're right or not?"

He seems entertained by my response. "Can't fool you, can I?"

Taking a sip of my drink, I scan the room again in case any other demons shielding themselves have wandered into the car, but for the moment I don't notice any. "How many more of your friends should I expect along this journey?" I ask, focusing my attention back on Rowen, my fingers playing with the rim of the wine glass while my other hand surreptitiously opens the rucksack, reaches inside, and removes one of the daggers.

He stiffens at the remark. "I'm here alone and plan on keeping it that way," he answers, his voice cold and unforgiving.

Dropping the hand from my glass and into my lap, I discreetly jab the tip of the blade into my index finger, drawing blood, which I use to scroll a crescent-shaped shield with a seven-point starburst at its center. I don't need to look at what I'm doing since I've drawn this banishment symbol many times before.

I scowl. "Too bad." Driving the knife into my palm, blood drips down onto the floor and I involuntarily grimace.

Rowen's eyes widen at the realization of what I'm doing. "Magdalene, don't!"

I press the wound against the underside of the table, covering the sigil. In a brilliant flash of blinding light, Rowen vanishes, returning to whatever hell cave he came out of. The people around me shriek, many terrified that a bomb might have gone off, only to sigh when they realize they're still alive. Some attribute the sudden glare to a passing lamppost outside, while others mumble that they've had too much to drink and return to their seats in the coach carriages.

I really don't care that my little stunt has frightened so many. Their lives are now safer because of my actions, though they'll never know it. And if there were any other of Lucifer's minions snooping somewhere on the train, they're now gone as well. I can't help but chuckle at Rowen's horrific expression. He was a fool to believe I would simply let him sit and chat me up like we're old friends. Demons are my enemy, regardless of how attractive and charismatic they might be.

With my uninjured hand, I signal the steward and request a towel. He momentarily glances at the now empty seat before me, so I comment that my friend went to use the restroom. By the time the steward returns, my wounds have healed, but I still need to wipe the blood off of my flesh and the weapon before placing it back into the rucksack. With the pelta shield marked on the underside of the table, the entire train is now protected from all hell spawn who wish to materialize and bother me. It also secures the chalice, even though it's at the far end of the train. If Rowen is truly after the sacred relic, I'm sure he'll reappear at the docks in Alexandria where I will have to dispatch with him again.

This might be a fun game of cat and mouse. Life does get boring without much needed fun, which I'm rarely afforded.

We arrive shortly after midnight, the air still unbearably warm when I step down onto the platform. After collecting my suitcase from the luggage car, I make my way to the bus that will ferry some of us to the boat. Many of my fellow guests on the ramshackle vehicle are with the exhibition to ensure every piece arrives pristine and unfettered in Athens four days from now. Thankfully, the boat wasn't at capacity, so I was able to book a room on the lower deck just above the cargo hold. Perfect for sneaking in and out without being noticed for when I carve a devil's barrier on the exterior box, safeguarding it when I can't physically watch the item.

Getting off of the bus, I head for the plank assigned for boarding passengers, and wait once again to have my travel papers and passport verified. I know Rowen is standing behind me without having to turn. His woodsy scent is a dead giveaway.

"That wasn't very nice," he growls in my ear, his hot breath tickling my skin.

"I just wanted to make sure there weren't any more of your kind on the train," I reply with genuine amusement.

He grabs my arm, spinning me around. "I'm not someone you should trifle with, Magdalene."

"Watch yourself, Rowen, or I won't be so nice the next time I banish you."

Releasing me, he storms off, disappearing behind several stacks of crates. I can't help but smile at his displeasure.

Once I've passed inspection and my ticket is validated, I place the papers and passport back into the rucksack and take my suitcase down to the cabin I've been assigned. I unpack some of my clothes, but not all, then spend the next hour applying protection sigils and hexes throughout the small space. The lengthy day starts to wear on me; however, I can't go to sleep just yet. I wait until the boat has left the port before making my way down to the cargo hold with one of the kards where I engrave a pentagram inside of a circle with runes between each of its five points onto the rough wood for the crate housing the chalice.

Back in my room, I change into cotton loungewear, brush my teeth, and slip under the soft covers, allowing the rocking of the boat to lull me to sleep.

Breakfast the next morning is served on the upper deck out on the veranda with the sun gleaming radiantly overhead. Today my attire consists of peach-colored palazzo pants with a matching blouson and white, open-toed shoes. I've decided to leave my hair down, allowing the warm breeze to billow it nicely around my shoulders. After having been seated at a table set for four beside the railing, I place the cloth napkin in my lap while the steward pours freshly squeezed orange juice into my glass as I look over the menu. Selecting eggs Benedict with a side of fruit as my entrée, I purse my lips when Rowen saunters over, claiming the seat across from me without being invited.

"I'll order whatever she's having," he says to the steward, who's started serving him juice.

Rowen cleans up well in black trousers and matching short-sleeved dress shirt. His hair is damp and perfectly frames his face.

"Smuggle yourself onboard?" I jest, sipping the refreshing drink, the acid biting my throat.

"If you must know, I have a cabin, and no I didn't wipe someone's mind to steal it."

Crossing my legs at the knee, I sit back in the cushioned chair, carefully holding the highball glass. "Why journey all the way to Paris when you can simply meet the exhibition there? This entire excursion seems like an awful waste of time for someone in your position."

He rests his elbows on the table, leaning forward just a bit. "Maybe this trip isn't merely about the chalice."

132

Lifting my brow, I study him very carefully. "What else is there?"

His demeanor changes from playful banter to something sullener. A longing and far away glint captures his eyes while his gaze drifts to the waters surrounding us. "Loneliness."

An ache tugs at my core, and my heart, but I try not to let it show. "How can someone such as yourself possibly be lonely? Surely there are female demons to whet your appetite."

The hazel in his eyes dims a bit while the corners of his full mouth droop ever so slightly. "There are, but they're more into fuck now and forget later." He stares intently at me, as if seeing deep into my soul. "I want the full gambit of being with someone forever. Knowing I've found the woman who will last an immortal lifetime. Never having to worry about being forgotten again."

I laugh, which obviously pains him. "That's an oxymoron, Rowen. Your kind live forever, there is no end." My tone turns abrasive. "Besides, demons don't love, they hunt, violate, and kill. What you're looking for doesn't exist."

Folding his hands together, he sits farther forward, practically on the edge of his seat. "Are hunters lives any different? They hunt, violate, and kill just as readily as demons do. You're also kept just as isolated, only permitted to leave the safety of your dwelling when called upon."

Trying not to slam the glass onto the table, I methodically and carefully set it back into place. "You know nothing about me, or my life," I say, seething, my face turning red from anger.

He reaches out to touch my hand, but I pull it away. "I know you were eight when your village burned, and that a demon named Belial murdered your parents. That you were trained from that moment on to be a relic hunter, and you're good at what you do. You've defeated legions single handedly, more than anyone in previous history. That it's more than Lucifer who has sought you out, and not simply to kill you."

I grow chilled by his words. Every one of them true. Choking on sobs desperate to escape, I ask through clenched teeth, "What do you want, Rowen?"

He doesn't smile or smirk, but merely gazes thoughtfully into my eyes. "To help you."

The steward arrives with our food, only I no longer have an appetite.

Standing, I throw my napkin into the chair. "I don't need it, or your pity." Then I storm back to my room, locking the door, and collapsing onto the bed in tears.

I hate being made to feel vulnerable, small, and insignificant. Loneliness does creep up every so often, but I rarely have the time to dwell on it. Being the only hunter of my kind has its drawbacks. The others I live with see me as something damaged, a thorn in their sides. I've begged and pleaded to be relocated, but I'm ignored and sometimes punished for my outbursts. It's a rough existence that I don't know how to escape from.

There's a soft knock on the door, so before opening it, I grab one of the kards I keep on the nightstand. Relieving the lock, I crack the door open, spying Rowen on the other side carrying a tray with our food.

"How did you know which cabin was mine?" I ask, holding the dagger out of view behind my back.

He nods to the graffiti on the walls, ceiling, and floor. "Those might repel us, but they also make us aware that you're here. I know you were taught to mark the premises, however it's not always beneficial for your safety."

"I'll keep that in mind."

Noticing the tearstains on my cheeks, he frowns. "I'm sorry to have upset you. Since I can't come in, and our breakfast is getting cold, perhaps we can go into the sitting room at the end of the hall and talk some more."

"There really isn't anything left to be said."

He's upset by the comment, heartbroken actually. "You still need to eat. At least take your plate. I'll feel much better knowing that you're not hungry."

I relieve it from the tray, then step back into the room. Just as I'm closing the door, he turns and heads toward the staircase at the opposite end, disappearing to the deck above. Setting the plate on the unmade bed, I eat even though I don't feel like it. When I'm finished, I set the plate on the carpeted floor of the hallway, then spend the rest of the day locked in my room, not daring to venture out.

Music wafts through the open window above my bed, rousing me from a nap. The sun has set, meaning I missed lunch and enjoying the views. Dinner tonight is to be a formal affair, which is traditional on the first evening. The dress I brought is a sage green, satin sleeveless with a V cut down the bodice to the breast bone. It exposes a good portion of my back, and wraps around my waist, secured with a discreet button on my hip. When I move, one of the sides swings open, exposing my well-toned leg, giving me a bit a femininity that I normally try to hide. I also made sure to bring heels that match.

Once I'm put together, I run a comb through my hair and try to find some way to carry one of the daggers, though that proves difficult given the slit in the hem. There is a sheath that I can strap around my thigh, only it'll have to rest on the inside of my leg, making walking a bit awkward. However, I don't want to chance being unprepared given the confinement of the boat and the safety of all those onboard. I'd rather it be noticed than go around unarmed.

Dinner is being served in the dining hall two decks above. The large space is decorated in royal blue, gold, and pearl accents. A five-piece orchestra plays in the corner, the melody soothing and inviting. Stewards in white tuxedos carry silver trays adorned with champagne flutes, so I claim one. A dance floor has been erected, limiting the number of tables available for eating, but still enough to satisfy the number of passengers onboard. There are approximately thirty people mingling with only a handful more already scoping out the buffet at the far end of the room. I keep to the back, hugging one of the open windows overlooking a narrow balcony, my focus on everyone else and the water behind me.

Rowen enters wearing a fitted black tuxedo, matching all others in attendance. My heart catches in my throat at the sight of him, the ruggedness and ease that pours off of him like water. He's left his hair hanging around his face, adding to his handsomeness. I can't help but blush as he approaches.

"You look amazing," he says, bowing ever so slightly.

Biting my lip, I state, "You're not too bad looking yourself. Who knew demons could clean up so well?"

He smiles. "I'll take that as a compliment." Then he extends his arm. "Would you care to join me for dinner?"

After wrapping my arm around his, he escorts me deep into the dining hall, snagging one of the more secluded tables. He pulls out my chair, which I thank him for while sitting. Before taking a seat, he waves one of the stewards over and orders a bottle of red wine.

"I know it's your favorite," he says, adjusting himself in the high-backed chair.

"What did you do all day?" I inquire, setting down the champagne flute.

"Well, I was going to attempt a robbery, but it seems someone has marked a certain crate with a devil's barrier. Now I'll have to wait until Paris in order to make my move." His wink is pleasing and plays with my tender heart.

"I can't say that I'm sorry you missed your opportunity."

The steward returns, fills our glasses, then sets the bottle onto the table.

Rowen grins wickedly. "Are we becoming friends?"

I chuckle. "That's stretching things a bit."

It's not long until we're able to queue up for dinner. He insists on carrying my plate, though I'm perfectly capable. We make small talk during the course of the meal. I have to nurse the wine because even though demons can't get drunk, hunters still can, and that's the last thing I need to happen. When the dishes have been cleared, the orchestra returns to playing and couples take to the dancefloor.

Rowen stands, pushes in his chair, then offers me his hand. "Care to join them?"

"I'm not much for dancing."

"Is it because you've never had a decent partner, or do you not know how?"

Furrowing my brow, I counter, "That sounds like a challenge."

Taking his hand there's an instant connection, a thread unraveling between us, linking our cores together, and intensifying with each passing second. Scared by the odd and unexpected phenomenon, I let go and the sensation vanishes.

"What's the matter?" he asks, bewildered by my sudden recoil.

"Nothing, it's ... it's just really warm in here and I could use from fresh air."

Turning, I head for the doors that'll lead us out onto one of the balconies that expands the length of the vessel. Rowen, with his hands clutched behind his back, stays by my side while we traverse the wooden floorboards in silence. Several feet from the dining hall, I stop and lean against the railing overlooking the dark waters, stars sprinkling overhead.

"I miss seeing skies like this," I comment, nodding to the one above us. "The stars over Cresidio were always so bright and blanketed everywhere you looked." Lowering my gaze toward the water, I continue, "It always felt like another layer to protect me when I was younger. A soothing embrace from the gods or goddesses who looked down upon us."

Rowen takes a position next to me. "Sounds lovely."

The wind catches my hair, pushing it away from my face as I turn to look at him. "What was your childhood like?"

Clasping his hands together, he leans farther against the railing. "It was a long time ago and not really worth discussing."

"Is it that you don't remember, or you just don't want to tell me?"

He snickers, his eyes glittering in the bit of light cascading around us from the lamps inside. "A bit of both, I suppose. Memories purposefully altered to preserve one's own sanity. I'm afraid it's a dull tale compared to yours." He moves until his back is now against the railing, his arms folded over his chest. "Besides, you might not believe me anyway. Demons lie all the time. Even about the personal things."

"Fine," I grumble, pretending to be annoyed.

He brushes his shoulder against mine. "Dance with me and I'll tell you my story." Again, he holds out his hand for me to take.

I hesitate, fearing the spark that ignited before will return and never allow me to sever from it ever again. The last thing I need is to be bound to a demon, whether intentionally or not. I've never actually heard of it happening, but there's a first time for everything.

Instead, I simply smile. "Thanks, but I think the food isn't sitting well with me. Perhaps it's best if I call it a night."

Disappointment tugs at the corners of his eyes, which have lost their glow. "Then I'll see you tomorrow at breakfast."

Making my way to the stairs, I know Rowen is watching, his thoughts as to my refusal incorrect and upsetting. He felt the bond forming like I had, and wants it to flourish. Whereas I'm apprehensive and feel as if I'm being pulled away from the task given to me. My main focus must be to protect the chalice at all costs. Nothing, and no one, can lure me away from that no matter how tempting.

An unnatural chill settles over me while I try to return to a restless sleep. My eyelids flash open at the realization that there's an unwelcome visitor onboard. Slipping on my sandals, I unsheathe the kard from its holster resting atop the dresser where I placed it after changing for bed. The loungewear I have on is cotton, though a bit thin because of the heat inside of the cabin. The cuffs for the pants dust the floor and the sleeveless shirt clings to my dampening skin. Stepping into the hallway, I keep the weapon down along my side and slowly follow the scent of death wafting from the upper decks.

The cabins I pass are darkened, so I shouldn't have to worry about stumbling across anyone, with the exception of the occasional deckhand or steward tending to the craft and preparing it for morning. Reaching the main deck, voices elevated in anger catch my attention. Rowen is arguing with another demon toward the back of the boat where the life preservers are stored. Making sure to mask my approach, I sidle up to the wall for the rear staircase, pressing my back solidly against the rough clapboards.

"I don't care what you want. This is happening my way," Rowen says sternly.

"You've had plenty of chances to deal with the relic hunter," his companion's deep voice booms in a German accent. "We grow tired of waiting."

Quickly glimpsing around the corner, I recognize the man as the same one from the train. He's shorter than Rowen by several inches and carries two daggers made from a bluish-black metal that curve slightly at the tip. The bottom of the blades by the grip are hollowed out, leaving a distinctive pattern should it be thrust into flesh. The woven grip itself appears to have small, shallow wings jutting out where the hilt meets the blade, and I swear there's a silver skull etched into the side.

"We reach Athens in a couple of days. Give me until then."

Something scrapes across the wooden floorboards. "You let that bitch ban you from the train and put a barrier on the crate. Your carelessness is going to cost you, Rowen."

I should slay them both right here. It won't take but a few seconds to turn them into ash with the single kard I carry, sending them to Lucifer's cages to rot for all eternity.

Peeking again, I catch a set of hazel-colored eyes staring in my direction, their shimmer being brought about by the full moon cascading its rays down onto the boat. Rowen bites his lip. "I know what I'm doing," he scolds, turning back to his counterpart.

The other demon raises one of the weapons, practically touching Rowen's face. "You had better."

The chill evaporates when the man disappears in a plume of black smoke, but not my unease. Stabbing my finger, I draw the crescent shape with its seven-point starburst onto the wall, but before I can pierce my palm to complete the sigil, Rowen is standing beside me. He grips my open hand with his, the kard posed inches above it. A charge of heat flows between us, enticing me to let go and give in.

"Don't bind that shield," he says, his voice quivering. "I can't protect you if you shut me out."

"You want me dead."

"If you honestly believe that, then go ahead and turn me into ash. Send me to the cages." Moving closer, he rests his forehead against mine, and I surprisingly let him. "But you know I speak the truth." He places his hands on either side of my face. "Magdalene, you felt the thread. It tugged me as well. The fact that a hunter and demon can be bonded together are extremely rare, but it does happen, and I know that thought terrifies you." He tucks a few errant strands of hair behind my ear, lighting up my insides. "I will never do anything to harm you. There's a reason I've been following you and it has nothing to do with the chalice. Please, give me a chance to explain."

Tears well in my eyes and an ache captures my heart as I discreetly pierce my hand, hiding the influx of physical pain with the emotional one seizing me. "I'm sorry, but I can't," I whisper.

In one fluid motion, I slap my palm onto the sigil, completing the shield, generating a bright light that takes Rowen from me. His screams echo through the darkness and continue to radiate in my ears even when he's gone. I slump to the floor, pull my knees up to my chest, and bawl.

I spend the rest of the voyage in my room except for meals. When we dock in Athens it's early morning, so just like in Alexandria, I share a bus with the exhibition crew as we make our way to the train station. This time I have a private compartment, and the first thing I do is add a pelta shield on the exterior facing wall for my room, protecting the entire train. Sitting in the lounge car, I monitor the activity outside, carefully observing the various crates and boxes being placed onto pallets and loaded into a cargo container at the rear while drinking a bitter cup of coffee.

140

It'll take roughly two days to reach Paris, which includes the various stops along the way to pick up and drop off fee paying travelers. Watching the scenery pass once we're underway, I try not to think about Rowen. It hurts too much. He's a dangerous distraction, and I honestly can't bring myself to believe anything of what he was saying. I sensed his thoughts, felt his heart shatter when I completed the circuit needed for the sigil to work. There wasn't any choice. At least, that's what I keep telling myself, knowing it's a full-fledged lie. Sitting in the cushioned chair, I raise my right hand and look over the healed wound in my palm, rubbing the spot where I eradicated all possible joy from my dark life, not even a scar to remind me of the deed.

After finishing the coffee, I return to my room and lock the door. Grabbing a pillow and blanket down from the small closet, I make myself comfortable on the over-sized seat, pull down the shades, and work on getting some much needed rest.

The squeal of metal grinding against metal jars me awake. We come to such an abrupt stop I'm thrown into the seat across from me. Orders are being barked loudly in Greek from the speakers in the hallway, but I understand every word that's being spoken.

"Guard the train. Ready your arms."

Opening the door, I find men with rifles in stiff military uniforms racing toward the rear. Stepping back into the room, I grab my kards and head in the same direction. A violent force rocks the train, causing me to fall against one of the outer windows, shattering it and cutting my arm through my long-sleeved, gray shirt. Loud footsteps can be heard running along the roof, followed by more shuddering and the noise of bending metal, this time throwing the train off the tracks and onto its side.

The impact with the wall in front of me breaks my nose and I briefly lose possession of the kards, but they sail back into my hands of their own accord. Blood runs down my face and I use my sleeve to wipe it away. Groans, screams, and breaking glass envelop the chaos unfolding. Standing,

I carefully make my way between the various cars, crawling across openings that are no longer tall enough for me to walk through. Up ahead are the armed men, regaining their footing from having been tossed around like the rest of us. I'm almost to their location when an explosion rips the entire compartment open. Wood splinters, shards of glass, metal fragments, and blood fly through the air. I drop onto what was once the exterior wall and crouch into a ball to protect myself.

Giddy laughter, tearing flesh, and shrieks of terror overload my senses. Pain that doesn't belong to me wraps around my brain like a vice, horrified voices mumble in the back of my head begging to be saved, and the stench of death overpowers my damaged nostrils.

Grunting, I reclaim my footing, step over the corpses of the men killed, and make my way toward the shafts of daylight that's bisected the car. The harshness of the sun burns when I stumble out into the open landscape, burning grass and smoldering vegetation the only signs of life. Once my sight adjusts, I spot the cargo container several cars down and completely detached. From the scorched and twisted debris, it's obvious the explosion originated there. Limping, I hurry over to the carriage, praying the crate with the chalice is still in one piece.

A demon materializes inches from the latched door, desperately prying it open. His back is to me, so he doesn't notice the kard enter his body until he becomes ash, the weapon quickly returning to my grasp as more like him appear. I cut them down while they randomly materialize, some armed to the teeth and ready for battle. Blades and other weapons fall from their hands when their bodies become nothing but dust. I'm nearly to the container when another explosion tears through its side, knocking me to the ground, and dispelling the cargo. The crates splinter and break, including the one for the chalice. Crawling over to it, a searing pain burns in my ribcage, stopping me. I scream as the blade is extracted. The toe of a boot slides under my shoulder, tossing me onto my bleeding back. The demon from the first train stares down at me, a satisfied grin on his cynical face. The weapon at his side is the same one he had on the boat, only now it's dripping with my blood.

"*Well, aren't you a hard bitch to trap,*" he spits, then steps on both of my wrists, preventing me from using the kards still clutched in my hands.

I scream from the agony, my bones crunching under his immense weight.

He chuckles. "*Where are those bastards now to help you? Don't the other hunters want to come to your rescue, or do they find you useless like the rest of us?*" Kneeling beside me, he grazes my cheeks with his rough, calloused fingers. "*Too bad when they do arrive, the only thing they'll find is your broken body.*"

"*Hey.*"

The man looks up and doesn't get a chance to shout for help when a knife similar to his cuts into his throat, splitting it wide open, and splashing blood all over me. Grappling for the wound, he drops his blades, staggers to his feet, and disappears in a swirl of black smoke.

Rowen's anxious face comes into view. "*Can you stand?*"

I nod, then whimper while using my damaged hands to push myself up. The bones are slow to reset, so Rowen places an arm around my waist and helps me to my feet.

"*You look like shit,*" he comments, his lips curling in a smirk.

"*Fuck off,*" I mutter, shoving him away, then go searching for the chalice, but the injury in my back causes me to collapse.

Rowen is beside me in seconds and notices the wound. "*Shit, we have to get you out of here.*"

"*I can't leave.*" The muscles in my chest and torso seize, making it difficult to breathe.

"*Stubborn ass,*" he complains. "*The chalice isn't worth your life.*"

"*Yes ... it ... is.*"

"*Bullshit.*" Cradling me in his arms, he gets to his feet just as sirens start wailing in the distance. "*Tuck those kards into your waistband. You don't want to lose them, and I can't touch them.*"

I do as instructed, then close my eyes and pass out.

The sound of chirping birds rouses me, my eyelids too heavy to fully open. A warm breeze drifts through open windows, bringing with it scents of fresh flowers and musty water. Lace curtains billow in the wake, dancing to their own music, almost like ghosts. Lying on my stomach, my head resting sideways on the plump pillow, I realize I'm on a queen-sized bed in a lavish bedroom that has lost its splendor. Peeling wallpaper in a brocade pattern barely clings to the walls, the oak wood floor is badly scuffed, and dust coats a few of the built-in shelves by a small seating arrangement, cobwebs draping from several corners along the ceiling. There aren't any light fixtures from what I can tell, but there are plenty of candlesticks in antique brass holders on the nightstands and dresser with wax stumps and burnt wicks.

Moving to sit up, I shriek from the excruciating pain, as if I'm being stabbed all over again.

Rowen rushes into the room carrying a tarnished silver tray holding a white porcelain bowl filled with water, a raggedy washcloth, and a bar of gray soap. "Don't move," he says, setting the procurements onto the floor, then kneeling to help me back into position. "It's best to stay lying still until the wound is thoroughly cleaned."

"Where are we?" I ask, my voice weak and gravelly.

"My home," he answers tenderly, carefully pulling up the back of my shirt. "It's an abandoned castle in De Lamar, France along the Durance River."

"Do ... do the others—"

He places a finger across my trembling lips, the spark between us instant, but I choose to ignore it. "No one knows about this place, so we're well protected. I promise."

I can't help but shake, confused by what's happening to me. "Why am I not healing?"

Wetting the cloth, he rubs it against the soap getting a decent lather. "The weapon used is called a clach. They're crafted from cursed steel and meant to inflict near fatal wounds on immortals. A few more inches higher and it would've pierced your heart."

"Wh-Who was that demon?" I grimace when he begins washing the wound.

"His name is Theron, and he's Lucifer's hunter."

"You led him right to me." The strength needed to convey the rage coursing through me isn't there, so it comes out as a simple whimper.

Rowen's face falls and he momentarily stops. "I'm sorry. That was never my intention."

"I heard what Theron said to you that night on the boat. You were supposed to deal with me."

He lets out a long, deep sigh, then resumes cleansing the wound after rinsing the cloth into the bowl, its clear water turning dark. "It's not what you think, Magdalene."

"Don't lie to me," I bark, immediately regretting the effort it took.

"I'm not," he snaps, then drops the washcloth onto the tray and rubs his tired face. "Look, we're both exhausted. Let me finish, then get some rest and we can talk later."

Grumbling, I turn my head away while he continues to clean off my back. After several long, tense minutes, he leaves, closing the door loudly behind him. Wondering where the kards are, I feel around the mattress beside me, but when I can't find them, I flip my head back around and visually search the floor, coming up empty.

"Shit."

Rowen must have taken them, or they fell out of my waistband on the way here. It really doesn't matter since I can't return home without them, or suffer further ridicule than I already do. Burying my face into the pillow, I yell out of frustration. Surprisingly, my back doesn't hurt like it did, so I try to move, albeit unsuccessfully. I'm not looking forward to being trapped here for who knows how long. Hopefully the injury heals quickly and I can get back to protecting the chalice, if it hasn't been pilfered already.

The sun has just about set when I start to feel more normal, though I'm caked in dirt, dried blood, sweat, and my clothes are ruined. There's just enough light coming in through the windows that I don't need to strike a match and ignite one of the pathetic candles. Gingerly sitting up, the pain and discomfort are almost gone, but not entirely, so I swing my legs over the side of the bed and tentatively stand. My limbs are a bit stiff, as are the muscles in my lower back and abdomen, but otherwise I'm fine.

Slowly heading for the door, I spot my blood-spattered shoes by a partially opened closet. Reaching for the brass doorhandle, something inside of the closet catches my eye, so I change course. I pull back the white bifold doors, and inside, dangling from a metal rod on a wooden hanger, is the dress I wore to dinner the first night on the boat, and it's in pristine condition.

"While you were resting, I went back to the train and retrieved your belongings," Rowen says, lingering in the now open door for the bedroom. "The rest of your clothes are in the dresser." He gestures toward the French provincial furnishing resting along the far wall.

"What about the chalice?" I ask, dreading the answer.

"It's with the Greek authorities, as are all the possessions from the exhibit."

Closing the bifold doors, I say, "I need to get to it."

I step toward the hallway, but Rowen stops me by placing his hands on my shoulders and blocking my escape.

"No, Magdalene, you don't. It's in well-guarded hands."

I push away from him. "They don't know how to do it properly."

"You still need rest, and a bath." He pretends to be put off by an imaginative odor.

Folding my arms over my chest, I scowl.

"All right, how about this ... get cleaned up, put on fresh clothes, and while you're doing that I'll make dinner. If you still insist on leaving after we've eaten, then I'll take you to where the chalice is being stored." A mischievous grin crosses his face. "Besides, you owe me a dance."

"Where are my kards?" I inquire, not amused by his attempt at levity.

His smile fades. "Downstairs in the kitchen."

"I thought you couldn't touch them?"

Brushing past me, he heads toward a closed door at the far side of the room. "They can't come into contact with my skin, so I used a cloth to carry them. I didn't think it prudent to leave them in bed with you."

Following him, we enter a lavish bathroom with white granite floors, robust red walls, gold accents and finishing, a duel vanity, working toilet, and a claw-footed tub. Rowen steps over to the gleaming porcelain and turns on the faucet, filling the deep basin with hot water.

"Turn around so I can check your wound," he says, once the water is shut off.

Rolling my eyes, I do, lifting my shirt just enough for him to glimpse the damage. Moving closer, his fingers caress the tender spot, causing heat to rise between us. His hot breath hits my neck as he bends down to get a better look. A lump catches in my throat when thoughts of the two of us together fill my mind, our skin rubbing against each other, adding to my already racing heart.

"It's nearly healed, but you will have a scar."

"Thank you," I say, lowering my shirt and moving to face him, my voice cracking, "for saving my life."

He straightens, reaches for the band holding my ponytail together, and removes it, allowing my long, raven hair to fall upon my shoulders and down my back. "You're welcome." His smile is enticing and warm. "Everything you need is in the cabinet." He points to a tall, three-paneled oak wood cupboard with open shelves filled with towels, soaps, and other toiletries.

As he goes to leave, I ask, "Why are you being so nice to me?"

"Because I care about you, Magdalene, and have for quite some time." The door closes quietly behind him.

Removing a soft, dark red towel from the stack, I claim a fragrant bar of soap, return to the tub, strip, then step into the steaming water. My muscles relish the heat seeping into them, relaxing more and more with each passing second. I don't bathe right away, wanting to enjoy the solitude, which I don't normally get to experience. It takes quite a bit of time to scrub my body and hair clean, turning the water almost an inky black. While the tub drains, I dry off, wrapping the towel around my body before stepping back into the bedroom. The sun has set farther and there are now numerous candles lit in the room, more than were in here before, in addition to the windows now being closed.

I can't help but grin at the thought that Rowen was just a few feet away as I lay naked in the tub. Shaking my head to clear it, I open the top drawer for the dresser, finding the clothes that had been inside of my suitcase neatly folded. Selecting clean under garments, black leggings, a lavender-colored shirt, and anklet socks, I dress quickly, hoping to stave off the slight chill enveloping the room. I use my fingers to work the tangles out of my hair before exiting into the dimly lit hallway, following the illumination from below cascading over the banister railing from a great room a floor below. Ornate tapestries depicting the family who must have once called this place home adorns the walls, their regal attire elaborate, stiff, and dated. The floors are covered in a thick, crimson carpet that muffles the sounds of each step. There are numerous other rooms in this part of the castle, but all the doors are closed, and I don't particularly feel like snooping. At the end of the lengthy hallway is a wide staircase that bends gracefully around a marble column, which extends all the way to the tall ceiling.

Candles line the gray marble floor, leading a path toward the drawing room where a blaze roars in the fireplace, easing a bit of the nippy air trying to seep in from the falling night. Like the bedroom, the furnishings in here are French provincial, but without the dust and cobwebs. Around a wide coffee table in the center of an elegant seating arrangement are stacks of pillows that look to have been purposefully placed. On top of the carved oak top are two place settings consisting of porcelain blue China, sterling silver utensils, and cut-crystal goblets. A lone red rose protrudes upward from a glass bud vase, adding a bit of elegance.

"Dinner will be ready shortly," Rowen says, startling me. Clutched in his hand is a bottle of red wine. "Shall I pour?" He raises the spirits, smiling while nodding for me to have a seat.

As I get comfortable on one of the pillows, he removes the foil around the cork, then extracts a corkscrew from the pocket of his jeans. After filling both of our glasses, he sets down the bottle and sits across from me.

"Do you always make meals such a formal affair?" I inquire, after taking a sip of the luscious liquid.

"Only when I have special guests, which isn't often."

I throw him a crooked smile. "I'm sure all the women you've entertained appreciate the gesture."

He bristles at the comment. "How are you feeling?"

"Sore, but otherwise fine. Once dinner is over, I'll pack my things and return to Athens where the chalice is currently being held."

Raising an eyebrow in surprise, he asks, "How do you know where it is?"

"Because it's the logical place for the authorities to have whisked the exhibition pieces off to for temporary storage."

Picking up his glass, he drinks a bit before saying, "I wish you would rest for at least a few more days. Having cursed steel pierce your flesh isn't an easy thing to overcome."

I set my drink on the coffee table, stiffening at the request. "Why are you so adamant that I remain here?"

He stares at me intently. "It's the safest place for you to be."

"I'm a relic hunter, Rowen. I'm not safe anywhere except at the home I share with the other hunters."

"Even though they despise your presence?"

I glower at him. "You don't know anything about what living there is like."

Sadness creases the corners of his hazel eyes. "I'm an empath, Magdalene, same as you. I see the pain that being with them causes to your soul, the dread upon your heart." He stares at me intently, his mood altering to one of mischief. "Hunters can sense their own, yet none have come looking for you. There aren't any sigils or hexes barring them from locating this place, so what's keeping them away?"

My breathing becomes heavier as my temper rises. Resting my hands in my lap, I ball them into fists, my nails digging into my palms, nearly drawing blood.

"They would've heard about the attack on the train by now. Surely someone knew you were onboard."

"What's your point?" I ask bitterly, my anger roiling just under the surface, ready to spring outward and slay him.

Finishing his wine, he smirks. "You've always hated being with them, but then again you never did fit in. You're not one to conform to their rules ... their rigid structure. You're like a vicious, wild beast held against her will. You pace in front of the wrought iron bars of your cage preparing to pounce, biding your time until someone forgets to click the lock into place. Perhaps now is that moment."

"Is that the real reason you've been stalking me? Hoping to turn me against my own kind? Start a war within the hunter ranks, tearing us apart so the rest of your friends can purge the world for their own enjoyment? Fill the rivers with blood, burn every last city to its foundation, then start anew?" Standing, I stretch both hands out behind me and within seconds the kards are in my grip, my fingers coiling around their welcoming ivory handles. "You picked the wrong one to fuck with, Rowen."

His throat bobs, but he tries not to let his nervousness show. "How many relic hunters have there been over the centuries, Magdalene? Your kind don't last very long. In fact, you've outlived all of your predecessors. A feat that has not gone unnoticed." He stands, then slowly approaches. "What I want is to make sure you remain the relic hunter and not get sent to one of those infernal cells where nothing but torture and death await you."

"And what do you get out of it?"

He stops so close I can easily kill him with the daggers, but the passion in his eyes keeps me rooted in place. Raising a hand, he brushes the hair from my face, his fingertips grazing my hot skin, igniting me inside. Leaning forward, he lowers his face toward mine, his mouth inches away. "The knowledge that the woman I care most about in this world will be protected."

I'm about to protest when he presses his soft, firm lips against mine, unleashing a fire down my spine that coils around my core, erupting into a welcomed hell storm.

Chapter Ten

The memory still clings to me as I run my fingers through Rowen's hair, tugging on his damp, wavy locks. He moans quietly, then pulls me down supine onto the mattress and presses his hard body against mine. His lips move momentarily down my neck, leaving goose pimples behind while his hands grip the pillow under my head, desperate to tear at more than the case covering it. Drawing him back, our tongues dance in each other's mouths, not quite able to fulfill the longing enveloping us. I want all of him, every last inch, his hot skin rubbing against mine in all the ways it used to, and I know he desires the same. He grapples with my clothes, anxious to remove them. However, the moment his hands wander up the back of my sweater, I quickly stop and move from his grasp, terrified that he'll discover more than the scar from the clach marring me.

"I can't," I utter, embarrassed and desperate to catch my breath.

He blushes. "I'm sorry. I shouldn't have done that."

I look at him adoringly, placing a hand on his cheek as the old feelings continue to return, consuming my every thought. "No, don't be." The smile that erupts on my face sparkles in his eyes. "It reawakened bits of our past. I recollect nearly everything about our time together, and how much we loved each other. That the horrors of the world fell away, and nothing else mattered. It was just us, and it was amazing." My expression falls. "There's just something I'm not ready to share with you yet."

Wrapping an arm around my waist, he presses his forehead against mine. "You can tell me anything, Magdalene. You know that."

I kiss him deeply, and it's hard not to stop, but I do. "I know." My gaze drops to the wounds on his chest, the tips of my fingers gently tracing their outlines. He quakes at my touch. "But my life has been so difficult this time that I bear scars worse than yours."

Placing his other hand under my chin, he lifts my face to meet his. "I love you, Magdalene. There isn't anything you can't show me."

Grazing his cheek with the back of my hand, I comment, "Maybe later."

He pulls me close and kisses me again, our passion reigniting, and it's not long until he has me pinned underneath him, more than just his muscles pulsating to be stroked. We're soon interrupted by a knock on the door. Rowen grumbles as he stands to open it, swearing about the poor timing, which causes me to laugh.

"Uh, Kagan sent me to fetch the two of you," Pierce says timidly, his American accent still odd to my ears because it's been years since I've been around one outside of my own. "We've been waiting in the library for the past five minutes."

Rowen tenses up while I continue to giggle. "We'll be down in a moment." He closes the door, then chuckles as he goes over to the armoire and removes a black, long-sleeved pullover. "We might have to create a 'Do Not Disturb' sign."

After extracting myself from the bed, I jab him playfully in the ribs while we head for the door, which causes him to snicker harder. When we reach the library, everyone is seated around the table with Kagan at the head, the fireplace lit behind him heating the chilled room. I take a seat beside Doreleska, with Rowen across the way.

"I'm glad the two of you could finally join us," the older man says, crossing his arms over his brawny chest, fuming. "Let me guess. More of Magdalene's memories are returning."

"Slowly," I reply, but the grin on Rowen's face and the lust in his eyes tells everyone a different story.

Hollis laughs, tucking a strand of blonde hair behind her ear, and Doreleska rolls her eyes, shaking her head.

Kagan clears his throat, which quiets everyone. "During our brief excursion to Kern, Magdalene revealed to me what the Watchers might possibly be after. They believe she's found something called a cardinal stone."

"What the hell is that?" Doreleska asks, kicking back in her seat, resting her long legs on the table, and clasping her hands with perfectly manicured nails in her lap. Her burgundy hair hangs loosely around her bare shoulders since the long-sleeved, red top she's wearing has cutouts exposing them. Her pants are black, tight fitting, and taper down to her ankles, a simple pair of socks covering her petite feet.

"I don't know," I answer. "The only thing I'm in possession of, besides the hunter blades, is a compass rose pendant."

Ulrich's ears perk up, and for once he doesn't have a book in his hands. He's dressed in jeans and a basic, plain white T-shirt, much like he was yesterday. "Can I see it?"

Reaching behind my neck, I unhook the chain, then reclasp it before handing it to him.

He studies it carefully, his long, nimble fingers rubbing the warped edge. Especially where the tips for the arrows have worn away. "This might be it," he says, his gaze still held by the object. "On a compass, the points indicating east, west, north, and south are called cardinal directions." He hands it back to me. "Where did you get it?"

I put on the necklace, tucking it back under the sweater. "I saw the pendant at the rynek and felt it was something of importance, so I did a few chores for the woman who owned it since I couldn't afford to purchase it. She gave it to me as payment."

"Dalma had it?" the older man asks, scratching his furry chin.

I nod. "It was buried under a mound of jewelry that she was selling. She claimed not to have realized it was in her possession, though I don't think she even knows what it's for... like I don't."

Doreleska watches me, her stare narrow and hard. "How did you discover the necklace if it wasn't in plain sight?"

Returning her intense expression, I reply, "It felt like the pendant was calling out to me. Beckoning me, actually. I wasn't sure why, but if it's a true sacred relic, then that's the reason."

"You hear them like voices?" Hollis giggles at her own question, leaning into the table as if to move closer to me.

"Something similar to that. It's an instinct, really. A knowing."

Ulrich clutches his hands together, setting them on top of the table. "Did you first notice the Watchers after you had the necklace in your possession?"

"No."

Kagan cocks his head to the side, arms once again folded at his chest. "When did you start seeing them?"

Glancing at Rowen, I hesitate to answer.

"Magdalene?" the older man queries, his tone harsh.

Avoiding Kagan's glare, I look down at the table. "It was the morning after Rowen arrived into town."

Everyone, but me, glowers at him.

"You think I drew them there?" His eyes widen in astonishment. "If that were true, then they would've found the castle by now, but they haven't."

"Maybe they were always in Kern, just biding their time," Hollis suggests, relaxing a bit in the heavily upholstered chair.

"For what?" Doreleska smirks.

She shrugs. "Perhaps they knew the pendant was in the market, but weren't able to garner it for themselves. It wasn't until Magdalene had it that they finally attacked."

"Then why bomb the café?" Rowen asks, appearing bewildered, then gestures to me. "She wasn't in it."

A hollow sensation eats away at my gut, the thought of Festus and all those people possibly being murdered over something so trivial as the pendant. "No, but I was heading there. A few more minutes and I would've been inside."

"And dead," Pierce adds bluntly, drawing ire and a sneer from Rowen. "Did you notice the Watchers before that moment?"

Besides detailing the two previous incidents of when they mysteriously appeared, I also go into detail about how I was headed to Safran to ask Festus about the journal he left for me at the hostel, divulging where and how many Watchers I had noticed before the explosion. Also, how I believed the one was smiling, even though I couldn't see it.

Kagan leans forward, resting his burly, heavily tatted arms on the table. "Dalma thought that book had been burnt up in the café and you didn't correct her. Why?"

"I didn't see the point since I no longer have it. The journal fell out of my hand when I was thrown backward from the blast. I didn't realize it was gone until I woke up here."

"Do you know what it contained?" Ulrich asks, interested.

"No. I never got a chance to read it," I reply, lying while the first line continues to haunt me:

If you're reading this, then I failed to stop him.

Until I'm able to determine who 'he' is, the others can't know anything about what might be contained within those weathered pages. I need to find a way of getting it back from the Watchers, if they do indeed have it.

"Perhaps it's mixed amongst the debris," Ulrich suggests, sounding hopeful.

Rowen shakes his head. "I checked yesterday shortly after Magdalene mentioned it was missing. It wasn't anywhere on the street or sidewalk."

"Could the Watchers have it?" Hollis inquires, her unpolished nails clicking against the table, which is starting to wear on Doreleska, who openly cringes with each rap.

"It's irrelevant now that we know what they're after," Kagan replies, waving away the thought. "We just need to keep that pendant out of their reach."

Hollis opens her mouth to speak, but pauses, then bites her lower lip.

Doreleska lets out a frustrated growl. "Out with it."

The young woman scrunches up her face. "Have we figured out yet why they're here? Did Lucifer send them? I mean, they work for him, after all."

Pierce groans. "We had this discussion yesterday. No, it isn't Lucifer since we're still here, and he'd have no interest in the relic hunter."

She glances at each of us. "Then who's behind this?"

"Maybe if we can determine what the compass rose does, we'll know." Ulrich stands and starts perusing the shelves, pulling out books he believes will be helpful, and piling them onto the table.

"Rowen, why don't you and Hollis head into the kitchen? I'm not sure about the rest of you, but I'm starving," Kagan says, rubbing his stomach for emphasis.

While the pair leave, Doreleska comments that she's going downstairs to the training room, so Pierce decides to join her. The older man stands, then makes his way toward the door, but at the last moment takes a seat beside me.

"What aren't you telling us about the journal?" he whispers in order to not draw Ulrich's attention.

"Nothing."

"If that were true, then you would've admitted to Dalma that you had the book at the time of the attack and not Festus. Instead, you kept that bit of information from her, meaning you're trying to hide something."

"Like I said before, I didn't read what was inside."

He scowls. "Didn't or couldn't? At least, not at that moment."

I roll my eyes at him pushing the subject. "It was written in hynafol glyphs and I wasn't able to comprehend their meaning in the brief time I was in possession of it. Why does it matter anyway? You said no one knows how to interpret that ancient language, with the exception of me."

"Because, besides Lucifer, there's another demon lord who can and he's the reason you're here with us." Kagan taps the table hard with his finger.

I stare at him, baffled. "Who?"

"That should do it," Ulrich says, forcing Kagan not to respond. "If the information isn't in one of these, then I don't know where we're going to find it."

"Magdalene, why don't you help him while I go check on the others?" The older man stands and hurries for the door, closing it on his way out.

Sitting, Ulrich passes a few heavy volumes over to me. "For once I don't have to do this on my own," he states cheerfully. "Thank God for that."

"Have you read all of these books?" I motion toward the numerous shelves lining the vast room.

"Well, all of us, with the exception of Rowen, have been living in Burmstone Castle for the last decade or so. I had to do something to pass the time, and knowledge has always been my passion. I find tremendous joy in reading."

Cracking open the worn hardcover for the first book in front of me, I ask, "What does everyone else do to keep themselves busy?"

Resting his head on the palm of his hand, he stares up at the ceiling like he's studying the rough surface. "Doreleska, and sometimes Pierce, prefer to spend their time training down in the former great room. She has an entire setup consisting of fighting dummies, an archery stand, old wrestling mats, and free weights. Kagan periodically joins them, but he travels a lot. Or at least he used to. Typically, Pierce will retreat to the living room and watch the news programs on the television when they're broadcasting." Ulrich points to the closed set of double wooden doors behind him. "Hollis prefers the outdoors. During the summer you'll find her up in the trees or down in the valley between the peaks swimming in the freshwater lake that's created from the winter runoff."

"And Rowen?"

His gaze returns to my face, but I'm not able to comprehend the expression etched on his dark skin. "He's only been with us for a few months and has spent every waking hour looking for you."

"Do you know how he found me?"

Ulrich shakes his head. "You'd have to ask him." Then, he starts rifling through his stack.

Returning to the volume before me, I carefully flip through the delicate, flaky pages filled with parables and folktales, none of which include references to either a cardinal stone or a compass rose. After setting that book aside, I select another, this one containing information on victories and losses during the crusades, in addition to what treasures were reclaimed, or outright stolen in some instances.

"Ulrich," I begin to capture his attention since he seems to be completely immersed in whatever he's reading, "what constitutes an object as being sacred?"

He pauses, placing a finger at the exact spot where he stopped. "Well, all relics are holy in some fashion, whether they were left behind by the polytheistic gods and goddesses of ancient Rome or Greece. Or the monotheistic lords of the modern era. It's the powers they possess which gives them life and credence."

"But not all have such abilities."

"That's true, though they don't necessarily require it to be considered valuable. Also, many artifacts have been destroyed over the centuries due to the numerous conflicts fought on these lands, including the Cleansing." He looks at me thoughtfully for a moment, drumming his fingers against the table much like Kagan did. "Perhaps the pendant isn't a true relic at all, but a means of finding one."

"Such as?"

He massages his stubbly chin. "We won't know that until we can determine who created the item, which at this point could be anyone." Dropping his head, he goes back to reading.

It's not long until Hollis returns, startling us by proclaiming loudly that food is ready. I follow her into the kitchen where individual bowls of a cream-based soup have been prepared. After taking a serving, I sit at the table along a panel of windows overlooking the front of the estate, noticing a stone terrace sweeping around the immense structure and toward a pebble-covered driveway that winds down the steep incline. The sky is currently overcast, and dusk is settling in, but the exterior lighting doesn't come on.

"It's so we don't draw people's attention," Rowen comments, sitting beside me.

"How did you know that's what I was thinking?"

He smiles. "Because I've always been good at deciphering your facial expressions." Then he winks, causing my cheeks to flush. "Any luck finding information on the compass rose?"

I consume a spoonful of soup before responding. "Not yet, but we've only looked through a few of the books Ulrich pulled from the shelves."

Rowen nudges his shoulder into mine. "Perhaps I'll help when we're done eating."

"I need you to take the first patrol of the night," Kagan states, joining us. "Hollis can assist in the library."

Rowen appears dejected by the order. "Why can't Pierce act as lookout?"

Kagan takes a seat across from me, his entire mass shaking the table when he sits. "He can, but I assumed that you'd want to make sure Magdalene was safe while she slept. After all, she's staying in your room."

Rowen grins wickedly, and I can't help but laugh.

"I've been thinking about what you said in regard to when the Watchers started to show in Kern," I say after a few minutes of silence. "There had been rumors for the last several months of them making appearances in town, snatching individuals off of the street in broad daylight, or dragging them down alleyways simply to disappear seconds later."

Kagan furrows his brow. "Did anyone actually witness these instances?"

"Vin did, supposedly, but just the one time. I did, maybe once or twice, prior to my own encounter. However, they never actually took anyone. There had been more occurrences reported to the local authorities. I caught gossip about it when I ate in the café, or Festus would tell me, so I'd be extra cautious on the street during the evening hours."

His spoon stops halfway to his lips when he asks, "How many?"

"At least a dozen or so, but not all of them happened in Kern. Several were in the towns and villages surrounding it."

The older man sets down his spoon and picks up his tumbler filled with a dark, amber-colored liquid. "Tomorrow, I'll have Pierce investigate. He has a knack for finding things out."

"While he's there, see if he can determine how the Watchers found Magdalene," Rowen comments.

"You mean besides through you?" Doreleska chides from her seat at the island, her rich voice thick with contempt.

Rowen slams his fist against the table. "I'm not the one who brought them to her!"

"How *did* you locate me?" I ask, leaning into him, soothing his anger.

His face softens. "I had a dream about you. It happened about a week ago. You were coming home late one night, and I saw the sign for the hostel flashing through a haze that was surrounding the building. It was just a brief glimpse, but enough to warrant a visit."

Doreleska snorts. "That's a bunch of bullshit. Demons don't dream. We barely even sleep."

"It's what I saw," Rowen snarls, balling his hands into fists.

Kagan's forehead creases and wrinkles form under his eyes. "I wonder," he mutters quietly.

I study him, speculating about what he's thinking and if it's the same idea that's suddenly popped into my head. "It wasn't a dream, was it?"

He appears stunned by my comment, his eyes widening in shock.

"It was a vision," I continue, completing both of our thoughts.

"We're not powerful enough to conjure those," Hollis finally chimes in from her perch beside Doreleska. "Only someone in Lucifer's position can do that."

Rowen grows ashen, trembling ever so slightly while setting his spoon into an empty bowl. "If that's true, then he knows I escaped and will be looking for me ... for us. He'll send the Watchers, or something worse."

"Calm your ass down," Kagan snaps. "Lucifer isn't sending anyone to drag us back to Hell. At least, not right away. But I think Hollis is correct about him being the one to have caused your vision. I wouldn't be surprised if he's also responsible for springing you, knowing you could find Magdalene a lot faster than any of us had been able to."

Doreleska crosses her arms over her chest, her face coloring in annoyance. "How can you be so confident?"

"Because Lucifer needs us here to help her." The older man points a rigid finger at me.

"I'm getting Pierce." Hollis rushes from the room, returning several minutes later with him and Ulrich, both of whom grab a bowl before sitting at the table. Since there's only one spot left, Pierce claims it, so Ulrich snags a stool and drags it over, prompting Hollis and Doreleska to do the same.

Kagan waits a few moments before continuing the conversation, probably trying to select his words prudently. "Fifteen years or so ago, Abaddon broke out of his cell."

Hollis gasps, her hand flying up to her mouth as she shakes. Ulrich wraps an arm around her shoulders while trying to balance his bowl of soup in the other hand.

"Who is he?" I inquire, having never heard the name before, as far as I know.

"A very powerful demon lord and rival to Lucifer," Pierce answers.

Kagan sees the confusion etched on my face, so he explains further. "Centuries ago, there was a great battle between Lucifer and Abaddon. It nearly destroyed the world, leaving much of it in ash and ruins. Lucifer, with the help of his brother, was victorious, thereby condemning Abaddon to spend eternity in the bowels of Hell."

"Why did God help him?" Hollis asks, unnerving Doreleska.

"Where do you think Abaddon would've struck next if he won? At least with Lucifer manning the dark realms, you know what to expect."

He must have been the one Kagan was referring to about being able to decipher hynafol glyphs.

"Why can't the demon hunters handle this?" Doreleska asks, crossing her legs and resting her elbows on top of her knees.

"Because the ones that are still alive have their hands full chasing Abaddon's followers all over the world, hoping to prevent them from bringing that arrogant bastard to the surface."

Pierce appears confused. "I thought you said he escaped?"

Kagan finishes his drink before responding. "He did. The problem is no one can find where he's hiding. They just know he's not above ground ... for the time being."

"Then the Watchers are probably working for him," Hollis states, her voice quivering.

"Doubtful," Ulrich counters, squeezing her gently. "They hate that asshole just like the rest of us."

"And we're supposed to stop Abaddon?" Doreleska huffs. "How?"

The older man stares into his empty glass. "Not us. Magdalene."

"With what?" Rowen fumes, his entire body stiffening. "Those hunter blades aren't powerful enough. He'll cut her down with the snap of his fingers before she can get close enough to him."

Kagan shrugs. "She's supposed to know what will work to defeat him. We're simply meant to protect her from other demons who might be aware of her arrival, such as the Watchers and whomever they're assisting."

"But I don't know." My heart races at the notion of going into battle ill-prepared. "I've barely scratched the surface of regaining my memories. How can I possibly fight? Right now, I feel like I have one hand tied behind my back and am running around blindfolded."

"It's almost as if you were sent here to fail," Pierce comments, then proceeds to shovel food into his mouth.

"That doesn't make any sense." Hollis collects the empty bowls, places them in the sink, then retakes her seat. "Why would He," she points skyward, "want her to fail?"

"Maybe you pissed him off." Doreleska chuckles, infuriating not only Rowen, but myself as well. She's one demon in this group I wouldn't mind using my kards on; watching her turn to ash would give me much pleasure.

"It isn't a 'Him' but a 'they'," Ulrich states. "Hunters are regulated by the divine edicts, or as some people refer to them, the heavenly council. They determine the fate of those they oversee, barring and punishing them if it becomes necessary."

"How the hell do you know that?" Doreleska inquires, shocked.

He glowers at her. "I read, which is something you should actually do for once."

I try to hide the smile creeping across my face as she seethes from the remark.

"Rowen, go upstairs and get your blade so you can start patrolling. Hollis, assist Ulrich and Magdalene in the library. The rest of you are with me." Kagan stands, indicating our impromptu meeting is over.

Hollis seems eager to help us search through the dozens of books scattered across the elongated, solid wood table. Retaking my seat, I continue examining the one I was in the middle of when food was announced, but I can't seem to focus. My thoughts keep drifting back to Pierce's comment about the edicts wanting me to fail. I don't understand why that would be the case, but it could explain why I have no memories of my past ... and why I was sent back as a child and not an adult.

It can't be anything that I've done, can it?

According to Dalma, I was always successful in garnering the relics before they fell into the wrong hands, or liberating them prior to being used. I ended wars, slayed monsters, and did what was instructed no matter the cost to me or others. At least, that's what I'm starting to remember. True, I'm not able to recall the moments after my victories, just the next battle or relic to save, which at most times was decades apart, if not a century or two. My last task was stopping Rowen from obtaining the Perpetua Chalice a century ago.

Then what is it?

Rising, I step over to one of the desks buried amongst the shelves and remove a piece of parchment and a pencil from the top drawer. When I'm back in my chair, I try to reconstruct the glyphs I saw in the journal. It takes several tries before I'm able to write the phrase that continues to baffle me. If I knew when the book was composed, then I could probably narrow down who I might be referring to, but without Festus that could prove difficult. Closing my eyes, I attempt to think back to the brief instance when I had the journal in my possession, forcing myself to focus on the other glyphs farther down the page, then blindly scribble them onto the paper.

"What's that?" Hollis inquires, interrupting my thoughts, her head close to mine while gazing at the markings, fascinated.

"Just a few of the symbols I remember seeing in the journal."

Her eyes light up. "Do you know what they mean?"

"Sort of, but at the moment they're not making any sense. I might have written them wrong."

Pulling out the chair beside me, she sits since she had been at the other end of the table. "Read it to me. Maybe I can help."

I forego the first line written and recite the one below it. "Sunrises cast hidden shadows, revealing dreams long forgotten."

She scrunches up her face, her flawless alabaster skin barely wrinkling. "Sounds like a riddle. What do you think, Ulrich?"

I didn't realize he was paying attention until I look over and notice the quizzical expression on his face.

"Very interesting, but we need to concentrate on the task at hand. One puzzle at a time." He goes back to reading, then abruptly stands, returning a few minutes later with a thick, colorful book, the map of the world embellished in gold foil on its hard cover. "I was thinking," he begins without prompting, "earlier we were contemplating whether the compass rose points to a relic instead of actually being one. Maps use the same symbol in their legends to denote directionality. Maybe it signifies a specific chart."

"There have to be thousands of those to look through," Hollis bemoans. "How will we know which is the right one?"

"I'm not sure. I just think it's another avenue that needs pursuing. Magdalene, would you mind if I borrow the necklace for a little while?"

After unclasping it, I toss the pendant to him. Sitting, he meticulously scrutinizes each drawing or print in the atlas, trying to match the marking against the one in his hand while Hollis and I go back to reviewing the books. Eventually, I grow tired, so I fold the paper with my notes and head up to Rowen's bedroom where I hide the parchment in my knapsack before getting ready for bed, putting on a pair of sweatpants and a T-shirt. I make sure all the lights are off, then get under the welcoming blankets.

Chapter Eleven

Thwap! Thwap!

The odd, faint noise pulls me from a restless sleep. I spot Rowen on the couch, the light from the fireplace enhancing his handsome features. Readjusting my pillow, I work on dozing off, but the sound has infiltrated my mind, piercing it into a dull ache. I'm surprised Rowen isn't disturbed by the sound since I thought demons had better hearing than humans, or at least hunters anyway. Tossing back the covers, I get out of bed and go to wake him, but he doesn't rouse. I shake him a little harder. Still, he won't respond. Placing my hand against his cheek and monitoring his chest, I feel his warm skin and note the rhythmic rise and fall in cadence with his heartbeat, so I know he's still alive.

Thwap!

Stepping over to the chair the scabbard is on, I remove my blade and exit into the hallway, then head downstairs. When I reach the bottom, I glance into the kitchen, finding Hollis sprawled across the stone floor, her sun-kissed hair fanned out around her. I rush over to her side, set down the weapon, and roll her onto her back. Pushing the hair that has now fallen away from her face, I check to make sure she's breathing, which she is. Like Rowen, she won't stir no matter what.

Picking up the dagger, I exit the kitchen and make my way along the lengthy corridor, the noise growing louder when I reach the winding staircase in the entrance hall. Descending, it's pitch black below because the doors for the training room are closed, a sliver of light shining under the gap between them and the cold floor. Pressing my ear against the polished, stained wood, the sound intensifies. I take a deep breath, stiffen my grip on the blade, and slowly open one of the doors, entering the stuffy training room.

Large landscape paintings occupy two of the walls. A panel of windows line the back of the room overlooking the lower portion of the sweeping walkway where the drive comes up to meet it, their panes devoid of adornment. Parts of the floor are covered in dingy gray mats, hiding the scratched wood underneath. Sconces shaped like medieval torches twinkle around the room, their bulbs flickering, mimicking the movement of candles.

At first there doesn't appear to be anyone inside of the dimly lit room until I reach a wide and deeply hidden alcove along the right. Several sackcloth dummies filled with hay take up the space while a young man with short, dark blond hair throws knives into their midsections. As the weapons sail back into his dexterous hands, I realize they're hunter blades just like mine.

"Took you long enough," he grumbles without stopping, his accent American.

"Who are you?" I ask, hoping he doesn't notice the tremble in my voice.

He waits until the daggers are in his hands before turning. I instantly recognize him as the man I encountered at Dalma's the other morning. His round face appears hardened through the jawline, his emerald-green eyes are a little lackluster, and the bulky sweater hides an athletic build. He sheathes the weapons into a belt around his waist, but I continue to hold onto mine, ready to strike if the moment calls for it.

Resting his hands on the grip of the daggers, he says, "My name is Avaris, and we're old friends."

Smirking, I reply, "I sincerely doubt that."

He takes a step closer, but still maintains a bit of distance. "Search your mind, Magdalene. The truth is lurking in there somewhere." His tone is one of condescension and bitterness.

Faint hints of recognition flicker to life, but quickly fade.

He chortles. "Still not ringing any bells? How about De Lamar and a cozy little castle along the shores of the Durance River?"

Even though I know the reference, I continue to stare at him since I'm not sure what his connection is to that place.

He rolls his eyes and lets out a deep, heavy sigh. "Are you still mad about what happened? Is that why you're not talking?"

Again, I don't respond. It's better to keep him prattling on and hope he slips up, or at least jogs a bit of my memory back into place.

"I was simply following orders." He sweeps his arms out to the side before recoiling them back to the blades. "You're the idiot who got wrapped up with a demon. It's not my fault you were caught and had to be dragged back home."

Although the memory isn't fully there, a hint of truth lingers in my mind. "You took me away from Rowen."

"Ding, ding, ding." Avaris crosses his arms over his chest, puffing it out in pride. "It took several of us to chain that fucker down so we could snatch you. Those damn things were heavy considering they were made from iron so he wouldn't escape." In the blink of an eye, the young man is in front of me, brushing the hair out of my face. His touch feels toxic. "How I would've loved to have witnessed your punishment. I hear the torture can be quite brutal, causing long-term damage. Sometimes even rendering the person useless, leaving death the only option for redemption." He smiles viciously. "But hunting never ends for people like me, so I wasn't permitted to stick around and watch."

I shove his hand away and take a few steps back. "I don't remember any of that."

"That's more than likely because of what was done to you. I will say that I wasn't expecting the aftereffects of your downfall to be so extensive. It's amazing you've managed to survive this long."

I kick him hard in the abdomen, which sends him flying backwards, and he lands with a thud on the mats. "You don't know anything about me," I say, seething.

He grunts while getting to his feet. "That wasn't smart."

With the wave of his hand, I'm sent crashing into the alcove, causing several of the practice dummies to fall on top of me, knocking the blade from my hand. As I shove the figures aside, Avaris grabs my ankle and drags me across the room, then straddles my waist and presses the tip of his knife against the soft part of my throat.

"Your skills need improving."

Instinctively, I raise my hand above my head, and within a matter of seconds, my fingers are curled around the ivory handle for the dagger. I bring the weapon up and rest it against his cheek, but don't break the skin. "Was that better?"

His laugh reverberates throughout the immense space. "Not by a longshot."

"Hers may be a little rusty, but mine are quite sharp," Kagan states, a gun now pressed against the side of Avaris' head. "Breathe wrong and you're dead, demon hunter."

The young man raises his arms, then stands and steps away. "How did I miss you?"

Kagan extends his free hand, helping me to my feet. "I wasn't in the castle when you knocked everyone out. Why not just kill them? Or do you enjoy playing games with your victims first?"

"You're one to talk." Avaris sheathes his weapon. "How many of my kind have you ruthlessly tormented before finally ending their lives? Besides, I'm not here for them, but to simply relay a message."

"And what is it?" the older man huffs.

"Get rid of Rowen or the deal's off."

Kagan relaxes his arm with the gun, allowing it to dangle by his side. "We never asked him to join us."

Avaris cocks his head and furrows his brow. "Yet you haven't banned him from the grounds either. He's a liability ... one you can't afford."

"What do you expect me to do? Kill him?"

The young man grins happily. "I can always do the deed for you if you're too squeamish."

The older man unsheathes a sword from the scabbard strapped across his back. "You're not hurting anyone in my home."

"How did you find us anyway?" I inquire, thinking perhaps it might be how the Watchers latched onto me.

Avaris' glare shifts from Kagan to me, his gaze scanning me from head to toe, leaving me feeling violated. "Hunters can easily sense their own kind, and there isn't a sigil preventing me from entering this place like there is for angels."

I narrow my eyes. "I'm sure you're not the only one out there, so how is it you're the first to locate me?"

"I could say it's because I'm better than the others, which is true, but in reality, it was from catching your scent during our brief encounter at Dalma's." He sneers, arrogance oozing from his pores. "I've been tracking you ever since that day. The others can't find you due to your misplaced hunter traits, and they don't know you as well as I do." Avaris winks, then changes his focus back to Kagan. "You have one week, or Lucifer will need to solve his problems another way since Magdalene will be rejoining us and made permanently off-limits to the rest of you." The young man vanishes in a swirl of white smoke.

"Prick," Kagan mutters, sheathing the sword. "Why don't you go upstairs since everyone should be waking now? I'll be along shortly."

When I'm in the entrance hall, I make my way to the library, finding Ulrich rubbing his head while sitting at the table appearing confused. Hollis enters a few minutes later, with Rowen quickly following.

"Are you all right?" he asks, wrapping his arms around me, pulling me against his chest.

"I'm fine." I relish the warmth of his embrace, the natural scent his body emits, and listen to his rapidly beating heart.

Hollis rubs the back of her neck as she takes a seat at the table. "What the fuck happened?"

"We had a visitor," Kagan responds, joining us. "Where are Pierce and Doreleska?"

The young woman giggles. "They're, uh, busy."

A few moments later the pair run into the room, both wearing hastily tied robes and looking flushed.

"Glad you could join us," the older man says sarcastically, leaning against the long table. "A demon hunter just left."

"I knew we should've added their sigil to the building," Doreleska complains, plopping down into one of the cushioned chairs in the seating arrangement.

"If we did that, Magdalene wouldn't be able to get inside," Rowen counters, still holding me, caressing my lower back.

Ulrich closes the book he had been reading. "Who was it?"

"Avaris," I reply, in case Kagan didn't know, or hear, his name.

Rowen's grip around me hardens and he quickly sucks in air. Avaris must have been the person who inflicted the wounds on his chest. Something other than a kard would've needed to be used to cause the damage ... like a clach. Otherwise, the blades would've sent Rowen to hell instantly, not allow Avaris to torture and mutilate him.

Doreleska licks her plump, red lips. "Want me to bring back his head?"

The older man clenches his jaw. "No. We don't need to start a war with the hunters when there are more important things that must be dealt with first."

Pierce takes a seat beside Ulrich. "What did he want if it wasn't to murder us the coward's way?"

"Him." Kagan points at Rowen. "The edicts know he's here, and if he doesn't leave, they'll take Magdalene away from us. We'll then be forced to handle Abaddon and his followers on our own, and without the proper relics, which only Magdalen can procure and probably wield."

"We don't even know what he's after," Pierce states furiously. "We're just assuming the Watchers are his, but they could be helping any number of disgruntled traitors. There are plenty to go around."

Doreleska tightens the sash around her waist. "How long do we have?"

"A week."

"It took years just to find Magdalene," Ulrich complains, his mouth falling open.

"And the edicts gave her to us defective."

"Fuck off, Doreleska," Rowen snaps.

She abruptly stands. "It's your fault that we're now in this mess with the heavenly council. You had to play hero and break out of Hell to rescue the damsel in distress. Why couldn't you stay in your prison like a good little boy?"

He goes to charge at her, but I hold onto him. "Stop it," I scold them, then move between the pair, focusing my next comment on Doreleska while twirling the hunter blade in my hand. "Call me damaged, or even a damsel in distress again, and they'll be digging your bones out of the cage I'll be sending them to."

174

She mutters incoherently under her breath, then storms from the room.

"Pierce, go make sure she doesn't do something stupid." Kagan nods in the direction of the hallway. "Hollis and Ulrich, continue searching the books for any reference on the compass rose. I'm going back outside."

Stepping toward the door to return to bed, Ulrich hands me the pendant, which I secure around my neck. Rowen says he'll be up in a few minutes and follows Kagan. When I'm back in the bedroom, I set the dagger onto the coffee table in the seating area, use the facilities, then slip under the covers. My thoughts automatically go to Avaris and how much he seemed to relish the idea of me being severely brutalized. I don't really remember the incident at the castle in De Lamar, or even understand why a relationship with Rowen would lead to my supposed downfall.

Then a sickening thought strikes me.

Getting out of bed, I enter the bathroom after turning on the light and go over to the vanity. I lift the back of my shirt, bringing it over my head, leaving my arms through the sleeves and the garment over my chest to hide it, then adjust my stance so I can view the scars created by the caretakers' belts in the mirror. The lines are dark, long, and slightly raised, covering most of the upper portion of my back, including the mark from Theron's clach. I have others across my chest, but not as many.

Beatings were an everyday occurrence in the orphanage, but on special occasions they would use devices to leave us permanently disfigured and broken. They never did explain why, and if we dared speak out, the punishments worsened.

I lower my head, close my eyes as the recollections become too much, and fall victim to another memory ... one I wish to forget.

Screams of torment rip down the narrow corridor with its high ceiling, peeling, light blue painted walls, and tarnished hardwood floors. The smell of fresh blood permeates the air, thickening the underlying aroma of death that's now rooted into these hallowed halls. It's a stench I've become accustomed to over the years. One that'll forever be embedded into my brain.

I should've known better than to help the young boy escape, like I have with so many others. Now he's dead, shot in the back and left to rot in the fields, while I'm hanging by my wrists from a tarnished, copper-plated ceiling, rusty chains biting into my cold, tender flesh as the punishment for disobedience commences.

This isn't the first time, but it certainly will be the last ... I hope.

I'm in a former dining room of a reclaimed mansion on a grand plantation somewhere among the many groves of magnolia and oak trees that line every waterway down in the south. The structure was taken over during the beginning of the wars when sides had yet to be chosen, and still aren't. Wrecked furniture has been pushed up against the battered walls, shattered glass from a full-length mirror lays strewn about the frayed, yellow carpeting, and brownish-red spatter clings to everything. A sign of the hell we call home.

Tears run down my heated cheeks, rage thumps in my veins, but all I can do is listen to the sounds of the others around me being abused, brutalized into anguished silence.

How many will die tonight? Could the gallows lining the river be getting new victims in the morning? Is the firing squad running out of ammunition? When will this nightmare end?

"Take her down," the magistrate, an older woman with long, silver hair, tobacco-tarnished teeth, and leathery skin orders.

Slowly I'm released, but allowed to fall hard onto my aching knees, triggering more pain, forcing me to bite my tongue for fear of allowing the cry of despair to escape my dry, chapped lips and be noticed. It would merely cause further problems. My short-sleeved, black T-shirt is torn, the tears aligning with the deep cuts emblazoned across my back. At least this time the abuse was minimal, not extensive like it has been before.

I refuse to meet my captors in the eye while being freed, denying them the satisfaction of seeing me weep. Two older boys pick me up under the arms and assist me from the room since I'm too weak to move on my own. We enter a former library, the books destroyed long ago, their shelves and walls devoid of all ornamentation. The boys gently place me down on a cot so my injuries can be tended to. One of the many things the magistrate demands is that everyone's wounds be treated, so new ones can be inflicted on healed skin, making the punishments that more severe.

A young woman—perhaps a few years older than me—with filthy brown hair and wearing tattered rags, carefully kneels beside the cot, lifts my shirt, and starts cleaning away the blood.

Leaning down, she whispers, "You need to stop acting out. Just do what they say and you won't be chastised."

"What they're doing is wrong, and you know it," I reply, my voice frail like the rest of me.

"Are you trying to get killed? Do you want to die?" she scorns.

I grimace at her touch. "I refuse to break for them."

She presses the cloth harder into my skin, washing away the blood while it continues to flow freely. "But how many more will pay the ultimate price for following you?"

"I don't ask them to."

She lets out a heavy sigh. "You don't have to. They see your courage, your strength, your resilience. The caretakers are no longer burying the bodies, but leaving them to rot where they fall so the others will be reminded about what's at stake if they decide to disobey. You saw that tonight with the little boy you were helping." Wringing out the rag into a cast iron pot, the young woman plunges the dismal piece of fabric back into clean water before continuing her work. "The magistrate plans on sending you to the firing squad tomorrow, along with a dozen or so more."

I finally look at the young woman, spying heavy lines around her tired eyes. "Who?"

"The children."

Grabbing the woman's wrist, she stops cleaning my wounds. "Get them out tonight. There's a secret passage in the kitchen that leads out to the swamp in front of the main house. The older ones will help you."

The young woman grows pale. "I ... they'll kill me."

"And what about them?" I gesture toward the hallway where the screaming continues, though not as loudly.

Trembling, she sets down the rag. "Why can't you just do what they want?"

"Because that's not who I am." Sitting up, I swing my legs over the side of the cot, grunting from pain while blood seeps from my wounds, and stand.

"Where are you going?" the young woman asks, clutching my hand in desperation to prevent me from leaving.

I shake her loose. "To end this."

My steps are slow and excruciating, forcing me to bite down hard onto my lower lip to keep myself from yelling, alerting the magistrate and her minions that I'm up and about, instead of cowering in a corner. When I reach the door for the hallway, one of the young men who brought me to the library leans against the wall as if waiting. Reaching behind his back, he removes a gun that had been tucked into his waistband and raises it in my direction. I stand firmly in the doorway, determined to survive no matter what happens to me tonight. He fires, and the bullet strikes the magistrate in the chest as she rounds the corner, killing her.

"The others would've heard," I mutter, taking the weapon from him. "Get the children and head for the swamp."

"What are you going to do?"

I check the number of rounds in the clip. "Destroy them all."

Hurrying away, he begins pounding on doors and shouting, rousing everyone from sleep, including the caretakers. A few of the young men emerge armed, as was the plan—having pilfered the weapons from the stocks in the cellar earlier in the day—while I return to the punishment room, shooting the tormentors as they continue to assault their victims. Others join me, freeing those too weak to move of their own accord, carrying them as best as they can out into the frigid night. Caretakers use young ones as shields, cowering behind those unable to defend themselves. Some have knives pressed against the terrified throats of the children crying in their desperate grasps.

Heat builds around me, practically choking the air, making it difficult to breathe, except I seem to be the only one who's unfazed. The older men and women clutch their throats, suffocating from an inferno that has started to consume their bodies from the inside. I don't know where the fire is coming from, but I'm glad to see it when it shoots out of their mouths, their eyes. Children flee in terror, rushing into the arms of their friends before escaping the house. Fire licks up the walls and rolls across the ceiling while I search for the bodies of the young already dead by the hands of the caretakers.

Not one will be left to perish in these flames.

I find a young boy stuffed under a bed, his throat cut, the man responsible for his death writhing on the floor, his flesh sloughing off from the conflagration that doesn't touch me or the dead child. Tucking the gun into the waistband of my pants, I pick up the boy, cradling him in my arms, then return to the corridor which is now a wall of fire. Behind me at the other end is a busted window. Carefully stepping through the broken panes, I make sure the glass doesn't harm him, but it winds up slicing my arms, which I'm fine with. The new wounds bleed in conjunction with the old, completing a sort of circuit, one that wraps around my body in warmth and grace. Once on the wraparound porch, I continue to carry the child down the narrow, wooden steps—windows bursting from the heat, the sound of wood crackling and splintering all around us—then head toward the front of the property where the others are supposed to have gathered.

For a brief moment I turn, relishing the blaze that's tearing through the two-story structure. Screams and cries echo through the night from the dying, but I instinctively know none of them are from any of the innocent. To me, this is only the beginning of our reclamation, our survival from these monsters and heretics. The Caltraves will rule no more.

"We got everyone out," the young man from earlier says, coming up alongside me. "Even the dead per your request."

"Good," I reply, gazing at the now crumbling mansion. "Bury them, but don't mark the graves. We don't need scavengers digging them up and using the bodies for some sadistic ritual. The rubble alone will be testament enough of the lives forever lost." Turning to face him, I place the dead boy into his awaiting arms.

"Some of the caretakers escaped." He nods toward the other young man who carried me to the library, signaling for him to approach. "Give her your weapon."

He nervously hands it to me.

"We'll wait for you."

Nodding, I head for one of the outer buildings where a few of the older men and women are hiding, but that's just the first stop. By the end of the night, everything on these lands will be burning. A fire to cleanse all souls and turn the Caltraves into nothing but dust and blood.

Opening my eyes, I take a deep breath as if coming up from narrowly drowning, a realization about the truth behind my imprisonment nearly unbearable. Panic seizes me and the room spins, forcing me to grip the edge of the vanity hard to prevent further collapse. Perhaps that's the reason I was a child when the divine edicts sent me here, and why I suspect I'm missing more than just my memories. They wanted me to die at the hands of the caretakers so I could be replaced. Eradicated from existence for someone more conforming, willing to do their bidding no matter who it hurts. Even if it's one of their own.

The true penalty for loving Rowen ... my demise.

The bastards couldn't do the deed themselves, so the Caltraves tried to do it for them. It was the same with Daimon, and is more than likely the reason his daggers never returned to him the last time he threw them. The edicts had grown tired of his conceit and recklessness, sending him to Cresidio to die, not to reclaim the scepter.

The choice for a new relic hunter had already been made by the time he strolled into the village. I was going to be his successor no matter what happened that night, and proved my worth by destroying the sacred artifact at the cost of hundreds of innocent lives.

So, who's my replacement if I've already lived well beyond the heavenly council's expectations?

Glancing up into the mirror, I notice Rowen standing behind me, immense sorrow weighing heavily on his face. He reaches out to touch me, but I move away, fixing my shirt, and begin making my way to the door, hastily wiping away the tears that have sprung forth.

"Who did that to you?" he asks, grief thick in his voice.

I stop, but don't turn to face him. "It doesn't matter. They're dead now."

"What was used?"

The lump forming in my throat threatens to choke me, and I find it difficult to speak. "A ... a leather strap with ... razor blades sewn into it."

He comes up to me, places a hand under my chin, and lifts my gaze to meet his. "I'm sorry I wasn't there to protect you."

I suddenly become very angry and shove his hand away. "I can take care of myself and don't require rescuing like Doreleska suggested."

"Magdalene, I realize that. It just hurts me to see you injured, knowing that I might have been able to prevent it."

"It was my punishment," leaning forward, I rest my head against his chest, "for loving you. Just as it was when the edicts stripped me of my memories, and why they sent me down here as a child. So I would die by the hands of those monsters who raised me."

He pulls me into an embrace and kisses the top of my head. "I wish they would all just leave us alone."

We remain wrapped in each other's arms for a few more moments, my crying easing with the slowly passing seconds, before we finally return to the bedroom.

As Rowen starts toward the couch, I grab his hand, desperate to cling on even longer. "Stay with me."

He smiles and nods, then moves around to the other side of the bed.

When we're both under the covers, I lie in the crook of his arm, nestling my head on his firm chest, enjoying the softness of his T-shirt, and the feel of him beside me. He gently strokes my back, easing away a bit of the tension I was feeling from Avaris. The air in the room heats up, slowly beckoning both of us to give in, but Rowen won't do anything until I'm ready. That I'm sure of. Sitting up slightly, I rest on my elbow and use my other hand to brush a bit of his wavy, brown hair away from his face, caressing his soft skin. My lips graze his, and he kisses me tenderly. The connection is immediate like before, tugging insistently on the thread between us, begging for us to let go and fall. Running a hand up the front of his shirt, I rest my palm on the stab wounds, absorbing their rough texture and wishing I could heal them. Our mouths battle for dominance, everything pulsing in desperation to be freed. I tug on his shirt, then help him remove it. Pressing him onto his back, my lips travel down his neck toward his chest, where I make sure to kiss every mark left by the clach.

I straddle his waist while our mouths reunite. This time when his hands wander up the back of my shirt I don't pull away, but instead remove it, tossing it onto the floor with his. He pushes me gently up to have a better look, tears forming at the corners of his eyes when he spies the scarring over my breasts. Sitting up, he leans me back slightly to kiss my wounds, his soft lips applying the littlest bit of pressure since he's afraid of hurting me further. A quiet moan escapes my mouth as he continues to enjoy me. I hold onto him tightly, pressing myself hard into him, hating the layers of clothes between us. He throbs at the notion, his nails digging into my exposed back, causing me to suck in a quick breath.

Gripping his face, I slam my mouth into his, nearly knocking him down. Holding onto my waist, he flings me over until I'm the one laying on the mattress. He runs his fingers through my hair with one hand while the other tugs on the elastic band for my sweatpants. I let him pull them off, my entire body quivering with desire and want. He quickly finishes undressing, our naked bodies pressed firmly against each other. The smoothness of him arouses me beyond restraint. I adjust my position, opening up for him, eager to have him. His fingers wander down between my legs, coaxing me further awake than I already am. I can't help but close my eyes and arch my back. The moment he enters, I gasp.

"God, how I've missed you," Rowen whispers into my ear, his hot breath tickling my senses.

I bend my knees so he can get deeper, allowing me to experience all of him. The bed thuds against the wall while we make up for lost time, leaving the others to know exactly what we're doing.

Chapter Twelve

When I wake, Rowen is snoring quietly beside me, his arm draped over my bare waist as his head nuzzles my back. I pull up the blankets, hiding ourselves for just a bit longer, not wanting this time together to end. How I wish we could stay in bed like we used to, when our lives seemed simpler, when we had nothing to truly worry about, and the world outside of our home didn't exist. After a few more minutes, I decide to get up and try to roll away when Rowen pulls me back.

"Where do you think you're going?" he teases, biting my shoulder.

I playfully slap his hand. "If you must know, to use the bathroom so my bladder doesn't explode."

Laughing, he releases me.

When I'm done, I rejoin him, snuggling myself in the crook of his arm, which he wraps lovingly around me. "Can I ask you something?"

He kisses my forehead. "Of course, my love."

Using my fingertips, I caress the cords of muscles forming his strong stomach. "What was I like before? I mean, did I have abilities similar to the demon hunters?"

He nudges me to lift my head, then kisses me passionately before responding, his free hand clutching my ass as he presses himself hard into me, obviously ready to continue where we left off from the night before. Eventually, he releases his hold on my body and lips. "You had some of their powers, such as moving rapidly from one place to another, like us demons can, but also ones uniquely your own." His fingers stroke my spine. "In addition to jogging your memories, how do we get those to return?"

A cloud of darkness starts to hover over me, the realization that I'll never be the same person I was long ago settling in. "The edicts are never going to let that happen. I'm surprised they haven't sent someone to kill me since it's obvious they want me dead. Otherwise, why take away everything important to me?"

"Shit, of course. Why didn't I see it before?" Rowen abruptly sits up, then swings his legs over the side of the bed. "Get dressed. We need to speak with the others."

While he rummages for clothes, I do the same, putting on black leggings and a long-sleeved, blue flannel, button-down shirt. I run a comb through my hair, place it into a ponytail, then don my only pair of sneakers and socks. When we reach the first floor, Hollis and Doreleska are sitting at the table in the library playing cards while Ulrich is still reviewing the pile of books from yesterday.

"You two sure had one hell of a night. We could hear you all the way down here," the horrid woman admonishes.

"Fuck off, Doreleska," Rowen snaps, then heads into the adjoining family room where Kagan is reclined on one of the dusty, yellow couches watching the television above the mantle for the dormant fireplace.

He briefly glances at us when we enter, a snarky remark forming on his lips, but he thinks better of it and returns his attention to the chaotic scene being displayed.

"Where is this?" Rowen asks, sitting and gesturing to the screen while I remain standing a few feet away.

"It's the city of Vineta where the ruling zealot was murdered overnight by a self-proclaimed spiritual warrior. This is his victory parade." Kagan snorts. "The bastard will either be dead by nightfall, or will have fled after pilfering whatever he can. I swear, these assholes are worse than us."

People donning tattered garments and severely weathered faces line a battered cobblestone road clamoring to reach and touch a man riding atop a dark brown stallion. He waves to the growing crowd, clearly enjoying the spectacle, and is flanked by scores of heavily armored guards, each of which is carrying a longsword. The entire display resembles fanfare from the Middle Ages, but is happening live according to the small caption scrolling along the bottom of the screen. As the crowd parts in a few places, I notice the only protective gear the man is wearing appears to be a dull helmet constructed from what might be iron. A ridge runs down the center starting from the base of the neck behind the head and stopping just above the cutouts for the eyes. There are hinges on either side to lift the faceplate, and a small latch to secure it closed.

I know instinctively what it is, and who's inside.

"Where's Pierce?" I ask, growing uneasy while continuing to watch the adoration being bestowed upon a man who doesn't deserve such accolades.

Kagan's gaze doesn't waver from the screen. "He's in Kern. I don't expect him back until much later today."

Rowen clears his throat, drawing the older man's attention away from the spectacle. "Magdalene and I were talking, and I think we're completely wrong about who's sending the Watchers after her."

Kagan glares at him, the creases at the corners of his eyes deepening. "What makes you say that?"

"Because of him." I point to the screen, drawing both of their attention.

He looks at me, dumbfounded. "You know who that is?"

"Yes. It's Daimon, the hunter I replaced."

The older man stares at me, shocked. "His face is covered, so it could be anybody."

"Only a relic hunter would go after the Armor of Rochelle," I counter. "The helmet protects its wearer against incurring any injuries. Demons wouldn't need it since they're impervious to harm, and the iron it's made from will kill them."

"Who's Rochelle?" Rowen inquires, curious.

The information spills from my mouth like water. "She was a young woman who helped defeat the French army during the revolutionary war at the Siege of Travion, and was the sole surviving soldier, saving the city from eminent destruction. When the fighting was over, she didn't have a single scratch on her while others bled to death from their wounds. The only pieces known to still exist are a shield and that helmet." Again, I point to the screen.

Kagan leans forward, resting his arms on his knees. "But Belial killed Daimon. Why would the divine edicts allow him to return?"

"Knowing him, and his ego, he more than likely made a deal with them to end my life so they'll make him a relic hunter for a second time. They want me dead. Why else would they send me to one of the worst places on Earth as a child without my memories or any abilities that I could use to properly defend myself?"

"The edicts promised you to us, that's why you're here," he grumbles, his face reddening.

"No, the offer was for a relic hunter to assist Lucifer in his civil war, not me specifically." I step away from the television, placing myself between it and Kagan. "Take me to Vineta. If Daimon is here to murder me, we kill him first."

"We can't touch him if he's wearing the helmet," Rowen states.

I smile. "Kagan won't be able to, but you will. The armor doesn't protect against hunter blades, and he'd never suspect a demon to be carrying one."

The older man glances between the two of us, his brow furrowed. "All right, but on one condition: you leave the compass rose here. We know the Watchers are after it, and if they are working for the heavenly council like you're suspecting, then we don't need Daimon getting his hands on it."

I unclasp the chain and give it to Kagan after he stands.

"Doreleska will accompany us while Hollis and Ulrich remain behind."

He moves into the library to inform the others while Rowen and I return to the bedroom to gather the blades. Since we don't want them noticed, I place mine in the outside pocket of the knapsack, which I strap across my back after donning my coat. Rowen sticks his under the waistband for his jeans behind his back, puts on a thick sweater, then we go back downstairs to wait for the others in the entrance hall. When Doreleska reaches the top of the stairs, she's securing two guns in a holster hidden under her knee-length leather jacket that matches her hair color.

"Kagan went ahead to scout out a location for us to trap Daimon." She doesn't wait for us and leaves.

I wrap my arms around Rowen, close my eyes, and we're thrust into bitter cold, once again the wind trying to latch on and rip me away. One of these days I'll need to see what happens during our travels so I can get used to the discomfort.

Something crunches under my feet, and when I open my eyes we're in an alley between two heavily damaged brick buildings, shattered glass and debris all around us, but it doesn't look to be from anything recent. The sky is a brilliant blue, not a cloud in sight to blemish it. Sounds of cheers and whistles soar through the air, pulling us toward a busy street lined with revelers, this group dressed in pristine attire with clean faces and highly polished shoes. A far cry from what was shown on television.

Just beyond them appears to be a main square where the liberator has dismounted his horse and climbed atop the base of a statue that's now lying discarded in pieces on the ground. His guards encircle him, making sure no one gets too close. The man is still wearing the helmet, pride oozing from his pores while he waves to his adoring fans. The sight sickens me.

Rowen takes my hand, and we follow Doreleska, who's moving effortlessly through the crowd, but I can't stop staring at the person responsible for my father's death. Rage consumes me, blocking out those who are praising him, so it feels like it's just the two of us. The rest of this war-ravaged town doesn't exist.

I pull free from Rowen's grip, unzip the pocket in the knapsack, wrap my hand around the handle of the blade, and step toward the marble base, pushing my way through the crowds. Removing the weapon, I hold it down along my side, my stare transfixed on the man who took everything from me. I'm nearly to the front row when our eyes lock and the world falls silent.

I sense him tremble, but only for a moment. He jumps down, and it's now I realize why there isn't any sound. Everyone has disappeared, the square and street are completely empty, with the exception of his guards, who remain poised in their position. Not even Rowen or Doreleska are anywhere to be seen.

"Have you come here to kill me, Magdalene?" Daimon asks in his odd accent, speaking the language of my ancestors, not bothering to lift the faceplate for the helmet. He saunters up to me, holding his hands out at his waist to show he's unarmed, though a sword is sheathed against his back.

"That depends on whether or not you sent the Watchers after me," I snarl.

He tilts his head to the side. "Why would I do that?"

"To regain what you lost." Raising my arm, I aim the tip of the dagger in his direction. "I know the heavenly council sent you, and I want to know why."

"Release me from your void and we can talk."

Furrowing my brow, I glare at him, confused. "I'm not conjuring this. The edicts stripped me of my powers. You know that. It's one of the reasons you're here."

He shakes his head. "This isn't my doing since I'm a mere mortal, and the demons you're with can't produce such tricks."

I grow concerned. "How do you know about them?"

He laughs, then turns and climbs back atop the marble. "I'll tell you, but first you need to end your hex, then meet me at the tavern on the outskirts of the city along the southern edge."

Suddenly, I'm surrounded by throngs of people, my name reverberating through the shouts of joy and jubilation, which is soon followed by Rowen tugging on my arm, pulling me back toward the sidewalk.

"Where did you disappear to?" he asks, panicked, once we're away from the crowds. "Why did you let go?"

"I-I don't know what j-just happened," I stammer, blindly placing the blade back into the pocket of my knapsack. "Daimon said I generated a void, which barred everyone from noticing us ... from me finding you."

Rowen holds onto my arm tighter. "What are you talking about? He never got down off the pedestal. It was you I couldn't see." His anxiety worsens, though he does what he can not to show it. "Come on, we need to find Doreleska and Kagan."

He starts to step away when I stop him. "Wait. Daimon wants me to meet him at a tavern so we can talk."

"Or kill you," Rowen utters.

"I don't think he does, since he could've easily done it while we were in the hex."

Scanning the crowds, he sighs heavily. "Let's get the others before proceeding over there."

We go in the direction Doreleska was heading, finding her and Kagan a few blocks away inside a dilapidated hotel. I explain what happened and Daimon's request.

"No wonder relic hunters don't last. They're all naïve and stupid," the young woman groans, crinkling her nose in disgust. "This is obviously a trap."

I seethe at her comment. "Then go secure the building yourself if you're so damn paranoid."

"And get stuck in a demon snare? Fuck that," she scoffs.

"I'll go since I can use the hunter blade to break any sigil or rune that may have been placed," Rowen says, then vanishes in a swirl of black smoke.

Doreleska rolls her eyes and steps outside, disappearing into the horde. Hopefully she's returning to the castle because I don't want her around. Kagan and I head back the way we came, passing the masses still celebrating Daimon's victory, though I no longer see him or the guards.

"How did you create a void?" Kagan asks to pass the time.

I shrug. "I have no idea. Maybe some of my powers are returning."

Taking my arm, he pulls me away from the festivities, tucking us into an alley. "That's not an ability a hunter has, Magdalene. They can't generate hexes, unless they're using runes or sigils, which you weren't from how you described the encounter." His stare bores into me, and I feel him shudder internally, which causes me to wonder.

Jerking my arm free, I step back. "You think I'm not really her. That the divine edicts sent an imposter to aid with the downfall of Lucifer, not help him."

Kagan grows pale, the light dimming in his eyes. "You read my thoughts."

"No, I sensed your emotions. Rowen can, too, which is uncommon in a demon," I say without thinking, going on nothing but instinct. "But you already knew that. It's why you let him stay, so he can alert you if the others decide to change allegiances."

The older man shoves a finger in my face. "Don't breathe a word of that to any of them, understand?"

Wrapping my hand around his wrist, I gently squeeze it. "I promise."

He holds my gaze for a few more seconds, then lowers his arm and we continue heading south where the buildings aren't so tightly packed together. The structure we come to is octagon-shaped with a high thatched roof, the exterior coated in disintegrating shingles. Inside, thick, wooden pillars hold up the vaulted ceiling, and the concrete floor is covered in dust, dirt, and dried leaves. Light fixtures dangle from beams crisscrossing overhead, some swaying in a slight breeze filtering in from gaps in the roof. Barrels topped with plywood act as tables, while wide tree stumps are used for chairs. Doreleska and Rowen are the only ones inside, but there are half-empty glasses scattered across a couple of the tables, as well as the chipped linoleum bar top lined with cracked leather stools.

"Everyone decided to leave when we arrived," Doreleska says, then chuckles as she steps behind the waist-high concrete bar that bends in an oval. She reaches underneath the counter and retrieves several shot glasses, along with a bottle of whiskey.

"I doubt they did it willingly," I chide, sitting at one of the tables clean of glasses, Kagan joining me.

"Does it matter?" She comes over and sets down the items. "This way, we have privacy for when we kill the bastard." She pours a drink, downs it, then serves herself another one.

Kagan covers the rim of her glass before she can consume it. "Go outside and stand guard."

"Killjoy," she grouses, swallows the last of her whiskey, and exits.

"Rowen, stay by the bar."

192

He nods just as Daimon and his guards enter.

The burly men are covered from head to toe in tarnished plated armor, every inch of their bodies and faces obscured, adding tension to the room. They take up positions around the establishment, even stepping outside to block the door. Daimon sits across from me but doesn't remove the helmet. Kagan reaches over, takes three of the shot glasses, and pours us each a drink, placing one in front of the former hunter.

"Not thirsty?" the older man asks after consuming the whiskey.

"I'm fine, thank you." Disdain oozes from Daimon's voice.

Kagan refills his drink. "It's awfully rude to sit at a table while still wearing the helmet. Didn't your mother teach you any manners?"

He points to the bottle. "I hope you intend on paying for the liquor."

The older man reaches into the pocket of his jeans, then slams several coins onto the table.

Daimon takes and twirls them between his fingers, turning his attention to me. "The edicts offered me a deal. If I found and killed you, they would grant me your powers and I could once again become a relic hunter. Seeing as it was better than rotting away in their horrid prison, I accepted."

"Why do they want me dead?"

"To replace you, of course." He smirks. "Like me, over the years you became defiant, balked at their incessant rules. Falling in love with a demon was the last straw for them."

"Who else did they recruit?" Kagan asks, leaning forward, resting his arms on the plywood.

Daimon shrugs. "That I don't know, but it could be anyone loyal to them."

"Like a demon hunter," I respond, the thought of Avaris invading the castle still fresh on my mind. "How come the edicts didn't slay me themselves when they had the chance? Why wait until now?"

"Because they wanted to punish you first. Also, a suitable proxy hadn't been determined yet. You can't simply allow a hunter's abilities to remain unseeded. They must be passed on immediately—such as mine were to you—or they'll be lost forever."

I stare at him quizzically. "But I don't have my powers. The heavenly council stripped them from me."

"If that were true, I would still be in my cell." He continues to play with the coins, which seems to soothe him, much like the obsidian rock calmed me as a child way back when. "Perhaps you found a way to hide your abilities, store them somewhere for safe keeping, and the only way for the edicts to garner them back is with your death."

"Which means you knew they were coming for us that night," Rowen comments, sounding aggrieved. "It also explains why you couldn't escape when those men broke into our home to take you away."

That must have also been the reason why I created the journal. So then, where are my powers and what does the compass rose have to do with any of this?

"It's obvious you haven't been actively searching for Magdalene. Why?" Kagan inquires, interrupting my thoughts.

"Because I don't want to return to that life, nor do I want the responsibility of reclaiming artifacts some self-righteous assholes should never have created in the first place. And since I'm a mere mortal now, those pricks who once dictated my life can't find me, just like they can't locate Magdalene." He lets out a deep sigh. "I've spent time looking for the Armor of Rochelle. It took me years to track down the helmet, and there's no way I'm giving it to you. The world, and I, need it."

"I see nothing has changed in regard to your egotism. How many people died because of it this time?" Finally drinking the shot that's been sitting in front of me, the liquid burns going down my throat, leaving a sour taste in both my mouth and stomach.

"Your father was an accident," he replies bitterly. "But if it wasn't for me, you never would've picked up the blades and avenged his death by obliterating Belial. Thereby, making you the fierce woman that you are today." He gestures pompously in my direction.

"Where's the shield?" I ask, ignoring his comment.

He chuckles. "You destroyed it. I think that's another reason why the divine edicts want to be rid of you. Relics don't remain intact very long in your presence. In place of restoring or reburying them, you raze the items until all that remain are tiny fragments, extinguishing the powers stored within them."

"Then you didn't send the Watchers," Rowen states from his perch on one of the stools, his hands clasped in his lap.

Daimon turns his head slightly toward him. "God, no. I can't afford to have them finding out I'm on the loose. Do you know how valuable a relic hunter would be to Lucifer? Even a powerless one? I still have the knowledge of what all those artifacts can do and how to find them. He'd torture me for that kind of information." The former hunter reverts his attention to me. "Which is why I'm surprised you're cavorting around with his deviants. Even bringing them to my doorstep." He snaps his fingers, and the guards draw their weapons from scabbards adhered to their backs. "Well, it's been fun catching up, but I've got a city to run and more lands to conquer."

He stands and turns to leave, but Rowen is there. In one smooth motion, he rams the kard into Daimon's abdomen, then forces him back into his seat before extracting the blade. I reach over and unlatch the hook to remove the helmet. Immediately, the guards vanish in a swirl of dust, leaving nothing behind, which causes Doreleska to bolt inside, her guns drawn. She smiles at the sight of the dying man's blood spilling onto the floor.

Astonishment creases Daimon's face while sweat beads across his scarred forehead. His damp, dark hair falls to his shoulders, and his olive skin is turning ashen. His cheeks are somewhat sunken, and his eyes have lost their luster. He resembles very little of the man who swaggered into Cresidio when I was a child, though his smugness is still overly abundant.

I stand, then move over to kneel on the floor in front of him. "Did you really think I was going to let you keep the armor?" Taking the weapon from Rowen, I show it to Daimon.

His eyes widen in astonishment and his mouth gapes.

"Hunter blades can cut through spells and hexes, such as the one for the helmet. Being a former hunter yourself, you would know that. I guess the edicts forgot to tell you that I bestowed one of my weapons to Rowen many years ago. That's something they were well aware of after I returned last time possessing only one. Perhaps it was you who was sent here to die, not me." I straighten up. "Enjoy Lucifer's cage. I'm sure you'll feel right at home there."

Gasping, he slumps sideways, takes a final breath, then dies.

"Told you he'd be dead before the end of the day," Kagan says jokingly.

"How come he didn't turn to ash like the Watcher?" I inquire.

"Because he's not a demon."

"What do we do with the helmet?" Rowen asks, reclaiming his weapon from me, then stepping over to the bar and grabbing a rag to clean it.

Doreleska holsters her guns. "I say we destroy it. It's far too dangerous keeping a relic like that around."

"Since Magdalene doesn't have her abilities and is easily susceptible to injury, I think she should wear it for protection," Kagan states, taking the coins from the dead man's hand and stuffing them back into his pocket.

She raises her eyebrow. "And the body?"

196

"Leave him," I reply.

Rowen rejoins me after placing the blade in his waistband. Wrapping one arm around his waist, I hold onto the helmet and close my eyes.

Chapter Thirteen

We return to the castle, arriving in the library, startling Hollis and Ulrich. The latter notices the armor and practically salivates.

His eyes dance with excitement. "Can I take a look at that?"

"Only if you put on gloves so the iron doesn't burn you," Kagan comments.

Ulrich rushes out of the room as I set the helmet down onto the table, returning a few minutes later with a pair made from leather.

"Is Pierce back?"

Hollis shakes her head. "What happened with Daimon?"

"Rowen did something useful for a change," Doreleska quips. "That's one less hunter we have to worry about."

After setting down the knapsack on the far end of the table, I remove my coat and take a seat next to Ulrich while he scrutinizes every pin and joint in the armor. Kagan and Doreleska leave, the former returning with the compass rose, which I secure around my neck. Rowen heads to the basement to properly clean his blade.

"This should have more pieces to it," Ulrich states, then flutters about the room, bringing back a heavily worn, brown leather-bound book.

Flipping through its immensely detailed pages, he stops when he comes to the story of Rochelle of Travion, an exquisite hand-drawn picture of her donning the armor in full glory. She has medium-toned skin and long, dark brown hair that sweeps over one shoulder as if being blown by an invisible breeze. The metal donning her tall frame appears heavy and severely dented—probably due to the battle—the tip of a blackthorn shield strapped in wrought iron digs into the ground at her feet, standing several meters high, and the helmet is tucked under her arm, the visor clasped shut. Her oblong face has high cheekbones, a narrow chin, firm lips, and is expressionless. Her steel blue eyes bore sharply into us as if we're right there in front of her, and not a portrait. A devastated land smolders in the background.

"It says here the body plating was melted down and used to create a sword, which is immortalized in the village square of Travion alongside her statue," Ulrich says, reading through the immense paragraph rather quickly. "The shield and helmet were interned with her remains in the catacombs under Ambrose Church, which is several miles outside of the village's boundaries."

"Daimon said I destroyed the shield, but I'd never grave rob to do that. It must have already been pilfered by the time I found it."

"Meaning the helmet was as well, so I wonder how Daimon discovered the location if you're the one who previously hid it after reclaiming the shield."

"That's if the pair were together at the time." Staring at the portrait, I can't help but focus on the shield, noticing a peculiar ornamentation in the center where the iron ribbing meets. "What's that?" I ask, pointing to it.

"Hmm." Ulrich stands, retrieves a magnifying glass from one of the desks, then retakes his seat and scrutinizes the area. "Well, I'll be damned. Here, have a look."

He passes me the magnifier and the book. It takes a few seconds for my eyes to adjust to the enlarged image and my mouth falls open. "It's the compass rose, but why would something like that be there?"

Reclaiming the heavy volume, Ulrich scans the next several paragraphs, locating the answer. "According to this, she requested that the compass be added to the shield when it was created. The pendant was the only possession she had of her father's, who died when she was a child. Rochelle believed it would guide her successfully during the battle, which it obviously did."

"Do you know if the church is still standing?" I inquire, becoming excited by the lead.

"I'm not sure. A lot of those structures were destroyed during the Cleansing so new ones could be built to accommodate the rising zealots and their devotees."

Picking up the helmet, I gaze into the closed faceplate, imagining Rochelle's piercing blue eyes staring back at me. A powerful disturbance erupts in my veins, tingling through every muscle as if setting them ablaze. Sounds of clashing steel reverberates in my eardrums, blocking out the world around me, and the scent of mud infiltrates my nostrils. Closing my eyes, I see a blood-soaked battlefield laid out before me, the war visible through the slit in the helmet adorning my head.

Moans and screams of pain spill from the mouths of the dying, both friend and foe. Metal armored guards strike down those desperate to murder the villagers and me. They appeared the moment I put on the helmet, but there was no time to question how or why. The enemy is unable to strike them down, causing several to flee into the forest while others fight against them to the death. Exhausted, I inhale deeply, absorbing the damp, moist air from the rain that continues to fall, making the ground beneath my heavily clad feet slippery and treacherous. Lifting my head skyward, droplets seep under the helmet, bathing me in their splendor.

Reaffirming my stance in the mud, I lower my head and stare down those who've managed to slip past my defenses. With a quick flick of my wrist a dagger sails out of my hand and drives into the enemy's chest, killing him before he has a chance to react. After the blade returns, I hold up the shield with my other arm to block their swords, then release my weapon again. It whips around my assailants, slicing through each before landing back into my grip. Moving toward the commander who sent his men to take over our homes, I'm hit repeatedly, my armor dented, but holding. The only protection I lack is around my drenched hands, which shiver from the cold, but I continue to hold the blade with confidence.

It was a wonder when I found the pair buried beside my mother's grave days before the French army arrived. The child's voice which flooded my dreams brought me to their location in the middle of the night. I didn't have to dig far beneath the soil, just a few meters, and I instantly knew they were meant specifically for me when the moonlight showed their magnificence. The armor and shield I stole when word that the battle was coming closer to Travion began to spread. I knew what had to be done and that I was the only one who could stop these invaders. It felt like I was born for this moment, my existence a necessity because it needed to be. Never had I sensed a better purpose than this one.

Stealing a moment from the fight, I look at the dagger, marveling its ivory handle and gold blade, knowing its twin rests in a sheath around my waist. I fill with warmth and pride, assured that this nightmare will be over quickly.

Startled, I drop the helmet onto the table and am pulled out of the imagery. My pulse races and my heart pounds rapidly against my chest while I try to catch a breath. Hollis appears terrified by the reaction, while Ulrich stares at me, a bewildered expression across his face. He goes to open his mouth when I abruptly stand and leave, heading for the small bathroom off the hallway leading into the library. I close and lock the door, flip on the light switch to illuminate the dark room, turn on the faucet, and splash cold water onto my scorching face. Gripping the edge of the sink, I bend forward at the waist to rest my forehead against the cool porcelain of the sink and try to convince myself that what I saw wasn't real … that I was simply witnessing everything through Rochelle's eyes and not my own. I reach under my shirt and clutch the compass rose while trembling at the possibility that I'm more than simply Magdalene Leech, the relic hunter.

Standing, I stare at my weary reflection in the mirror while still holding onto the pendant.

In the glass, the room dissolves around me and is replaced by a clapboard covered one with well-worn furnishings and a fire burning warmly in the hearth. A young girl around eleven or twelve, with short, dark blonde hair wears a raggedy nightgown that dusts the wood planks under her bare feet as she traverses across the dank, dimly lit room. She wrings her hands nervously while approaching the man standing by a window constructed from warped panes. His attention is focused on the many lanterns parading in the middle of the night along the dirt lane in front of their home, each one headed toward the village square where he knows he ought to be.

"Papa?" she asks, uncertain whether to disturb the man or not.

He turns, the worried expression on his face replaced by one of adoration. His features are identical to that of the girl's, right down to the color of his eyes. "My sweet, you should be in bed."

"Mama is crying."

Kneeling in front of the child, he places a hand on her arm. "I know. Why don't you go to her?"

The child looks past him, her focus now on the lanterns. "What's the matter?"

"Nothing you need to worry about." But the pain in his eyes tells her something different. "Here," reaching into his pants pocket, he removes a silver chain with a compass rose pendant dangling from its links, "hold onto this for me." He drapes it around her neck and tears well in his eyes.

She looks at the item thoughtfully, caressing the warped silver between her small fingers, then returns her gaze to her father.

202

"The pendant will guide you always, like it has me. Use it with care, Rochelle." He kisses her gently on the cheek. "And remember, if you should ever get lost," he taps the compass rose resting in her palm, "this will show you the way." Standing, he turns for the door and disappears into the night.

The reflection in the mirror reverts back to normal, and I release my hold on the necklace. I know where I must go next. Follow a path laid out for me over a century ago when I suspected the edicts wanted me dead. A way to guarantee my return and survival without their interference. It was a calculated move, one that still needs to be navigated carefully if I'm to be successful.

Exiting the bathroom, I return to the library, pick up the helmet, and tap Ulrich on the shoulder since he's nose deep in the thick book. "Are there any satchels I can use to carry this in?" I ask, indicating the armor in my hands.

"There's a linen closet on the second floor that has a few bags. One of them should work."

I head upstairs, locating the closet between Ulrich and Rowen's bedrooms. It's a small walk-in filled with hand-carved shelves holding various colorful towels and bedsheets. Along the back wall are dozens of leather bags hanging from hooks welded into the brick. After several attempts, I finally find a rucksack large enough to hold the helmet, then return to the library where Kagan is nervously pacing and Rowen is trying to calm him down. He's shed the sweater, and the black T-shirt that had been underneath accentuates the ripples of his muscles, causing me to ache.

"He should be back by now," the older man bemoans, twisting his hands together.

"I'm sure Pierce is fine," Rowen replies. "There's a lot of ground to cover and he has to be discreet about how he asks the questions. Nobody is going to voluntarily claim to have seen the Watchers because it'll put their life in jeopardy."

Moving to the other end of the table, I put on my coat, pick up the knapsack, and strap it, along with the new bag, across my shoulders.

Rowen turns his attention to me, staring at the unfamiliar rucksack. "Are you going somewhere?"

"I need to visit Travion, France, the birthplace of Rochelle."

Everyone glares at me.

"Why?" he asks, his tone harsh and blunt.

Taking the book away from Ulrich, I get nearer to the pair, turn to the page depicting the valiant young woman, and point to the compass rose embedded into her shield. "I know what this does and it's telling me to go to Travion."

Kagan, Rowen, and Hollis come closer, studying the image.

"Rochelle's father told her that if she ever got lost, the pendant would show her the way home."

Rowen glowers at me. "How the hell could you possibly know that?" He puts all of his weight on one leg while crossing his arms over his chest, puffing it out.

"Because I saw her memories just now, which triggered more of mine." I take a deep breath to settle myself before continuing, "I'm the one who stole the shield and helmet from Rochelle's catacomb, then hid them before I was dragged back to the edicts by the demon hunters when you and I were in De Lamar. Knowing what was in store, I removed the compass rose before dismantling the shield, using it to mark the location of where I hid my powers."

"That's a pretty big assumption," Kagan states. "It could be a trick by the edicts to lure you away from the castle if Avaris told them how to find you."

"Then why haven't they sent the Watchers?" I counter. "There's no sigil or rune keeping them from infiltrating the grounds."

Hollis scrunches up her face. "Maybe they're not the ones ordering the Watchers to capture you."

204

"You said relic hunters don't rob graves," Ulrich interjects before anyone can dispute Hollis' remark. "Or at least you claimed not to have."

Glancing at each of them, I reply, "Is it really stealing when the tomb is your own?"

"What?" Rowen utters, his jaw dropping.

"I was Rochelle, and I'm guessing a few others during the times when the relic hunter wasn't needed. How else can you explain me knowing everything about her life? When she fought the French. The weapon she used wasn't a sword, but the kards. I saw it ... I remember it. That's why there's no record of what she fought with, only what was used to defend herself." I tap on the picture of the shield for emphasis. "The moment the fighting was over, she hid the daggers for her—rather me—to find later, which I did."

"Let's say, for the benefit of the doubt, that what you're telling us is true." Rowen holds up his hands as if to ward off an impending argument. "It's still not safe for you to leave the castle while the Watchers are out there."

"But I have the—" I start to rebuff his claim when the gasp from Hollis stops everything.

Turning, we all gape at Pierce, who's leaning against the doorframe into the library from the hallway. Dirt and sweat streak his face; his clothes are disheveled, filthy, and torn. His left hand is pressed firmly against a gash in his side, blood seeping between his fingers and spattering onto the floor. Kagan and Rowen rush toward him, carefully balancing Pierce between the two of them.

"He's alive," the beaten man mutters, his head lolling against his chest while his shoulders slump forward. "He's alive."

"Rowen, help me take him to his room." The three vanish in a swirl of black smoke.

After removing the bags and setting them onto the table, I race upstairs while Hollis goes to fetch Doreleska. When I reach the bedroom, Kagan is stripping off Pierce's shirt and Rowen dashes into the bathroom to fill a basin with water, returning with a washcloth and a bar of soap. I loiter by the fireplace at the far end of the room, staying out of the way. Doreleska and Hollis burst in a few moments later, the former crawling into bed beside Pierce.

"Why isn't he healing?" she hollers, glancing desperately between Kagan and Rowen, who's busy cleaning the wound. "How the hell could he have gotten injured?"

"He's alive," Pierce continues to mumble between painful moans, his harried gaze settling on me. "He's alive."

"Who?" Kagan asks as Doreleska helps wipe away the blood while Rowen continues to work.

Pierce locks eyes with the older man and grabs his wrist, leaving a bloody impression behind. "Belial." Then, he passes out.

The world around me shatters.

Clutching my stomach, I practically bend over as if I've just been gut punched, and use my other hand to support myself against the back of one of the cushioned chairs in front of the hearth. "No ... no, that can't be."

"Rowen, take Magdalene down to the library. Doreleska and I will tend to Pierce," Kagan orders, snatching away the cloth and soap.

He's at my side in a matter of seconds, wraps an arm around my waist, and escorts me out of the room. When we're back downstairs, I take a seat in one of the upholstered chairs. Rowen pulls another closer to mine to use, then takes my hand.

"No," I whimper, tears erupting from my eyes, blurring my surroundings as everything spins out of control. "That's impossible." Bending over, I clutch my stomach and begin to rock back and forth in the chair.

"What's going on?" Ulrich queries from his seat, confused.

"Pierce ran into Belial while in Kern," Rowen answers. "We won't know more until he wakes up."

"I killed him. Burnt him to ash," I mutter, continuing to grip my abdomen, tears dripping into my lap. "He's dead. Pierce has to be mistaken."

Ulrich comes over, kneels on the floor, and grasps my free hand, squeezing it. "How could he have escaped?"

Rowen rubs my back, hoping it'll soothe me. "Would Abaddon have freed him?"

"It makes more sense for Belial to have released the greater monster from his dungeon. Not the other way around."

I close my eyes while the two discuss the Prince of Darkness, who's horrid stare seers into me through wisps of fog encircling my memories. His dark, narrow eyes the only thing between reality and me slipping into an unescapable abyss. The pungent odor of his foul breath hits me square in the face as the nostrils of his wide nose flare. I'm thrust back to the instant just before I plunged the kard into the Scepter of Ignis. Odd shadows are cast from the flames flickering around us, and the stars are blacked out by the thick, heavy smoke. I feel the fate of the entire world on my young shoulders, lives that will forever be altered with the simple stroke of a blade. My parents are dead, leaving me alone in a broken land never to properly heal.

"Do you fear me, Magdalene?" he asked, though I barely saw his lizard-like lips move.

More of my recollections from that night return. I didn't plunge the kard into the gem right away, but hesitated, terrified of what was about to happen, knowing that I had to do it no matter the price.

"No," I answered fiercely, though it was a lie.

He cocked his head to the side, amused by my response. "Why?"

The parched air made it hard to speak, and a headache formed behind my overly dry eyes. I swallowed as best as I could, praying the words I were about to utter wouldn't be my last. "Because Olwen and others like her will protect us all from beasts like you. Evil will never defeat them ... nor me."

The ground beneath my knees was hot as I bent down to destroy the scepter. Belial nearly had a clawed hand on my arm when the blade destroyed our lives, sending him and his knights to Hell ... or so I had believed.

Opening my eyes, I wipe away some of the tears, lift my head, and glance between Rowen and Ulrich, both of whom stare at me with concern etched deeply on their faces. "Where do creatures like Belial go when they've been overpowered?"

"To the pit," Rowen replies, resting his head against mine. "It's worse than the cages hunter blades send us to. There, you're simply locked away to suffer and rot. In the pit, you're chained to the molten-lined walls, spewed with unrelenting fire, and tortured for eternity by any means at the Watchers' disposal. Hardly anyone ever escapes, let alone is released from their bindings."

"But when they are?"

He clears his throat, obviously uncomfortable by the question. "It can't be of their own doing. Another demon must give themselves over as an indentured servant, and eventually take their master's place when called upon."

"Has anyone, other than Belial, been freed from the pit?"

"Not that I know of." Rowen turns to Ulrich, who's shaking his head.

"Why would anyone willingly do that?"

"Beings in high command can be very persuasive to those seeking the same status." Ulrich stands, patting the back of my hand, which he still clings to. "Power is often sought by those too weak to control it. Demons are no different than humans in that respect." He releases me, returning to his seat.

I wipe the remaining tears off of my face, stand, and retrieve the kard from the knapsack, holding it down along my side. "How do I locate the one responsible for releasing Belial so I can kill him or her?"

"That's the job of a demon hunter, Magdalene. Not you." Rowen joins me at the table. "Let them handle it."

"No." I move away from him. "Their kards won't be able to touch him. Daimon tried in Cresidio and failed. Belial batted down the one thrown at him like it was a feather. He side-stepped to avoid the other, its blade hitting my father, killing him. I used the Scepter of Ignis to destroy him and his knights. Simple hunter blades will have no effect. It has to be me like the last time."

Ulrich focuses his troubled attention solely on me. "Then you'll need an extremely powerful relic, and without your memory fully restored, we won't know where to start looking for one."

"Pierce is going to need to be monitored, so Doreleska will be staying with him," Kagan announces after entering.

Hollis a few steps behind. "What did Belial use?"

"A clach," Rowen replies, surprising the others, but not me. "It's a serrated dagger made from cursed steel, which is why it can harm demons." His eyes become sorrowful while turning his focus exclusively to me. "The wounds on my chest are from the same type of weapon, but mine were inflicted by a demon hunter, who then used his kard to send me to the cages." He doesn't mention the time Theron stabbed me with is, which I'm grateful for.

"While iron chains held you to the bed," I add, then kiss him lovingly on the lips. "It was Avaris, wasn't it?"

He nods.

Ulrich leans back in his chair, crossing his arms over his chest. "What do we do?"

"Prepare the room," Kagan orders sternly.

Tucking the dagger into the back of the waistband for my leggings, I retake my seat in the cushioned chair after removing my coat while the four of them go about closing the shutters over the stained-glass windows. They also move the main table and chairs, placing them into the family room, along with the heavy, woven rug that's underneath, exposing charred wood with a large disturbing depiction of two circles—one inside of the other—containing six different runes carved equidistant between each other into the floor. At the center of the inner circle is an upside down triangle with an 'x' starting at the top corners and branching down beyond the shape, the lines extend and curl into what look like overlapping horns.

"Magdalene, hide behind one of the bookcases," Rowen instructs, closing and locking the door for the hallway, while Hollis seals the connecting door into the family room.

I stand, head for the farthest corner, and bend down, adjusting a couple of the books on a lower shelf to better see what's happening.

Kagan, Hollis, Rowen, and Ulrich each position themselves next to one of the runes, then the older man passes around a knife, but I can't tell what it's made from. They slice their palms, then kneel onto the scorched wood, placing the exposed wound against the rune beside them. A red radiance flows from the markings, around the two circles, and finally into the center, illuminating the entire sigil, casting an ominous glow about the room. Their eyes are completely black, just like Rowen's were when he killed the Watcher. The hairs on the back of my neck prickle, and the heat in the room intensifies with each passing second.

Red smoke rises from the image in the floor, churning the air, creating a powerful breeze that threatens to knock the books from their shelves. The sharp smell of sulphur permeates my senses, making it difficult to breathe, so I lift the collar of my button-down, blue flannel shirt to cover my mouth and nose. The smoke solidifies, transforming into a tall creature with red skin, hooves for feet, claws for hands, a shortened, horse-like face, and sharp horns protruding from the top of a bald head. His muscular body is bathed in a dark red silk cloak, pooling at his feet like blood.

"Ah, my children," the thing growls as the wind eventually stops, and I spot the four bowing their heads in subjugation. "What news do you have for me?"

"My lord," Kagan begins, keeping his gaze toward the floor, "we've learned Belial is among the living. He attacked Pierce, nearly killing him."

Lucifer is about to speak when his nose wrinkles, but not in disgust. He sniffs the air, then extends his long, scaley tongue and licks the invisible scent that's caught his attention. "You have her," he states, smiling. "Bring her forth."

"No!" Rowen shouts, standing, drawing angry stares from his fellow demons. "Magdalene is safe where she is. This conversation doesn't need to concern her."

The creature raises his arm and points a sharp talon at the defiant young man. "I'll decide what matters, boy. Your freedom from the cage was purely to assist with locating the relic hunter, which has been done. I can easily place you back inside of your prison if I so wish, but I sincerely doubt she'll cooperate if you're down there with the rest of the rule breakers."

Rowen shudders, lowers his head, and drops down to his knees.

"Perhaps, my lord, it would be best to alter your appearance," Hollis suggests, her sweet voice now abrasive and cruel. "One more appropriate for the problem at hand."

It bothers me to hear them refer to Lucifer as their lord, even though he is. The actuality of who they truly are hadn't sunk in until this very moment. When Hell and Earth are isolated from each other, it's easier to mentally separate the demons from their master. But now with the two plains briefly merged, it chills me to the bone knowing that I'm in love with one of them, and that it can all be taken away in an instant.

The beast smirks. "I suppose it couldn't hurt." His body transforms into that of a tall man around Kagan's age with short, dark brown hair, pale skin, rugged features, firm physique, and solid black eyes. The cloak changes into simple red dress pants, a matching long-sleeved, button-down shirt, and loafers. The thick sulphur odor diminishes, but doesn't leave completely. "Magdalene, come out and join us." His voice is hypnotic with its sultry blend of accents, making it impossible to determine an exact one to listen to.

Before stepping out, I make sure the compass rose is tucked under my top to keep it hidden, and close an extra button near my throat for good measure. I leave my hiding spot and go stand at the end of the sigil by an unoccupied rune. He smiles at my approach, lust heavy in his leer, but I have a feeling that's normal for him. Sensuality and desire ebb and flow from him like cologne, which is most likely how he attracts so many followers. The dark abyss of his eyes pulls me in, enfolding me in their charm, beckoning me to fall into their cavernous waters and obey his every command. Reaching behind my back, I wrap my hand around the handle for the kard, but don't remove it. I just need to feel it in my grip, an affirmation of my true existence, and draw strength from the ivory to help overcome my shortfalls.

"You're very beautiful. Just like your mother." He licks his lips.

"You know nothing of her or me," I say through clenched teeth.

"I know everyone who once lived, and is currently living, whether they wind up in my den or not. It's the same for my brother, but you already knew that." He steps forward, coming close to the edge of the inner circle, but something tells me he can't move any farther than that or he'll disappear. "How I've longed to meet you. I just wish it was under better circumstances." Placing his hands behind his back, he turns and retreats to his original spot. "Yes, I'm aware Belial is out there roaming the lands, and he has been for quite a long time."

"Why have you continued to allow him?" Kagan asks, raising his gaze to meet that of his master's.

"At first, I hadn't intended to, but then a thought occurred to me. What better way to introduce my Legion onto an unsuspecting world than by using him? It was the opportunity that I'd been waiting for, and with the demon hunters busy murdering my irrelevant followers, as well as the relic hunter being under so-called house arrest for her poor judgment in lovers," Lucifer glowers at Rowen, who's keeping his head down, "there was no one left to mind the ship while the rats took over."

"Who, or what, is a Legion?" I inquire, terrified to know the answer, but desperate too as well.

With the flick of his wrist, an invisible force propels me across the floor and into the heart of the sigil, where I stop mere inches from him. "They are several of my most devoted disciples. Demons capable of bending wills and minds with ease, molding the world into whatever I can possibly imagine while I'm stuck toiling down there." He points to beneath his feet. "One of them is responsible for the Cleansing, my dear. Orchestrating it by harnessing the greatest fears which dwell in most hearts of humankind." He chuckles. "I was quite impressed with how you slaughtered several factions of the Caltraves, which my Legion created—along with many others—foolishly believing you were doing the world a favor. It took a bit of time to replace those loyal men and women. Your efforts, I'm afraid, were to no avail."

The corners of my mouth curl into a wicked smile. "Then why are you trembling?"

He frowns, irritation filling the creases now lining his face.

I narrow my gaze. "It's not only Belial and Abaddon that you fear, but your Legion as well. You're worried they've betrayed you."

He tries to cover up his discomfort by loudly clearing his throat. "You're an empath. What an unusual gift for a hunter."

Tightening my grip on the kard, I say, "I'm full of all sorts of surprises."

Tilting his head to the side, he reaches out, seizes my arm, and pulls the limb forward, exposing the weapon. Through the material of my shirt, the heat his hold generates hurts. I'm sure if my skin was exposed, it would be burning.

The grin now on his face is tantalizing and alluring. "I must say you're smarter than most of my commanders. Of course, this kard won't work on me like you want it to." He bends my wrist, causing me to wince and to drop the blade onto the floor, then he grazes my cheek with a sharp fingernail, cutting my flesh and drawing a bit of blood, which he places on the tip of his tongue. "Sweet." He releases me. "This damn war would be over so much faster if you were mine. Perhaps someday soon you will be."

Glancing back at Rowen, I notice his hands are now balled into fists and he's baring his teeth, but remains the ever obedient servant and stays on the floor.

"Continuing our discussion about Belial, it wasn't until the Watchers deserted their posts that I fully understood the treachery befallen upon me. He's the one who lured them away. I can only guess he made promises to them that he has no intention on keeping."

"You didn't even notice when Abaddon was freed?" I ask, incensed by his arrogance.

Lucifer paces around me like a dog in heat. "That coward has always been unfettered, hiding in his little hole in the bowels of the underworld and well out of my reach." Stopping, he places a hand on my shoulder, his lips practically touching my ear. Fluttering rises in my stomach, much in the same way it does when I'm with Rowen, and I don't care for it. "In a way, I'm glad this is all happening. It gives me a chance to destroy that bastard once and for all. Rid him from existence."

"How did you get the edicts to go along with your scheme?"

"I didn't. There's no way those pricks would've ever listened to me. Now my brother, on the other hand, can be very persuasive, and, after all, they work for him." He moves in front of me, his hands clasped behind his back. "You see, my dear, I bring balance to an otherwise stale world, which is why I'm permitted to remain. Abaddon will usher in nothing but destruction and chaos. The wars will continue for eternity until the only things left are ash and blood. I know when to pick my battles and who to leave alone. He doesn't." Lucifer steps closer, towering over me, his hot breath hitting me square in the face. "If I lose this fight, then we all do."

Looking into his eyes, I can easily stumble and fall into his powers, joining those subjecting themselves on the floor around me. "What am I supposed to use to stop him since the kards won't work?"

Smirking, he affectionately presses his palm onto my cheek. The heat of his skin has now become tolerable, so it doesn't burn or hurt like I believed it would. "A relic, of course. One capable of causing the extinction of creatures like him and me. Isn't that why you're known as the relic hunter?" His thoughtful gaze lingers, drawing me in further. When he finally pulls away, the trance I was succumbing too disappears, leaving me feeling empty and dejected. "However, I did hear from one of my spies that you've lost your special abilities. Stolen by the very council who sent you down here to die at the hands of those self-righteous zealots Lethe created so you can be replaced by another more desirable candidate. If you become mine, I'd never treat you with such disrespect, Magdalene." He cups my face in his hands, the desire returning, infiltrating my soul. If he says the right words, I might just break. "I can give you so much more than they ever would permit you to have. Even allow your relationship with Rowen to flourish well beyond these walls."

The proposition tantalizes me, but I find myself stepping backward, breaking the connection before it can fully consume me. "Who released Belial from the pit?"

He drops his arms down along his sides, a red heat pulsating between us, desperately trying to reattach itself to me. "That I don't know since he had a lot of devotees readily to serve him when called upon. No doubt one of them is responsible." Reaching toward me, he grabs ahold of my hair, takes down the ponytail, and tosses the elastic band onto the floor. "Much better." He runs his fingers through my loose locks, causing me to quiver with heightened anticipation. "Accept my offer, love, before it's too late. Don't let the edicts destroy you. Their pens are far worse than mine." He caresses my face with the back of his hand. "But, then again, without your powers you're simply mortal, able to die by the weakest of weapons. You'll be inaccessible to everyone if that were to happen. It would be a shame to lose someone so cunning and determined to a repairable flaw." He steps back. "Let me know when you're ready."

With his elbows locked against his side, he raises his arms, which pulls forth the wind from earlier. The sigil glows and red smoke envelopes him, drawing him into the symbol. A calm settles over the room as the radiance dissipates, but there's an invisible current throbbing in the air, connecting all of us.

Rowen is quickly at my side, pulling me toward the door for the hallway when all I want to do is remain. "We have to leave this room," he says, struggling to keep his feet moving, mine dragging reluctantly.

Pulling him to a halt, I wrap my arms around his waist and kiss him passionately. Our cores ignite into an inferno. He pulls me tight against him, every inch of him quaking with excitement. I want nothing more than to get naked and fuck him, not caring that the others are in the room with us.

After several intense seconds, he manages to wrench himself free. "We need to go."

"But I want to stay." Grabbing hold of his shirt, I start to tug it off, anxious to see his firm body, feel it pound against mine, hear the sensual noises escape his lips like they did last night.

"No, Magdalene, not here." He shoves my hands away, then starts to unbutton my top. Shaking his head, he ceases. "Come on."

Again, he pulls me toward the door. When he grabs the handle to open it, I turn and notice Hollis plastered between Kagan and Ulrich, both undressing her hurriedly. She leans her head back against Kagan's shoulder, closes her eyes, and moans as Ulrich strokes her between the breasts, while Kagan desperately undresses.

216

Rowen pushes me into the hallway, slamming the door behind us, then drags me into the bathroom. The door is barely closed when he has all of the buttons on my shirt undone, and I'm working on the zipper for his pants, our mouths unable to release each other. The moment we're both naked, he pins me against the wall, pushes my hips up, and takes me forcefully. I cry out, but not from pain. Sweat rapidly covers our hot bodies and the room heats up to near combustion.

Ogling him, I notice something odd. "Your eyes are still black," I gasp.

"It's why we needed to get out of the library." With my legs wrapped around his waist, he moves me onto the tiled floor. I have to use my hands to brace myself against the wall so he doesn't ram my head into the plaster. "Lucifer has powerful emotions, which affect everyone he's near. His hunger for you charged all of us."

Rowen's lips cover mine. I place a hand on the back of his head and tug on his hair, which escalates things. Closing my eyes, I revel in the intensity of the moment, wishing it to never end. Rowen howls like a wolf when he reaches his end, matching pitch with the sounds emanating from the library. When I open my eyes, his have returned to hazel. He smiles, kisses me some more, then rests his head on my sweat-drenched stomach.

"Will Hollis be all right?" I ask, working on catching my breath.

"She's used to this. That's the reason we closed off the room, so the infection wouldn't spread to Pierce and Doreleska. There was no telling what was going to happen, but we couldn't take any chances. If Lucifer had become angry, everything would've turned into a bloodbath. We can all heal, except you."

I stroke his dampened locks. "And if we stayed with the others?"

Rowen sits up and kisses me again. "I'm not sure you want to know that answer."

I grin. "Demon orgy."

The laugh escaping his lips brightens his face. "I, for one, do not want to see Kagan naked. Also, I get jealous very easily and there's no way in hell I'd ever allow anyone to touch you so intimately."

Placing a hand on his cheek, I say, "Then it's a good thing we left, otherwise Hollis might have frowned at being sent to a cage since I feel the same way about you."

We kiss each other fervently, not wanting the deep desire to subside.

Rowen is the first to let go. "Let's get dressed. I'm dying of thirst."

With our clothes back on, we exit the bathroom and head to the kitchen. I pour glasses of juice while Rowen scrounges for something to cook for an early dinner. Just as the food is ready, the others join us, behaving as if nothing out of the ordinary happened. When we're done eating, Rowen and I return to the library, which has been restored to its original arrangement. I find the kard kicked under a bookshelf, so after reclaiming it, I place it into the knapsack, pick up my coat and the rucksack, then take everything upstairs, depositing them on the couch. We spend the rest of the evening in bed dispelling Lucifer's charm.

Chapter Fourteen

"I can't believe you summoned him," Doreleska bemoans while we all sit in Pierce's bedroom the following morning.

"Sounds like it was a good time. Too bad we missed it." Pierce playfully pokes her in the ribs since she's beside him on the bed. He's propped up against the headboard in clean clothes looking a bit better, but still not completely recovered.

I was the same way after my encounter with a clach, though I tried to push myself into believing the wound was nothing more than a scratch. It took several days to fully heal, just like Rowen said it would.

She swats at him. "What did he say?"

"Apparently, Belial has been roaming the Earth for quite some time," Kagan replies from his perch by the window overlooking the front of the castle, a storm raging outside, intense thunder rocking the structure while fierce lightning glances off the tops of the trees. "Lucifer claims to not know who released him from the pit, but I find that hard to believe. He also stated that it wasn't until the Watchers disappeared that he realized he'd been deceived."

"Bullshit." Doreleska pulls her long, burgundy hair behind her head, tying it into a knot. "Nothing escapes Lucifer's notice. I wouldn't be surprised if he instructed the Watchers to join Belial as a way to monitor what he's reporting to Abaddon."

"Then why are they after Magdalene if she's already assisting him?" Rowen queries, the two of us sitting on the couch facing the bed. My feet are tucked under me while his arm is draped around my shoulders, holding me against his side.

"Pierce, did Belial say anything to you when you found him in Kern?" Kagan stands, placing his hands on his hips.

Staring at me, a pained expression crinkles his square face. "He wanted to know where Magdalene is hiding. He's aware she's being guarded by demons, but not the exact location or which one of Lucifer's devotees have her."

Rowen squeezes me tight. "What does he want?"

Pierce appears sheepish when he responds, "To kill her, but only after absorbing her abilities so he can become the next relic hunter."

"And help Abaddon rule the world," Hollis mutters from the corner by the door, shivering at the notion.

"How did he find you?" I ask while lightning flashes brilliantly outside, the rain pouring down, more than likely soaking Ulrich, who's patrolling the grounds per Kagan's orders.

He shakes his head. "I don't know."

Doreleska places a hand on his arm. "Tell us what happened."

Before speaking, he reaches over to the nightstand and picks up a glass of water, drinking its contents. "When I arrived, the town square had been cordoned off for the authorities to investigate the bombing at the café. The only place I could inquire about the Watchers was at the market. I simply wandered around and listened to those discussing the incident. No one mentioned seeing them the day of the attack, which I found rather odd. I asked a few people if anything unusual had happened before then and they all told me the same thing: nothing. Kern has been quiet ever since the Cleansing ended for them several years ago when the Kulls were defeated and executed."

"But I saw several people get dragged into alleys by them. Vin claimed to have as well," I utter, becoming defensive for no reason.

"Maybe it was all an illusion," Doreleska says, grinning wickedly. "A simple demon trick played on the weak minded."

Rowen becomes incensed and is about to get up when I place a hand on his arm. "What would be the reason?"

"To scare you, of course," she chortles. "Make you run again, like you did when you fled the States. It obviously didn't work, which is why they took drastic measures."

I scowl. "Your theory is flawed, but that really doesn't surprise me considering how narrow-minded and conceited you are."

She snarls at my remark while Rowen chuckles.

"The Watchers knew about the cardinal stone and what it does before I did. How?"

Kagan comes over and sits next to me. "Was anyone with you when you took apart Rochelle's shield and hid your powers?"

"No, I don't think so."

Doreleska glowers at us. "Not even the boyfriend?"

"What's your problem?" I ask, fuming.

She sits up, jabbing a finger in my direction. "I don't like hunters, or anyone who willingly associates with them. Regardless if Lucifer asked for your assistance. The sooner you're gone, the better off we'll all be."

"Can I finish what I was saying?" Pierce interjects, annoyed, his irritation aimed at Doreleska.

She leans back against the headboard, crosses her arms over her chest, and pouts.

"When I left the rynek, Belial's knights were waiting for me in the parking lot. One of them stabbed me with a weapon I haven't seen before, then I was draped in darkness and taken someplace else, but I don't know where. They used cursed chains, not iron, to bind me to anchors embedded into a damp, stone wall. Belial kept asking where Magdalene was and sliced me open a few times with an odd-looking dagger made from bluish-black steel, and I was struggling to heal. Even insisting that I had no idea what he was talking about, he kept attacking."

Hollis moves from her spot and over to the bed, clasping one of the wooden posts that reaches up toward the ceiling, clearly enthralled by the tale. "How did you escape?"

"Avaris. He cut down several of the knights with his kards, then loosened the chains, and I fled."

Sitting up, I place my feet onto the floor, rest my arms on top of my thighs, and furrow my brow. "Why would he do that?"

"To keep you out of Belial's reach," the young man says, emerging from the shadows surrounding the roaring fireplace. His hands are wrapped around the grips for his daggers while they're sheathed at his waist. The jeans and long-sleeved, gray shirt adorning his body look like they've been slept in, his emerald-green eyes appear tired, his short, dark blond hair is badly disheveled, and his round face deeply worn.

Kagan stiffens. "How long have you been eavesdropping?"

"Just a few minutes." He hobbles over to one of the cushioned chairs alongside the couch and sits. "Do you have something hard to drink?"

Animosity consumes the room while we all stare at him until he removes his hands from the knives.

"I'm not here to fight." After taking off the belt containing the sheaths, he sets it on the coffee table.

"Hollis, get him some brandy," Kagan instructs, then stands and takes possession of the worn leather belt, moving it out of Avaris' reach while the young woman saunters over to a glass and gold filigree cart where several filled canisters and cut-crystal tumblers are kept. "Why are you here?"

He waits until the drink is in his hand before responding. "To help." In one gulp, the amber-colored liquid is down his throat.

"We don't need it," Rowen seethes, moving to sit where Kagan just vacated, putting himself between Avaris and me.

He chuckles. "Tell that to the demon hunters when they arrive."

"The bastard sold us out." Doreleska jumps off of the bed, opens the drawer for the nightstand on her side, and removes a sword breaker blade. "Let me gut him."

Kagan holds out his hand, stopping her. "How do you know they're coming?"

Avaris turns his attention solely to me. "The edicts know you're here. They saw what happened in Vineta yesterday since one of them was there to slaughter Daimon for reneging on his deal. His little parade got their attention, and so did you killing him. They caught your scent like I had at Dalma's and followed it." He shakes the empty glass.

Hollis takes it from him, refills the tumbler, and hands it back.

This time, Avaris sips it slowly. "They told me in the hopes that I'll turn you over to them before you become inaccessible, should you die by the wrong hand, and prior to you locating your misplaced abilities."

Reaching behind his back, Rowen removes the kard tucked into his waistband. "Like hell you will."

"Settle your ass down. If I was going to obey them, I would've snatched her already." He finishes the drink. "So here I am, warning you."

Taking the blade from Rowen's grasp, I stand, then go over to Avaris. "They want you to replace me. You're simply here to finish what they started."

Rolling the glass between his thin fingers and leering at me, he says, "Perhaps, at one time, I did relish the idea of becoming the relic hunter. But I don't anymore."

Kagan moves beside me. "What changed your mind?"

"It's more of a who, actually," he replies haughtily. "Dalma did, if you must know. She took exception when she discovered the edicts were planning to send a hunter to murder Festus for aiding Magdalene instead of betraying her like they had hoped. However, the Watchers got to him first."

"Where is she?" I ask, lowering the weapon.

His anxious gaze bores into mine. "She's safe ... for now."

"How long do we have?" the older man inquires, a bit of sweat beading above his brow.

Avaris nods toward the window.

We hurry to it, spotting dark hooded figures emerging from the forest that lines the front of the property.

I inhale sharply, my hand going up to my throat, my fingers tightening around the chain for the pendant. "Those aren't hunters."

"Shit, Watchers. Get Ulrich," Kagan tells Hollis, who swiftly disappears.

"How the hell did they find us?" Rowen laments, then grabs Avaris by his shirt collar, hoists him out of the chair—which causes him to drop the glass onto the thick, woolen rug covering the floor—and slams him into the dresser. "You led them straight here."

The young man appears startled by the violent altercation, his eyes widening in shock. "No, I didn't. They must have followed Pierce."

Kagan points a finger at the pair on the bed. "Doreleska, take him and go to the retreat."

"Let me fight," Pierce insists, grimacing while trying to move.

"I need you to live," she says, quickly pushing him back onto the mattress. "Let me pack a few weapons, then we'll go." She darts from the room.

"Rowen, you and Magdalene head off to another location. It'll be safer if we separate for the moment."

"What are you going to do?" I ask Kagan while handing Rowen his kard.

"Set off a few of the traps we laid out the other day to buy you all some time. Avaris, come with me."

"Why?" He nervously snatches his leather belt away from Kagan and secures it around his waist.

"I'm not going to kill you, if that's what you're worried about. There are weapons down in the basement we can use to defend the grounds, and I need you to help me."

The pair leave, with Rowen and I quickly behind them, but we head to our bedroom instead of the main staircase. While I'm donning my coat, Rowen is rushing around the room shoving clothes into the duffle bag. After putting on my boots, I secure the knapsack around my shoulders—my kard safely tucked into its pocket—as well as the rucksack containing Rochelle's helmet. The door bangs open, surprising us, a Watcher on the other side. Removing the dagger, I throw it at the figure, transforming him to ash. The weapon returns just as another cloaked figure appears.

"We have to go," Rowen says, grabbing me, the duffle bag slung over his arm.

The Watcher raises his hand, which expels an unseen force, sending Rowen flying back into the mirror above the dresser, destroying it. His navy blue sweater is shredded from the shards, but he otherwise appears unharmed, though slow to rise. I'm about to release the dagger when it's pulled from my grasp and into the creature's hand. My eyes widen in horror.

"Give us the stone," it hisses.

Rowen moans, drawing the Watcher's attention, who hurls the kard in the demon's direction. I pitch myself sideways, stretch my arm out as far as I can, snag the grip by the tips of my fingers, and land hard on the floor. The thing charges, but is killed by Rowen's dagger.

He reaches down to help me up with his free hand. "Let's get out of here."

A chill overtakes me, and an ache begins to throb in my stomach, a dull pounding encasing my head. "We can't. He's here."

Rowen grows ashen. "Belial?"

I nod, rubbing my temples in the hopes of preventing the headache from growing.

Screams rise from below, prompting us to venture downstairs, finding Hollis in the hallway nursing a gash in her arm, one of Belial's knights dead inches from her, a bluish-black, steel-bladed knife covered in blood still in his fist. Ulrich, drenched from the heavy rains and holding an iron sword with a leather-bound grip, stands poised to strike again.

"Where's Kagan?" I ask, assisting her to stand as she keeps her wounded arm pressed against her side.

"He's outside with that demon hunter. Doreleska and Pierce have already left," the terrified woman replies.

"Ulrich, take Hollis to the retreat." Rowen is about to snatch my hand when I bolt for the front door. "Magdalene, don't!" he calls after me.

The second I step outside onto the front balcony, which winds down to the drive, I'm soaked to the bone. Avaris is throwing his blades at anything in a black cloak, while Kagan swings two swords at Belial's knights, doing little to no harm. Through the torrent, I spot segments of scorched earth, charred robes lying on the ground void of remains. In the distance, a man with a bald head and hefty muscles lingers, waiting, watching ... smiling. Theron. His black trench coat flaps in the wind as the storm intensifies, exposing his matching pants and shirt underneath.

He's not alone.

226

Belial stands beside him. His gray scales glisten in the rain, his round face and piercing black eyes alight with amusement. The horns on the top of his head twitch as if directing the thunder clashing above.

"We need to go," Rowen insists, snatching my arm, rain dripping down his soaked face.

I shake him loose and run toward the melee while removing Rochelle's helmet, donning it and tossing the rucksack aside. Over a dozen guards rise from the muddy soil, their heavy swords brandished. They wield them against the knights, the sound of clashing metal overpowering the noise from the storm. Through the slit in the visor, I take aim at the Watchers and drive my kard deep into those distracted by the guards, covering myself in ash. After dropping the duffle bag onto the soft ground, Rowen joins the fight, helping Kagan. Avaris is able to defend himself against the Watchers' tricks, but I'm not.

One manages to separate me from the group, flicking his wrist until I'm several feet in the air, my arms splayed outward like they had been after the bombing. I scream from the pain, but the others are too busy fighting for their lives to be of any help.

"Give us the stone," the thing hisses inside of my head, spreading his fingers.

I feel as if I'm being gradually dismembered. The dagger is stripped from my hand, landing somewhere in the distance. The helmet rises, obscuring my view for only a brief moment before coming off, causing the guards to instantly vanish. In a split second the iron is crushed by an invisible might and falls into the mud. Out of the corner of my eye, Belial's knights circle Kagan and Rowen, while the Watchers batter Avaris, who struggles to keep a grip on the slippery ivory handles of his weapons.

"Magdalene, so nice to see you again," Belial croons, shoving the Watcher aside with the brush of his hand, after having left the safety of the forest.

I tumble to the ground, moaning from pain, my arms practically useless.

A firm hand grips the back of my jacket and hoists me onto unsteady feet. Cold steel presses into my neck, threatening to split it open. Theron's rancid breath hits me in the face, while his other arm wraps tightly around my waist, forcing me against his thick, muscular frame.

Belial stands in front of me, grinning in triumph. "You have something I want."

"Leave her alone!" Avaris shouts as several Watchers pin him to the ground, his weapons nowhere in sight.

The Prince of Darkness moves alongside me, allowing the others to view me without obstruction. "With a simple stroke of Theron's clach, I can easily end your pathetic life and become the relic hunter Abaddon is desperate to obtain," the vile creature sneers. "Or, you can watch your lovers die and become my master's prisoner and puppet like he wants." His hot breath seers my eyes as he leans in closer. "Which one will it be, Magdalene?"

"Fight him!" Rowen shouts, then is struck hard across the face by one of the knights. His head violently snaps back, and he drops to the ground, not moving. I can't tell if he's breathing.

Staring past the carnage before me, I spot a yellow, glowing orb dancing in the still air of the forest, slowly moving toward me. Though the storm continues to rage around us, I feel none of its affects, almost like I'm cocooned by my own thoughts, sheltered by the mysterious power now coursing through me. As the orb gets closer, I realize it's a ball of fire, rotating so the flames whip around in a dazzling spiral. Various shades of yellows spin in a hypnotic sway, stealing my attention until that's all I can see. My skin grows hot—though it doesn't hurt—and the world around me turns an eerie orangish-red.

Theron hollers since he can no longer tolerate the heat I'm somehow generating, and let's go. Turning to face the Prince of

Darkness, I snap my fingers, which causes the orb to split into small fragments and spread its glowing talons, grabbing hold of the knights, the Watchers, and even Theron, burning them alive. Their shrieks become deafening and the smell of burning flesh permeates the air, nearly smothering us. Kagan grabs Rowen by the collar of his sweater and hauls him away from the knights as they crumble, while Avaris scrambles to get out of the reach of the Watchers, each desperately lunging at anything to help ease their torment. After a few moments, all that remains is ash. Not even Theron's bones are visible. They're simply powder.

I stare at Belial, who's gray skin has tremendously whitened. Raising my hand to touch his rough, scaly cheek, he suddenly vanishes in a plume of dark smoke. My vision gradually returns to normal and the fires that remain are extinguished by the pouring rain.

"What the hell was that?" Avaris utters, an expression of absolute shock covering his face as he stares at me in bewilderment.

Ignoring him, I rush over to Rowen, who's slowly regaining consciousness. I throw my arms around his neck and bury my head in his shoulder while kneeling beside him.

"I'm all right," he whispers, returning the embrace.

Releasing him, Kagan helps me stand, then I go about searching for my kard, which is buried in the mud. After tucking it into the knapsack, I bend down and retrieve the helmet, annoyed by the damage done to it.

Avaris joins me, dragging his fingers over the coarse surface. "This can be fixed."

"We should leave," Kagan states, sheathing his swords in the dual scabbard strapped to his back. "There's no telling when they'll return." He turns to me, his bearded face scrunched up in confusion. "I thought you were powerless?"

"I am," I reply, snatching the rucksack from the ground, shoving the helmet inside. "I don't know where the fire came from."

"That's most definitely not a hunter quality," Avaris remarks, placing his weapons into his belt after digging them out from under the charred remains for several Watchers. "Maybe it's some sort of demon virus you developed from becoming their lackey."

I raise my fist to punch him in the face when Kagan snatches my arms, pulling them behind my back. "We can't produce such tricks, Avaris, and you know that. Stop goading her into a fight."

Rowen claims his kard from the remnants of Belial's knights, fetches the duffle bag, then relieves me from Kagan. "We'll meet up with you later."

The demon hunter elbows his way between the two of us, placing a steady hand on Rowen's chest. "Don't take her there."

"Why not?" he gripes, stepping back, while I tuck the helmet into the rucksack.

"The edicts know about the castle in De Lamar. I wouldn't be surprised if there are hunters waiting for you. They'll capture her the moment you step foot inside and take her directly to the heavenly council. Lucifer will lose his war without her ... we all will." His face contorts, the truth behind his words too much for him to accept without anguish.

"Then we'll go to the retreat."

"Magdalene won't be able to enter," Kagan states. "There's a hunter protection seal in every room." He kicks the ground in frustration. "Since it appears the Legion has sided with Belial, therefore Abaddon, I'm wondering if we should even go there at all. They can easily get to us because the retreat is known to every demon roaming the lands."

Rowen chuckles. "At least Theron is now down in the pit."

The older man isn't as amused. "But for how long? Without the Watchers monitoring the prisons, Belial will be able to easily move between the two realms and release him without having to resort to promises or allegiances. Magdalene won't be safe until she can reclaim her abilities, which needs to happen sooner rather than later."

"Are you blind?" Rowen raves, motioning at the charred remains. "She did this!"

"You don't know that for sure," Kagan counters, shoving a finger into the young man's face. "Besides, what would've happened if Theron slit her throat before the conflagration? She'd be dead with no chance of resurrection. We can't take any more risks with her life."

Avaris lets out a low groan. "I know a place where we can go."

Rowen glowers at him. "We?"

Noticing the revulsion in the demon's eyes makes Avaris snicker. "You heard right."

"Why should we trust you?" I snap.

He gestures to the small battlefield around us. "You'd all be dead if it wasn't for me. So, you're welcome." Sighing, he places his hands on his hips. "Look, the longer we stand around and debate this, the sooner Belial will be back with more Watchers. Or the hunters might actually show up."

"Fine," I growl, then wrap my arms around Rowen's waist.

"Try to keep up," Avaris chides.

I close my eyes, the rain now feeling like sharp projectiles as we travel through the storm. It doesn't last long, and I sense warmth spread over us. After several long minutes, our feet touch solid ground, and when I open my eyes we're surrounded by lush olive groves, the sun shining in a pristine cerulean sky.

"Where are we?" I ask as Avaris leads us down a row of trees toward a cottage in the distance.

"Saltrani in what was once Italy," he replies, glancing briefly behind him as we follow. "The Mediterranean Sea is twenty miles southwest of here. The closest town is thirty miles that way." He points to what I can only assume is the east given the position of the sun.

When we approach the structure, I notice a deep, circular rut carved into the earth filled with an abundance of white rocks. The single-story house sits in the center plastered in off-white stucco, and red clay tiles form the roof.

"How do you know we're safe here?" Rowen comments, furrowing his brow.

"Because the foundation sits on the center of the angel protection sigil I dug into the earth before building the cottage. The divine edicts don't know about this place, and even if they do, we're well protected. They can't get past the ring of rocks."

Carefully stepping over the rut, we cross several feet of lush, green grass and traverse up a small stoop. Avaris opens a screen door into what appears to be a mudroom complete with a washbasin, water pump, scrub board, and clothesline, which dangles across the wood paneled ceiling. Tucked in the corner is some sort of boiler to heat water. The hostel had one down in the laundry room, but on a much larger scale.

"Leave your things in here since they're covered in mud," he suggests, removing the belt with his weapons, hanging it on one of the pegs embedded into the wall.

After setting down the bags, I take off my boots and notice a door on the right going into a workroom complete with a thick, wooden table, tools, saws, and vices. The doorway in front of us leads into the kitchen where we venture to next. I'm surprised to find a wood burning stove and an old-fashioned icebox, since the rest of the room has a more modern, though still dated, décor. The cabinets and counters are made from walnut, and a steel sink sits under the lone window overlooking the yard. The only illumination in the dank space is from a small light fixture secured to the dull, gray ceiling.

Avaris smiles. "It's not much, but it's home."

Next, we enter a front room adorned in ivy-covered wallpaper where a hand-carved table with four seats is off to the side. Two couches upholstered in dark red tartan with matching chairs are the focal point of the room, a walnut coffee table in the center. Along the far wall is an array of floor-to-ceiling built-ins filled with various knickknacks and weathered volumes of differing thickness. Avaris shows us the single bedroom, though only he steps inside. Sensing the devil's barriers, I hold Rowen away from the threshold. When he questions my actions, I point to the ceiling around the queen-sized bed blanketed in a handmade quilt, much like the ones I saw being sold at the rynek. A large pentagram with runes between each of the star's five points encompasses the entire area.

"Magdalene, you'll stay in here."

I glare at Avaris. "Thanks, but I'll sleep on the couch."

He bristles at the remark. "Fine, whatever. The bathroom is over there." He points to the door on our left in the front room. "The boiler doesn't hold a lot of hot water, so you're going to want to bathe quickly. You can also heat up a bucket on the stove in the kitchen if the supply runs out. There are logs along the side of the house and an area a few yards from here where more can be cut." He gestures toward me. "You take the bathroom. Rowen and I will get cleaned up in the mudroom."

"I'll bring you something to wear." Rowen kisses me wistfully on the lips, then retreats while Avaris remains a few seconds longer than necessary, looking upset, before joining him.

Closing the bathroom door, I flip on the light switch, igniting the sconces above the vanity, illuminating a rustic room adorned with dormant candles and glass jars filled with various oils and lotions. I'm thrilled to see a functioning toilet, which I use before rummaging for a towel and bar of soap since there isn't one already in use. A claw footed bathtub rests against the back wall, so I turn on the water and let it run cold for a few seconds. It's not overly brutal, but I do turn it a bit warmer, drop my mud-ladened clothes onto the floor, and step under the spigot that rises from a metal pipe out of the faucet for the tub, then close the cloth curtain encircling the bath. It takes several passes with the soap, both over my skin and through my hair, to get rid of the filth. Just as I turn off the water, the door for the bathroom opens and closes. Parting the curtain barely an inch, I spot Rowen standing there holding something for me to wear. He's freshly scrubbed and donning jeans and a tight, black shirt. I can't help but gawk.

"Avaris went to town to stock up on a few supplies," he says, blushing from my leer.

Setting down the soap on the wide lip of the tub, I pick up the towel from the floor, dry off, then wrap it around my body before opening the curtain the remainder of the way, and step out. "I don't want to be here longer than absolutely necessary. Perhaps just a day or two."

"Good, because I don't relish the idea of being confined with a demon hunter." Rowen hands me the clothes but doesn't leave. Instead, he smiles wickedly. "Do you think he'll be gone long?"

I laugh. "You're incorrigible." After dressing in the black leggings and heather gray sweatshirt he packed for me, I drape the wet towel over the rack by the sink.

Wrapping his arms around my waist, he leans his forehead against mine. "That's because I love you so much." He kisses me, then lifts the pendant out from under my top and places it in his palm, leaving the chain around my neck. "So much trouble for such a little thing."

Staring at it in confusion, I mutter, "How could any of them have known about it?"

Placing a hand under my chin, he lifts my gaze to meet his. "Do you remember everything from the moment you disassembled Rochelle's shield?"

"Just a few flashes, but nothing concrete."

He nudges me to follow him out into the front room, then we sit beside each other at the table on the far side by the kitchen.

Taking my hand, he lovingly strokes the back of it, waiting patiently for me to continue.

Before I can utter any words, I start to tremble and sweat, terrified of what might be lurking underneath these brief recollections. Swallowing hard, I do my best to keep my voice steady. "It was the middle of the night. I think a day or two before Avaris and the hunters arrived at the castle in De Lamar. You were asleep in our bedroom, and I was alone in the lower level."

Brushing the back of his hand across my tender cheek, he asks, "Which room?"

I scrunch up my face in thought. "The wine cellar, I think, but can't recall anything after that. Including what I transformed the shield into. It's almost like my memories have been segregated, only to trigger at certain moments and not all at once. I wonder if visiting the castle might help."

He leans into me. "Maybe we can sneak out one night and go there while Avaris is either sleeping, or is just unconscious from having his head bashed in."

Kissing him in agreement, I can't help but dwell on Belial's remark about my lovers. Pulling away, my gaze falls to the table, and I study the grain of the wood as a way to sort out my thoughts, navigating the various veins as if they were rivers. Besides referring to Rowen, was he also indicating Avaris? It had to have been an assumption on the demon's part, but what if it wasn't?

"Hey, are you all right?" Rowen asks, placing his hand on my thigh.

Looking up into his enchanting hazel eyes, I force a smile. "Yes, I'm fine."

He narrows his gaze. "Magdalene, I know something is bothering you. Please tell me."

Since I'm not sure if he caught Belial's comment, I decide to mention something else that's also troubling me. "How was that Watcher able to take possession of my kard?"

"They're technically not demons, even though they can die like us, which explains why handling it didn't hurt him." Rowen shrugs. "It never really occurred to me what, or who, they actually are, and I'm not sure who would know the answer to that."

I scowl in frustration.

Draping an arm across my back, he asks, "Did you still want to visit Ambrose Church?"

"Yes, but after the helmet is repaired."

He stands and takes my hand. "Why don't we clean our weapons?"

Entering the mudroom, we claim the kards, then clean them in the wash basin. I also take the time to empty the knapsack and scrub the cotton fibers as best I can, while Rowen does the same with the duffle bag, after setting our things down onto one of the cushioned chairs in the front room. The rucksack is easier since it's composed of leather, so I simply wipe off the mud with a clean cloth. After hanging up the damp sacks along the clothesline, we take our mud-laden clothes and do the same, then retreat to the kitchen just as Avaris returns with a box containing a freshly roasted chicken, potatoes, green beans, and a bag of freshly baked rolls. He places everything on the table while Rowen fetches us drinks, then we each take a seat and eat while the food is still hot.

With our bellies full, I put away the leftovers while Avaris takes possession of the helmet and Rowen decides to make a quick trip to the retreat to check on the others. I follow Avaris into the workroom where he places the helmet into one of the vices welded to the table, picks up a small ball peen hammer, and works on removing the dents from the inside.

"Thank you for warning us," I say, hovering several feet anxiously behind him, not relishing the idea of being left alone with him.

He doesn't bother to look at me when responding. "You're welcome." His voice is flat and emotionless.

I move to stand in front of him, clutching my hands behind my back. "How long have you had this place?"

He keeps his focus on the helmet, his nimble hands coaxing the iron back into shape. "For a while."

His abrupt answers grate on my nerves. "Has anyone else ever lived with you?"

Pausing, he looks up, a cross expression on his face, and his emerald-green eyes harden. "No."

"Not even a girlfriend?"

"They're not worth my time." There's an underlying hint of resentment and rage as he returns to hammering. I'm about to leave when he gingerly touches my arm. "Why are you with Rowen?"

I've been preparing for someone to ask me that question. I just didn't want it to be Avaris, but I'm not sure why. Biting my lip, I don't answer right away, which only causes the animosity between us to build. "Because I love him."

He scowls, clearly displeased by the response. "Is that what he told you, or do you actually remember?" Avaris sounds both angry, bitter, and jealous.

Crossing my arms over my chest, I reply, "I recall how we met, all the way up to being dragged back to the heavenly council by your friends."

His face turns cold, irritated. "Nothing before then?"

Perhaps Belial was correct. My stomach falls at the notion of being with someone like Avaris. I do what I can to prevent the bile swimming up my throat from coming out. "My memories are returning sporadically, like when I touch an object or a person. But I doubt they'll be fully restored until I reclaim my powers."

"Do you know where they are?" he asks, his tone softening a bit.

I shake my head.

"Just make sure it's a true memory of Rowen, and not a demon trick." Stepping around the vice, Avaris reaches for the compass rose, which I forgot to tuck under the sweatshirt. "Where did you get this?" He caresses the warped metal, his eyes unwavering from mine.

I find myself unable to break away, a twinge of regret pinging deep in my core. "It belonged to Rochelle of Travion. Dalma gave it to me."

He stares at it as if mesmerized. "Is this what Belial is looking for?"

"I don't know," I lie. Still not trusting Avaris, I hold off on revealing too much.

"Why did Dalma give it to you?" He releases the chain, allowing the pendant to swing back against my chest, his now tender gaze enveloping me.

"It was payment for helping her with a few things." I shove the compass rose under my top. "How come you're limping?"

He hobbles back behind the vice. "I was injured fighting to free Pierce. It's not a big deal. I'll heal."

"Hey," Rowen says, standing in the doorway, briefly glaring at Avaris before focusing his attention on me. "Kagan is here, and he wants to talk to you."

"Why didn't you just invite all of them to my home?" Avaris fumes, setting down the hammer and rolling his eyes.

The demon chortles. "Maybe next time I will."

Following Rowen into the front room, I find Kagan sitting at the table covered in dried mud and looking worn. The three of us join him, though by the expression on Rowen's face, Avaris wasn't technically invited to the gathering.

"My house," he says, seething, reading the animosity in the demon's eyes.

The older man stares uneasily at me, his body quivering ever so slightly, but I'm not sure why. "What, exactly, is in that journal you created?"

Holding his serious gaze, I reply, "I don't know. Like I said before, it was in my possession for just a few minutes."

"What journal?" Avaris asks, leaning forward in his seat, resting his arms on the table.

"But you saw something," Kagan continues, ignoring the hunter, as well as my question. "You were able to translate a bit of the first page."

Frowning, I cross my arms over my chest, my legs at the knee, and sit back in the chair. "Hollis told you."

"Does it matter?" Rowen comments, mimicking Avaris' posture.

The older man glances between me and the younger demon. "If the journal reveals anything about sacred relics, regardless of which side they belong to, it might be a roadmap to finding them." He focuses his attention solely on me. "You thought the hunters were coming to collect you that night at the castle in De Lamar, which is why you hid your powers beforehand. It's probably also the same reason you created the book."

Fury roils under my skin, and my stare hardens. "What are you getting at?"

"Belial can read hynafol glyphs just like Abaddon and Lucifer. Since the Watchers are obviously working for him and they have the journal, it might lead him to relics that can be used to aid his master in rising to the throne and bringing about the downfall of Lucifer. There's a couple of items Ulrich discovered in his readings back at Burmstone that can change the tide of this encroaching war, but that depends upon who finds them first." He rubs his tired eyes, bits of dirt flaking onto the tabletop. "What did you translate?"

Standing, I head over to the chair where Rowen placed our belongings, grab the folded piece of paper that had been in the knapsack, and hand it to Kagan before retaking my seat.

Rowen tries to peer over the man's shoulder. "What does it say?"

Since it's written in glyphs, he hands the note back to me. I clear my throat before reading it. "Sunrises cast hidden shadows, revealing dreams not yet fulfilled."

Avaris snorts. "That's cryptic."

I glower at him. "It was meant to be."

"Could the entire book be written in this manner?" Kagan points to the paper.

"Perhaps, but I don't know for certain."

He lets out a tentative sigh. "Let's hope it's enough to confuse Belial."

Rowen fidgets in his chair. "What relics did Ulrich find?"

The older man hesitates in answering, letting several tense seconds pass. "The first thing he discovered is the Calsaign shroud, which allows its wearer to remain hidden from those around him, except the ones he wishes to interact with. The other is Solomon's ring. It has the power to control demons, regardless of allegiance."

A brief hint of recognition surfaces, but I can't tell which item it's for.

"Did the books reference their last known locations? Or at least hint at it?" Rowen asks after clearing his throat.

Folding his hands on top of the table, Kagan replies, "The shroud is purportedly buried under the ruins of Lingley Manor somewhere in the British Isles. Of course, that place has been deemed simply mythological since it stems from around the time of King Arthur and his rule over Camelot. The location of Solomon's ring isn't referenced anywhere, simply that it exists. My concern is, could these be mentioned in your journal?"

I shrug, not knowing what else to say or do.

He lets out a long, exasperated sigh.

Avaris stares at Kagan. "If Magdalene does find these artifacts, what are you going to do with them? Use them for yourself?"

The older man clenches his jaw and narrows his eyes. "How else are we going to stop Abaddon?"

"Thereby giving Lucifer unlimited power to reign over all." Avaris balls his hands into fists. "His Legion are already controlling parts of the world, slaughtering demon hunters whenever possible. He'll be unstoppable if she finds those items for you." He gestures angrily at me.

Kagan leans far forward, resting his solid arms on the table. "That's if you're assuming we'd tell him they exist in the first place."

Avaris appears taken aback by the comment.

"This is why Magdalene is here. To fight for us using the relics, not for Lucifer or any other demon lord, or the Legion, to overtake the world." Kagan turns his attention to me. "Do either the shroud or ring sound familiar?"

Biting the inside of my cheek, I lie, but only partially. "No. I've never heard of them."

The inkling of recognition returns, solidifying ever so briefly on the shroud, which I reclaimed from a man intent on using it to overthrow King James VI. The memory is fleeting and gone as quickly as it started.

"What about the ball of fire at the battle today? If it wasn't Magdalene, then I'd like to know where it came from and how it was able to destroy the others effortlessly," Rowen comments.

Kagan furrows his brow. "So do I. It had a supernatural appearance to it. Something I've never seen before." He hesitantly glances at me, then abruptly changes the subject. "Do you still intend on visiting Ambrose Church?"

I have to swallow the lump building in my throat before answering. "Yes. The compass rose is pointing me there."

Pushing back his chair, Kagan stands. "Let me know when and I'll accompany you."

"Before you go," I say, interrupting his departure, "do you know who the Watchers actually are, besides guards of the underworld?"

The older man stares at Avaris before answering, "Rumor has it that they're condemned demon hunters. Betrayed by the divine edicts and forced into unholy servitude for all eternity, but I'm sure he can tell you for certain." Kagan nods at Avaris, then disappears in a swirl of dark smoke.

The young man grumbles and leaves without saying a word, heading back to the workroom while Rowen and I remain at the table.

"You're holding something back," he says, stroking my arm.

My gaze follows Avaris, though he's no longer in sight. "It's nothing, really. Just thinking things through."

After a few seconds, I get up and start rummaging for blankets and pillows the two of us can use when we finally decide to go to sleep. Rowen moves the coffee table to the other side of the room, then creates our makeshift bed out of the couch cushions. When the night starts to wind down, I step into the bathroom to use the facilities and change, reemerging to raised voices.

"Just tell me where it is," Rowen shouts, standing in the doorway to the mudroom, leaning against the frame wearing only sweatpants.

"Why does it matter?" Avaris counters. "I'm not going to use it."

"What are you two arguing about?" I utter, relaxing against the wall by the door across from Rowen.

Avaris is sitting on a small stool, cleaning his kards. "Your boyfriend is paranoid. Thinks I might stab him when he's not looking." He gives a mischievous expression. "Rowen is worried that I'll use the clach in my possession, but not these." He holds up one of the hunter blades, water dripping from its surface and onto the floor.

"It's not me I'm concerned about," Rowen snaps.

Avaris scowls, fury holding firm in his eyes. "If I wanted to hurt Magdalene, I would've done it already." He reaches for a towel and then dries off the weapons. "Fuck, man. I didn't bring either of you here to be killed. What would be the point with Belial running around out there searching for artifacts that can bring about the end of the world? That takes precedent over any issues that I might have with the two of you."

Rowen stoops down and jabs a finger close to Avaris' chest. "Because I don't trust you."

"All the more reason for me not to tell you where the weapon is hidden." He sheathes the kards back into their holster—which has also been cleaned—and stands. "Now if you don't mind, I'd like to get some sleep." Swinging the belt over his shoulder, he pushes past the two of us and slams the door leading into his bedroom.

Rowen pulls me into his arms, and I wrap mine around his waist, placing my cheek against his chest, listening to the rhythmic beating of his heart. "I wish there was someplace else we could stay."

He kisses the top of my head. "Me too. The retreat is the safest spot, but it's heavily protected against hunters."

"Maybe there's some sort of rune or sigil that'll allow me entry."

"I'll ask Ulrich or Kagan about it tomorrow. Why don't we get some rest?"

Smiling, I take his hand, and he escorts me into the front room. Once the lights have all been turned off, we nestle into each other under the blankets, wishing we were alone.

Chapter Fifteen

*M*y palm grazes the tops of tall, spindly grass after I emerge from a dense forest and into an expansive field. Thousands of stars twinkle overhead, and the moon hangs high above the sea off to my right, waves lapping serenely against the hidden shores. Round huts with thatched roofs lay spread out amongst the weathering land, each grouping with a small bonfire to fend off the cold that I can't seem to feel. Villagers bundled in heavy pelts mingle about, talking and laughing while children play with handcrafted toys before bedtime. Their hot breath breaks the chill with a puff of white.

Mine doesn't.

Everyone appears happy and joyful, breaking my heart since I know instantly I'm in Cresidio, and this is thankfully just a dream.

No one seems to take notice as I wander down the many winding paths, making my way toward the temple where I'm hoping to find my father. Candlelight glows from the open doorway, so I step inside and am greeted by the familiar fall scents of spice and cinnamon wafting up from an offering plate on the altar. Lanterns adorning the walls light in a welcoming affection. The building is empty, but I continue my approach, feeling drawn to the shiny, black rock resting beside the metal plate. Picking up the obsidian stone, I caress the smooth surface, discovering it warm and comforting. It reminds me of the one I had as a child, and find myself praying to see my parents again, even if it isn't real.

"Taking a stroll down memory lane?" someone taunts behind me.

Turning around, I spot Belial standing between the last row of benches, the horns on his head shuddering ever so slightly. He's wearing a simple, dark gray robe, which conceals his feet and any weapons he might be carrying.

He holds up his hands as if in surrender. "Don't worry, I'm not here to hurt you, just to talk. I thought a familiar setting would lessen the hostility between us."

"How are you doing this?" I ask fearfully.

"I have tricks up my sleeve the same as you." He winks. "Conjuring the fire of Olwen was tremendously impressive. It seems to naturally obey you. Almost as if the sun goddess herself were flowing through your veins. Of course, I took offense at you trying to burn me like you did the others."

Attempting to bring forth the ball of flame like before to extinguish the monster in front of me leaves me exhausted and strained, so I stop. "Where's Theron?"

"He's running around here somewhere." Belial gestures haphazardly. "He was most upset to have been burned alive, so don't be surprised if the next time you two meet he severs your head clean off your body."

"What do you want?" I snarl.

Stepping closer, he lowers his arms. "You're already well aware what I'm looking for, and I know for a fact that you have it." With a razor-sharp fingernail, he points at my chest.

Glancing down, I notice the pendant is dangling exposed outside of the long-sleeved, red flannel shirt I wore to bed.

His smile is cruel and calculating. "And, I know what it does and where it leads."

The obsidian stone still in my hand, I clasp it tightly as if it were a lifeline. "How is that even possible?"

He chuckles. "I'm privileged with information, my dear child. The knowledge I've acquired over my extensive existence would astound you. I've roamed these lands far longer than either of my masters, garnering wisdom most mortals crave to obtain." His grin is snakelike. "In regard to the compass rose, a little birdie told me all about it. What a fascinating story. You having been the great Rochelle of Travion, who single-handedly defeated the French army, thereby saving her tiny, pathetic village. Genius to incorporate your previous lives with that of the relic hunter. I'm sure it's more than artifacts that you've intertwined yourself with."

Lifting his hand, he places a finger against his parched lips. "Want to know a secret? You've barely tapped the full extent of your abilities. Some are starting to show, but not the kind several of your emissaries are vying to obtain by any means necessary." His black eyes sparkle in the candlelight, the flickering flames reflecting deeply in his irises. "Desperate as you are to find your gifts, they'll come when the timing is right. There's still much for you to discover before the truth is revealed and your trial begins."

"If you already have the means to bring forth Abaddon, then why come after me?"

His grin widens as he once again approaches. "Because I don't. At least, not yet." He stops inches from me. "Also, I need you to reclaim your abilities in order to take them. They can't simply be stolen, like many other things in this world. Someone has to willingly give them to me, just like the divine edicts bestowed them onto you."

"No one is taking anything away from me, and there's no way in hell I'd voluntarily give them to you," I say, seething. "You have no followers here."

The laugh that escapes his mouth curdles my blood. "Such lies you tell yourself, Magdalene. How do you think I was freed from the pit in the first place all those many years ago? I know Lucifer told you about it. Wouldn't you like to know who it was that did the mischievous deed?"

I do but am fearful of the answer.

"Didn't think so." He turns as if to leave.

"You have something of mine."

Drumming his fingers together, he returns to the altar. "I must say, you were very clever in disguising the location for every relic known to exist by using those glyphs in such an obscure and befuddling fashion. At least, *that's what I'm assuming the journal is meant to decree, besides outlining the many lives that you've lived outside of the relic hunter persona. The phrases make absolutely no sense to me, so I'm at an utter loss. Though, I am curious to know who you were unable to stop, per the first line at the beginning of the journal. Was it the boyfriend, or someone more ruthless and cunninger?"*

I remain silent.

"Most intriguing." He chuckles. "Are you willing to trade for its return?"

Out of curiosity, I ask, "What did you have in mind?"

The lines around his eyes crinkle. "Let me think about it." He snaps his fingers.

I wake up lying on the make-shift bed constructed from blankets and couch cushions, which are now on the floor where the coffee table had been. Rowen is curled up alongside me, his arm draped over my waist as he softly snores. I'm surprised to find him asleep since demons don't require a lot of rest, but it's comforting to have him there. The door to Avaris' room is closed and the rest of the house is dark. I'm deeply troubled by the encounter with Belial. He's convinced I conjured the ball of fire, but I didn't. At least, I don't think I did. Then again, Daimon claimed I placed the two of us into a void when I confronted him in the village square. Both abilities hunters aren't capable of possessing. So, where did they come from?

The Scepter of Ignis produced the fire needed for Olwen's temple. I destroyed the relic, engulfing everyone and everything in flames. Could I have absorbed the gem's power during that firestorm? And according to Kagan, the Calsaign shroud hid its wearer from all except with whom they're specifically interacting. Did I destroy it as well? Is that how I created the void when we were in Vineta?

Not wanting to disturb Rowen, I carefully slide out from under his arm, toss off the heavy, woolen blanket, get up, and wander into the workroom, feeling my way around in the dark with only the faintest light from the moon's rays filtering in through the discolored windows to guide me. The helmet is still secured in the vice, the iron cool to the touch, the surface rough and still badly uneven. I doubt it will ever return to its once pristine condition, but that might not be such a horrible thing. No one will be able to wear it, allowing Rochelle's guards to stay slumbering for eternity. Never did I imagine that a being could crush iron, much less a Watcher, and without touching it. What other powers could they have?

What about me?

Exiting out the back door into the cold night, I don't wander far since I want to remain inside of the protection of the angel sigil, but I need to try and conjure the ball of fire to see if Belial is correct. I don't want to do it inside, should I lose control and burn down the cottage.

Holding my hand palm up, I block out my surroundings and try to build a flame from my flesh. A tiny ember rises to the surface, then levitates a few meters above my skin. It swirls into a slow, hypnotic sphere while growing in size. The yellows and oranges lick at the air, thirsting for a drink, but I prevent it from becoming too big, and can't help but stare at the glow, awestruck by the capability I seem to possess. Loosening my grip on the power, it eventually vanishes, leaving a warmth inside of myself that the cold can't touch. Blinking a few times so my eyes adjust to the encroaching darkness, I catch Avaris standing in front of me, a perplexed expression on his face.

"How long have you been there?" I ask, surprised by his sudden appearance.

"A few minutes. I tried getting your attention, but apparently you failed to notice." He cocks his head to the side, furrowing his brow. "Why are you out here?"

Studying him carefully, I reply, "I needed some fresh air since I was having trouble sleeping. What about you?"

"I heard the door close and came to investigate." In his hand, which hangs down by his side, I notice a long, serrated dagger made from bluish-black steel ... a clach. Probably the same one he used on Rowen when the hunters came to steal me away from him.

"What's that?" I ask, pointing to the weapon, pretending not to know.

He doesn't even bother to glance at it, his cautious gaze piercing me. "Just something I keep on hand."

Scowling, I narrow my hardened stare. "The weapon Rowen was looking for earlier. The one you used on him in De Lamar."

Avaris frowns, his fingers tightening around the grip. "He told you."

"Of course he did," I scoff. "You were already going to kill him with the kards, so why use that?"

Pride and arrogance flash in his eyes. "Because the heavenly council instructed me to, and I was more than willing to oblige them."

"For what purpose?" My voice rises out of anger.

He grins, taking a step closer to me. "To scar him. Mark him for the monster that he is."

The urge to punch Avaris is strong, but I don't. "You're an asshole."

I'm heading back to the house when he forcefully grabs my arm, spinning me around. "Why did you lie to Kagan?"

I yank out of his grasp. "I didn't."

He smirks. "Yes, you did. I saw the look on your face when he mentioned the shroud. It was one of absolute fright."

"You're imagining things."

I have the door into the mudroom partially open when Avaris says, "I was with you when the cloak was destroyed."

Slowly closing it, I turn back to face him while stepping down off of the stoop. "That's not possible."

He approaches carefully, sensing my agitation. "The edicts sent me and another hunter to London so we could infiltrate a demon den. It was during our raid on their camp when we heard that two of them had been dispatched after you to secure the shroud."

The memory that had been merely fleeting returns with such force that it momentarily blinds me, searing my head in unimaginable pain, forcing me to stumble back onto the ground. Avaris kneels in front of me, cupping my face in his hands, his lips moving without any sound coming out, appearing genuinely concerned. All I can do is close my eyes and relive that awful night.

It had taken me weeks to hunt the thief, disparaging myself in one of the brothels that fill London's seedier side along the Thames for information as to the man's whereabouts—slitting a few throats along the way, stealing their coins to make it look like a robbery for when the bodies were discovered. The lengths I'll go to for a stupid relic is beyond fathomable, but if it allows me to avoid being sent to the cells of Malum, it's an unfortunate necessity. Nobody escapes those cages alive.

Clutching the linen garment with its dark embroidery under my arm, I slip out of the second story window of a private dwelling. The man had intended on using the Calsaign shroud to commit treason. My orders are to return to Lingley Manor and hide it in a new chamber, one buried deep in the cellar of the large estate, and new protections applied, hopefully for it to never be found again. Using the drainpipe along the side of the building, I shimmy down it, careful not to make too much noise and wake the traitor up. My boots scuff the pavement when I land, but merely the owls seem to notice. The cold wind howls, whipping dead leaves into the air, triggering my black cloak to snap at my back while I rush down the cobblestone-filled street. *Bare branches of the dormant trees clack together when I reach the outskirts of the sleeping hamlet, the only illumination being the lighted lampposts, their candles burning behind closed, frosted glass orbs. I don't reduce my stride until I'm a good distance away, fearful I might get caught, but not by the thief I've stolen the garment from.*

Ever since arriving, after having followed the man's trail from Pickling where he stole the shroud from another robber, it feels like I'm being watched. Dark, haunting eyes I can't see, yet know are there.

This isn't the first time I've sensed such an intrusion. The heavenly council warned me that I might be targeted by others—demons mostly—which is why I carry two kards around my waist at all times. Since my transformation into becoming the relic hunter all those years ago, this is the eighth artifact I've reclaimed from someone who wishes to do the world harm by controlling the mystical powers embedded within these sacred objects. It makes no sense to simply hide the relics again only for them to be found later by another raider.

It's a never-ending cycle, and one that should be broken. Nothing good could ever come from having such commanding items at the world's disposal.

Especially this one. The ability to shield oneself from their enemies, cut down their foes without being noticed, or overthrow a monarchy with the flick of a blade is far too dangerous ... too tempting. Such items should be destroyed, razed from the earth of which they were forged. Too bad they weren't sacrificed like those of the gods and goddesses who created them. The world would be a much better place.

Stopping to catch my breath, I lean my back against a thick tree trunk, a stitch forming in my side. I can easily transport away from here, but I want to know who's trailing me and I can't do that if I disappear into a swirl of white smoke. Bending down, I use the low-lying brush as cover and peer back the way I came. A twig snaps off to my left, so I unsheathe the daggers after securing the shroud around my neck, using its nickel-plated clasp to hold it in place.

"I think she went this way," someone utters, the deep voice a bit muffled.

"Then flush her out," another retorts, this one female. "We need that cloak."

"Don't tell me what to do."

Footsteps gingerly approach my position, so I slip on the hood for the shroud, knowing it'll conceal me. Out of the corner of my eye I catch a sliver of movement. A tall figure clad in worn leathers steps into the slight shaft of light cascading through the canopy from the full moon overhead. His long, gray hair is tied into a plait at the base of his neck, the wrinkles on his face are deep, and he walks with a profound limp. He isn't carrying a weapon, but that doesn't mean he's unarmed. I hold my breath the closer he gets, praying the enchantment is working. From out of the darkness a gold blade with an ivory handle sails into his chest, then as it retreats the man disintegrates into dust.

"I've got the other one," a young woman calls somewhere behind me. "Check if there are any more."

Even though these two new companions appear to be hunters—because of the weapons they carry—I can't allow them to see me. I wait patiently for them to leave, but the one who killed the male demon doesn't move from his hiding spot. The air is unsettlingly still where it wasn't a moment ago. Lowering the hood, I carefully stand, scanning the woods for the slightest movement. An arm wraps around my throat, squeezing ever so gently while something sharp presses into my back.

"Causing trouble as always. You still have a lot to learn, relic hunter," my captor says, his new world accent odd to my ears.

"So do you," I reply, using the same tone since I can mimic many.

Blinding light engulfs us, flames erupting between our bodies, setting the shroud on fire, which wasn't my intention. The young man hollers, staggering backwards to avoid the blaze. I'm not injured as the garment continues to burn, causing my own clothing to become engulfed in flame, all while a profound sense of isolation envelopes me. In a matter of seconds, I see and hear nothing at all.

My heart races as reality comes back into focus, a lump caught in my throat, and sweat drenching my back.

Avaris continues to stare at me, his hands fidgeting to touch me, worry deep-seated in his eyes. "Are you all right?"

Wrapping my arms around myself, I reply, "I saw it. The night I reclaimed the shroud, the confrontation in the woods, and the garment's destruction." I glower at him, furious with how he treated me in the memory. "Why did you put an arm around my throat and press a knife into my back?"

His eyes widen as he sits back on his heels, stunned. "I didn't."

Rage courses through me at his lie. "The other hunter with you was a woman, right?"

"Yes, so?" he answers, ill-at-ease.

"She went to check for other demons while I waited for you to leave, but you didn't When I removed the hood for the shroud, you placed me into a chokehold and shoved the tip of the kard into my back. You were the only person there. Who else could it have been?"

Standing, he runs his fingers through his dark blond hair, disquiet filling his troubled gaze. "Maybe you're remembering an encounter with someone else."

I shake my head. "I'm not. It was you." Quaking from anger, I wring my hands together to keep from lashing out, though I don't know why I'm holding back. "You said I still had a lot to learn. The shroud burned while I was trying to get away from you. It was destroyed unintentionally."

Bending over, he instinctively pulls my hands apart, clasps and squeezes them with care. "No, you did it on purpose because you didn't see the point of hiding the garment simply for it to be found later by another graverobber. I agreed with your decision and didn't tell the edicts about it."

Shoving him away, I rise to my feet and utter, "I don't believe you."

"Magdalene, it's the truth. I would never do anything to hurt you." Reclaiming my hands, his fingers briefly intertwine with mine while a hint of sadness touches the corners of his emerald-green eyes, making me tremendously uncomfortable. "I'm not the enemy, but your friend. Please believe me." He reaches up to stroke my cheek, keeping his other hand clasped in mine, when I back away, but not completely out of his grasp.

"I need to get some sleep," I say, my voice cracking.

He releases me and we both enter the house. Avaris watches me for a few seconds, then closes the door to his bedroom while I lie down beside Rowen, an unsettling feeling washing over me.

It's now obvious where my extra abilities are coming from, which makes me wonder how many relics I've destroyed over the years and what underlying powers still lay dormant. It's no surprise the heavenly council want me dead, or at least under better control. I can easily destroy them with a simple snap of my fingers if I should wish to do so.

Another thought crosses my mind regarding Avaris. He was adamant that the vision I recalled isn't accurate, but I don't see how that's possible. Memories can't be altered. However, what bothers me most is the fact that I don't remember him at all, even though it seems like I should. Hunters know each other, and I'm sure if I run into another one I'd recognize them ... or would eventually, given the right circumstances. So why don't I remember Avaris? I can't even be certain it was him I saw in the woods when I reclaimed the shroud. I simply assumed it given the situation, and him confirming he was there.

Shaking my head, I try to clear it and get some much-needed rest, but my thoughts keep dwelling on Avaris.

Chapter Sixteen

The sun has barely broken the horizon when Rowen rouses me, his lips grazing mine. "How did you sleep?" he asks, now nuzzling my neck, his hand caressing my stomach underneath the shirt, dangerously close to the waistband for my lounge pants. One slip and we won't be able to stop ourselves.

"Horribly." I bury myself into his chest, allowing his fingers to continue grazing my hot skin. "Belial got into my head."

Rowen lifts my face to meet his widening hazel eyes. "He manipulated your dream?"

"He claimed to merely want to talk, so he took me to Cresidio at a time when it was flourishing." I go on to explain what transpired, leaving out the rest of the night, including the memory about the shroud. "I didn't know demons had that capability."

"They don't ... at least not that I'm aware of. I'm glad the journal is no use to him, but let's keep that bit of information to ourselves for the time being."

I nod in agreement.

Kissing me tenderly, he moves on top of me, pushing our entwined hands above my head. "I think we should visit Travion today. Do it early before Avaris wakes."

"Or, we can keep doing this."

He smiles. "I love how your mind works." Then he parts my lips with his tongue, pressing his firm body harder into mine.

At the moment, I'd give anything for Avaris to disappear, but I worry his door will creak open any second. Glancing briefly at it, I notice it's still closed.

"No peeking," Rowen teases, having caught me.

I nip at his nose. "We should get going. I'll dress while you fetch Kagan."

Groaning at having his fun interrupted, Rowen rushes to change out of his sweatpants and into jeans, in addition to a sienna-tinted turtleneck. After his boots are on, he makes sure to grab his kard from the mudroom before leaving. I take the black leggings I wore yesterday, along with a dark cyan Henley shirt, and slip into the bathroom where I use the facilities and swap out my clothes. Returning to the front room, I toss the ones I wore to bed onto the chair with the rest of our belongings, and work on combing the knots out of my hair, pulling it back into a ponytail.

"Going somewhere?" Avaris asks, lingering in his now open doorway, legs crossed at the ankle, arms hugging his brawny chest.

I roll my eyes at him being awake. "We're leaving for Travion once Rowen returns with Kagan."

"It's not smart to go there, but when have you ever taken my advice?" He saunters into the front room. "Just don't do anything stupid."

"Is the helmet fixed?" I ask, ignoring the condescension in his tone.

He exits, reappearing a few minutes later with the helmet tucked inside of the rucksack.

Taking the bag from him, I strap it across my shoulders, not bothering with my outer coat since it's still wet from being washed yesterday.

"You're going to need this as well." He holds out my kard, which is lying flat in his palm.

I hesitate in reaching for it, unsure of what type of reaction I might get if I graze his skin, though nothing happened last night when we touched. Still, I wonder if my memories of him will ever be restored ... if they do in fact exist. Time passes slowly before I finally reclaim the weapon, putting it into the rucksack, and inwardly smiling.

Avaris seems disappointed, but tries to cover it up with a sheepish grin. "Be careful." He heads back into his room and closes the door.

It's not long until Rowen and Kagan return, the latter with his dual scabbard strapped to his back. Gripping Rowen's waist, I close my eyes and feel the wind whipping around us, the warm air replaced by cold. For a brief instant, I open my eyes, noticing nothing but black smoke swirling around us, obstructing much of the scenery below. Occasionally, I catch glimpses of buildings and waterways miles beneath us. The speed at which they pass is almost disorienting. Firming up my hold on Rowen, I close my eyes to keep the nauseating sensation at bay. Perhaps this will eventually get easier once I'm able to transport myself.

A few minutes later, we arrive in what remains of the village of Travion. It's a far cry from how I remember it. Gone are the quaint cottages, rustic adornments, and the people. The lane we're on is flanked by deserted homes, many of which have broken windows, warped exteriors, and sunken roofs. A few are completely burned down to their foundations. Debris and garbage litter the street, along with several demolished cars and ravaged carcasses of dead animals.

"I had Doreleska scout the area already," Kagan states, obviously trying to qualm the apprehension we're each suffering. "The town is abandoned, so we shouldn't run into anyone."

The three of us stroll cautiously down the center of the road with me between the two beefy demons. The only sound to be heard is from the rustling of leaves as they skitter across the cracked pavement. At the end of the road, before it branches off to the left, we come upon a massive graveyard where large mounds of dirt try to mask the thick scent of death and decay. Hastily erected stone markers indicate the names of those who died during the Cleansing and are now buried in the neglected field, almost like a memorial to their shortened, pitiful lives. Bouquets of dead flowers cling to the granite like tentacles, clutching for any signs of life to give them purpose. The last remnants of anyone showing compassion for the slaughtered.

"Which group do you think is responsible for this massacre?" Rowen inquires, breaking the unsettling silence.

"The Tirans," Kagan replies, his gaze never wavering from the graves. "We'll need to keep an eye out in case any of them are still lingering around. Those bastards can be tricky."

"How so?" I ask, unable to take my eyes off as well.

"It's a faction mostly made up of syrthies—fallen angels—not normal humans like many of the other clans Lethe created for the Cleansing. Though they're led by one or two of them. These beings specialize in brutality and torture, and belong to Orcus ... the god punisher."

A shiver runs down my spine thinking about the Caltraves and what they did to all of us in the orphanage. "That explains a lot." I swallow the bile rising in my throat. "How many belong in the Legion?"

Kagan scratches his head as either a way to help him come up with the number, or he's got fleas. "Six, if you count Belial, but now isn't the time nor the place to discuss them."

I make a mental note to remind him about it later.

We follow the road deeper into the village, finding more of the same decimation and carnage. When we reach the main square, nestled in the center of a roundabout is a park with slumbering brown grass, a couple of misshapen wood-plank benches, and a statue no taller than me topping a pedestal. Crossing the road, I take one of the small pebble-filled paths leading to the monument, while Rowen and Kagan keep a sharp lookout for anyone who might possibly be lurking in the shadows that are desperate to remain given the rising sun.

The statue stands on a thick column of white granite, the figure itself made from a tarnished metal. In the growing sunlight the sculpture glistens, exposing every intricate detail of Rochelle's beauty and grace. Her long hair hangs down around her shoulders, gilded armor covers her firm body, a shield rests against her muscular legs, and her right arm points skyward, but the semi-closed grip is empty. A plaque is adhered to the base, written in French, but I can easily understand it.

Rochelle Garnier

Birth: 27 May 1785

Death: 8 September 1803

Savior of Travion

"She didn't live very long," Rowen comments, glimpsing the dates. "I wonder why."

"That I don't remember," I say, then point to the empty hand. "Her sword is missing."

Kagan scowls. "That could've been stolen during the Cleansing. Hopefully you won't need it."

"Which way to the church?"

He points to the right. "This way."

Kagan leads us down one of the connecting roads where desolate shops congregate, many of their hand-painted signs having faded with time and dangling precariously from rusted chains. It's a haunting and unnerving sight. Makes me long for the bustling crowds in Kern.

We round a bend coming upon another town square, this one much smaller and containing chunks of blistered concrete, bent metal rods, heavily charred structures, and dried blood spatter. The only building still standing is a small, old church constructed from dark gray stone, poorly stained wood, and colorful glass windows. The steeple at the entrance reaches at least several stories high, a large, brass bell situated under the twisted spires. Three elongated, narrow steps rise to the dual front doors constructed from pine, which are currently closed.

Rowen ogles the edifice suspiciously. "Do you think there's anyone inside?"

"I'm not sure. Doreleska didn't check," Kagan replies.

Staring at the tiny basilica, I can't help but feel frightened by it. The grandeur something Rochelle never would've wanted, or even ask for. "I don't like this," I mutter.

The older man turns his attention toward me and away from the building. "We can always do this another day."

I shake my head. "No. You two stay out here and keep watch. I'll holler if I need you."

"Are you sure?" Rowen asks, taking hold of my arm.

"It's a church," I reply, my voice wavering a bit. "I think even fallen angels have their limits since they left the structure intact. I should be fine."

He releases me, and I head up to the entrance, pulling open the heavy door using its thick, brass handle. My senses are immediately assaulted by the thick aroma of frankincense, and I'm not even in the main part of the sanctuary. The vestibule is decked out in deep, plush, red velvet carpeting, and the walls are painted off-white with pine wainscoting. A sideboard table rests against the wall on the left, adorned with dead candles in small, red glass jars caked in dust and a few cobwebs. A lone painting of an angelic looking woman wearing a pale blue gown holding her wee babe swaddled in only simple cloth hangs crookedly above. Looking up, I notice the steeple

260

is wide open, exposing the bell secured by thick ropes to knotted beams. Two sets of staircases wind up either end of the entryway, probably leading to a choir loft, or something similar. In front of me are a series of partially ajar doors with paper-thin glass paneling, each marking the beginning of an aisle heading toward the altar in the center of the apse at the far end.

Moving to the inner portion of the sanctuary, the carpet transitions into rough, gray stone, matching that of the exterior. Rows of worn wooden pews sit empty; many have been violently upheaved, torn right off the bolts securing them to the floor. Tattered song books with torn pages are tossed onto their scuffed seats, brown splotches covering the hymns, their lines of music warn and fading. The only light being cast is from the rising sun filtering in through the dozen or so stained windows, each depicting stories that few still believe in. Although the exterior of the church seems to have withstood the Cleansing, I can't say the same for the rest of the interior.

Shattered marble statues and broken vases rest in alcoves, their debris caked in dried blood, monumental streaks of which encompass the floor, spreading toward either transept where additional exits are located. I wouldn't be surprised if people sought refuge in here not realizing this was to become their tomb. These hallowed halls are undoubtedly more haunted than the village beyond the front doors. The entire back portion of the sanctuary has been slashed and shredded. Wood shards, fragmented metallic candle holders, and damaged tapestries lay strewn around the cracked altar—its once pristine white tablecloth now a dark coffee-color—along with smashed bottles of oil and wine. The only thing untouched by the atrocity are the stained-glass windows. Their height being the lone saving grace to their continuing existence.

Wandering slowly and carefully around the edges of the sanctuary, I study the pictures depicted in brilliant colors and warped panes. Phrases transcribed in Latin are penned in makeshift scrolls, highlighting the importance of the sceneries on display ... mainly the people in it. The one above the altar catches my attention over all others. It's without a true marker and shows a wooded landscape with ankle-high green grasses, blossoming flowers, and a lone stone and wood structure sitting in the center of the tranquil view. There's very little ornamentation on the building, simply a few windows lining the walls and a modest slab of slate leaning against one of the columns supporting the roof. It's void of any sort of embellishments, adding to the mystery.

Outside, the sun continues to ascend, bathing the image with unobstructed light and beauty. Gradually, the slate tile shimmers as if giving off waves of radiating heat, enhancing the unique illumination. After a few minutes, the sunlight captures an odd engraving on the slab that wasn't noticeable before. It appears to be a hollow circle with dozens of twisting rays of flame radiating outward like the sun.

A breath seizes in my chest.

The symbol for the goddess Olwen.

"Sunrises cast hidden shadows, revealing dreams not yet fulfilled," I mutter to myself.

"*Until the rays reach the tomb, then all will be revealed,*" a long-forgotten voice sings in my head.

Rochelle.

"Can I help you?" a quivering voice inquires in French behind me.

Spinning around, I'm greeted by an old man dressed in a black cassock with a starched white amice under his collar. His tan features are sunken and wrinkled, his short, white hair is plastered against a thin head, and he's slightly hunched over, his fingers curled practically into knots.

"I was wondering if the tomb for Rochelle of Travion was open," I reply in his dialect.

His parched lips crack when he smiles, a hint of joy touching the corners of his tired eyes. "No one has asked to see her in ages.

Of course, there isn't anyone around to visit the young lady either. What brings you by?"

Reaching into the rucksack, I remove the helmet. "This is hers and I'd like to return it." Though I had previously planned to keep the item, it feels right to place it back where it belongs.

He hesitantly touches it, almost nervous, as if the metal itself might harm him. "Where did you find it?" Caressing the damaged relic, he quakes.

"In Vineta. A thief was using it to command control over its people."

"What about the shield?" Hope lingers in his sharp, brown irises.

"I'm afraid he just had the helmet."

The old man frowns. "That's most unfortunate." He breathes shallow for a moment. "Would you like to see her crypt?"

I nod, then follow him through an archway at the far end of the apse, which brings us to a winding staircase leading down into a blackened sub-basement. The air is damp and freezing the farther we travel. The walls are held up by disintegrating stone pavers, moss growing between each acting like a natural cement. When we reach the bottom, the priest extracts a match from one of his pockets and lights a torch on the wall, then gingerly carries it in his feeble grasp. The entire floor is covered in loose dirt, easily caking my already filthy boots. Various catacombs line both sides of the lengthy chamber with its low ceiling, a miniature statue depicting the individual buried in each of the vaults. Rochelle's is simple, much like the others, but blocked by a heavy, wrought iron gate.

"We had to install this to keep the grave from continuously being robbed," the priest comments, fishing out a set of keys from his other pocket.

After turning the lock, the gate swings open and we step inside. A shield similar to the one she used in battle is carved into the lid of her final resting place. Handing me the torch, the priest steps farther inside, placing the helmet into a niche in the wall, then returns, relieving me of the light.

"She'll be most pleased to have her guardians back to protect her," the older man comments, sighing with great relief.

"Can I ask how she died?"

Still gazing at the grave, he replies, "No one knows. She simply vanished one day, never to be seen or heard from again. It deeply startled the villagers. The crypt is really a homage to her legacy and a place for her devoted followers to pay tribute, though there aren't any left." He grows sullen at the notion, his heart fracturing a bit more than it already has. One more crack to his fragile soul and he may never recover.

"Then, how were her shield and helmet found?"

He perks up a bit. "Oh, those were left in the stables behind the home she once shared with her parents, making her disappearance even more suspicious. Rumors spread that she'd been kidnapped by a royal sympathizer, but they were never substantiated. This church was dedicated in her honor."

I furrow my brow. "But why is the symbol for the goddess Olwen embedded into the glass window above the altar?"

He stares at me, mystified. "You're very astute, miss. I don't think anyone has ever noticed that image before. Of course, many don't know the story of Olwen and her temples."

"Was this one of them?" My heart races at the notion.

After closing the gate and locking it, he waves for me to follow him back upstairs, making sure to extinguish the torch before leaving the catacombs, as well as stuffing the keys into his pocket. Once in front of the altar, he gestures gracefully toward the window, my gaze following his gnarled fingers.

"The tale of Olwen is one not often told, but the massacre suffered at the holiest of shrines is known by all who studied ancient theology, such as me. Before it became illegal." His face falls at the thought. "Many people died that horrible night. It's believed that their spirits still haunt the sacred grounds, beckoning for the one who murdered them to return and take pity on their souls."

My eyes widen and my heart catches. "This depicts Cresidio?"

He startles at the question, practically jumping, then glares at me. "Who are you?"

I clear my throat, hoping to free the lump that's formed. "No one of consequence. Just an admirer of ancient dogmas."

"Her name is Magdalene Leech," a strong, female voice answers behind us, an odd accent escaping her mouth. "She's a relic hunter."

Turning, I notice the elegant woman stands around my height, is slender with medium-length, caramel-colored hair that's swept up into a chignon, light blue eyes, a pinched nose, high cheekbones, and plump, ruby lips. She's wearing a cream-colored, tunic-style dress, her figure lacking any sort of jewelry. There's an aura about her. One that prickles my skin.

Reaching into the rucksack, I grip the handle for the kard, but don't remove it. "Do I know you?"

She chuckles, her eyes scrunching ever so slightly. "Under normal circumstances you would, but these are extraordinary times, and you've misplaced your memories."

"They were stolen from me," I reply, fuming.

"Not all of them, apparently." She smirks, cocking her head to the side.

Studying the woman, it dawns on me who she is. "You're one of the divine edicts."

Her smile is reptilian, much like Belial's. "My name is Sadaina, and we've been searching a long time for you, Magdalene. Who knew you'd return to one of your former homes, restoring an item that rightfully belongs to you." She gestures toward the door leading to the catacombs.

I harden my stare. "How did you find me?"

Grasping her hands behind her back, she responds, "We've been chasing you ever since you had Daimon killed in Vineta, but to no avail. That is until now."

Fury consumes me. "Avaris told you where I am."

She laughs, her cackle echoing eerily around the decimated chamber. "Don't be ridiculous. He's gone into hiding and refuses to follow orders, much like you." Her face darkens. "He'll have to be dealt with eventually, but that's all in good time."

My pulse pounds in my head, aggravating an underlying headache that began down in the vault. "What do you want?"

"To finish what was started fifteen years ago ... your demise." Lifting her arm into the air, I'm pulled off of my feet, then in one smooth motion I'm flung across the room, crashing into cracked vases, broken candlesticks, and several pews, knocking them over.

I'm badly cut by the debris. Glass and metal slice my pant legs open in several places, cracking my knee on the stone floor. I holler from the pain shooting through my body, blood dripping from my open wounds.

"Magdalene!" Rowen screams upon hearing the noise.

"No!" I instinctively thrust my hand out as if to stop him, though I can't see him.

Every single door in the church slams shut, the thuds echoing throughout the building in tandem. The door handles for the front entrance rattle while pounding reverberates, my name shouted by both Rowen and Kagan, their voices sounding distant and desperate. The priest runs for the closest exit ... however, it won't open. There isn't anything barring the door, at least not visibly. He takes refuge under the altar, terror etched on his weathered face.

"Friends of yours?" Sadaina croons, nodding toward the pair desperately trying to enter.

"Leave them alone," I moan.

Lifting her hand, she flings me to the other end of the transept. My shirt tears, allowing my flesh to scrape along the rough flooring, shredding my skin. Blood cakes my clothing, in addition to the many abrasions I now have on my face. Panting, I clamber to my feet, my hand still clutched on the kard inside of the rucksack. Every nerve inside of me begs me to use it, to slay a member of the heavenly council just out of spite alone. But I need to prove to her, and the others, that I'm stronger than they ever thought possible.

With the twirl of her finger, Sadaina manages to open up my healed scars from the caretakers. Blood pours down my back and front, soaking my shirt, dripping down my leggings and onto the floor in pools. The scream escaping my lips is the same one I expelled when the lashes were first placed upon me. The razors of the leather belts tearing open my flesh over and over again. Rowen shouts louder, agony clutching to my name as he shouts it.

Though my consciousness is waning due to blood loss, I refuse to bend, to fall, to fail. Seeing my stubborn refusal to die, the woman charges, wraps a hand around my throat, and squeezes. Flailing in her grasp, I use both hands to claw at her arm to no avail. Darkness slowly settles in around me, beckoning me to succumb. Reclaiming my hold on the kard, in one swift motion I stab her in the abdomen. She releases me and stumbles backward, but doesn't yield. Coughing, I try not to wretch as my stomach tightens and I gasp for air, the world around me swirling into a never-ending void.

Bending down, Sadaina picks up the weapon, which had fallen out of my grasp, her wound rapidly healing. "This ends now," she says, seething.

Using the blood that's pooled on the floor, and without a clear mind, I intuitively dip my fingers into it, then draw a circle, striking three lines horizontally and another three vertically. As she barrels toward me, I recall the weapon from her hand with the flick of my wrist, then jab the tip of the blade into the center of the sigil I drew.

A white flash erupts from the floor, sailing outward along it, snatching Sadaina in its talons, and setting her ablaze. The woman's shrieks hurt my ears, the stench of burning flesh overpowering everything, causing my stomach to wrench once more, but thankfully nothing comes up. The white glow around her intensifies before exploding into a brilliant shockwave that destroys every window, causing slivers of glass to rain down, as well as break the bell loose from its rope, sending it careening from the tower and into the vestibule.

Sadaina is gone. Not one piece of her remains. Not even ash.

Collapsing onto my side, I hear the doors open, followed by the rush of heavy footsteps.

"Magdalene!" Rowen brushes a few loose strands of hair away from my face, noticing my distress, clutching me in his arms while he kneels on the floor beside me.

"They know where I am," I whimper, the light from the sun fading from my sight, though it's radiating through the broken windows.

"Who?" he begs, his voice cracking with emotion.

Tears well in my eyes. "The edicts. I … I just killed one of them." With the kard still in my hand, I do my best and use it to point at the symbol on the floor.

Kagan steps back to get a better look while Rowen readjusts his hold, the mark a bit smudged from their boots.

The older man's face grows pale. "A mortality curse," he mutters. "It annihilates supernatural beings, except for the one who casts the spell. And I don't just mean sending them to any cell, cage, or pit, but it completely and utterly obliterates them. If you hadn't sealed the doors, Rowen and I would've been affected. H-How did you know to do this?" He gestures to the sigil.

"I don't know." I moan from the pain pulsating through my entire body while I continue to bleed, wishing they'd stop asking questions and tend to my injuries. "It was a reflex."

"What about the doors?" Rowen asks, firming up his grip under my legs and around my tender back, carrying me in his arms while Kagan helps him to stand.

I shake my head as it lolls to the side, banging lazily against his chest. "No idea."

He glances at the older man. "We can't stay with Avaris after what's just happened. There has to be a way we can get her into the retreat."

The older man scratches his head. "I ordered the others to find a new location before we left this morning, so for the moment I don't know where they went. We'll have to wait at the cottage for now."

"But you still plan on protecting the place against hunters."

Using a torn page from one of the song books, Kagan picks up my kard and places it into the rucksack still strapped across my shoulders since it had fallen out of my hand when Rowen picked me up. "Let me do some research." He vanishes, the plume of dark smoke drawing the priest out from his hiding spot.

"Demons," the terrified man murmurs, quaking. "Get out of my church!" Shoving a hand into the pocket of his cassock, he removes a flask and unscrews the cap.

"We're not going to hurt you," Rowen says, trying to qualm the poor man's fears.

He threatens to throw the flask's contents—which is probably holy water—onto the two of us. "Leave!"

"All right, we'll go."

Not wanting to startle the priest any further than he already is, Rowen decides to use his demon flying outside of the church. Carefully making our way down one of the aisles, we pass the crashed bell, it's brass deeply imbedded into the floor, the carpet buckling underneath it, and head out into the chilly morning that's now fully upon us. We hardly make it ten feet from the front steps when five armed men saunter out of the shadows of the imposing structure—one of whom carries a gilded sword with an embellished silver guard, a gold and black grip, and an enlarged compass rose for the pommel.

The sword from Rochelle's statue, the one made from her melted down armor.

Of the five men, two are larger than Rowen in both height and girth, while one is rather sickly looking with overly thin arms, torso, and an elongated face. Their clothes are filthy, their faces scarred, and their eyes pure black. Each carry a different weapon in their grip ranging from Rochelle's sword to clachs to a mace that looks to have never been cleaned.

They encircle us, blocking our route back into the church. The only way to escape is by flying, but something tells me they'd follow us, and there's nothing at Avaris' cottage to keep them out. Fallen angels don't adhere to the same laws or sigils that Dalma or Festus would, so the protection symbol underneath and surrounding the cottage won't work on them.

Rowen holds me tighter, which only aggravates my wounds and causes me to wince.

"Look what we have here," the man with the sword says, grinning, his accent muddled. "New victims."

His companions chuckle.

Rowen stiffens. "Stay away from us." Without looking, I know his eyes have turned solid black, and he snarls with each syllable.

The sickly-looking man on the right jabs a finger in our direction. "Do you know who we are, boy?"

Gently setting me onto my feet, Rowen makes sure one hand is still secured around my shoulders, holding me up and plastering me against his side, though I feel like buckling. I'm not sure how much longer I can force myself to remain awake and alert. It's taking every ounce of energy I have left just to keep my eyes open.

Using his newly freed hand, Rowen reaches behind his back, wrapping his fingers around the handle for the kard tucked under his shirt. "Tirans."

"Keep your hands where we can see them," the leader demands.

Reluctantly, Rowen obliges.

The lofty, burly man on the left whistles in amusement. "It's not often we get new toys to play with."

"We're just passing through." Rowen's voice begins to fade as darkness ultimately clouds my vision.

"That's a nice weapon you have," someone close to us says, assuming he's referencing the kard tucked into the waistband of Rowen's jeans.

"I wouldn't touch it. You won't like what happens."

Conjuring enough force to open my eyes, I spy the man ignore the warning. He goes to remove the kard and immediately starts screaming as his flesh first smolders then burns. Within a matter of seconds, he's nothing but ash, the weapon now on the ground. While the others look on in horror, I somehow manage to reach into the rucksack, remove my blade, and throw it at the man with the sword. To my horror, it doesn't touch him, glancing off an invisible shield around the arrogant man. Flashes of what happened to Daimon when he confronted Belial slam into my mind, causing my stomach to wretch. The dagger does an about face, returning to my grip. Noticing the ineffectiveness of my weapon, Rowen moves toward the demon after having reclaimed his kard from the ground, leaving me to wobble dangerously on weakened legs. Without missing a beat, I hurl the dagger at one of the other three, turning him to dust, which causes the remaining two to vanish in plumes of dark smoke.

Clutching the weapon, I stay in my spot, monitoring the fight, looking for any weak spot the demon has. Though he carries a sword, it's obvious the man doesn't know how to properly wield it, making his movements clumsy and awkward. Also by the lack of injuries, he's more than likely being afforded the attributes of the armor, with the exception of the guards, making the sword a lethal weapon for any demon to have in their possession. Rowen swings his leg high and wide, making contact with the sword itself, knocking it from the demon's hand. Before he can reclaim it, I throw the kard. He doesn't get a chance to scream as he disintegrates.

Securing his blade under his waistband, Rowen picks up the sword, then makes his way over to me. I shove my kard into the rucksack before he wraps an arm around my shoulders since he can't pick me up due to the sword.

"For the moment, let's go back to Avaris' and get your wounds looked at." He holds me firm against his body, then we disappear.

Chapter Seventeen

"What the hell?" Avaris bellows when we enter the mudroom, rushing over to help Rowen after noticing the amount of blood covering my horrendously torn body. He first relieves him of the sword, leaning it against the wall by the backdoor, then holds the interior doors open for Rowen as we make our way inside.

The pair assist me into the bathroom, laying me gently onto the cool, tile floor, which is soon smeared with the filth clinging to my clothes. Grabbing a towel from the rack by the door, Avaris folds and places it under my head while I lie on my uninjured side, shaking from the cold as I gradually, finally, go into shock. Rowen hurries from the room, returning a few seconds later, his arms laden down with blankets, which he places on the floor by his feet, unable to wrap me in them until my wounds are bandaged.

"We ran into some trouble," Rowen comments, noticing the furious glare from Avaris, then goes about gathering soap, a washcloth, and filling a porcelain basin with water. Kneeling beside me, he peels away my clothes piece by piece to clean my injuries, triggering additional pain and cries now that bruises and clots are forming, while also making sure Avaris doesn't see things he shouldn't.

"I'll say. What the fuck happened?" the hunter raves, leaning over to scan the rips along my back as he holds me steady so Rowen can work.

Words fail me and I eventually pass out, Rowen's voice trailing me into nothingness.

Stirring from a nightmare infested sleep, I find myself in clean, cotton lounge pants and a long-sleeved flannel shirt, soiled bandages cover my entire upper body under the clothing, and I'm nestled under several layers of blankets on the couch now that the cushions have been returned to their proper positions from having been on the floor earlier. Darkness seeps in through the windows, the only light is being cast from the one in the kitchen, which isn't very bright. Glancing at the couch across from me, Rowen is out cold, his arm draped over his exhausted looking face. Avaris sits on the floor against one of the chairs, twirling a kard in his hand, almost like he's on guard.

"What time is it?" I croak, my throat scratchy and parched.

The demon hunter slides over to me, staying on the floor and placing the weapon in his lap. "Almost midnight. I'm supposed to wake Rowen when you roused."

"He looks beat. Let him rest. Is Kagan here?"

"He was for a few hours, but he'll be back in the morning." Avaris' voice is barely above a whisper. "Do you need anything?"

"I could use some water."

Smiling, he tenderly touches my face with the tips of his soft fingers, stands, and retreats into the kitchen. When he returns, he has to hold the cup to my mouth and help me drink. Setting the glass down, he goes over to the kitchen table and comes back with a pill bottle.

"Kagan brought these from the castle. He thought you might need them." After unscrewing the cap, Avaris dumps two into his hand, then assists me in taking them. He props my pillows so I'm sitting up slightly, but I can't help to grimace from the slight movement. Placing the pill bottle and his kard onto the coffee table, he drags one of the cushioned chairs closer, taking a seat. Leaning forward, he rests his arms on the tops of his thighs while his hands hover in the air, eager to clamp onto mine. I sense heartache and fear in his soul, along with rage and madness for the wounds I've suffered. If I didn't know any better, I'd say he actually cared. "What happened back there?"

I roll my head to the side to better see him and the anguish on his face. "Didn't Rowen tell you?"

"He was about to, but the second you passed out he kicked me from the bathroom. I think he was afraid I'd hurt you further." An aggrieved expression crosses his face, darkening his bright emerald-green eyes.

"I'm sure he just wanted to make sure my modesty remained intact," I reply, grinning slyly.

Avaris ignores the baited remark. "Where did you get all those slash marks? Weren't Kagan and Rowen with you?" His voice rises a bit while fury takes over his emotions, distorting his face, turning it a foul shade of crimson, his hands balling into fists, their knuckles going white.

I use whatever ounce of control I have left not to snap, knowing he'll defend the people responsible for my suffering. "You mean the ones on my back?" I narrow my hate-filled gaze. "Your beloved heavenly council had them bestowed upon me when I was young. They sent me to the Caltraves—one of the warring, so-called, religious clans in the States—to be brutalized in the orphanage they operated, along with hundreds of other children. Leather straps lined with thin, sharp razors was their weapon of choice since it inflicted the most damage. They relished our screams, our blood as it flowed down our battered, broken bodies. I lost count of how many died over the years by their hands."

He appears genuinely shocked, disturbed by the notion of such cruelty.

I furrow my brow, my ire rising at blistering speed. "Didn't the edicts tell you their grand plan for my downfall?" I do nothing to hide the disdain in my voice, wanting Avaris to hear every spiteful sound aimed at him. "You made it abundantly clear when you appeared in Burmstone Castle the other night that you knew all about it."

His face falls, and as he goes to open his mouth, only silence escapes his trembling lips. Dropping his gaze to avoid the loathing pulsing in my irises, he sucks in a breath, his entire body shuddering as he expels it.

"Why are you so cruel to me?" The question parts my mouth before I can stop it, but I'm also glad that it did.

Lifting an enraged stare to meet mine, his eyes are damp, filled with tears desperate to be shed, clinging to the lip of his eyelids. "You'd understand if you had your memories." He abruptly stands, shoves the chair back into place, and leaves, slamming the screen door in the mudroom behind him, which disturbs Rowen.

Noticing I'm awake, he comes over and sits on the edge of the couch, taking my hand in his. "How are you feeling?"

"Sore and tired. Avaris gave me something for the pain." I nod toward the bottle on the coffee table, the kard now missing. I didn't even notice him take it.

Rowen gently pulls back the blankets. "Let me look over the bandages. They might need to be changed."

Blood has seeped through a few of them, so Rowen goes into the bathroom to grab more, along with a healing salve Kagan brought from the castle when he went to retrieve the books for Ulrich.

"Is it safe to go back there?" I ask while the demon removes the old bandages, applies a heavy amount of ointment onto all of my wounds, then wraps them up tight in clean white cloth.

"Not for long periods of time. According to Kagan, Theron and quite a few Watchers are wandering the grounds hoping we'll return. For now, he's the only one permitted to venture there since he knows where all the hidden entrances and tunnels are located."

Resting against the pillows now that my wounds are freshly covered, I mutter, "Shit. I was hoping we could search the library ourselves."

He looks at me quizzically, discarding the excess cloth and ointment onto the coffee table. "For what?"

"To find information about what can be used to defeat Belial. I doubt there's a book out there with that knowledge, but I want to try to find one."

"There isn't a weapon that can annihilate a demon from existence, other than the mortality curse you used," he states rather nervously.

"Then what does Abaddon intend on utilizing to overthrow Lucifer? He can't use the hex because it'll wipe out all of his followers. Also, he's not simply going to send his rival down into the pit where loyalist will have easy access to free him. Abaddon will want Lucifer eradicated, thereby eliminating any threat of his return, in addition to proving his power as a leader by instilling fear into anyone who might want to try their hand at ruling, or even challenge him."

Rowen bites his lip. "Don't you think if there was such a weapon, Lucifer would already be in possession of it?"

I try to shake my head, but it's too painful. "No, because he would've hidden it in much the same way all the others have. He can't go looking for it without someone spying, and he won't be able to say anything to us out of fear of being overheard."

Letting go of me, he wrings his hands. "Perhaps we can get him to hint about the item, maybe even its location without giving too much away."

I scrunch up my face, then scowl. "Do you really want to bring him back up here? He could grow angry with us trying to manipulate him, triggering a bloodbath that I can't heal from."

Rowen lets out a deep sigh. "I'll go ask Kagan." He kisses me on the forehead. "Why don't you get some more rest?"

In the blink of an eye, he's gone, and thankfully I'm alone. Getting comfortable under the blankets I barely have my eyes closed when I hear Avaris storm back into the room, steam practically coming out of his ears.

"Were you wearing the helmet at the time you were attacked in Travion?" He stands beside the couch, towering over me, his hands on his hips.

I glower at him, irked by the interruption. "No."

"How come?" he rants, his face reddening even more than it had before.

"Because I'd already returned it to Rochelle's grave."

He glowers at me.

"I wasn't comfortable carrying it around. Besides, I didn't think I could still get it over my head due to the damage of the metal."

He tosses his hands into the air in frustration. "It was still a little banged up, but perfectly fine to wear. None of this would've happened if you had it on."

"Don't give me a lecture," I bark, which doesn't help my aching body.

Taking several deep breaths, he works on relaxing himself a bit, then sits on the coffee table, putting some much-needed distance between us. "How were you injured, other than your back? I thought you went to Travion simply to have a look around."

"We did, initially, until Sadaina found me." I purposefully neglect mentioning seeing Rochelle's tomb, discovering the stained-glass window depicting Cresidio, and what the priest said about the church being one of Olwen's temples. All out of an abundance of caution since Avaris hasn't been forthcoming with information and knows more than he's letting on. I don't need him putting the pieces of the puzzle together before I do.

He appears tremendously disturbed by the news. "How is that possible?"

"At first I thought you led her to me," I answer honestly, which causes him to scowl at the accusation.

Suddenly standing, he kicks the side of the couch I'm on, rocking it. "Why the hell would I do that?"

"I don't know. You've had something stuck up your ass since the moment we met. You despise Rowen and me for some absurd reason, you're fucking sneaky about everything, and you lie whenever it suits your needs. So, yes, I'm going to assume the worst of you." I want to keep battering him, yelling at him, tell him exactly what I think, instead I go with the truth. "But the edicts know you're hiding and are unwilling to take orders, so I'm not sure how she knew where I was."

This seems to appease him slightly, so he moves to sit on the edge of the couch much like Rowen did, allowing his arms to hang between his knees. "What happened when she found you?"

"After flinging me around the transept a couple of times, she tried to kill me by opening old wounds and stab me with my own dagger. I somehow managed to use a mortality curse on her."

Avaris' eyes widen in horror. "She's gone? Goddamn it, Magdalene! What the hell were you thinking?"

"Are you serious?" I snap, merely to have it come out as a whimper due to the headache blossoming and my throat parched from shouting. "Did you not hear what I just said? What was I supposed to do? Let her murder me?"

"No, of course not." He runs his fingers through is dark blond hair. "Fuck, this is bad. Where were Rowen and Kagan while this was going on?"

"Outside," the older demon responds as the pair materialize before us.

Avaris quickly jumps to his feet, moving to the far end of the room, noting the hostile gaze from Rowen at how close he was to me. "How did you two not succumb to the hex?"

Kagan glances at me briefly before answering. "The doors to the sanctuary became locked and we couldn't open them. That is until whatever spell was sealing them closed broke. Sadaina had already disappeared by that point."

Rowen reclaims the seat by my side, grazing my cheek with the tips of his fingers, lighting me up inside. "If the heavenly council wants to replace you, then why is the kard returning after each use? Don't they control them in a way?"

"There's one out of the seven who would prefer Magdalene to remain the relic hunter," Avaris replies, sounding sorrowful. "For the moment, it's probably his influence that's allowing her to keep them. But we don't know how much longer that might last."

"Good thing she has the sword," Kagan states, gesturing toward the mudroom.

Avaris furrows his brow. "Where did you get that?"

I wait for the older man to retrieve it before responding. Handing it to me, I wrap my tender fingers around the supple grip, leaving the tip touching the floor. A power, much like the one I felt while wearing the helmet, courses through me, but to my disappointment—and that of both Rowen and Kagan—no guards appear. "It's made from Rochelle's armor and used to be attached to her statue in the main square of the city. However, it doesn't seem to have all of the same properties much like the helmet. I might not be able to use it in replace of the kards."

280

"At least it's something," Kagan comments, tapping me on the shoulder.

"The syrthie carrying it didn't know how to handle the weapon. He was easy to subdue once I kicked the sword from his weak grip," Rowen chides.

Avaris comes closer, resting his hands on the back of the couch while looking down at me. "Fallen angels? You ran into one of them?"

"Several, actually," Rowen responds, acknowledging the hunter directly. "They're the ones responsible for the horrors the people in Travion have suffered."

"Goddamn it." Pushing away, Avaris begins to pace the room having paled slightly.

"What?" I ask, noticing the unsettling expression rumpling his youthful face.

He comes around to the other side of the couch, forcing his way between Kagan and me. "Did any of them escape the encounter?"

I nod.

"Did they recognize you?" He presses his lips firmly together, thinning them out.

"I don't believe so. They didn't act like it."

"Mind explaining all the questions?" Kagan demands, agitated, gripping the back of Avaris' maroon-colored, V-neck shirt, pulling it tight against his throat.

The hunter yanks free, but doesn't retreat from his spot. "If they realize Magdalene is here, they might try to use her to gain entry into Malum and overthrow the edicts who banished them to Hell."

"What's Malum?" Rowen asks.

"It's where the heavenly council resides, in addition to housing their courts and prisons. It was once referred to as Mount Olympus, but that was during ancient times."

He glares at Avaris, seething. "How do you know this about the syrthie?"

"Because the edicts warned me that it might be a possibility."

"And you chose now to tell us?" Standing, the demon shoves Avaris hard in the chest. "Don't you think that's something we should've known before going to Travion?"

"When did they tell you?" I ask, grabbing the hunter's arm before Rowen pushes him too far from my grasp.

"The same time they gave me the message to relay about you needing to ditch Rowen."

Kagan claims the sword from me, raising it is if to strike. "Anything else you've neglected to mention?"

With a flick of his wrist, both kards soar into Avaris' hands from the kitchen where he must have left the one and moved the other. "No, now get out of my house."

The older man's jaw tightens, his tongue clicking against the roof of his mouth. "I'll be back in a few days when Magdalene is healthy enough to travel." He focuses his attention on me. "Ulrich wants to examine the sword to see if it can be used against Abaddon." Turning, he heads for the mudroom, then out the back door.

Glowering at Avaris, I ask, "Where's my kard?"

"He put it back into the knapsack after cleaning it," Rowen answers, his eyes boring into the hunter. "I'll get it." He briefly steps out of the room, returning quickly with the bag in hand, along with his own kard clutched tightly in his grip.

Rolling his eyes, Avaris heads for his bedroom. "I'm turning in for the night. Don't do anything stupid." After shutting the door, we hear the lock fall into place.

"Asshole," I mutter, setting the bag onto the floor. "I don't give a damn about my wounds. We need to leave tonight."

Grunting, I push myself up into a sitting position. Rowen places his hands on my shoulders and settles me back down. "We can't chance it. I'm afraid we're stuck here for a few more days."

"Did Kagan say anything about us getting into the library?" I ask, pulling the blankets up under my chin, conceding to the idea of remaining with Avaris a little longer.

"That's why he took Rochelle's sword. Ulrich thinks there might be a chance it'll work, but he wants to test it first."

"Do I even want to know how he intends on accomplishing that?"

Rowen chuckles. "No, you don't." He kisses me fervently on the lips. "Go to sleep. I'll keep watch and make sure you're not disturbed."

He heads into the kitchen, turns off the light, then sits on the floor beside me, his back resting against the couch. I can't help but play with his hair, sending shivers down his spine.

"If only we were alone," I whisper, his head now tilted back onto my lap.

"Given your condition, Magdalene, I don't think sex is a good idea."

I grin wickedly. "There was another time where you were in far worse shape than I am now and couldn't keep your hands off of me."

Turning, he rests his cheek on my stomach and smiles. "You remember."

I tap him on the nose with the tip of my finger. "We weren't alone then either."

He laughs. "True, but we weren't in a tiny cottage with an exceedingly paranoid demon hunter a few feet away."

I chuckle timidly, the horror of that day filling my mind, the smirk on my face fading. The one time we ventured away from De

Lamar, other than to purchase food, was the day Lucifer sent a pack of hellhounds after Rowen for not returning when ordered.

We had been picnicking beside the Durance River a mile downstream from the castle during a decently cool summer day. The fruit we ate was juicy, the wine intoxicating, and the lapping of the waves soothing. We had placed a queen-sized cotton bed sheet onto the soft ground, and I was nestled in the crook of his arm, desperately trying not to fall asleep while he stroked my back. Growling from the thicket of trees behind us alerted us to the beasts' presence, even though we couldn't immediately see them.

I still remember their rancid, searing hot smell, the way their coarse fur abraded my skin, and the coagulated drool that dripped from their sharp canine teeth. Rowen pushed me out of the path of the first one that attacked. It tore at his arms, legs, and torso, gouging the flesh open nearly to the bone in some places, turning the floral print sheet crimson. I tried using the kards against the other two that leapt out of the shadows, but the weapons did nothing. Not even penetrate the tough skin under the mounds of bristling fur, startling the hell out of me. Eventually, I was pinned down, their jowls inches from my throat when a shockwave wrenched through the earth, slashing the hounds apart and sending them back from where they came.

Panting, I tucked the kards into the waistband of my shorts and crawled over to Rowen, who was barely conscious, his flesh jagged and mangled, and his moans scarcely audible. A twig snapping had me going for one of the daggers, but the man who emerged from the foliage was armed with a crossbow pointed at my head, its tip covered in a green, foul-smelling substance. He was several inches taller than Rowen with broad shoulders, beefy, muscular arms, an oval face, a hooked nose, long, platinum hair that lay in a braid down his back, and sun-kissed skin. The truly unnerving thing about him were his mismatched eyes. The iris for the right was pure black, no light seemed to touch it, and appeared to be filled with nothing but malice and murder. While the left was a deep, untainted crystal blue, radiating warmth and intelligence.

The world shook at his presence.

He didn't say a word when he put his weapon away and tended to Rowen's injuries, which were extensive. I didn't even learn this name until we were back inside of the castle. The ambush by the hounds was the reason I decided to give Rowen one of the kards.

"Where is Wraith?" I had heard a few stories about him before the day we met, and was awestruck by the man upon finally encountering him. His intimidating stature and might would make any demon, or hunter, think twice about confronting him, and somehow Rowen was able to befriend the reclusive man, a story I've yet to learn.

Rowen's demeanor sours. "I haven't seen him since the night he left. Two days after we were ambushed. Fucker never said anything when he took off. Sometimes I wonder if he's the one who told the edicts where to find us since it was just a short time later when Avaris brought the hunters and carted you away."

"I hardly think a demon would go running to the heavenly council."

Rowen snorts. "Don't forget, he's also half angel. His loyalties rest with no one."

Slipping gingerly onto my bruised side, I pat the couch cushion for him to slide in next to me, then drape the blankets over him once he's removed his boots and wraps an arm around my waist, our faces practically touching. "How did you initially run into him?"

"Believe it or not, I saved his skin. The idiot chose to pick a fight with Theron of all people." Rowen rests his forehead against mine, and I relish his touch, the softness of his skin. "Several centuries ago, Lucifer's hunter, me, and a few other demons were in a tavern for a small hamlet in Shrule, Scotland looking to recruit, make deals with those too drunk and desperate to know any better during a time when England was warring with itself."

A twinge rattles through me, one that drives hard into my core, threatening to cleave it in two. The room becomes suffocating, made even worse by Rowen's closeness. Taking shallow breaths, I work on easing the panic rising, hoping he doesn't notice, but he does.

"Are you all right?" He clasps my clammy hand in his warm and dry one, while the other rubs a spot on my back that isn't bandaged or injured.

"I'm fine. Just need some water."

Briefly sitting up, he reaches for the cup on the coffee table, which isn't empty, and hands it to me. I down the contents, he replaces it on the table, then lovingly kisses my forehead. Squeezing his hand, I indicate for him to continue with the story.

"Well, we'd heard about the half-breed—which many referred to Wraith as back then, and still do—but never actually encountered him or met anyone who had and lived to tell the tale. That night when he entered the tavern, everyone went silent ... mortals and demons. We all waited until he sat at an isolated table in the back corner before continuing conversations and drinking. As the hours wore on, Theron had managed to trick three men into handing over their souls to Lucifer when the time came, but I couldn't keep my attention off of Wraith. You knew he was studying you even if his focus seemed elsewhere." Rowen shudders a bit. "When he realized what Theron was up to, Wraith took exception and nearly snapped the hunter's neck after punching him hard in the face. Of course, this initiated a full brawl in the tavern. Throats were slit, limbs were shattered, and people fled as quickly as possible before they became casualties."

I try my best not to grimace at the images he's painting but to no avail. Instead, more memories thunder to the surface of a young woman with chestnut eyes, a freckled, oval face, button nose, full lips, and long, curly red hair. Her name rests on the tip of my tongue, but refuses to be spoken or acknowledged. Grasped in her steady, nimble hands is the cane Dalma was using, only I can't remember how it came into her possession, or even what it's called

286

since I know it has a name. Closing my eyes, I push the recollection away for the time being and focus on what Rowen is saying.

"Wraith was so preoccupied with the fighting that he didn't realize Theron had convinced the other demons in our group to use their clachs on him, with the intension of bringing the great behemoth down for good. Something inside of me cracked, and I killed the others before they could inflict more damage, but unfortunately left Theron merely severely wounded. I knew what punishment Lucifer would bestow if I killed his hunter. Wraith stumbled out into the chilly night, and I never saw him again until the hellhounds."

"Were you punished for slaughtering the others?" I ask, nuzzling my head into his chest.

"No, but Theron was for not leaving when Wraith first arrived. He was leading our little party and should've known better than to continue recruiting with the half-breed in the same room. Of course, Lucifer's hunter never let me forget my part in the whole thing. I'm sure he still holds a grudge."

"I wonder why he was there," I utter, more for myself than Rowen, who doesn't respond, but instead places a hand under my chin, lifts my head toward his, and kisses me passionately on the lips.

Hiking up his shirt, I run my nails up and down his tight, muscular back, causing him to quake with anticipation. "I don't want to hurt you," he moans in my ear, his hot breath riling my senses.

"You could never."

We adjust positions so I'm supine on my back and he's completely on top. His hands work fast at removing my clothes, easing them off in such a way not to aggravate my injuries—which, thankfully, have stopped bleeding—or loosen the bandages. His soft, warm lips take to my neck while I fiddle with the zipper of his pants, and he involuntarily moans when I take his firmness into my hand.

"Shh," I whisper, chuckling a little.

"I can't help it." His mouth returns to mine, his tongue diving inside.

Our clothes drop onto the floor into a comingled pile. I arch my back as he enters, gasping from the intense sensation. After only a few minutes, sweat glistens off of our skin, our heartbeats thud rapidly together, and I pray we're not disturbed.

The sun's rays hit me square in the face as they plunge through the window, alerting me that morning has arrived. Rowen is sleeping on the sofa across from me wearing only his jeans, while I'm fully dressed. He must have put my clothes back on after I fell asleep from our subdued lovemaking. Tossing the covers over the back of the couch, I grunt while moving into a sitting position, my body stiff and sore. I force myself to stand, then make my way to the bathroom to use the facilities. After washing my hands, I splash cold water on my face and take down the ponytail that's left my hair tangled and a mess. Running my fingers through it to loosen the strands, I slip the black elastic band around my wrist so not to lose it, then turn for the door. Avaris is standing inches from the threshold when I open it, his entire body rigid, including his face, which is filled with wrath and derision.

"What are you doing up?" I inquire, disquiet settling into my nerves.

"I had a hard time sleeping due to all the racket the two of you were creating." The bitterness in his voice can't be concealed and he does everything possible not to hide it, as well as emphasize the disgust and fury flowing through him.

I blush from embarrassment. "Sorry." I try to move around him, but he continues to block my escape, his arms folded over his chest as he bites the inside of his cheek. "Let me by," I snap, annoyed that he won't allow me back into the front room.

"Not until we discuss a few matters."

"I have nothing to say to you." I'm in the process of prying my way past when he snatches my arm and drags me into his bedroom, shutting and locking the door. Breaking free from his tight grasp, I stumble a bit, my muscles groaning from the effort. "Are you fucking crazy?"

"Just shut up and listen for a minute." He presses his back into the door, afraid the lock won't be enough to contain me. "I wasn't lying the other night when I said we were together the night you destroyed the Calsaign shroud. And I know why the doors in the church sealed themselves yesterday."

The light from the sconces in the room becomes uncomfortably bright, causing me to squint. "You couldn't possibly."

Stepping forward, he says, "Prometheus' chains. Sound familiar?"

Furrowing my brow, I stare at him. "No. What are they?"

"They're supposed to be unbreakable manacles used to keep supernatural beings confined and weak. Theron used a pair on me down in his dungeon. The same place I found Pierce, which is why I knew where to look for him." Avaris rubs his face, and I now notice dark circles under his red, puffy eyes. I would swear he's been crying.

My stomach twists into knots at what he might be suggesting. "Cursed steel is destructible when it goes against a kard," I counter, hoping it's true since I can't recall that bit of detail, then I tilt my head to the side. "How did Theron capture you?"

Avaris takes another step closer. "They're not made from cursed steel, but something much more sinister and otherworldly. I don't know their history because I wasn't the one searching for them, you were. The edicts sent us together: you to collect and hide the chains, and me to protect you at all costs." He starts to pace the room like a wounded animal. "Theron and a few of his men had been pursuing us for days. No matter what traps, runes, or sigils we used to ward off our scents and hide our tracks, they still managed to find where we were. I distracted them while you escaped, knowing I wasn't going to be coming out of that tomb alive."

He settles himself against the door, crossing his feet at the ankles, and hiding his hands behind his back. "I was unconscious when they took me, and woke up bound to anchors embedded into a damp, stone wall. Theron procured the chains from the tomb before we were able to and used them." His gaze turns distant, lost. "Unimaginable pain blistered throughout my entire body. It felt like thousands of needles were being speared into every cell. I shrieked until my voice was raw. Theron simply laughed. He never even laid a finger on me. It was all Prometheus' chains."

Focusing his attention back on me, sorrow crinkles the edges of his eyes, and a wrinkle knits his brows together. "I don't know how long they were planning on keeping me, or what their intentions were in the first place, but it became apparent after a while that Theron was waiting for you, using me as bait, knowing you'd come. What he didn't anticipate was you sneaking into the barracks and dungeon unnoticed, using the power you had absorbed from the Calsaign shroud to mask your entry." A smile touches his lips. "You made your appearance known to just me. The guards in the room didn't realize something was amiss until the chains disappeared."

The knots in my stomach tighten, coiling tighter, constricting everything inside, making it difficult to breathe. "How...how did I destroy them?"

"At first you tried using the kards, including mine, which you had retrieved from the tomb after Theron and his men left." In the blink of an eye, Avaris is in front of me, fondly taking my hands in his. "When that didn't work, you gripped them with your fingers and screamed. I begged for you to let go and leave, but you refused to abandon me. I thought for sure the guards would hear you, but the power from the shroud masked your voice as well. A brilliant light erupted around you, encasing you in a dazzling glow. I was forced to close my eyes so I wouldn't go blind. When I opened them, the chains were gone and you were on the floor, practically lifeless. The spell for the shroud had vanished, exposing you to the guards. Picking up the kards, I turned them to ash, then cradled you in my arms after securing the weapons and took you back to the hunter stronghold. It took days for you to recover."

Stepping back, he releases me, my arms falling to my side, my face paling in disbelief.

"The doors in the church sealed because of the abilities you took on after destroying the chains, fastening them shut until whatever happened to Sadaina dispelled the enchantment."

Turning away from him, I wrap my arms around myself in the hopes of warding off the chill slithering down my spine. "Why would I go back for you?"

His warm hands embrace the upper part of my arms, while his sultry breath tickles my ear and neck. "Because you loved me, and I can prove it." He nudges me over to the antique cedar dresser with its fluted legs, heavily polished drawers, and brass handles. "There's something here that belongs to you ... to us." Releasing me, he moves to my side, hope radiating from him.

Scattered across the top of the dresser are several various knickknacks ranging from small statues to pieces of tarnished jewelry to empty perfume bottles. It reminds me of the crucifix test Dalma had me perform. One item instantly jumps out at me: a square, cherrywood music box with beveled edges, small, spindle legs, and gold filigree laced in an intricate scroll pattern on the lid. It's no bigger than the size of my hand. Picking it up, I can already hear the soothing melody that will play when I open it. The tinkling of the comb scraping along the drum brings back fond memories of warm summer evenings and cool ocean breezes. However, they seem distorted, not quite in focus, which I find puzzling. It's almost as if they've been altered or tampered with, but I don't see how that's possible.

"This is mine." I turn to face him. "I thought I'd lost this years ago. Where did you get it?"

Closing the lid, Avaris' hand remains on top of it. He steps closer, heat and desire exuding from his body like a fine wine. When he lifts his other hand and caresses my cheek, I feel him trembling with not only eagerness, but a long held-yearning. "I've always had it, Magdalene. It was a present for when you agreed to marry me."

Shocked, I stagger backwards, putting a bit of distance between us, the music box still clutched in my hands. "You're lying."

"I'm not." He comes over, removes the item from my grip, and turns it upside down. Engraved on the underside are our names and a date: 25 December, but no year.

My head spins, the room swaying before me, forcing me to sit on the edge of his bed to steady myself. "You could've had this made just to trick me. This doesn't prove anything."

"Maybe this will." Kneeling down on the floor, he sets the music box onto the mattress, then cups my face in his hands and kisses me ardently.

I vehemently shove him away. "What the hell are you thinking?"

"You said you could recall your past by touching things. I thought if I kissed you, then you'd remember us!" he raves, sounding heartbroken, then his frustration turns to rage. "How can you remember Rowen and not me? Me? Us? We were together for years. Long before he ever entered the picture!"

"I-I don't know why." Rapidly rising to my feet, I sprint for the door, momentarily forgetting that it's locked, the handle unwilling to budge in my quivering grasp. "I recollect the music box and the tune it plays, but not you or the reason behind the gift."

Slamming himself against the hard wood, he thrusts my hands away from the handle. "That's not possible. We had our lives planned out, aspirations for the future. We were both looking forward to the day we could finally be free from the heavenly council's rule." His hostile stare darkens. "Are you lying to me because of him?" Avaris nods to the person who rests on the other side of the door, the madness in his eyes terrifying me.

"No, I swear." I shake my head adamantly.

"We'll just see about that." He storms over to the bed and reaches behind his pillow.

I don't wait to see what he removes and hurry to unlock the door, throwing it open, then quickly retreat to the front room to rouse Rowen, but he doesn't wake no matter what I attempt.

"What did you do to him?" I demand, standing next to the slumbering demon while Avaris comes at me, a kard in his solid, unwavering grip.

"He'll wake when I want him to. If he lasts that long." Snatching my arm, Avaris pulls me away. "We're not done talking about this." He drags me back into the bedroom, then locks the door once it's shut.

Noticing the handle for the clach sticking out from behind a vase on top of the nightstand closest to the door, I snatch it and hold it in my shaking grip. "Don't come near me."

"Put down the dagger," he demands.

"Let me go and perhaps I will."

"Not until you hear what I have to say." He takes several deep breaths, obviously to steady himself. "I built this cottage for us, so we could have a place of our own instead of being stuck inside of Sealgair with the other hunters. The edicts sent you to monitor the Perpetua Chalice while it was traveling the world since they heard rumors that someone was after it. You were gone for months, and I remained here constructing our home. I didn't know anything had gone wrong until I was called back to the sanctum on Malum and ordered to hunt you down." Tears well in his eyes. "When I found you and him together, it ... it tore me apart. You acted as if I was nothing. Pretended like you didn't know me." The tears burst forth, raining down his heated cheeks.

"I wasn't pretending, Avaris. I have no real recollection of you at all."

His face flushes scarlet. "Rowen fucked with your mind, Magdalene! Can't you see that? He did all of this!" Spit flies from his mouth and a vein bulges in his neck. "Manipulated it somehow to erase any idea of me ... of us."

"Why would he do something like that?"

"To take you away from me and make you one of his ... a demon whore." He expels the words like venom. "I'm sure you're not the only one he's done this to, but you will be the last. He's going to pay dearly for it. When I'm through with him, there will only be pieces of him remaining. I'll use a rune to make him temporarily mortal so he doesn't turn into ash the moment the golden blade touches him. No cage this time. Straight to the pit."

"No!" I scream, then as Avaris turns for the door I throw the dagger, hitting him in the upper back just beneath his right shoulder blade.

He hollers and drops his weapon as he falls to the floor onto his stomach. Rushing over to him, I kick the kard out of his reach, lift the back of his shirt, dip my fingers in the blood surging out of the wound, and draw a vertical line on his skin with two diamonds along the shaft, the top one left partially open.

"What the hell are you doing?" he moans, his body spasming.

"Placing a binding hex on you, so you can't access your powers."

When I'm done, I use his shirt to clean my finger, stand, and unlock the door. Rowen grumbles as he wakes, the sedation spell wearing off. I quickly start packing, not bothering to change out of the clothes I slept in.

"What happened?" he asks, rubbing his head.

"Magdalene!" Avaris shouts, causing Rowen to stare quizzically at the partially closed door.

294

"We need to go." Taking his hand, I pull him to his feet and hand him a sweatshirt.

We put on our shoes, then Rowen checks to make sure nothing has been left behind in the mudroom.

"Where to?" he asks, returning to the front room where I nervously wait, hoping Avaris doesn't find a way to undo the hex.

"Anywhere," I reply, wrapping my arms around his waist.

I close my eyes, and we disappear in a swirl of smoke. The air eventually turns bitter cold, nearly paralyzing. Snowflakes hit our faces, and when I briefly open my eyes, I spot mountains soaring below us. We start our descent, my teeth chattering together while I desperately cling to Rowen. The ground we land on is rocky and covered in several inches of snow, the wet soaking through our clothes. We're on a ledge of a large mountain range, a cave looming in the darkness ahead of us.

"The new retreat isn't too far from here," he says, making his way toward the opening with me closely in tow. "I'll get a fire started to keep you warm, then fetch Kagan."

"I thought demons hated the cold," I comment, dropping the bags to the ground next to the duffle once we reach shelter.

"We do, but it makes a great hiding spot. Hunters never expect to find us in their own territory."

While he gathers firewood from the forest below, I add on layers, making sure to bundle up as much as possible.

"Where are we?" I ask upon his return, rubbing my hands together to prevent them from freezing.

"The mountainous region of Siberia." He sets out the wood, and while he's rummaging for something to light the fire, I summon Olwen's flame and ignite it, then take a seat on the cold, hard ground. "How did you do that?" he asks, astounded.

"I'll tell you later." Scooting closer to the heat, I bring my knees up to my chest to help maintain a decent body temperature. "Get Kagan. I don't want to be in here all night."

Rowen leaves. Thankfully, the shelter of the cave prevents much of the biting winds roaring outside from entering. Otherwise, it would knock out the flames, leaving me to freeze to death in a matter of seconds. The pair return carrying blankets, which I gratefully take. After adding on his own layers, Rowen wraps one around his shoulders and sits beside me while Kagan remains standing, a puzzled expression on his face.

"That was a short stay," the older man comments. "How are your wounds?"

"F-Fine," I stammer, unable to remain warm.

Pulling me under his blanket, Rowen adds his body heat on top of mine, thawing me out a bit. "We need a room in the retreat."

"Ulrich is still working out the details on that. Now, tell me what happened."

"Avaris ... he's..." My mind is racing so fast that I'm struggling to come up with the words. "H-He sedated Rowen using the same charm he did back at the castle when he first visited, and was going to kill him. He's under the impression that my memories aren't accurate because of some demon mind trick Rowen is using on me, but he's not. The memories I do have are accurate. I know it."

Shifting his weight onto one leg, Kagan folds his arms over his chest. "Why does Avaris believe that?"

"Because he's convinced we were engaged at some point during our supposed many years together. That it all changed when I was sent to guard the Perpetua Chalice. He even has an old music box of mine to prove he was telling the truth. Before he could attack Rowen, I stabbed him in the back with the clach that he has and drew a binding hex on his back using the blood from the wound."

Kagan lifts his brows in astonishment. "How did you know to do that?"

"I'm not sure. It was instinctive." Biting my lip, I hesitate in telling them about what happened the night prior and how I discovered the cause of my additional powers, but do. Including what I recall about the Calsaign shroud, and the abilities I currently possess from destroying that relic. Even the tale Avaris wove about Prometheus' chains. When I go on to explain the dream Belial instigated, Rowen buries his face in my shoulder to avoid Kagan's penetrating stare.

"Shit," the older man mutters. "I didn't know he could manipulate dreams. Abaddon and Lucifer can ... however, they're more powerful than the Prince of Darkness. Fuck."

I look at him with optimism. "Now what?"

He frowns, his body going rigid. "I'm sorry, Magdalene, but I can't allow you inside."

"Why the hell not?" Rowen rages.

"Since Avaris can sense her, she isn't safe anywhere, and I'm not about to jeopardize the cabin by damaging one of its sigils, placing us all at risk."

Rowen abruptly stands, pitching blankets onto the ground. "You can't just abandon her like this."

"Until Ulrich can figure out what will work to get her past the hexes, I'm sorry, but the answer is no." He gestures to the bags beside me. "You two are going to need to keep moving should Avaris free himself." With one last look of sorrow, Kagan disappears.

My body somewhat thawed, I alter my wardrobe, removing the clothes I slept in while keeping the blanket tightly clenched around me. I put on black leggings, a matching tank top, and a burgundy sweater with long sleeves, then run my fingers through my hair and secure it into a ponytail before slipping my boots back on and stuffing the rest of the clothes into the duffle bag.

"Where do you want to go?" I ask, securing my outer coat closed.

"We can't go to De Lamar. That'll be the first place he looks." Rowen bends down to fold the blankets and is almost done when Doreleska suddenly appears wearing a black fur coat and knee-high boots, startling us.

"Good, you haven't run off yet," she snickers, her plump lips twisting into a hostile cackle.

"What the hell do you want?" I seethe, itching to use the kard on her.

She cocks her head to the side, surveying me from head to toe. "I came to offer my assistance with your little dilemma."

I eye her suspiciously. "Why?"

She clasps her hands in front of her. "Let's just say that I was quite impressed at hearing about how you destroyed one of the edicts. I really didn't think you were capable of such deceitfulness."

Not trusting her, I cautiously ask, "How can you help?"

Turning her attention to Rowen, she says, "Wait for us inside of the retreat."

"Are you insane? I'm not leaving her alone with you."

Doreleska scowls, her smokey eyes darkening. "Do you want my services or not?"

He rolls his eyes. "Fine." Reaching into the duffle bag, he retrieves his kard, handing it to me so I have both, which I place into the canvas knapsack since I left the rucksack behind. "Be careful." His lips press hard against mine, gathers the blankets, slings the duffle bag over his shoulder, and leaves.

Doreleska holds her hand out, which I take begrudgingly. "Don't let go," she teases, then we vanish.

Chapter Eighteen

$\mathcal{P}$lumes of gray-stained smoke billow out of the dark stone chimney for the quaint, rustic cabin we approach, snow drifting over our boots from the harsh gusts rolling down from the expansive mountain range around us. Wide bluffs rise up the sidewalk leading to the wooden structure, lights blazing inside behind partially closed curtains.

Doreleska releases my hand before we climb the elongated steps to the tiny porch. "Let me do all of the talking. Joran can be temperamental around strangers. You'll also need to wait out here. His home is covered in hunter traps, much like the retreat."

"Then why did you bring me to this frozen tundra if I'm not allowed inside?" I snap, ice seeping into my bones.

She rolls her fiery eyes. "There's a shed in the back where you can wait, though I doubt it's any warmer than outside."

Shivering, I go in the direction Doreleska indicates with a firm jab of her finger while she ascends the few steps to the front door, knocking on the thick timber, the sound deadened by the falling snow. There isn't a direct path, so I create my own, prodding through ankle-deep snow, soaking my leggings. When I reach the rear of the house, I spot the shed tucked between two heavy pine trees, their snow-laden branches lying across the roof tearing away a few of the dark shingles. Gripping the door handle, I scowl when it doesn't turn. I peer through the window beside the entrance, noticing walls constructed from bark-less pine logs, badly scratched wood planks for the flooring, and numerous mounted animal carcasses, their hides fraying while a few detached antlers are being used for chandeliers, their bulbs dormant. A wood burning stove sits nestled in the corner, logs scattered around it.

Along the back wall are shelves containing jars of ink, several menacing devices containing needles, and a horribly stained worktable. On the adjoining walls are racks of swords, knives of every design, a couple of machetes, and a few maces, their spikes looking rather dull.

I don't know why Doreleska thought the shed would be unlocked considering the arsenal inside. Turning to head back, a pair of hostile voices shatters the stillness of the air and I nearly collide with a tall, bulky man with long, curly, dark brown hair, and broad face. His entire body is covered in blue flannel from head to toe, fur-lined boots adorn his massive feet, a matching hat covers his head, and in his beefy hand is an ax swung over his shoulder. The tool, or weapon depending upon how he intends to use it, looks freshly sharpened, the metal gleaming in the veiled sunlight.

His cruel eyes slink up and down my frame. "What did you bring to my doorstep?" he asks in Russian, his voice gravelly and harsh.

"A friend," Doreleska replies in the same dialect, her tone matching his.

He snorts. "Hunters aren't friends." He turns to glare at her. "Why you hanging around one anyway?"

"Believe it or not, she works for Lucifer. Traded sides when she realized how much better we are than those pathetic assholes." Her plump lips grow into a sly smile.

He goes to study me again, but I don't seem to impress him any with supposedly changing allegiances. "Why you here?"

Crossing her arms over her chest, either for comfort or for warmth, Doreleska replies, "She needs to be branded with a hex breaker."

Joran smirks, the corners of his tight mouth curling ever so slightly. "Who she piss off besides her own kind?"

"Just them. She can't currently go into hiding until she gets her scent masked, which a hex breaker tattoo will be able to accomplish."

His stare bores into me, adding to the chill overtaking my senses. "Still, what makes her so special to warrant protection?"

"It's not for protection," I reply in Russian, shocking him and angering Doreleska.

He raises his brow. "Then you intend on breaking a sigil." Lifting his free hand, he waves it dismissively. "I don't brand for such things. It would make me a target by not only hunters, but other demons as well. Is too risky." He turns and starts to walk away.

"What's your price?" I ask before he's rounded the corner.

Stopping, and without glancing in my direction, he replies, "You can't afford it."

"Try me."

Coming back over, the grin on his face makes my soul shiver. "A sword renowned for protecting it's wielder. One only familiar to a few, most of them dead. The last I heard a Tiran leader was in possession of it, though I wouldn't be surprised if he doesn't realize the magnitude of the weapon he has. I doubt you have the balls to go against someone like him. A lowly little hunter like yourself fighting a syrthie."

Doreleska goes to open her mouth when the piercing glare I throw her way halts all movement. "If I'm able to procure this sword, will you tattoo the mark on me?"

"And then some." He bows with great exaggeration. "I'll be your humble protector should you survive the battle."

I force myself to bite the inside of my cheek to keep from smiling. "Doreleska, can you go back to the retreat for me? It looks like I'm going hunting for a sword and will need provisions."

Her face remains expressionless as she leaves, swirling the snow that had been under her feet into a small vortex that quickly dies down.

I gesture toward the door of the shed. "Mind if we wait inside? This hunter is freezing her ass off." Wrapping my arms around myself, I quiver for emphasis.

Chuckling, he removes a brass key from his pocket, places it into the lock, and turns the handle. The interior is just as cold as the exterior, so Joran puts a couple of logs into the stove and lights them. I take a seat in a chair covered with red tartan, hidden in the corner closest to the door, which is flanked by a spruce table and glass oil lamps, each one flickering inside their hourglass shaped shades after Joran ignites their wicks.

"How many demons have you branded over the years?" I inquire, nodding toward the heavily stained table.

Taking a seat at the lone chair for his workbench, he leans a beefy arm onto the wooden surface. "A few."

"What do they request?"

"The usual protection sigils. Not that it does them any good against hunter kards."

I smile. "But you still get paid."

He laughs. "Dumb bastards. They never learn." Scooting the chair closer, he tilts his head like the walls have ears. "What's the real reason you want a hex breaker?"

"To go into hiding," I whisper, playing along. "It's not wise for someone in my position to be so exposed. Lucifer wouldn't want me to get hurt."

302

He slides back over to the table and hoists his thick legs onto the top, the wood creaking a bit from the weight. "What did you do to warrant his favor?"

Crossing my legs at the knee, I casually drape my arms over the rests for the chair and look Joran dead in the eye. "I murdered a divine edict."

The swarthy man pales, a visible lump forming in his throat. "You're going to need more than a hex breaker to protect your fine ass."

I can't help but grin. "We'll see."

The knock on the door prompts Joran to rise and answer it. Doreleska stands there empty handed, which infuriates me until I spot Kagan behind her, a double scabbard strapped to his back. I hope Rochelle's sword is in one of them. The young woman nervously steps into the room, leaving a path for Kagan, who fills up the entire doorway.

"Joran," he says, his deep voice booming around the cramped space, "I was wondering if this is where Magdalene was taken." He glowers at Doreleska, who's surprisingly recoiling into the stones encasing the wall behind the stove, then turns his attention back to the other demon. "If I'm to understand correctly, you're willing to mark Magdalene with a hex breaker if she retrieves a specific sword for you, in addition to serving as her protector?"

"I think it's fair trade." He smirks, folding his arms over his puffed-out chest. "That's if she lives after meeting the Tirans." He cocks his head to the side. "Why are you here, Kagan?"

"To make sure you keep your word." After stepping into the shed, he reaches over his shoulder, unsheathes the sword with a compass rose pommel, and hands it to me.

Still weakened by the attack from Sadaina, I try not to drop the hefty weapon, resting its tip into the planks covering the floor and clutching the grip with both hands. "Is this what you wanted?"

Joran's eyes widen while his face falls. "How did you get that?"

"Took it from a syrthie when I was in Travion yesterday visiting an old tomb."

Moving away from the door, Kagan closes it to keep the icy air outside. "What Doreleska neglected to mention was that Magdalene hunts relics, not demons. But she does need the hex breaker so she can stay with us and out of the hands of the heavenly council now that she's killed one of their own. Every hunter will be searching for her, which won't help Lucifer retain his throne."

"What are you talking about?" he barks, stomping his way back to the table, slamming the blade of the ax into the floor close to Doreleska's feet, making her jump.

"Abaddon."

Rubbing his face, Joran mutters incoherently, then plops into his chair. "Fucking bastard. I refuse to fight him, and anyone he rallies to his side."

"Right, because there's no profit in it for you. You'll sidle up to both and pledge loyalty to whomever wins," I grouse.

His face reddens and his eyes turn solid black. "Look, little girl, I've fought in more wars than you've been alive. Got the scars to prove it. Tell me what you've done besides slaughter a pathetic, whiney edict. Nothing."

Sensing Kagan choking back laughter, I step forward, thumping the sword against the floor as I go. "Who do you think sent Belial to the pit all those centuries ago? Or destroyed Melek when he went searching for the Crown of Thorns?" All three flinch at the mention of one of the Legion, a memory that didn't rise until this very moment. "Why do you think no one can locate the most sacred of relics? Because I burned it along with that son of a bitch. Used a mortality curse on both of them. I can easily do the same to you."

"And if you continue to refuse," Kagan pipes in from behind me, "then I'll have Lucifer pull your chain back underground since he's been searching for you a long time." Again, his focus changes to a still shaken Doreleska.

"Fine," Joran growls, turning to grab a jar of ink off one of the shelves, along with some cruel-looking device, which he inserts a fresh needle into. "Take off your coat and top so I can brand the mark on the back of your shoulder."

After leaning the sword against the wall, I do my best not to groan from spasms of dull pain while reaching back to pull my hair into a ponytail, then I toss my things onto the chair, but keep the tank top on and shiver from the underlying chill still in the room.

"Hang on a minute," Kagan mutters, stepping up behind me, tugging on the bottom of my shirt, lifting it up. "It looks like some of your wounds are still bleeding and a few of the bandages are coming loose. We'll take care of them afterwards." He releases me just as Joran stands and waves for me to take his seat.

He turns on the device in his hands, a low hum emitting from the needle as he dips it into the ink. "This is going to sting."

Slouching forward a bit, I rest my arms on the table. "Pain and I are old friends."

He snorts, then starts by pressing the needle into my flesh on the left shoulder blade. I try not to flinch as he carves through the skin, a burning sensation following every twist and turn that he makes. There's only brief relief when he adds more ink into the needle. After he finishes, he cleans off the excess ink from my back, then applies a healing salve.

"Now what?" Joran grumbles, while I put my sweater and coat back on, draping the knapsack across my unmaimed shoulder.

"Doreleska will help you pack, then you'll come to our place. You'll bunk with Ulrich since we don't have enough rooms to accommodate everyone." Kagan gestures to me. "Let's go, Magdalene." He steps over to the door and holds it open.

Once we're outside, I grip tightly onto his hand and close my eyes. Flying is getting easier, but it still terrifies me. We arrive at the foot of the steps leading up to a porch that expands the entire front of the house, its dark red bricks matching the tone of the wood planks and overhang. A double door with glass side lights awaits us, the sun glistening off the falling snow at our back. I hesitate in climbing up the few inches, Kagan waiting patiently by the door.

"What if this doesn't work?" I ask, staring at the house with great trepidation.

"You can go back and kill Joran. Lucifer would appreciate you putting that asshole in a cage." The older man smiles, but it's pained.

Taking a deep breath, I square my shoulders, step up onto the porch, and hope the hex breaker works. The brass handle is bitterly cold in my grip, yet turns with ease. I brace myself for whatever the sigils strewn about the home will dispense upon me, but when I move across the threshold, nothing happens. Kagan enters behind me, closing the door with a gentle nudge.

The interior of the house is warm, a fire blazing in the fireplace in front of an arrangement of brown leather sofas with a walnut coffee table in the center. The walls are covered in a light blue and cream-colored wallpaper with a pencil stripe pattern. The floors are wide plank hardwood that look to have been freshly polished. Simple pendant lighting with bronze piping and frosted glass shades are scattered throughout. The living room expands into the dining area and kitchen, the basic color scheme continuing along the way. Toward the middle of the structure is a hallway that turns right off of the living room and into another hallway that runs parallel with the rest of the house, leading to all of the bedrooms and baths.

Lifting my gaze upward, I spot two 'H's intersecting—one forward, one reversed—the sigil to protect against hunters. It's stenciled above each room, and though the hex breaker is working, I can still sense the power of the symbol throbbing through the air, trying to push me out. Swallowing the lump that's formed in my throat, I ignore the unsettling feeling and step farther inside.

Rowen is sitting on the couch, hands clasped together, staring anxiously into the fire. Hollis and Pierce are in the kitchen making themselves sandwiches, while Ulrich sits at the dining room table pouring over the several books Kagan had retrieved for him. Kagan clears his throat, which garnishes everyone's attention, then brushes past me and enters a study just off the dining area, setting the scabbard inside where I notice many of the weapons are currently being kept.

"Oh, thank God." Rowen comes over and pulls me into a tight embrace. "I was so worried, but Kagan wouldn't let me go with him when Doreleska came for the sword."

"Where is she, by the way?" Pierce asks, sitting across from Ulrich.

"She'll be along shortly." Kagan heads into the kitchen and starts assembling his own meal. "Ulrich, you'll be sharing your room. We have an unwelcomed guest joining us."

Hollis takes the seat beside Pierce. "Who?"

Lifting his head up from the sandwich he's constructing, Kagan replies, "Joran."

A shudder rattles Hollis' thin frame, then she stiffens and clenches her jaw, but it seems I'm the only one to have noticed it since the others don't comment on her reaction.

"Rowen, take Magdalene into your room. Her wounds need to be rebandaged." The older man nods in the direction of the bedrooms.

Clasping my hand, Rowen leads the way. When we reach the hallway for the bedrooms, he turns right, then another right at the end and into one of the rooms at the front of the house. It's not as nice, lavish, or big like the one at the castle. The furnishings are simple, an off-white carpet covers the floor, and the walls are done in sky blue. On the ceiling is the hunter sigil, it's pull waning the longer I'm inside of the retreat. The duffle bag sits on the end of the bed partially unpacked. Setting the knapsack beside it, I remove my coat, sweater, and tank top so Rowen can take a look at the wounds. Thankfully, the thick, blackout curtains are closed, otherwise if we had neighbors they'd be able to see me.

After closing the door, he comes up behind me and gently unwraps the soiled bandages, setting them on the dark blue comforter covering the mattress. "The downfall about this place is we have to share a bathroom with Ulrich and Hollis." Rowen's soft, delicate fingers trace around the tattoo while his other hand brushes my hair across my other shoulder. "This is beautiful." He burrows his forehead into the back of my neck, his hot breath tickling my senses.

"What is it? Joran never told me."

"It's a thistle." His soft lips graze my skin, his hands gripping onto my hips, fingers tugging at the waistband for my leggings. "Lie down while I get some more ointment and cloth," he utters, forcing himself to break away from the desire building between us.

I do as instructed while he steps out of the room, returning a few minutes later with the supplies. Taking his time to clean off the blood and lather my skin with the ointment, I think about everything that's happened in the last several days. Mainly the clues laid out before me with regard to where the compass rose might possibly be leading.

I know it's to bring me to the spot where I've hidden my powers and memories, but where? My hope was that visiting Rochelle's tomb might give me a bit of insight. However, the only thing I learned was that the church had once been dedicated to the sun goddess, Olwen. The stained-glass window depicting Cresidio and its temple, then Rochelle finishing the phrase I had written down in the journal, echoes in my brain.

"Sunrises cast hidden shadows, revealing dreams not yet fulfilled. Until the rays reach the tomb, then all will be revealed."

Why did I write down just the first half of the saying and not the entire thing? And how come Rochelle knew it? Have I been entwining my past lives with that of the relic hunter, leaving myself breadcrumbs as a road map to reclaiming what I've lost?

Tomb.

Could the stanza be referencing the vault my father kept the Scepter of Ignis? Is that where I need to go next? Back to Cresidio where my life as young Magdalene Leech ended and this new one began?

Pushing myself up onto my elbows, I take hold of the pendant as it dangles between my breasts, resting the warm, warped metal in the palm of my hand, and closing my eyes, concentrating on the memories that have already surfaced, forcing those still lingering underneath to rise.

Just one takes the bait.

I try to work quickly, not knowing how long I have to create my treasure box, which is how I've decided to refer to the puzzle before me. Pieces of Rochelle's shield lay scattered on the makeshift workbench I erected down in the musty wine cellar of the castle I share with Rowen. Thankfully, he's passed out up in our bedroom after I slipped something into his wine at dinner. I had to. Otherwise, he'd stop me, and neither of us can afford that. I know they're coming, it's just a matter as to when, and the visit won't be a pleasant one.

Wraith wasn't specific on the details when he showed up uninvited the other day while Rowen was out. He simply stated that the edicts know where I'm hiding and plan on sending hunters after us. My intentions were to rejoin them once I'd secured the chalice ... however, a life I've been missing—stolen from me, actually—has awakened and I don't want it to end.

But now the heavenly council want me dead, replaced like Daimon. That can't be accomplished, nevertheless, if I'm not at full strength, so here I am constructing a box just large enough to house the thing I treasure most in this world. An item I've carried with me throughout time. One that reminds me of what life should've been like before Belial and his soldiers invaded.

Glancing at the obsidian stone resting beside the compass rose I removed from the shield, I can't help but pick it up to caress its smooth surface one last time. A pulse flows throughout the rock, causing it to vibrate ever so gently in my hand, my powers begging to be released from their new confines.

But they can't be. Not yet.

The edicts must fall before I can rise again.

"I know where my powers are," I say after opening my eyes and releasing the necklace from my grasp, allowing it to swing back into place.

Rowen pauses in wrapping the new bandages around my chest and torso, kneels on the floor beside the bed, and cups my face in his hands. "You do?" His smile is broad and full of hope, relief flooding his enchanting hazel eyes.

"Yes, but you're not going to like it."

His expression falters as he sits back onto his heals, his hands falling into his lap. "Where?"

"Cresidio."

He frowns. "Are you sure?"

I nod.

Letting out a heavy sigh, he says, "Let me finish, then we'll go tell Kagan." Standing, he returns to wrapping the fresh bandages around my chest and torso, though I can tell his mood has drastically changed.

There's a coldness about him that I can't explain and it worries me. He's not normally like this, and I thought he'd be happy to know we're close to figuring out one of these damn puzzles, but somehow I get the feeling that it's the opposite.

As I'm putting on a clean sweatshirt, I decide to say something. "Why do you sound disappointed?"

"I'm just worried," he replies, keeping his head down while collecting the soiled bandages and the tube of ointment from the bed. "The edicts will be able to track you once your abilities are restored, and so will the other hunters."

"The thistle will mask all of that."

Facing me, his cheeks flush with anger. "And what about Belial? He'll kill you for those powers the moment he discovers you're back to being a fully restored relic hunter."

"I need to be if we're going to stop Abaddon from rising," I counter, my own fury showing. "What's your problem? I thought you'd be happy."

He sets everything on top of the dresser, comes over, and wraps me in his arms, resting his head on top of mine. "I don't want to lose you again."

Putting my arms around his waist, I lean into him. "You won't."

The tension in the room doesn't subside the longer we stand there holding each other, which greatly troubles me. After a few more seconds we exit the bedroom and return to the dining room where everyone has gathered, including Joran. Rowen skirts his way around the other side of the table to claim Kagan's attention while I take a seat on the couch in the living room. The two join me, Doreleska and Pierce staring at us from across the way, curiosity in both of their eyes.

Resting my arms on top of my legs, I sit forward in the seat to get closer to Kagan, who's occupying one of the armchairs, Rowen beside me. "I know where my powers are. They're in Cresidio."

The hair on the older man's beefy arms bristle and he tugs on his beard. "I was afraid they might be."

"There's more," I interject before he can continue. "I want to search the library in Burmstone Castle."

"Why?" His voice booms, alerting the others to our conversation if they hadn't already been listening.

"To see if there's a book on weapons that can kill Abaddon. My kards won't work on him, so something must. Otherwise, what's the point of Lucifer requesting my help?"

"Maybe restoring your memories will resolve that problem. If it doesn't, then we'll venture to the castle, but only if Theron and the Watchers are gone." He stands, running his fingers through his hair. "We'll go to Cresidio tomorrow."

"It should be before sunrise."

Placing his hands on his hips, he asks, "Any particular reason?"

"Remember the glyphs I wrote? It's a clue about how to locate the box I stored my abilities inside of."

He narrows his gaze, clearly uncomfortable with the idea. "All right," he finally relents. "But I'm limiting the length of time we're there and who will be accompanying us." Turning, he glances at the others. "Pierce, Hollis, and Ulrich will remain behind. The others will go with, and I want you all heavily armed. There's no telling what we might run into in that haunted village."

"Ghosts don't carry weapons," Doreleska quips.

"No, but they might not be the only ones there," he retorts. "We need to be ready for anything."

I want to feel confident that tomorrow will go smoothly, but dread overwhelms me to the point where I forgo dinner when it's time and head straight for bed. Rowen cradles me while I try to sleep, my anxiety worse than it's ever been.

Chapter Nineteen

It's still dark when we leave the retreat. The kards are secured in a holster around my waist, hugging my hips, along with my black leggings. It shouldn't be as cold along the Adriatic Sea, so I leave my heavier coat in the bedroom and put on a simple, long-sleeved Henley shirt in dark blue, my boots laced tight around my ankles. Rowen and Kagan both have dual scabbards against their backs, along with additional knives strapped around their waists. Doreleska is armed to the teeth with sword breakers, dirks, daggers, and a Sai—a three-pronged blade with a thick grip—which are either being held in a holster similar to mine, or tucked into hidden pockets of her floor-length, burgundy leather trench coat, her hair braided down her back like mine. Joran has two axes secured across his back and machetes in each hand.

I cling to Rowen as we make our way to the haunted village, the bitterly cold air gnawing at my exposed skin, threatening to chip pieces of it away. It gradually warms the farther southwest we go, but not by much. I regret not wearing something thicker to stave off the bitterness. However, if I must fight, the additional garments will simply make moving cumbersome. Rowen holds me firmly in his grip, squeezing me for comfort since I'm severely nervous about what we might encounter.

Kagan had suggested just before we left to arrive along the northern edge of the forest that acts as the village's boundaries. He doesn't want us setting foot onto the hallowed ground until he can guarantee we're the only ones there. Touching down on the leave-strewn soil, the trees have thickened and are much taller since the last time I saw my home. An ominous fog hovers over the area, concealing the village in a hauntingly darkened shroud.

"I don't like this," Doreleska states, standing beside us. Joran and Kagan join a few moments later. "Why couldn't we wait until the sun was out?"

Stepping free from Rowen's grasp, I can't help but stare at the thin layer of mist ebbing and flowing through the air as if it were alive. "Because the vault will only appear when the sun's rays hit it as they rise."

"Then how were your parents able to locate it all those years ago?" Kagan inquires, removing one of his swords from the scabbard.

"The Scepter of Ignis always led the way for those seeking guidance from Olwen. Until the day I destroyed it. It was how Belial's guards were able to get to it after murdering my mother." Gripping the gold handles of the daggers at my waist, I unsheathe them, holding the weapons down along my sides.

Rowen moves beside me, his gaze focused on the mist that continues to wander over the ground like a wave, rising and falling as if breathing. "How did you locate it when you hid your powers?"

I'm so entranced by what's before me, that I don't bother glancing at him when I respond. "I didn't. Someone did it for me."

Seizing my arm, he turns me to face him. "Who?"

Smiling, I place a hand on his cheek. "An old friend."

Sorrow creases the corners of his eyes as he releases me.

"Joran and I will scout the perimeter," Kagan says, just as children's laughter tickles my ears.

"What was that?" Doreleska barks, each hand now carrying a sword breaker.

314

The laughter sounds again, and is accompanied by a lulling melody I haven't heard since my childhood. Turning, I step nearer to the edge of the forest, then close my eyes and let the welcoming sounds wash over me. I find myself humming along to the tune, becoming more enchanted the longer I listen.

Opening my eyes, I spot a small glow in the distance, a light showing me the way home. "They know I'm here." I'm about to move forward when Rowen snatches my arm.

"Don't go in there," he scolds, the song and laughter continuing, though merely as an underlying current pulsing through the still night.

Placing my hand on his, I gently remove it. "I have to." Rising up onto my toes, I kiss him tenderly on the lips. "It'll be all right, Rowen. They won't hurt me."

Before the others can stop me, I breach the fog. It parts, allowing me entry, then quickly solidifies, sealing me inside, blocking out Rowen, though I hear him shouting for me to come back, his voice a good distance away. A moment ago we were feet apart, now it seems much farther, though I haven't moved far from the forest edge. The laughter and singing abruptly stop, while the fog takes on a brittle texture. It scratches at my face and tugs on my clothing, almost like I'm treading through a briar patch when I venture forward. The light I noticed seconds ago has also vanished, plunging me in unnatural darkness that even Olwen's flame can't penetrate when I call it up in my palm after securing one of the kards into its holster.

The only sound I hear is my own breathing. Rowen's voice a distant memory. I slowly make a path through the charred grasses that have never recovered from that fateful night, going deeper into Cresidio. Silhouettes of huts begin to form off to my right and left, harsh whispers emanating from their doorways.

"Murderer ... thief ... betrayer."

Something firm brushes against my shoulder, shoving me backwards. I'm hit again, this time in the back, then the arm. It doesn't hurt since I know it's merely the ghosts that haunt these lands alerting me to their presence. I don't blame them for being angry, or even vengeful. Most were on their way to safety when I shattered the stone with the kard, ending all of their lives. Tears trickle down my cool cheeks as I continue to make my way, stopping only when I spot the hut that was once my home.

Crossing its threshold, the mist ceases. This dwelling, along with the others, should be in ruins, burnt husks of an ancient world. Instead, it's perfectly intact, no sign of devastation. I know this is simply an illusion, being either cast by my memories or those who still live here, causing me to wonder what other trickery I might come across.

The ruggedly woven grass mats lay on the floor exactly how they were every day, including the blankets my mother tossed aside from rousing me that night. Dirty clothes are rumpled in the corner, while baskets of dried goods sit next to the doorway. A lone lantern dangles from the ceiling, its flame the only light being cast around the homey space. Moving farther inside, the chill that has been following me dissipates and is replaced by a soothing aroma of lavender.

"Hello, sweetheart," a soft, familiar voice whispers behind me.

Whirling around, I find my mother standing in the doorway wearing her traditional short sleeved dress made from textured sackcloth that's dyed dark blue. Her long, black hair is handsomely braided down her back, yellow flowers woven into the delicate curves. She looks exactly how she did the last time I saw her, minus the blood from the wound in her torso Belial's guards inflicted when she went to claim the scepter.

"Mom," I choke out, the tears flowing rapidly down my face, a lump forming in my throat while I blindly secure the remaining kard into its holster.

She holds out her arms, and I rush into them. "It's all right, dear one." Wrapping me in a loving embrace, she rests her head against mine. "It's going to be all right."

"I'm so sorry, Mom. I ... I never meant for any of this to happen."

"I know you didn't. We all know that. Those voices you hear aren't from the villagers, but something far more sinister that also claims these lands as home." She holds me at arm's length. "But you need to listen to what I have to say. Your destiny has yet to be decided, regardless of what the heavenly council tells you. What happened here in Cresidio is their fault, not yours."

"How ... how do you know about them?"

She shakes her head. "It doesn't matter. I don't have long, since the others don't want me telling you this." Glancing behind her, she shudders at something I can neither see nor hear. "It's imperative that you stop the edicts. They were never supposed to exist in the first place. A mistake you must ratify." She kisses me lovingly on the forehead. "You're His warrior, Magdalene. You've always been since the moment you were born. The edicts didn't choose you as the relic hunter. He did. They did." She gestures toward the ceiling. "All of the gods and goddesses that have ever lived selected you to be their heir. That's why you're so fervently sought after by those who will do anything for power and control. It's also why the relics call to you. They belong to you, and only you. No one else." Trembling, she releases me. "Find the Kamin, sweetheart. It's the weapon that can end all of this, but you must hurry. He grows more powerful with each passing day." She abruptly turns and disappears into the fog.

The flame for the lantern sputters out and smoke rapidly fills the hut. Rushing outside, I escape just as fire erupts up the walls and swallows the floor. Ash rains down from the sky when everything around me bursts into flame, forcing me to run for the other end of the village where the vault is located. With the conflagration, the fog that had been masking Cresidio vanishes, exposing the hidden community to the world. My name reverberates through the groves, Rowen's voice the loudest amongst them, but I ignore their calling and forge on, slipping into the forest just as the sun's rays begin their ascent.

The entrance to the underground cavity isn't far, if memory serves me correct, so I linger close to the first row of trees and patiently wait. The rays brush along the ground, coating the fallen leaves in a shimmering yellow glow. Small flakes of glistening gold rise from the earth like tiny balls of fire. I follow them a few meters to the right, and nestled between two wide tree trunks are narrow stone steps covered in moss descending several feet into the ground. I struggle to secure my footing due to the slipperiness of the moss and the developing morning dew, so my trek down the steps is precarious at best. When I reach the granite door at the bottom, there's a combination lock securing the latch for it to the disintegrating wooden frame.

"Shit," I mutter. "Damn it, Festus. How the hell am I going to know what numbers you used?"

Forgoing the lock, I examine the wood, noting the heavy cracks and termite damage. Locating the section with the worst rot, I push the heavy door, rocking my body against it to loosen the hinges. The frame groans, finally giving way. The door falls inward, with me on top of it. I grunt when we both slam into the granite floor, my shoulder throbbing from the impact, dust flying everywhere. Getting to my feet, I brush off the bits of wood from my clothes, then bring forth a ball of light from my palm, illuminating the dank space. Tucked on the lone shelf at the back of the vault is a heavily embellished wooden box in the shape of an octagon, the top indented with the image of the compass rose.

I don't recall the shield I dismantled to create the box being so beautifully and intricately carved. Festus must have done this after I gave it to him because I recognize the detailed patterns from ones I've seen him design on cakes. Leave it to him to ensure the treasure box was unique in its own right. Extinguishing the flame, I take the container and sit on the floor, resting my back against the granite wall. The memory of Festus' visit returns, and I welcome it.

"Are you sure you want to do this?" he asks in his native Hungarian, the two of us standing in the drawing room for the castle, him holding the treasure box in his beefy, sweaty hands.

Clutching the journal against my chest, I glance nervously upstairs, praying Rowen is still sound asleep. "Yes."

"What about that?" The older man gestures at the leather-bound book.

"I'm hiding it here." Stepping over to the dormant fireplace, I remove a brick that I'd been loosening for the last several days just below the mantle, then place the journal into the cavity behind it. "You'll know when it's time to retrieve this." I point to the journal before securing the brick back into place.

He lovingly tucks an errant strand of hair behind my ear like a father. "Be careful, Magdalene. The powers you're messing with can bring about the downfall of us all."

"I know, but what other choice do I have?"

Smiling, he pats my cheek. "I hope to see you again. Soon.

He brushes past me, but I keep my eyes focused on the brick in the fireplace while he leaves, gently closing the front door behind him.

If this fails, I'll lose everything. Including the little bit of freedom that I currently have. Making me not only an enemy of the heavenly council, but also my fellow hunters. However, this needs to happen if he's to be stopped.

Even with that little bit of memory surfacing, I still don't recall who 'he' is. It could be anyone I know, or someone I don't remember yet. Either way, I went through an awful lot of trouble to prevent something horrid from happening. At least, I think that was the purpose behind my actions.

Removing the necklace, I rub my finger over the pendant, take a deep breath, then flip the compass rose over so it fits the slots I carved into the precious wood. Turning it to the left, the lid clicks, then opens, revealing a black obsidian rock sitting on top of a bed made from tuft covered in red silk. I hesitate in touching it, afraid of what might happen when my abilities return, or what memories have yet to resurface ... mainly those of Avaris.

Wrapping my shaking fingers around the warm stone, a tremendous power seizes me, coursing through my veins and muscles with such force that I feel as if I'm being torn into shards. I bite my lip to muffle the scream desperate to escape. My body stiffens and I fall onto my side, unable to release the stone from my tightened grasp as everything inside of me starts to spasm. Crackles of lights flash behind my eyes and my hearing wanes, but no memories return. Not even a flicker of recognition about who I am ... or was. No connection between what I remember to what's still missing.

If I'm not responsible for my lost memories, then who is?

My head lolls to the side, I open my fist, and the stone tumbles out. Gradually, the debilitating aches cease, my sight returns to normal, and my hearing is restored to Rowen desperately shouting my name. Sitting up, I remove the pendant from the box and secure it back around my neck, then tuck the stone into my boot since my pants don't have pockets. I set the box onto the floor as I have no intention of bringing it with me. It takes me several long seconds to stand and crawl out of the vault into the dazzling sunlight. The sun is much higher than I'm expecting, so I wonder how long I was down in the crypt. It felt like just a few minutes. Grabbing for the nearest tree, I straighten up, my legs wobbly for some odd reason. Looking to my left, I spot the remains of Cresidio, the shattered temple the only structure still distinguishable among the scorched landscape.

In order to move, I have to focus on where I plant my feet, reminding myself which leg to use, as if I'm walking for the first time. Clearing the forest, I enter the village, spotting Rowen running toward me, but I don't see the others.

"Are you all right?" he asks, taking hold of my arm to steady me, his gaze raking the length of my body, looking for injuries.

"I'm fine," I reply, my voice weak, my gaze fixed on the temple and the creature emerging from it. "Where are Kagan, Doreleska, and Joran?"

"I don't know. We got separated."

Glowering at the demon that I love, my heart wrenches in two. "Why are you lying?"

He stumbles back, eyes widening in shock. "I'm not."

"Then explain him." I point to Belial, who now stands in front of the temple, a satisfied expression on his gray, scaly face.

Paling, Rowen whips his attention back to me. "You have your powers?"

I nod.

"Run, Magdalene. Get far away from here, and never look back."

Conflict rises inside of my devastated heart. Hatred for being betrayed by someone I thought truly cared a great deal for me, and deep-seated sorrow for what I wanted to be real for so long. The tears that had ceased when I fled from the burning hut return, but now they land on heated cheeks.

"You released Belial from the pit," I state, practically sobbing. "That's why Lucifer sent the hellhounds after you when we were in De Lamar."

Rowen reaches for me, but I step back a few feet. "I can explain all of this. Just not right now. You need to flee before it's too late."

My soul crumbles into pieces, my entire world once again shattering beyond repair. "Why?"

His eyes well with tears and his lips curl downward. "You wouldn't understand."

Staring at the man I would've given everything to, I unsheathe the kards. "Going after the chalice was a ruse. A way to get me out in the open so Belial could find me."

"Yes." His voice cracks as his cheeks become wet.

"Theron was there to keep an eye on you, wasn't he? It's why I caught the two of you arguing that night on the boat from Alexandria." I raise my arms, the daggers poised to strike.

"Please, Magdalene," he begs. "Don't do this."

I'm in the process of releasing the first weapon when powerful arms wrap around me, shoving mine against my sides, preventing me from flinging the kard. Throwing my head back, I come into contact with the chest of my captor. The laugh escaping his lips terrifies me.

"Good, Theron," Belial praises, sauntering up to us. "Thank you, Rowen, for keeping her distracted."

Removing one of his swords, the demon turns to face his master. "Let her go."

The monster chuckles. "You know I can't do that. She has something I want."

Rowen reaches for the compass rose around my neck, yanks the chain, breaking it, and tosses it to Belial. "Here. Now leave her alone."

Tucking the pendant into the pocket of his robes, he smiles. "That's not exactly what I was meaning, but seeing as you're now interfering with my plans, I think it's time you began serving my sentence." Belial snaps his fingers, and Rowen screams while his body turns to cinders as he disappears.

"I'm going to kill you," I utter, seething.

"Maybe one day, but that won't be for quite some time." He moves in front of me until we're mere inches apart. "Now, let's see what's inside of that pretty little head of yours." Placing his rough hands on either side of my skull, his eyes turn black and a paralyzing pain splinters my mind.

The shriek that leaves my mouth vibrates along the ground, causing the remnants of the temple to collapse and all ability to use my newly restored powers evaporates. Breathing becomes difficult while Belial probes my memories, searching for information that isn't there. When he finally releases me, the kards fall out of my grip and I sag to my knees, Theron bearing all of my weight.

"What a disappointment you are, Magdalene. All that effort, and for what?" He gestures for Theron to release me, allowing me to fall to the ground unencumbered. "Looks like I'll have to find Abaddon the relics he requires on my own. Or perhaps your journal will come in useful after all if I can decode your little passages."

"Which ones does he want?" I mutter hoarsely, my throat raw. I sit up and desperately claw for the kards that seem to be slightly out of reach.

Belial laughs. "You'll just have to find out." Bending down, he puts a finger under my chin and raises my gaze to meet his. "I do hope we meet again, but I'm sure the edicts won't be letting you out for quite some time." Without another word, he and Theron leave in a plume of black smoke.

Finally getting hold of the weapons, I tuck them into the holster around my waist, then try to stand, which takes a couple of attempts. Emerging from the forest off to my right are Kagan, Doreleska, and Joran, their weapons drawn and covered in blood. The Watchers must have been keeping them distracted while Belial played his little game. Sweat coats their brows and their clothes are torn in a few places. They stop several feet away, obviously unsure about how to handle me now that the truth about Rowen has been revealed.

Kagan is the only one who approaches. "Magdalene."

But I leave before he can continue with whatever sorrowful remark he intends to make. I'm enveloped in white smoke while traversing across the sky, heading to the last place where I was genuinely happy, although now I know it was nothing but a trick that I stupidly fell for.

The castle in De Lamar has seen better days. Many of the windows are broken, and the stone pavers for the circular driveway are either badly smashed or missing. Part of the roof has collapsed in the east wing, and most of the enormous structure is overgrown with weeds or vines, a good chunk of them snaking up the steps and into the foyer where the front door is barely hanging on by its rusted hinges. The once pristine yellow exterior is now dull and nearly brown from age and deterioration.

Making my way inside, mold creeps up the walls and the floorboards are horribly warped. Wallpaper peels from distended sheetrock and spray paint covers exposed beams. The furniture has been ripped open; the stuffing caked over the floor like snow. Heading into the drawing room, I find much of the same destruction, the fireplace and its chimney the only thing undisturbed. Except for the one brick Festus would've had removed to garner the journal. I wonder who Dalma sent to procure the item for him. Not that it really matters now.

I go carefully upstairs, doing my best to avoid the holes in the risers. One false step and I'll fall to the floor below. Wandering the lengthy hallway, there's just one room I want to visit.

The door to the bedroom is partially open, so I nudge it the rest of the way with the tip of my boot. Much like the remainder of the building, there's heavy water damage along the ceiling joists and on the floor. The bed has collapsed, the mattress and sheets missing. Turning for the closet, I reach out to clasp the knob, hesitant to expose what's inside. It takes a few tugs to get the door open, the sage green, satin dress I left in there well over a century ago now moth-eaten and in tatters.

"You still owe me a dance," *Rowen says one night after we're in the castle for a week.*

"And what makes you think I'll honor you with one?"

He laughs. "Because you're curious to see if what's happening between us is real." Taking my hand, he kisses the back of it. "And the easiest way to do that is getting up close and personal. Dancing can be very intimate, if done correctly."

I scrunch up my face and cross my arms over my chest. "What do you have in mind?"

Rowen smiles wide. "Give me an hour, then come downstairs in that dress and meet me in the ballroom."

When I'm ready, I hurry my way to the first floor, anxious to see what he has planned. The entire length of the room is decorated in red roses and candles. An old victrola, which he found somewhere in the cellar, plays a wartime record from the 1940s. Dinner consists of roasted duck, potatoes, and fresh vegetables.

I fell for him completely that night. Right into his arms and his bed. After our first kiss, I was still questioning his altruism. However, the night we danced put all doubts aside.

How foolish I was to have believed him, to fall for his deception, to allow myself one iota of happiness. Whatever happens to me now, I deserve it.

"I always thought you looked stunning in that dress."

I don't bother glancing behind me to acknowledge Avaris. He doesn't need my affirmation.

"I was wondering what happened to it."

Releasing the closet door, I let it swing shut, though it simply bangs against the warped frame. "How did you find me?"

"Where else would you have gone once you discovered the truth?"

I finally turn to face him. "Don't pity me."

"Don't worry, I'd never do that," he says scornfully. I notice the kards secured around his waist and the clach in his clenched fist. When he realizes I've seen it, he lifts it to his face. "I'm surprised this didn't give Rowen's real self away. All of Belial's loyalists carry this weapon. This is his, by the way. I took it the night I sent him to the cages." He lowers it, his knuckles turning white from his grip tightening. "I take it you found your powers. Otherwise, how else would you have gotten here?"

Anger builds inside of me, and I don't bother hiding it. "What do you want?"

His stare hardens. "You've been summoned to appear before the heavenly council."

"And you're the one they selected to come and collect me?" I ask mockingly.

"Actually, I volunteered."

Circling around him, I notice the blood seeping through his shirt, a badly applied bandage bulging underneath. "How did you escape the binding hex?"

Limping, he moves to keep me in front of him, wincing as he does, which satisfies me. "I called in a favor."

"Who would possibly help you?" I ask, stopping by the door to the bedroom, which I had left open.

A devilish grin crosses Avaris' lips. "Him."

Turning, I discover Wraith standing in the doorway looking exactly like he did the day he warned me that the hunters were coming. His sun-kissed skin is even darker due to the lack of light in the room because the sun is still rising on the other side of the building. His platinum hair nearly glows, and the blue iris of his left eye gleams like it were a pool of water. The pure black right eye bores into me, hate radiating, penetrating my every nerve.

As I reach for my kards, Wraith strikes out, landing a punch into my abdomen that sends me flying across the room, knocking the air from my lungs. Coughing, I roll onto my side and try to get up, but the large man kicks me in the back, sending me careening into the wall. The room spins and my head pounds from slamming into the sheetrock covering the bricks that were originally used to erect the castle. Lifting my hand to my forehead, my fingers are immediately sticky, covered in blood, and some drips from my nose, but it doesn't feel broken. Using the chair rail along the wall, I grip it as best I can and pull myself up.

"Just stay down," Avaris comments, knocking my legs out from under me.

I manage to free one of the kards, but it's jerked from my grasp by Wraith, surprising me considering he's half demon. Before I can unsheathe the other one, Avaris removes it. Because of his proximity, I swing wide with my legs, sending him to the floor, the dagger and clach skittering across the hardwood. As I'm crawling over toward the latter, Wraith stabs me in the lower back with my own weapon. I holler as blood spills, pooling around me.

Grunting, Avaris gets to his feet and reclaims the lost knives. "Pick her up," he demands. "They're expecting us."

Wraith bends down, picks me up, and flings me over his shoulder. Lights flash before my eyes as the room dissolves and all I hear is silence.

Chapter Twenty

I don't bother lifting my head when we arrive at Malum. Wraith's boots pound heavily on the cement floor, each step echoing in unison with Avaris', who must be in front of us since I can't see him. Lining the dark stone walls are iron doors, hefty padlocks holding them closed, a thin slat at the bottom along the floor, and a lone window toward the center of the door with its own set of bars. The only way to see inside. Gas lanterns adhered to the walls cast very little light, adding to the ominous surroundings. We stop, and the sound of metal grinding against metal pierces my ears. Wraith continues forward while Avaris stands by the door, holding it open.

The first thing that hits me is the musty smell, followed by the odor of urine and feces, a bucket in the corner the likely source. Wraith drops me onto the floor, and I cry out from the shock and pain. Rolling onto my side so I'm not facing either of them, the back of my shirt rises.

"What's this?" Avaris inquires, his voice rising slightly in confusion. "You got a tattoo?"

Shit. Please don't know what it means.

"Why? Was it Rowen's idea?" Disdain drips from his tongue like acid.

"It's none of your business," I croak, my voice still raw from Belial's torment.

Grumbling, Avaris dips a finger into the blood still escaping from the knife wound in my back, and draws something between my shoulder blades.

I know what it is without having to ask.

"You should recognize this room," he comments, coming around to my front and kneeling before me after dropping my shirt back into place. "It's the same one you occupied last time."

I keep my mouth shut, knowing whatever I say is only going to rile him further.

He grazes my cheek with the tips of his fingers, and I flinch at his touch. "Now that your powers are back, your memories have to be as well." He lowers his face until it's nearly touching mine. "Recall me yet?"

With my last bit of strength, I slam my forehead into his, knocking him on his ass. "No, you bastard. I'm not the one responsible for my missing memories. I never was."

Rubbing his head, he groans, "Goddamn it, Magdalene." Getting to his feet, he gestures for Wraith to leave, his weighty steps reverberating on the way out. "I told you that demon was fucking with your mind."

I want to curl up into a ball, cocoon myself like an infant, but I'm in too much agony to move, and I'm sure any additional motion will tear the wound further. "Go away," I mutter, having lost my will to fight.

"With pleasure." He storms away, slamming and locking the door behind him.

With the door closed, darkness settles in since there isn't any source of light in the cell. Though I can easily call up a ball of fire due to the thistle on my back, I don't want to draw attention to myself. Instead, I bury my face in my hands and bawl until there are no tears left to shed, and start to wonder what plans the edicts have in store for me. What means of torture will they subject me to, much like the caretakers at the orphanage? Or will they outright execute me? Either way, it's going to be excruciating.

I'm not sure how much time passes before I hear loud voices arguing in the corridor, then the lock gives way and my cell door opens. But I don't move, determined to ignore whoever has come to harass me.

"This is no place for Magdalene to be," Dalma growls, her teeth clacking in disgust.

"Just get her cleaned up and take care of her wounds, but don't touch the binding hex on her back. That needs to remain," Avaris barks.

Knowing who my visitor is, I decide to move ever so carefully, rolling onto my other side to watch the heated exchange.

"Why the hell does she have it? Isn't the one you painted on her door enough?" The old woman shuffles into the room, a scowl carving deep lines in her soft face, her hands holding a cherrywood tray containing bandages, medical tape, a bar of soap, a bowl of water, a bottle of what's probably alcohol, and a fat candle lit on a wooden base, its wax collecting at the bottom, cementing the candle to its stand.

"She's due in front of the council shortly and we don't need her burning the entire sanctuary down." He closes the door, locking the pair of us inside. "Shout to the guard down the hall when you're done, and he'll let you out."

"When did you turn into such an asshole?" she snaps, setting the tray onto a spindly wooden table in the far left corner that I hadn't noticed before.

Glowering, he leaves without answering.

"Prick." She places her hands on her hips and changes her attention to me. "Why are you just lying there? Get up."

"I can't because I was stabbed in the back and it hurts too much to move. Or did you miss the pool of blood around me?" I nod to the mess and the filth covering my clothes, as well as the dingy concrete.

Huffing, she picks up the tray, walks behind me, and gets settled onto the floor. "What weapon was used?"

"My own kard."

She snorts, then shoves my braid over my shoulder. "I told you to be careful about who you bequeathed your daggers to."

I hear her fussing with the items on the tray, then she lifts the back of my shirt, tucking it under my bra strap, and applies something cold and caustic to the wound.

My intake of breath is sharp due to the immense stinging from more than likely the alcohol. "Rowen isn't the one who stabbed me. Wraith did."

She pauses. "Why would he do that?"

"Avaris probably told him to as payback for me shoving a clach into him."

Dalma resumes cleaning the wound. "So, that's why he's favoring the one side. Were you two arguing?"

I try not to wince while she works. "He was convinced Rowen had manipulated my mind, and wanted to torture the demon, then send him to the pit. I panicked and impaled Avaris with the clach. I also drew a binding hex on his back so he couldn't follow us when we fled his cottage."

"It looks like you were starting to heal on your own, but the mending has stopped. Probably due to the binding hex. Am I to assume that you found your abilities?"

Nodding somewhat, I reply, "Yes."

"Good." She places and adheres a bandage to my back, then moves around to the other side to clean the blood off of my face. "Can you really blame Avaris for how he reacted? Rowen destroyed his world." Setting down her blood-caked rag, she cups my face in her hands. "He took the one thing that meant the most to him and toyed with it until it couldn't tell the difference between reality and fiction."

I push her hands away. "Avaris is nothing to me, or I to him."

After picking up the rag, she dips it into the stained bowl of water and dabs at the cut on my forehead. "Nonsense. If that were true, then he wouldn't have warned the heavenly council that the Watchers had found you."

Puzzled, I ask, "How did he know they were after me?"

She starts wiping the dried blood from my nose. "Festus told him. That's where the cowardly man went after shuttering the café. He went running to Avaris."

I stare at her, recalling what Avaris had said about Dalma's change in loyalty after learning what the edicts had planned for Festus for aiding me instead of turning me over into their hands. "Why are you here?"

She ignores my lingering gaze and keeps her focus on the rag in her hand. "Where else am I supposed to go?"

Studying the lines on her face and the way they've deepened since I last saw her, it dawns on me. "Which cell is yours?"

Setting the rag on the tray, she grunts while standing. "The one at the end of the hall by the stairs." She reaches for the tray, which is still on the floor, but I grab her wrist, stopping her.

"Avaris told me you were someplace safe."

She shrugs. "He probably does consider Malum to be a safe sanctuary. Of course, he's never witnessed what the edicts due to those who defy them. Unlike you and me."

Feeling a bit better, I slowly sit up after releasing her. "My mother told me they were never supposed to exist."

Her eyes widen, and she carefully lowers herself to the floor. "When did you see her?"

"Maybe a few hours ago. I'm not sure how long I've been in this cell." I go on to explain what happened in Cresidio, all the way up to Belial sending Rowen down to the pit.

"It all makes sense," she mumbles, placing a trembling hand over her thin, parched lips.

"What does?"

She doesn't get a chance to answer when someone pounds on the door.

"Time's up, Dalma," a man with a husky voice snaps. The lock clicks and the door is pulled open, but the guard remains in the shadows so I'm unable to see what he looks like.

She rushes to gather the tray and get to her feet, but before she's close to the door, I ask, "Where's your cane?"

Pausing inches from the threshold, she glances back and replies, "The same place where I found it."

When she's in the corridor, the door closes and locks, and I'm alone in complete darkness. Scooting against the wall, I bring my knees up to my chest and wrap my arms around my legs, hugging them tightly. It's not long until Avaris returns with Wraith, the latter entering the room alone, who's carrying shackles.

"Seriously?" I bemoan. "I'm not strong enough to fight both of you."

Wraith looks over at Avaris loitering in the doorway. "Maybe this is a bit much."

The young man scowls. "Danais wants her chained, so that's what we're going to do."

Sighing, Wraith comes over, stoops down, and slips two of the binders around my ankles. "I need you to sit forward, Magdalene," he says, his voice meek and low, which isn't normally like him.

"What made you decide to turn against me?" I ask, not daring to move just yet. "You warn me that the edicts are sending the hunters a few days before they showed up in De Lamar, but now you have no qualms about, quite literally, stabbing me in the back?"

His blue eye dulls a bit and his chin stiffens. "That was a mistake."

"And was it the same with saving Rowen from the hellhounds?"

I catch Avaris' pause while making his way inside, more than likely to assist in binding me some more.

"It was a debt that I owed him. Nothing more."

Fury bubbles up inside of me when I realize who sold us out. "Is that why you betrayed us to the edicts? A way to clear your conscience?"

"Enough." Avaris grabs my arm and flings me to the floor face down, then holds me there while Wraith drapes the chains between my legs and secures my hands behind my back. "I knew you were lying about what you remembered. More lies spewing from your mouth in order to get me to believe you. No more, Magdalene."

Each take a limb and haul me to my feet. "I don't give a damn what you think, Avaris. Let's just get this over with."

I struggle to walk between them because of the limited mobility the shackles provide. In the corridor, we turn right and head toward the stone staircase at the end of the hall. Dalma spies us through the bars of her door, her eyes moist and her cheeks damp. I wish I could tell her that I'm sorry for what's about to happen to the both of us, but words fail me, and I can only hang my head in shame.

The stone staircase winds its way up several stories, the brightness from whatever lays waiting above cascading down, shattering the din. When we reach the top, we pass under a white marble archway with flecks of gold, and into a rotund space constructed from similar material with a dome ceiling and towering carved windows, which line the entire room. At the far end is a raised dais covered in red velvet with twelve marble thrones, six of which are unoccupied.

"Put her there," the woman in the center orders, gesturing firmly to an invisible spot on the floor. She's wearing a gold linen robe, much like the ones that the ancient Greek and Roman gods and goddesses were rumored to have donned. Her long, wavy, light ash brown hair is parted along the side, most of it draped over her right shoulder. She has a diamond-shaped face, chestnut-colored eyes, a Nubian-style nose, and thin, red lips. Given the four men and one woman flanking her, each wearing a similar gown but in white, she must be Danais.

Once I'm positioned to her satisfaction, both Wraith and Avaris step toward a console table made from wrought iron and white oak with cabriole-style legs. An etched glass vase filled with red roses is the only ornamentation. They stop, then turn and face me instead of the edicts, their hands clasped behind their backs like obedient little soldiers. Wraith is no longer in possession of my kard—or any weapons for that matter—and Avaris has just his knives strapped around his waist. Missing is the clach, which surprises me.

"Magdalene Leech," the horrid woman begins, her voice shrill and harsh, her accent mixed. It draws my attention away from my guards and toward her. "You have been brought in front of this council to answer for the murder of the edict, Sadaina. Before your sentence is carried out," she looks over at Avaris, "show me the mark."

Unsheathing a kard, he saunters over, then spins me around until my back is toward the council.

"Where's your clach?" I whisper as he takes the knife and cuts my shirt open, starting at the collar. "Afraid the edicts will find you in possession of a demon lord's weapon?"

He purposefully knicks me, drawing blood, adding another wound to my already battered body. After ripping the garment down to the waist, he tears off the left sleeve, discarding it to the floor. I expect him to return standing beside Wraith, but he doesn't.

"A hex breaker," one of the men utters in astonishment.

"That can easily be remedied," Danais says, her arrogance showing.

The cut Avaris inflicted on me suddenly grows, cleaving the skin covering my left shoulder blade in several places. I scream and drop to my knees while blood seeps down, soaking my leggings and collecting onto the floor. Tears run down my cheeks and panic rises inside of me, nearly suffocating. After several agonizingly long seconds, the brutalization ceases, but the pain remains.

"Get her to her feet."

Wrapping his arm around mine, Avaris pulls me into a standing position, though all I want to do is crumble. He turns me to face the council, then releases me and goes to stand next to Wraith, sheathing is weapon along the way. Keeping my head lowered, I refuse to look at any of them.

"Never in the thousands of years that we've been leading the hunters has one ever dared attack us. Let alone slay their master." I don't have to see Danais' face to know it's red with rage. The hatred in her voice says it all. "She went to retrieve you, bring you home, but instead you inflict a mortality curse, assassinating her. You killed an innocent woman."

"Innocent?" I rave, lifting my heated stare toward hers, fury coursing through my veins like bile. "Sadaina was sent to execute me, not retrieve me."

A plump, old man with a round face, green eyes, a concave nose, and short, white hair sitting to the right of Danais bristles at the remark. "I'm sure the demons you were cavorting around with influenced you to believe such nonsense." He picks at his robe, adjusting the creases across his lap until they become smooth. The way he holds himself, all that's missing is a crown of laurels over his head and he would resemble a deity from ancient times.

My mother's words resound in my mind.

"All of the gods and goddesses that have ever lived selected you to be their heir."

336

It's soon followed by another conversation.

"Malum was once known as Mount Olympus." Avaris mentioned it when he and Rowen were discussing the syrthie attack in Travion.

Twelve thrones right in front of me for the twelve Olympians who once occupied them.

"You're His warrior, Magdalene. You've always been the moment you were born."

The Perpetua Chalice was rumored to have been used at the last supper where the twelve apostles ate with Christ.

"The shroud is purportedly buried under the ruins of Lingley Manor somewhere in the British Isles," Kagan commented when we were discussing the Calsaign shroud.

The time of King Arthur and the twelve Knights of the Round Table.

Twelve. Twelve. Twelve.

Why does that number seem important? What am I missing? Remember, Magdalene. Force yourself to remember.

"It is this council's decision ..." But Danais' voice fades into the background of my thoughts.

"The edicts didn't choose you as the relic hunter. He did. They did."

They did.

Not just the gods and goddesses, nor the singular one many various religions worshipped until the Cleansing, but all those who once roamed these lands leaving their mark. Including myself.

"It's also why the relics call to you. They belong to you, and only you. No one else."

I return to the present when the feel of metal against my throat startles me. My braid is wrapped in Avaris' grip as he tugs my head back slightly. Any second now and the blade will sever me clean.

"Who's going to stop Abaddon from rising?" Not bothering to wait for a response, I continue, "I'm the only one who knows how to find the sword that'll defeat him and Lucifer. Leaving the world and all souls for you to reign over. Even the demons will be yours to command and control."

Danais raises her hand, pausing my execution. She then gestures for Avaris to let go and step back, but still remain close. "Explain."

"No matter who you select to take my place, they won't have the capability to wield the mighty weapon. A sword called Kamin."

An older man with a square face, coarse features, salt and pepper hair, and brown eyes sits straighter in his seat next to the self-proclaimed leader. "I've heard of this weapon. It's believed that the power coursing through its hearty metal can cripple the simplest of men. No mortal can handle it without certain death. Even those who have abilities like ours struggle to control it."

Danais narrows her uncertain gaze. "What makes you so certain that it's you alone who can possess this sword?"

Firming up my stance, I hold my head high. "Because you didn't choose me to be the relic hunter. Those who came before you did. The ones you crave to aspire to and will do anything to accomplish that task ... even send a child to be slaughtered at the hands of the enemy."

Her jaw tightens and she curls her hands into fists, her knuckles turning white.

I look at Avaris. "Or remove the memories of a loved one with the hope that when he finds his beloved with another, he'll kill her." Turning my attention back to the edicts, I continue, "Ridding you of the thing that frightens you the most. Me."

Unclenching her hands, Danais places an arm on the armrest of her throne and drums her fingers, her nails clacking against the cool stone. "What guarantees do we have that you won't use the Kamin against us?"

"I'll pledge my loyalty to this council. And after the demons and their lords have been defeated, I'll sever all connections with the outside world until called upon to serve."

"Magdalene, don't," Avaris says, grabbing my arm, tears in his eyes.

I sense regret and shame in his soul for having believed the lies the edicts fed him all these years. It's too late, though. They succeeded in destroying anything that might still have been between us.

Smiling, Danais turns to the man beside her. "Rhodes, restore Magdalene's memories. Wraith, retrieve Dalma so she can remove the binding hex from the relic hunter's back."

The half-breed retreats down the stairs while Rhodes approaches, shooing Avaris away. The young man moves like a wounded animal, limping toward the console table, his back arched and his head down.

Rhodes places his hands on either side of my head, then gently pushes, returning everything that was stolen from me. The memories of Avaris were taken when the council assigned me to guard the chalice, knowing a demon had been sent after it, hoping I would fall for him like I foolishly did. Those are the hardest to bare. The joy and happiness Avaris and I had together was nearly as strong as what I felt with Rowen. We did truly love each other and were looking forward to leaving the hunter stronghold, living out our days in the cottage he built. I was always afraid he'd be taken from me. Killed by a demon during one of his hunts. Neither of us realized that the threat was much closer to home.

"How are you feeling?" Rhodes inquires when he's finished.

"Whole again."

He nods, then returns to his throne just as Wraith reappears with Dalma, who's carrying the same tray she had earlier. Setting it on the floor, she soaks a clean rag into the fresh water of the bowl, rubs it against a bar of soap, then lifts up my shirt to scrub off the dried blood making up the sigil.

"Where are my kards?" I ask, while the old woman continues to work.

Danais nods toward the table with the flowers. The weapons appear, and within a matter of seconds, they're back in my hands. I don't have any means of securing them, so I simply hold them in a tight grip, afraid they'll be stripped from me again.

When Dalma finishes, she works on cleaning the new wounds, which are now healing, but is immediately reprimanded.

"That'll be enough," Danais orders, causing the old woman to tremble. "Come forward."

Setting the rag down onto the tray, Dalma steps around me and approaches the dais, her entire body shaking, her hands clenching and opening almost in a nervous tick.

The spiteful woman scrunches up her face in disgust. "You disobeyed us, Dalma, when you went in search of the relic hunter. It was explicitly known that she was off limits to those in your position, which is why we had planned on sending a hunter after Festus since he befriended her instead of informing us of her whereabouts. However, the Watchers took care of that problem for us." The smile on her lips roils my blood. "You were given the same command and selected not to follow it."

Picking at the drab brown dress adorning her feeble body, she says, "I ... she had to know the truth."

"That wasn't your decision to make," Rhodes scolds.

From his prominent position beside Danais, and the way he's speaking more freely than the others, I take him as her second in command. Studying his poise, and recalling that his convictions are strong when it comes to those who humbly bow at his feet, he might be a powerful ally if I can sway him to go against the others. Particularly Danais, but I wonder what it'll cost me and if the toll will be worth the effort.

Danais crosses her legs at the knee, a smug expression creasing her face. "We don't take these matters lightly. To defy your masters is beyond treacherous. If the others had discovered what the two of you were up to, they might have followed in your foolishness. So, in accordance with our laws, your punishment is death."

"No!" Avaris shouts. "You can't do this."

Turning to glare at the demon hunter, Danais asks, "Would you rather take her place?"

He stares at me, desperation heavy in his eyes, but there's nothing I can do, so he remains silent. Sorrow tugs at my heart. Dalma knew this was a possibility given that she wound up in a cell. It baffles me that Avaris didn't come to the same conclusion.

"Magdalene, to prove your obedience and devotion to the heavenly council, you're tasked with her execution, which will happen now."

I want to be shocked by the command, but truthfully, I'm not. "Relic hunters don't slaughter angels."

She chuckles. "You do now." Then her tone turns serious. "Obey, or meet the same fate."

Swallowing both the bile and hatred threatening to spew from my mouth, I nod in compliance.

When Dalma turns, the calm and peace floating over her isn't anything I'm expecting. Stepping in front of me, she places a soft, warm hand on my cheek, her tender fingers wiping away my tears as they fall.

"It's all right, Magdalene." Reaching for my hand, she wraps hers around it and the grip for the kard, raising it toward herself. "I'm not afraid, and neither should you be. Follow your instincts, let your heart lead you, and everything will be all right. The answers you need are already inside of you." Taking her free hand, she taps a finger against the center of my forehead. "This isn't the end, but a new beginning for all of us. One that only you can make a reality." Releasing me, she takes a step back. "I'll give Festus a hug for you."

My entire arm quakes as I lift it above my head, aiming the tip of the blade for Dalma's heart. She closes her eyes, tilts her head back, and beams. The knife plunges into her ribcage, splitting it open. An impulsive gasp escapes her lips before she dissolves into white ash, her remains being carried away on a breeze that flitters through the room from the windows since they are devoid of glass. The glare I give Danais should cut in her in two, but she simply continues to smile with immense satisfaction. Flicking her hand, my kards are jerked free from my grasp and sail through the air into Avaris' open palms.

"You'll get those back when you earn them," Danais quips.

Cocking my head to the side, I smirk. "You already don't trust me?"

Her smile turns into a scowl. "To ensure that you follow orders, you'll be assigned a sentry. He'll be responsible for your training, accompany you on hunts, and dole out discipline when warranted."

I furrow my brow. "Who?"

She snaps her fingers, and a quarter-inch black line with intricate scroll marks circles around the ring finger of my left hand, snaking its way up my arm before splitting at the top of my bicep. I feel one spiral of it penetrate my shoulder blade, while the other crosses my collarbone, then dives down into my chest, piercing my heart. The ends connect inside of me, creating a circuit, tethering me to another soul. Avaris grunts, so I look over at him. Since he's wearing a short-sleeved shirt, I easily notice the identical mark on his left arm.

"What is this?" he asks, puzzled.

"A ligare mark," Danais responds, once again grinning. "A symbol used to connect souls for all eternity."

"You're binding us together?" I rave, unable to control my anger any longer.

"Avaris will know immediately when you're using your powers. Including the ones we didn't give you."

"But he won't have access to them," Rhodes adds, angering Danais.

She glowers at him for several long seconds before returning her attention to me. "Your sentry will dictate your life, your actions. Ensuring your complete and utter loyalty to us. If one of you dies, then so does the other. The mark can never be removed. It is forever a part of you now, so I suggest you embrace it."

Looking for an arrogant expression on Avaris' face, I'm shocked when I don't see one. That is until the entirety of our new situation sinks in. The realization of the power he now has over me. However, being the relic hunter, I know things the edicts don't. The trick becomes using my knowledge against them and freeing myself from the cage I've been placed into. It all depends on what happens next.

"Avaris, take Magdalene to Sealgair where she can bathe, get into fresh clothes, and rest. Starting tomorrow, her new training will begin."

Tucking my kards into his waistband, he approaches, wraps his arm around mine, and we leave. The warmth of Malum is soon replaced by the bitter cold of the Ural Mountains where the hunter stronghold is kept. We bypass the main gate and head right for the dormitories. Particularly the fifth floor where my room is kept.

The stale smell of the ancient stone and wood building hasn't changed in all the centuries that I've lived here. The narrow halls are poorly lit by gas lanterns, their glass smoke-stained and desperately in need of cleaning. Antiquated Grecian rugs line the cold floor, adding to the dank and dreariness that seems to permeate the entire structure. Traversing down the corridor, there are ten rooms, five on each side, and each laid out and furnished the same. We come to the room second to last on the right, a vertical line with two diamonds along its shaft, the top diamond open is heavily stenciled on the wooden door.

"Is that really necessary?" I bemoan when Avaris lets go.

"It's to prevent you from fleeing in the middle of the night." Reaching into his pocket, he extracts a brass key, then places it into the lock, the gimbles give way. "I also intend on placing a guard at your door, so you can't slip out without notice." Turning the brass handle, he pushes the door open onto a room that resembles chaos with books, maps, and parchment strewn about not the floor, but the top of a profusely nicked desk under a set of closed windows that overlook the court below.

The room is warmer than the hallway, and more inviting since it's my personal sanctuary. Strolling around, I pick up a book or stray map, loving their soft feel against my rough fingers.

"I forgot how horrible you kept this place," Avaris comments from the doorway.

"Somehow I doubt that, considering there isn't an ounce of dust or any signs of cobwebs like there should be for such a derelict chamber." Setting down the book and map onto the desk, I turn to face him. "How often did you come in here while I was away? Every day? Once a week?" I take a step forward. "Did you sleep in my bed? Smell my scent on the clothes that were left behind?" I gesture to the wardrobe, its door partially open. "Rummage through my notes like a good little spy?"

"You have no idea what my life was like when you were gone," he says, seething. "How lost I felt without you. The missions I would take hoping not to return from them."

"And all while I wallowed away in my cell, uncertain about my fate." Standing in front of him, I grip the side of the door. "You could've stopped them, Avaris. Prevented all of this, but instead you reveled in self-pity. Lamented for a life that was never going to be allowed. You're a coward, and will always be." Slamming the door in his face, I lean my head against it and let out a deep breath to calm myself.

As the lock glides into place, sealing me inside, I return to the desk instead of heading for the bathroom. Pulling out the ladderback-style chair with its red paisley cushion, I retrieve the black stone from my boot and place it on top of one of the piles, then sit and sort through the mess, making stacks of each so I can properly begin my search for the relic that will free me from all of this.

End of Book One